FOREVER ISLAND

and

ALLAPATTAH

A Patrick Smith Reader

Novels by PATRICK D. SMITH

THE RIVER IS HOME

THE BEGINNING

FOREVER ISLAND

ANGEL CITY

ALLAPATTAH

A LAND REMEMBERED

FOREVER ISLAND

and

ALLAPATTAH

A Patrick Smith Reader

PINEAPPLE PRESS, INC.
SARASOTA, FLORIDA

Inquiries should be addressed to:
Pineapple Press, Inc.
P.O. Box 3889
Sarasota, Florida 34230

www.pineapplepress.com

Library of Congress Cataloging-in-Publication Data

Smith, Patrick D., 1927–
    Forever Island and Allapattah

"A Patrick Smith reader."
1. Seminole Indians—Fiction.   2. Everglades (Fla.)—Fiction.
I. Smith, Patrick D., 1927–   Allapattah. II. Title.
PS3569.M53785F6   1987   913154   87-15407

ISBN 0-910923-42-6

ISBN-13: 978-0-910923-42-2

First Edition
20 19 18 17 16 15 14 13

Printed in the United States of America

*To Rick and Danny
and to Lois S. Doty*

and

*To my Seminole friend James Billie, and to all
American Indians who have suffered greatly because
of the unjust cruelty of others*

CONTENTS

Introduction by Ed Hirshberg ix
Forever Island 3
Allapattah 189

INTRODUCTION

Soon after Charlie Jumper, the hero of *Forever Island*, learns that the patch of swamp he has occupied in the Everglades for sixty years is to be cleared to make room for a housing development, he poles his ancient dugout deep into the swaying River of Grass. He gazes into the peaceful sunset, surrounded by the natural beauty of his land, and he thinks about the past:

> Charlie . . . had seen the white man come into this land and slaughter the egret for its feathers, shooting them only when nesting on the rookery, killing them by the hundreds of thousands, and leaving the young either to die in the nest or be eaten by vultures . . ., the water around the mangroves turning red with blood; and he had seen the white man come into this land and slaughter the alligator, shipping out their hides fifty thousand at a time to be made into wallets and shoes . . .; and he had seen the white man come with his mules and his curses and his saws and his puffing trains and strip the land of the giant bald cypress, cutting them down like fields of sugar cane; and he had seen the white man wipe out the tree snails so that their shells could be sold as trinkets; and he had seen the white man dig the canals and drain the land and come closer and closer until he was now here again, once more telling the

Seminole that he could not live on this land because the
white man wanted it.

This passage strikes the theme of both of these
books. They are about the encroachments of "civiliza-
tion," in the form of the white man's greed and rapacity,
on one of the nation's last natural strongholds, the
Florida Everglades. The white man is the unregenerate
villain, with his utter disregard for anything except his
own welfare, his own profit, his own law.

Patrick Smith writes both novels from the point of
view of the native Indians who inhabit the Everglades,
the final refuge where they have retreated after their
defeat and decimation by the white man in the mid and
late 19th century. They have found a way of life that is
a sort of compromise between white and Indian. Some
live in chickees and eat fish and turtle stew; their sons
live in abandoned buses, have jobs on road crews, drive
old Ford pickup trucks and sell native souvenirs to the
tourists. There is an uneasy peace between them and the
white man — there has to be, in order for them to survive. And when the white man wants more land,
regardless of previous agreements or contracts or
assumptions, the Seminole has to give in.

Both of these books were written during the 1970's,
a critical decade for the Everglades, when governmental,
environmental and developmental forces were at logger-
heads, when the very existence of the River of Grass was
on balance. *Forever Island* and *Allapattah* addressed the
stark realities of what could happen if the plans of what
John D. MacDonald once called "the uglifiers" were

allowed to go forward. When Toby Tiger in *Allapatta* argues about God with his preacher father-in-law, who urges him to forgive the whites for what they have done, Toby says, "I know that God is everything. God is the land and the water and the trees and the animals, and they are destroying Him. God will soon be dead." Toby is a young version of Charlie Jumper in *Forever Island*. Both protagonists know that the way of the white man is the way of death, as far as the Everglades are concerned. The choices that both of them make, in these essentially tragic stories, are highly symbolic of what is actually happening in south Florida.

Patrick Smith himself seems to be a prototype of the villain he despises. Reared in Mississippi, he has an accent as thick as molasses and all the obvious accoutrements of white Southern manhood: degrees from Old Miss, good white-collar jobs in public relations, a fine wife and family. Yet he has never toed the prototypical line. In his actions as well as his writings he has stood up for the minority, the down-trodden, the misbegotten, rather than for the conventional values of his class, having to do with the acquisition of status and property. Back in Mississippi he wrote *The River Is Home*, a novel about the very poor and their determination to survive despite their poverty. Soon after he came to Florida, in 1967, *The Beginning* appeared, dealing with the crisis between blacks and whites that was dividing the South into two armed camps. It was a plea for understanding and tolerance, espousing a view that did not always sit well with many white Southerners. Between *Forever Island*, first published in 1973, and

Allapattah (1979) — also about a cause, the Indians' conflict with white developers, that was not particularly
popular — he did research for and wrote *Angel City*,
published in 1978, which concerns yet another cause
that is not dear to the hearts of many white people, the
plight of the migrant workers, most of them blacks and
Latins, who pick the fruits and vegetables on Florida's
vast farms and orange groves. Finally, *A Land
Remembered*, which came out originally as a Pineapple
Press hardback in 1984, is a splendid novel presenting
the panorama of Florida's history but again shedding a
not very favorable light on what the real estate developers have done to make sure that their profits from
Florida's growth continue to rise — again, a delicate
subject, since the book questions the sacred doctrine
that growth is necessarily good.

Recently Smith has flown against yet another rooted
middle-class convention. He has been on friendly terms
with the Russians. Two of his novels have been published
in Russia, and he has been there twice as a guest of the
Soviet Writers' Union, in 1983 and 1986. He feels strong-
ly that the only solutions to the problems that confront
the world lie in dialogue and communication, not in
additions to already overloaded atomic arsenals — in
some circles, again, an almost heretical sentiment.

An interesting thing about Smith's writing is that,
though you always know which side he is on, his
characters for the most part are credible and not all one-
sided. Though the general thrust of what white men
have done and are doing is evil, the individual white men
are not necessarily all bad. The young game warden who

picks up Toby Tiger in *Allapattah* for killing a deer out of season to provide meat for his grandfather is not an evil person; he is just doing his job. So is the judge who puts Toby in prison; and so is Mr. Riles in *Forever Island*, who is just a real estate man, not an avenging angel who sends bulldozers into the swamp to destroy it. What Smith tries to do is to show that all his characters are human beings, not just the blacks, the Indians and the Latins who are the downtrodden victims of white perfidy and deception. Sometimes, as they must, these victims emerge as almost too saintly, but Smith has a point to make — his readers cannot sympathize with characters whom they do not admire.

Smith has a deceptively simple narrative style that is remarkable in its directness and economy. There is a sort of epic inevitability in the events his stories describe. You know almost from the beginning that Toby Tiger and Charlie Jumper are doomed. The forces they struggle against are like mythological gods — all-powerful but invisible, faceless. When Charlie offers to pay for his land with fish and animal hides and snake skins, Mr. Riles says, "The owner of that land is not a man; it's a corporation. I can't speak to a corporation about fish and pelts and snake skins. They'd think I've lost my mind." Charlie cannot understand why his offer is unacceptable, why, if he agrees on a fair compensation, he can't continue to stay on the land he has occupied all his life. The conflict between his way — the Indian's way — and the white man's way is irreconcilable. Inevitably, he must give in.

Patrick Smith's writings have been nominated for a Pulitzer Prize and a Nobel Prize in Literature. There is no question that he deserves one or both. He has produced a small but extremely powerful body of work about subjects that need to be talked about and thought about if we who inhabit this fragile planet are to survive. Especially these two novels, *Forever Island* and *Allapattah,* are worthy of a much wider readership than they as yet have had, because they address head-on the complications and results of "civilized" man's wanton and continuing destruction of his native habitat, than which there is no more important a subject.

> — Dr. Edgar W. Hirshberg
> Department of English
> University of South Florida
> Tampa, 1987

FOREVER ISLAND

CHARLIE JUMPER stopped the dugout canoe in a pool of black water and watched the fish as it came out of a clump of pickerel weed. He picked up the spear and waited as the gar swam closer, its long snout poking into the decayed matter beneath it. It moved in a slow circle, coming nearer and nearer, until finally the old man smashed the spear into the side of the fish. He flicked the gar into the bottom of the dugout, put down the spear, and poled the canoe to the next clump of weeds.

He muttered, "Must have two gar. Little George might be hungry today." High overhead, a flight of crows cawed noisily as they winged their way eastward across the swamp. The old man stood rigidly erect, squinting into the still water, then again the spear slammed downward and a gar was brought into the dugout, its blood spilling over the bottom of the cypress canoe.

Once again the old man poled the dugout swiftly across the water, causing little waves to form behind and make rippling sounds as they spread outward into the cypress knees. He was moving deeper into the swamp, and the growths of live oaks, dwarf cypress, and cabbage palms, heavily laced with vines, blocked out the sun and caused the stream and the woods to be bathed with a soft yellowish tint. Ahead of him, the white heron lifted itself from the water's edge and glided away from his path, and the gallinule and rail scurried away into the grass.

The narrow stream turned and widened out with no visible bank, and at this point the old man turned right, entering an area of dwarf cypress and slimy water. The water mark on the cypress indicated that here there was normally two feet of water, but now the water was down to eight inches. The trunks of the trees were dotted with air plants, and scattered throughout the area were clumps of button bush and pickerel weed.

The old man traveled for a half mile across the green water and then turned into a slough covered with water lilies. This led into a pond of about two acres, most of the pond leading again into the dense swamp but the south portion covered by a mudbank. The dugout glided to within thirty feet of the mudbank and then stopped.

Lying atop the bank was a giant alligator at least eighteen feet in length, its body partially sunk into the muck. Aside from its size, it was different from any other alligator because of a scar that ran across the back of its head. Where its right eye had once been there was now a grotesque clump of scar tissue.

The old man and the alligator faced each other, the two eyes locking into the one eye as if in a greeting, then the man said, "You will eat now, Little George. I have brought you two nice garfish."

When the man threw one of the fish from the dugout, the alligator slid from the mudbank and came forward, his tail pushing him through the water. The fish made one brief chomp for his massive jaws, then the second garfish was thrown to him. When he finished this one he hesitated for a moment, waiting to see if more fish would come from the dugout, and then he turned and climbed back onto the mudbank, his one eye again locking into the eyes of the old man.

"You like it, heh, Little George," the man chuckled. "Next time I will also bring you a swamp rabbit. I will see you again in a few days."

The alligator continued to watch as the old man turned the dugout and started retracing his way across the pond and into the swamp.

Charlie Jumper was a Mikasuki Seminole, eighty-six years of age, living in the Big Cypress Swamp, the northern entrance to the Florida Everglades. His wiry body stretched only to five-nine, and his skin, baked deep brown by the many years of the Florida sun, resembled the bark of the cypress tree. His once black hair was now flecked with white.

Charlie Jumper had lived for the past sixty years at the same spot on the bank of Gopher Creek. He could remember once living in a glade deeper in the swamp, and he remembered an earlier life on a hammock in the River of Grass, but before that he was not certain.

He could not say for sure where he was born, but he knew he was a youth in early manhood when the century turned, and he could be older than the eighty-six years he claimed.

The old Indian now lived alone with his wife Lillie Tiger, but one mile away was the home of his youngest son, Billy Joe, and Billy Joe's family. Twenty-two years ago Billy Joe had gone to the real estate agent in Immokalee and asked if he could buy some of the land and put it to use. He had been told that the land was not for sale but that he could rent what he wished, and he had signed a rental agreement for ten acres at a cost of ten dollars per acre per year. Two acres of the land he had cleared for a truck farm, and on the rest he raised hogs and a few cows.

When Billy Joe had built the wooden frame house a mile away, his father had refused to come and live in the house. Billy Joe asked Charlie several times, but he finally accepted the fact that his father would never abandon the camp on the bank of Gopher Creek.

Billy Joe had married Watsie Cypress during a celebration of the Green Corn Dance, and now they had two children, Lucy, nineteen, and Timmy, twelve. Billy Joe was forty-two and Watsie five years younger.

Three other sons had been born to Charlie and Lillie Jumper. One was buried on a hammock in the marsh, and the other two had once gone to Oklahoma to attend an Indian trade school and had never returned.

In refusing to abandon the old ways, Charlie Jumper was not unique. There were many other Seminole chickees, or huts, on scattered hammocks throughout the Everglades and in remote sections of Big Cypress. The needs of these people were simple, and their lives were tied to the animals and the water and the land. They had no desire to live elsewhere. Charlie Jumper himself had no thought of leaving his chickees on the bank of Gopher Creek, for to him the swamp was eternal and indestructible.

When Charlie reached his camp he pulled the dugout onto the bank and began cleaning a black bass he had speared on the way home. Lillie was at her sewing machine on a small raised platform in the cooking chickee.

The Jumper camp was composed of a cluster of three chickees, one for sleeping, one for cooking and eating, and one for storage. Frames for the chickees were dwarf cypress poles, and the pointed roofs were made of palmetto fronds. The sleeping chickee had a raised cypress plank platform three feet off the ground, as did the storage one. The floor of the cooking chickee was dirt except for the small raised platform at the north end that served as Lillie's sewing area. The storage chickee had three palmetto frond walls, and the other two chickees were open on all sides.

In the center of the cooking chickee there was a large iron grate held up by two walls of limestone rock, and on the grate sat two skillets and a cast iron dutch oven. Under the inside eaves of the structure Charlie had constructed shelves which held the various pots and pans, such staples as coffee, sugar, salt, flour, and

cornmeal, and the few canned goods that were purchased at the store in Copeland.

The chickees were built beneath a huge live oak,
and the clearing was ringed by magnolia, dwarf cypress, cabbage palm, and wax-myrtle. There was a
clump of banana trees that Charlie had planted, and a
small plot of ground was used for growing corn, tomatoes, beans, squash, sweet and Irish potatoes, and cu-
cumbers. A flock of chickens roamed the clearing, and
off to one side there was a hog pen which was no
longer used.

All of Lillie's time when not cooking was spent at
the foot-pedal sewing machine, which had been given
to her fifty years ago by a white woman who had
opened an Indian mission in Everglades City. Lillie
made colorful Seminole jackets, skirts, and blouses
which Billy Joe sold for her to the souvenir stands
along the Tamiami Trail. Her pieces always brought
a good price, for she was one of the few Seminole
women left who could hand-weave into the cloth the
exact designs on the backs of the now almost extinct
tree snails. Lillie would spend at least six hours each
day on the sewing platform, and her work produced almost all of the cash money available for purchases of
staples and cloth.

Most of Charlie's time was spent roaming the
swamp and marsh in search of fish, turtles, squirrels,
rabbits, turkey, and ducks. It was seldom any more
that he hunted the swift deer or the bear. He also gathered the guavas, blueberries, wild grapes, plums, black-

berries, and wild orange, and tended the vegetables he grew in the garden plot.

Although Charlie had abandoned the old mode of dress in favor of dungarees, Lillie had not. Her thin body was covered to the ankles by the colorful long dress, and a multi-colored cape was always draped around her shoulders. Her hair was balled on top of her head and held fast by a hairnet, and the silver eardrops came down to meet a dozen strands of glass beads that she wore around her neck. She was extremely shy and quiet, and would not speak to a stranger even in reply to a question. It was seldom that she said more than a few necessary words even to her husband or son, and it was only the grandson, Timmy, who could make her laugh.

Charlie was joined in his fish-cleaning chore by a large raccoon that jumped onto his shoulder and started clawing his head frantically.

"You stop that now, Gumbo," he said. "Don't I always give you a piece of the fish? Can't you have patience? You will get your share."

He had kept the 'coon as a pet for many years, and it had the free run of the chickees. It often took its meals at the same table with them, sometimes eating from Charlie's bowl. A hunter had shot the animal's mother and left it lying on the ground where it had fallen, and Charlie had named the small one Gumbo because he had found it on the limb of a gumbo limbo tree. The 'coon kept scratching at Charlie's head until he handed it a strip of fish, which it turned over and over in its paws before it began to eat.

The old couple did not have any set meal times and ate only when hungry. There was always food cooking on the grate, and now the smell of a turtle stew made Charlie's nose twitch. He came over to the cooking chickee, put the cleaned bass in a pan, and dished himself up a bowl of the stew. Just as he started eating he heard the rattle of a vehicle coming along the gravel road. An old 1960 Ford pickup turned down the narrow trail leading to the clearing and stopped. Billy Joe Jumper got out of the truck and came over to the chickee, closely followed by Timmy.

"Hello, Pappa," Billy Joe said, taking a seat on one of the cabbage palm stumps used as chairs.

"You want to eat?" Charlie asked. "We have a fresh turtle stew."

"No thanks, Pappa. I'm not hungry."

"Will you take me fishing, Granpappa?" Timmy asked quickly. He always got excited when he came to the camp of his grandfather, for he loved to go into the swamp with the old man in the dugout canoe.

"It is up to your father," Charlie answered. "You must ask him first."

"I guess he can stay," Billy Joe said. "I've got to carry the rent money up to Immokalee. I came by to see if you need anything from the store."

"I need a bolt of the blue cloth and three spools of red thread," Lillie said. "I have the money here." She got up from the sewing machine, took a tin can from the overhead shelf, and handed a roll of bills to Billy Joe.

"Is that all you need?" he asked.

"We need a can of coffee and a sack of the plain flour," she said. "And I have one finished jacket you can sell."

"It won't bring as good a price in Immokalee as it would in Naples or down on the Trail. Keep it here and I will sell it for you later this week."

Billy Joe got up to leave, then he turned to Timmy and said, "You mind your grandfather, you hear? And don't pester your grandmother. And don't pull Gumbo's tail. I will come back for you this afternoon."

Billy Joe turned the pickup west on the narrow limestone road that led from the swamp to Turner River Grade, a gravel road that ran north through the Copeland Prairie to Alligator Alley, the Everglades Parkway toll highway. Instead of turning north when he reached the Grade, he turned west again on the state road to Copeland, where he would sell a hamper of tomatoes to the Janes Store. He did not want to take the tomatoes all the way to Immokalee because the intense heat would make them soft, and the price would not then be as good.

When he reached the store in Copeland, which was on Highway 29 three miles north of the Tamiami Trail, he sold the tomatoes and purchased the things his mother wanted. Just above Miles City the highway intersected Alligator Alley, and he stopped for a few minutes and watched the stream of speeding cars heading east and west across the two-lane toll road that connected Naples with Fort Lauderdale.

The hot May sun was causing heat waves to rise

from the asphalt, and because of the long drought there was little water in the drainage ditch that paralleled the highway. There had been no rain for almost eight months, and the fields and pastures were burned a deep brown. Even the fronds of the cabbage palms that bordered the highway seemed to be smoking.

When he reached Immokalee he went to the small concrete block building that housed the office of Riles Real Estate Agency. At a front desk he gave the rent money to a secretary, and while she was writing his receipt, Kenneth Riles came in. He was a young man of twenty-nine who had inherited the real estate business when his father died five years ago.

"How are things with you, Billy Joe?" Riles asked, handing a sheaf of papers to the secretary.

"Drought is beginning to hurt bad," Billy Joe said.

"Yes, it's sure bad. We really need some rain. And by the way, Billy Joe, I just received a notice that ten thousand acres of the land that belongs to the Potter Estate in Miami has been sold. That section includes the land where you live. I wouldn't think that the rent price would change, but if it does I'll let you know. Until we learn more about the plans of the new owner, just keep making the rent payments here the same as usual."

"I will, Mr. Riles. And if the rent goes up, I'd appreciate your letting me know right away."

Billy Joe then drove to the office of the Everglades Gazette, which was owned by Albert Lykes. Lykes was also an attorney although he practiced little law any more. He was in his late fifties and devoted most of his time to the small weekly newspaper.

When Billy Joe had purchased the pickup truck from a used car lot in Naples he had been overcharged two hundred dollars on the finance charges. When Lykes learned of this he had recovered Billy Joe's money and then refused to accept a fee for doing so. Lykes was known as a lawyer who would handle legal matters for the Seminoles at no cost, and he counted most of them in the area as his friends. Billy Joe always brought him something when he came to Immokalee.

Albert Lykes was sitting at a desk in his small cluttered office when Billy Joe entered. He did not look up from his work quickly, for in the jeans, faded blue denim shirt, boots, and cowboy hat, Billy Joe resembled any of dozens of other men to be seen on the streets and in the businesses of this cattle center. When he finally recognized who had entered he pushed the papers away and said cheerfully, "Well, hello, Billy Joe. Have a seat. How are things with you?"

"I brought you some beans and some okra," Billy Joe said, handing Lykes a brown paper bag. "It's not much, though. The drought has about ruined my whole vegetable crop."

"Yes, we're really beginning to hurt everywhere. The fires have already burned thousands of acres in the southern Glades, and some of the fires have burned down so deep into the muck that they say it will take years for them to burn out even after we get rain. What we need is a pure flood."

"I sure hope the fire doesn't break out in the swamp. I don't see how it could ever be stopped there." Billy Joe pulled up a chair, sat down and said, "Mr. Lykes, they just told me down at the real estate office that ten thousand acres of land out there where I live have been sold. Why would anybody buy that much land so far out in the swamp? Most of the cypress has already been cut a long time ago."

"Who told you that?" Lykes asked quickly.

"Mr. Riles. He said he didn't know if the rent would change or not, but he'd let me know as soon as he heard something. I sure hope it doesn't go up. After this drought killing my crop I'd have a real hard time getting up more money."

"I don't know why anyone would want that land, Billy Joe, unless they're just speculating. It's an awfully isolated place. If I can find out anything I'll let you know."

"I would sure appreciate it, Mr. Lykes. And you come see us. We'll take you fishing."

"Thanks for the vegetables," Lykes said, "and anytime you're in town, come by to see me."

As Billy Joe turned back down Highway 29 towards home he was troubled by the news of the sale of the land. He just didn't understand why anyone would want to buy it.

As soon as his father had left, Timmy dipped a bowl into the turtle stew and began to eat ravenously, although for breakfast that morning he had eaten hot biscuits, corn grits, and fried ham. His mother could not cook the wild game and the turtle as well as his grandmother, and he often slipped off and came down to the chickees to eat an extra meal. His grandmother made the corn bread in a five-inch deep loaf, and he broke off a chunk of the steaming-hot pone and dipped it into the juice of the stew. The turtle meat was sweet and tender, and he licked his fingers after each bite.

Charlie watched in silence for a few minutes, then he said, "You eat like a hungry panther. It is good for you. Make you grow big and strong."

Timmy had the same Seminole features as his father and his grandmother, the high cheekbones, the deep brown color, the slightly slanted, piercing eyes. But unlike his grandfather, his eyes were searching and excited rather than tired and squinting.

He finished the bowl of stew and said, "Are we going into the swamp now, Granpappa?"

"I have not finished my food. If you are in such a hurry, you go and dig the worms for the bait."

Timmy jumped up and ran to the storage chickee, took out a shovel, and headed for the area of the abandoned hog pen. He came back shortly with a can filled with worms and put them, along with two cane poles, into the dugout. The poles were equipped with lines the same length as the poles, turkey quills, and small hooks. Charlie used them only when fishing with Timmy for the bream, for when he hunted the black bass and the garfish, he used the spear.

As they started down Gopher Creek, Timmy sat in the front of the dugout and watched his grandfather move them swiftly across the water. He studied each stroke of the pole in his grandfather's hands. He had always been fascinated by each task Charlie performed, even the seemingly simple things like removing the shell from a turtle or cleaning a fish or carving a bowl from a block of cypress. He had a deep love for his grandfather and hoped that someday he could be like him.

He finally broke the silence and said, "Where are we going, Granpappa?"

"We will fish for the bream in the otter pond."

"Will you take me to the big tree?"

"We will go to the tree first and fish on the way back."

They moved quickly along a narrow winding stream bordered on both sides by growths of oak and willow and dwarf cypress and wax-myrtle, laced overhead by a dozen varieties of vines. The landscape then changed suddenly and they were in the open area of the dwarf cypress swamp where Charlie had turned right that morning on his way to the giant alligator. This time they went straight ahead, and on the far side of the clearing they found a stream that led back into a dense area of swamp.

After another mile this stream widened out and spread its black water across the entire land; and rising up before them, towering a hundred and fifty feet into the sky, was a giant bald cypress that had escaped the saw when the loggers had ravished the swamp several decades before.

Charlie poled the dugout close to the base of the tree, and when Timmy looked up it seemed to him that the trunk went out of sight into the clouds. Around the base of the tree, which must be at least fifty feet in circumference, the cypress knees grew so thick that the canoe could not pass through them.

Timmy said excitedly, "Can I climb it, Granpappa? Please let me climb it this time. You promised you would let me do it someday."

Years ago Charlie had built a ladder up the side of the tree, driving the rungs in one at a time with nails, moving slowly upward and driving in the cypress rungs until he had no more, then climbing down to the canoe and going back up with more rungs and more nails, moving steadily upward until finally he had reached the top where the limbs forked outward and upward in graceful curves. From the top he could see above all the other trees, across the roof of the swamp, past the point where the trees suddenly stopped and the great sea of sawgrass began, over the River of Grass dotted with the thick growths of the hammocks as far away to the horizon as the eye could see.

He thought for a moment and said to Timmy, "Not this time. You will climb it, but this is not the time. You must be strong, or your arms would give way before you reached the top."

"Can you see Forever Island from up there?" Timmy asked.

"No, you cannot see Forever Island. You can see the way, but it is too far. It is many miles to the south."

"You will let me climb it someday, won't you, Granpappa?"

"Yes. I promise you, you will climb the tree."

Timmy sat back down in the bottom of the dugout and the old man poled them off in a westward direction. He left this swamp by a different stream and soon came to a pond dotted with dwarf cypress and pickerel weed. He stopped close to a clump of weeds and said, "We will try here for bream, but you must be very quiet. The bream will run away if they hear a sound."

Timmy put a worm on the hook, adjusted the turkey quill to a depth of two feet, then threw it out close to the weeds. As soon as the hook had sunk, the quill darted downward and the line became taut. Timmy pulled in a fat bream and dropped it into the dugout. Each time a hook hit the water the same thing happened, and soon they had boated more than a dozen fish.

Charlie wrapped his line back around the pole, dropped it onto the bottom of the dugout and said, "We will quit now. You have all the fish you can eat."

As Timmy wrapped his line around the pole, Charlie watched a heron pecking at minnows along the edge of the water. The flat was also being worked by wood ibis and water turkey. He pointed to a nearby mudbank and said, "You see the marks there. It is where the otter slides down into the water to play. They have been watching us catch their fish. Would you like to see them?"

Timmy finished wrapping the line and put it down. "Yes, Granpappa. Maybe we can catch one and I can carry it home with me."

"You will not catch the otter with your hands. He is

too fast. Only the alligator can catch the otter, and he cannot do it unless the otter's mind is elsewhere."

Charlie picked up one of the fish and threw it to the edge of the water. Almost instantly, a brown otter shot down the mudbank, grabbed the fish in its mouth, stared intensely at the man and boy, then scurried back up the bank. The otter paused for a moment more, again staring at the intruders, then he scurried out of sight into the brush.

"Sometimes they will come out and play for you," Charlie said. "They have even come into the chickees. If we stayed here longer, they would not be afraid. But we must go now. We have fish to clean for your supper."

Timmy lay on his back and looked upward into the trees and the sky as his grandfather poled the dugout toward home. It made him dizzy to watch the limbs and the vines and the clouds fly by overhead, and hear the rippling of the water as the ancient canoe sliced through the swamp. High up in the sky he could see a flight of white ibis winging its way south toward the marsh country, and, although he could not see it, he listened to the deep-throated croak of a great blue heron. He draped one leg over the side of the dugout and let the water swirl across his bare foot. In a moment he was asleep and was awakened only when he became aware that the movement of the dugout had stopped.

When Timmy pushed himself up he did not see his grandfather. For a moment he was startled, then he looked up a shallow slough and saw Charlie snatching something from the bottom and putting it into his pocket. He soon returned to the canoe and said, "Crawfish. They are for Gumbo. These are for him like candy is for you. He could eat a gallon if you would give it to him."

When they started to leave, Charlie suddenly stopped the dugout again and walked back up the slough. He noticed a fresh gash cut into the side of a tree, then he waded further up the slough. As far as he could see into the swamp there was a line of fresh gashes cut into trees. He wondered about this for a moment, then he turned and retraced his path back to Timmy.

As soon as the bow of the dugout touched land at the chickees, the 'coon jumped in and smelled the fish, then he climbed to Charlie's shoulder and started scratching his head. Charlie put him out of the dugout. "The fish are not for you, Gumbo," he said. "They are for Timmy. This is what I brought for you." When he took the crawfish from his pocket and dropped them on the ground, the 'coon let out a high-pitched yell, almost like a chuckle; then he grabbed one and turned it over and over in his paws.

Lillie was still at the sewing machine when Timmy scampered up the bank and to the chickee. "Can I have some more stew?" he asked eagerly.

"You can have what you wish," she said, smiling. "There is plenty. It is good for you to eat."

He dipped a bowl of the stew, broke off a large piece of corn pone, and again ate with relish.

TWO

SETH'S FISH CAMP was two miles eastward on Gopher Creek from Charlie's chickees, and the narrow limestone road ended at the camp. The owner was Seth Thompson, who had been born on the campsite and had lived all of his sixty-five years there except for a period of time in his youth when he had been a commercial fisherman during the catfish boom at Lake Okeechobee.

Seth's father had bought the ten-acre homesite from a mail-order advertisement in 1890, had sold his small farm in Georgia, and headed south to Florida and the land of milk and honey which the advertisement guaranteed. It pictured tomatoes that weighed five pounds and okra two feet long and sugar cane twenty feet tall and soil so rich that, if you threw a stick on the ground, by the next day a tree would have sprouted.

John Thompson arrived south of Lake Okeechobee six months later with an ox cart filled with plows and axes and dreams, and the further south he traveled the deeper the water became and the more impenetrable the swamp. He finally abandoned the cart and the oxen and waded onto his property with only an axe and a rifle. For the next year he slept on the wet muck and swatted millions of mosquitoes while he built the small house from the stand of virgin bald cypress. He drew his bare living from the swamp and sold the pelts of the animals he killed for food.

Many times he thought of abandoning his property and seeking out the real estate company that had tricked and fleeced him, but he stayed and gradually hacked a small piece of the land from the jungle and grew a few six-ounce tomatoes and three-inch okra.

In 1906, while on a trip to Okeechobee City, he married the daughter of a fisherman and brought her back to the cypress house in the swamp. She stayed just long enough for Seth to be born, then she left man and child and swamp and was not seen again by John Thompson.

Seth and his embittered father had no father-son relationship, and his father looked upon him as something he could not swat dead only because of the law. He tolerated the boy for thirteen years, and then Seth ran away to Lake Okeechobee and secured work in the catfish industry.

Seth would occasionally come back home and give his father what money he could spare, and the relationship gradually warmed. It was during such a brief visit in 1931 that Seth found his father dead in the small tomato patch. He buried him in the cemetery at Copeland.

Seth came back to the property and brought with him a new bride from Moore Haven, and then he experienced the same thing as his father. One week in the dilapidated cypress house and the mosquito-infested swamp was enough, and on the eighth morning Seth awoke to find that his bride had vanished. Unlike his father, though, he was not embittered. She had been unable to cook and had refused to chop logs and skin animals, and it suited him that she was gone.

By this time the great catfishing boom at Lake Okeechobee had played out, and there was still much of a demand for fish, so Seth began commercial fishing in the creeks and sloughs of the swamp and in nearby Turner River. As he grew older and lost his taste for the long hard hours of commercial fishing, he added rental boats and sold his services as a guide, and gradually Seth's Fish Camp became known to the sportsfishermen of Collier County. He would now do commercial fishing only when he needed the money.

The old house was still as it had been when built in 1890, with the sagging front porch, thick plank floor and hand-hewn shingles. To the left of the house there was parked a Ford pickup truck and a swamp buggy with its huge airplane tires. Close to the creek Seth had built a shack that served as his store. Here he sold such items as fishing tackle, beer, soda pop, candy, and cigarettes, but he drank a great deal more of the beer than he sold. A dozen flat-bottomed rental boats were pulled onto the bank of the creek, and everywhere around the clearing there were piles of fish nets and traps.

The only modern conveniences added to the place were the electric lines, the cooler for the beer and soda pop, a refrigerator, and a big Coca-Cola sign across the front of the store that read Seth's Fish Camp. He still cooked his meals on an open grill in front of the house or on a wood-burning stove in the kitchen. There was an outdoor privy in the woods back of the house, and baths were taken in a wooden tub on the rear porch. He did, however, have an electric pump to draw water into the house and to the stand on the edge of the creek where fish were cleaned.

Seth had an assistant known only by the name of Slim, a gangling man of forty who had walked into the camp ten years ago and asked for a meal and had never left. Seth had never known where Slim had come from or where he was going or if he had any other name, and he had never asked. Slim became a faithful helper around the camp, ate little, and did whatever he was told to do without question, and this was enough for Seth. He lived in a room Seth had built for him on the back of the store, and it was obvious that he had no intention of ever leaving.

The one thing that distinguished Seth's place from any other part of the swamp was the nine acres of virgin bald cypress surrounding the camp. No timber had ever been cut except for the one acre where the earlier gardening venture had been tried, and those trees went into the building of the house and sheds. Now the somber trees reached high into the sky, with boughs so thick that no sunlight ever came through, and the ground was covered with cypress knees of all shapes and heights and tall graceful ferns and sphagnum moss. There were ponds filled with water lilies; thick growths of palmetto and wild orchids; and there

was a quietness that was almost unearthly. Many people came to the camp just to walk through these
woods.

Seth Thompson at sixty-five was a rotund man,
five feet eleven in height and carrying two hundred
and eighty pounds, a modern-day Falstaff, always smiling, dressed only in a pair of faded overalls. Even
when he made trips into Naples or Everglades City or
Fort Myers or Immokalee to sell fish or buy supplies he
donned neither shirt nor shoes, and if he had, he would
not have been recognized by those who had known
him for many years. He was accepted for what he was,
both by those who came to his camp and by those who
came into contact with him in the towns and cities,
and he was no more of a curiosity than any other of
the white men or Indians who made the Big Cypress
their home.

Seth was daubing tar on the bottom of a rental boat
when Charlie pushed the bow of the dugout onto the
bank. He always stopped by to visit with Seth when on
this part of the creek. As soon as the canoe touched
land, Gumbo jumped out and started shaking a gourd
rattle. Charlie sometimes took Gumbo with him on the
shorter trips into the swamp, and the 'coon would run
up and down the dugout, shaking the rattle to frighten
the birds. Charlie had made it for him from a dried
gourd and little limestone pebbles. But he never took
Gumbo with him when he went to feed Little George,
for he knew if the 'coon jumped out of the dugout, he
would make one good bite for the giant alligator.

Seth looked up and said, "Well howdy, Charlie. How about a beer?"

He always offered the old Seminole a beer, and Charlie sometimes accepted. He relished the taste of the cold brew, but he seldom drank more than one for fear that his head would swim.

Seth put down the tar pot, looked toward the shack and shouted, "Slim, git on out here and bring us a couple of brews."

The lanky man sauntered from the store with two cans of beer. He was dressed the same as Seth except that he wore an oversize pair of brogan shoes. He handed the cans to Seth and said, "Howdy, Charlie. How's yore folks?"

"They are fine," Charlie replied, taking one of the cans from Seth. Slim turned and went back into the store.

Both men got up and moved into the shade of a moss-festooned oak whose limbs nearly covered the house. They squatted on their haunches and faced each other, Seth's huge stomach bulging out so far that he could not see his feet. Charlie took a drink of the beer and said, "It is good. It makes my stomach chuckle."

Gumbo ran up and snatched at the can, and Seth said, "Give him a little snort, Charlie. It won't hurt him none."

Charlie held the can down while the 'coon put his mouth to the rim and sucked. Then Gumbo jumped back, scratched, twitched his nose, and scampered onto the seat of the swamp buggy.

"Guess he's going to take a little ride now that he's likkered up," Seth laughed. He took a deep drink from the can. "Shore mighty hot and dry. They's places I can't even get into anymore in a boat. Water's down two feet and more, and in some of them little ponds they ain't but a few inches left. We need a regular flood of rain."

"Are you fishing now?" Charlie asked.

"Ah, I'm doin' a little, catchin' some catfish and some mullet over in Turner River. Ain't many fishermen comin' out here now and rentin' boats with the water so low and it so hot and dry. So's I thought I might as well sell a few for pocket money whiles I'm not doin' too much around the camp."

"I saw a strange thing this morning," Charlie said, suddenly changing the subject. "There is a slough southeast of here, about five miles, where the birds feed, and I went there to cut some small pond cypress. There were two ducks that were dead, and a spoonbill that could not move itself, and it died too while I was there. They were young birds, and they had not been shot."

"Well, I guess even the critters can get sick and die before their time. I've seen dead birds before in the swamp. Could be something they et."

"Maybe so."

Seth sucked the last drop of beer from the can. "You ready for another?" he asked.

"This is enough. This one was good, but if I have another I might point the dugout toward Cape Sable instead of home."

"Ah, you better have another. A man can't travel on one leg, you know."

"Thank you, but I must go now."

Seth got up and followed Charlie down to the creek bank. "What you going to do with them small logs?" he asked.

"I am going to hew out the little dugout canoes to be sold to the tourist places on the Tamiami Trail."

"How come?" Seth said, laughing and digging his elbow into Charlie's side. "You ain't got a woman somewheres that's hittin' you up for money, have you?"

"No woman would want even money from such an old dog as me," Charlie said. "Lucy, the daughter of Billy Joe, is going to marry Frank Willie, and Billy Joe wants to give them the television for a present. He has lost his crop to the drought, and he is worried that he cannot now do this. So I will help, and Lillie will help, and we will not tell Billy Joe until we have earned the money. The little canoes will bring a fair price."

"Shoot, if that's all that's botherin' you, I'll help too. Me and you can gather some cypress knees, 'cause they bring a good price too, and I know a place down in Miami that'll buy all the snake hides you can get, and we can get some frogs and sell the legs. Shoot, them frog legs is high as a cat's back now. I ain't doin' much of nothin' around here now, so I'll help. You just let me know when you want to get started."

"It is kind of you to offer, Seth. I will let you know. And I thank you for the beer." He turned to leave, then he stopped and said, "Have you been marking a trail on the trees anywhere in the swamp?"

"What you mean, Charlie?" Seth asked, puzzled.

"Cutting gashes on the trees with a hatchet."

"Shoot, no. I got better things to do than that. How come you ask?"

"It is nothing, I guess. I saw such a fresh trail the other day, but maybe it was a hunter who feared losing his way."

"Ain't no hunters out here this time of year and you know it," Seth said. "But I don't know what kind of a fool would go around choppin' on trees."

Charlie then put Gumbo into the dugout and pushed the slim craft out into the creek. "We will see you again soon, Seth," he said.

"You come back anytime, Charlie. And you just let me know when you want to get started raisin' that money for the television."

THREE

CHARLIE WAS SITTING on the ground striking chips from a miniature dugout when
he heard the sound of an airboat coming
down the creek. He put the work aside and watched as
the craft came around the bend and approached the
chickees. It was Fred Henderson, the game warden.
He cut the engine and guided the bow of the boat onto
the landing.

Henderson was a youthful looking man of thirty-
five who had worked this area of the county for the
past nine years. Six years ago he had been shot by alligator poachers, but this had been before the law was
strengthened, making alligator poaching a felony pun-
ishable by up to five years in prison. This new and
more drastic law, combined with a vanishing market
for hides, had made poaching almost a thing of the past,
although a few alligators were still killed or captured
illegally. But it would never again be the booming business it once was, and now the wardens could spend
more time enforcing the game and fish laws.

Fred Henderson stepped from the boat and said,
"Hi there, Mr. Charlie." He always visited this camp
when traveling the area of Gopher Creek.

"Hi there, Fred Henderson. You want tea?"

"Sure," the warden smiled. "I came twenty miles out of the way to get a mug of that special brew of yours."

Charlie got up, went to the cooking chickee, and returned with two steaming mugs of a dark colored brew.

Henderson took a sip. "Man, that's good. Really makes your motor run."

"It is the secret Black Drink," Charlie said. "It cleans out a man's innards. It is good for you." Charlie then chuckled, for it was only harmless sassafras and not the legendary Black Drink used during the Green Corn Dance festival to purge all the males.

"Well, if it's what you say, I better give it back, 'cause I've got a long ride ahead of me out in the sawgrass, and you know what would happen if I hung my bottom over the side of the boat and some of that sharp sawgrass got ahold of me." Henderson then laughed also, for he knew exactly what was in the brew.

Charlie said, "Only the Seminole knows how to do his business in the sawgrass and come away without injury."

"I can believe that," Henderson said. He looked about the clearing and asked, "Where's Gumbo?"

"He is right above you."

The warden looked up and the 'coon was coming down an oak limb, just about ready to pounce upon him. One leap and Gumbo straddled his shoulders.

"Man, you've gotten fat, Gumbo," Henderson said, taking the 'coon from his shoulders.

"He eats only ten meals each day," Charlie said.

"Well, you better watch him. Some big 'gator sure would like to have him for a meal." The warden finished the drink and got up. "You want to ride with me? I'll bring you back in a couple of hours."

"Yes, I will go," Charlie beamed, for one of his greatest pleasures was riding in the swift airboat.

Charlie was still grinning when the engine thundered to life and the craft moved off slowly down Gopher Creek. They made their way through the shallow ponds and the sloughs and then into the vast River of Grass, the open Glades that stretched southward all the way to Cape Sable and to Florida Bay.

When they reached the open marsh the boat picked up speed and crashed through the razor-sharp sawgrass, which was sometimes as high as ten feet and sometimes only two feet. Dotted over the landscape there were hammocks filled with cabbage palm, oak, lancewood, poisonwood, gumbo limbo, all interlaced with vines.

Sometimes the warden guided the boat along open paths through the sawgrass which were mostly trails wallowed out by alligators; and sometimes they would break through a wall of grass and suddenly come into small ponds filled with water lilies. Here the alligator eyes peeked up at them out of lily pads. Ahead of them the coots and the ducks scurried out of the way, and once they surprised a little coot that went under the boat and came out behind them uninjured but with a ruffled pride.

They made a wide circle through the marsh and

then turned back north. They could see just how much the towering royal palms overshadowed the other trees. Their slick trunks rose upward for a hundred and seventy-five feet and their green down-turned tops resembled tiny umbrellas above the roof of the swamp. From this distance it seemed that the swamp's mixture of trees formed a solid wall that could not be penetrated, but as they drew closer, many openings came into view.

When they entered the swamp, Charlie signaled for Henderson to stop. He idled the motor and Charlie said, "Have you been by Muscadine Slough?"

"Not in a good while," Henderson replied, "but I know where it is."

"I saw several dead birds there yesterday. They were young, and they had not been shot."

"Well, let's take a quick look. Can we get there with the airboat?"

"The water is low, but I went there in the dugout. I do not believe the airboat will have trouble."

They moved very slowly, Henderson guiding the boat around decayed logs and fallen limbs, following narrow paths when he could, sometimes gunning the powerful engine and shooting over the shelves of shallow mudbanks, pushing through beds of the deadly cottonmouths and making the snakes run from the thunder of the engine.

The east end of the slough was narrow, but as it turned a bend it widened and formed a pond of about ten acres. The water level was down from a normal four feet to a scant six inches, and there was no water

movement in or out of the area, making the entire
pond stagnant. Birds scattered into the swamp at the
approach of the airboat.

Henderson came into the main pond, cut the engine and looked about. "Good God," he exclaimed in
puzzlement, "what has happened here?"

There were dead birds lying everywhere: Florida
mallard, ringnecks, blue-winged teal, coots, black-
necked stilts, white ibis, American egrets, grebe, gallinule, gull-billed terns, Louisiana heron, skimmers, glossy
ibis, and roseate spoonbills. Many others were para-
lyzed, not yet dead but unable to move, their wings
outspread and their beaks turned upward, struggling
to move.

Henderson just sat and stared silently until Charlie
said, "It was not this bad yesterday. There were only
three."

"It must be getting every bird that stops by this
pond. I've never seen anything like this. Dead birds,
yes. But not this."

The warden took two metal containers and scooped
them down into the water and the muck, then he
sealed them and put them aside. "I'll move around the
edges and you pick up about a dozen of the dead
ones," he said to Charlie. "As soon as we get back I'll
rush them and the water samples to the lab. They can
probably figure it out pretty fast."

After they had gathered the dead birds, Henderson
pushed the airboat through the swamp and toward Gopher Creek. He moved faster now, and he and Charlie
had no more jokes nor conversation. Charlie got out at
his landing and the airboat shot away up the creek.

FOUR

Timmy had run down the dirt lane to the chickees early the next morning, and Charlie was just finishing a breakfast of biscuits baked in the dutch oven, hot corn grits, and slices of fried turtle meat. He was pouring a mug of coffee as Lillie busied herself preparing a pot of fish chowder.

Even before he said "Can I have one?" Timmy had grabbed a hot biscuit, broken it in half, stuffed it with crisp turtle meat, and plopped it into his mouth. Between munches he said, "Can we go into the swamp this morning, Granpappa?"

"I must go to the camp of Seth Thompson, and then I have work to do, but you can go with me to the camp, and maybe we can come back through the swamp."

Timmy heard a rattling sound and looked up, and Gumbo was on top of the chickee, shaking the gourd. "Do not pay him any mind," Charlie said. "He has eaten twice already this morning. He is worse than a hog. Now he is just wanting your attention."

When Charlie finished his coffee, they got into the dugout and started up the creek. This time Timmy sat in the furthest point of the bow, looking ahead and skimming his hands through the cool water. It did not take the sleek craft but a short time to move the two miles to the fish camp.

Seth was inside the store when they arrived, and he came out with a can of beer in his hand. He greeted Charlie in the usual way, "How about a can of beer?"

"Not this time, Seth. It is too early in the morning for me. I thank you anyway."

Timmy ran across the clearing, jumped onto the swamp buggy, grabbed the steering wheel, and made sounds like the motor running. Charlie squatted down and said to Seth, "When are you going down by the Trail again?"

Seth plopped down in front of him, his huge stomach almost touching the ground. "I got to make a trip down to Everglades City tomorrow morning. You need something?"

"I have one of the little canoes finished. Billy Joe could sell it for me, but I don't want him to know of this until we have our share for the television. And Lillie has two jackets."

"Shore, I'll take 'um down with me. How much you want for the canoe?"

"I do not know. What do you think?"

"Well, I've seen them things sell to the tourist for about thirty dollars, so you ought to get fifteen. I'll do the best I can. I ain't no fool when it comes to dealing with them crooks down on the Trail."

"We will have the things ready when you come by."

"Shoot, long as I'm makin' a haul for you anyway,

why don't we go out tonight and get a mess of them frog legs. I could sell 'um to the Rod and Gun Club down in Everglades City. Some folks pays as much as two or three dollars for a plate of them things, and they ought to bring at least sixty cents a pound, maybe more."

"We will go if you have the time."

"I got the time, Charlie. 'Bout all I've got ever night is time. I'll pick you up sometime after dark."

The sound of an airboat stopped the conversation, and Fred Henderson turned in to the camp when he saw Charlie and Seth together. He cut the engine and got out.

"How about a beer, Fred?" Seth asked.

"Thanks, but no thanks," the warden replied.

Seth and Charlie both got up, and Henderson said to Charlie, "Got a call early this morning from the lab down in West Palm. It's a bacteria killing those birds. They said that when the water gets real low, this bacteria can multiply and really do some damage. It'll take rising water to stop it. They told us to go in there and burn all the dead birds and try to keep the others away from that area. We've got a man who's going to stay in there and fire a shotgun to scare the birds off. The bacteria might be in just that one pond, so the important thing is to keep the birds out of there. Beyond that, they say there's nothing we can do, except maybe pray for rain."

"Is that the place you told me about, Charlie?" Seth asked.

"Yes. It is the east end of Muscadine Slough. I went

by there again yesterday with Fred, and we found many dead birds, maybe eighty or a hundred. And others were sick."

"If either of you run across this somewhere else, please let me know right away," Henderson said. "I'll be running this area for the next few days. And we sure thank you, Mr. Charlie, for pointing this thing out. Something like this could happen out in the swamp and we wouldn't know about it until it's too late to do anything."

As soon as Henderson was gone, Charlie and Timmy got into the dugout and started back down the creek. About halfway home Charlie stopped the canoe and said to Timmy, "Look very close there in the mud-bank."

Timmy peered into the water and could see that a large snapper turtle had buried itself in the mud with only its head showing. Its mouth was open, and two appendages inside its mouth were waving gently in the slow moving current.

Charlie said, "Little fish will think those are worms."

Timmy continued to watch as a small bream slowly approached the waving tentacles, then it suddenly darted to them. The turtle's mouth snapped shut.

"The turtle has now had his dinner," Charlie said. "I will come back sometime and take the turtle for my dinner. It is the way of all things in the swamp. We all depend on each other."

Timmy frowned for a moment, then he said, "It

seemed like a bad trick, Granpappa. The little fish did not know better."

As Charlie pushed the canoe away and continued downstream, he repeated, "It is the way of all things, Timmy."

When the evening meal was finished, Charlie and Lillie sat around the flickering fire in the cooking chickee. From far in the south a rumble of dry thunder echoed through the swamp. Lillie was rocking back and forth gently, her hands in her lap, looking as if she were half asleep.

She turned to Charlie and said, "Why do we not have the electric line brought to the chickee? It passes here on the way to the fish camp."

At first Charlie didn't know what to say in reply, for she had never mentioned this before. For a few moments he remained silent.

She spoke again, "If we had the electric line I could be sewing now. My eyes cannot see by the firelight anymore."

He finally said, "It would cost money each month. Billy Joe has to pay the first of each month."

"It would not be much. We could pay it from the things we sell. And later we could buy the electric box to make ice and to keep the meat and the fish from spoiling."

"Then we could keep the cans of cold Coca-Cola like Billy Joe, couldn't we?" For a moment he became silent as if in deep thought, then he said quickly, "We

will do it! I will speak to Billy Joe and have him make
the arrangements for us."

Just then Seth came out of the darkness of the
creek and rammed the bow of his boat onto the landing. He walked to the chickee and eased himself slowly
onto one of the palm stump seats.

"We have just decided to have the electric line
brought to the chickee!" Charlie said triumphantly.

"You ought to have done it long before now," Seth
said. "I've seen them chickees all up and down the
Trail with electric lines runnin' to them. Ain't no sense
you sittin' here in the dark ever night."

"And we will later buy the electric box to keep the
fish and the meat and the cans of Coca-Cola."

"Shoot, you can pick them things up mighty cheap
second hand. I don't see how folks nowdays gets along
without a refrigerator. I know we used to, but I swear
I don't know how we did it in all this heat. The fish
and the meat won't keep no time without one. And besides that, it's mightly fine for beer."

"Do you think it is time for us to go?" Charlie
asked.

"Well, they ain't no hurry, but we could mosey on
into the swamp. It'll be a while yet afore them big
frogs gets to stirrin' good. It wouldn't hurt, though, to
get there a mite early and be ready for 'um."

Charlie went to the storage chickee and returned
with his gig. Seth got up and said, "Miz Lillie, I got a
cooler of cold beer down there in the boat if you would
care for one."

"I thank you, but I do not believe so," Lillie said.

"Beer is for the men only. It does not seem right for a woman to belch loudly, and I have seen and heard what you men do when you drink the beer."

"Well, I guess you're right," Seth said, thinking that this was the longest speech he had ever heard Lillie make. "We'll see you a little later on."

Seth sat in the back of the boat and Charlie in the front, Seth guiding with a paddle and Charlie leading the way with a flashlight Seth had brought. There was also a gasoline lantern in the boat but they would not light it until they started the gigging. An outboard engine on the stern had been pulled out of the water and locked into position.

As they moved slowly into the outer edges of the swamp Charlie was riding two feet above Seth, for Seth's weight, plus the weight of the motor, had sunk the rear of the boat to within two inches of the water and shot the bow high into the air.

Seth reached into the cooler, took out two beers, opened them and handed one to Charlie. "Man can't travel on one leg on a dark night like this," he said.

The moon had not come up yet and the sky was covered with a thick cloud formation, and there were still rumbles of thunder coming from the south. The beam of the flashlight cut through the darkness like a drill, illuminating only a ten-foot-wide area at its furthest point.

The day creatures were now silent and the swamp was echoing the sounds of the night creatures: the chilling cry of the limpkin, the shrill squawk of the night heron, the fluttering wings of the night hawk in pursuit of mosquitoes, the gentle call of the hoot owl, and the terrifying scream of the screech owl. The alligators were beginning to bellow, and this, combined with the distinctive croaks of the bull frogs and the tree frogs, made a symphony of mis-matched melodies.

Seth stopped the boat momentarily and said, "Where you think we ought to go, Charlie? This boat don't draw much water, but my big butt's got her down by the stern. I'd shore hate to get stuck in a mudbank and have to wade out of here with them 'gators chasin' cottonmouths all over the place."

"The deepest place would be the pond just to the east of the big cypress. There is two feet and more of water there, and that pond has always been a good place for frogs."

"Well, from the sound of it they's plenty of frogs right here in the creek. But we'll start in the pond and work our way back." Seth threw the empty can onto the bottom of the boat and took another beer from the cooler. "You ready for another yet?" he asked.

"No. Too much beer would make me pee in my britches."

"Shoot, if that's your only problem, have another. You can always hang it over the side of the boat and let go. Who's going to see you out here in the swamp in black dark?"

"The alligator might see me and think it was a snake. Then I would be in great trouble."

"At your age that wouldn't matter none either. But I shore ain't got your problem. I got a set of kidneys what can hold five gallons. You decide you want another one, it's right there in the cooler."

As they left the creek and turned right, Seth had to dig the paddle into the muck and push them over an area of shallow water. When they reached the outer edge of the pond Charlie turned off the flashlight and they were immediately immersed in a sea of total darkness. Not one beam of light drifted down from the sky, and Seth could not even see the lantern sitting at his feet. He found it with his hands, put a match to the wick, and an orange flame sprang forth and put a globe of dim light about the boat.

Charlie put the lantern in the bow of the boat, and Seth moved them slowly around the edges of the pond. The frogs were croaking everywhere, and in each area the light touched, the yellowish glint of eyes came from behind every lily pad and from each foot of mudbank. Charlie stood up and gigged the frogs, then passed them back for Seth to take off the gig prongs. Seth was in semidarkness and sometimes had to feel for the frogs with his hands.

Within a half hour they had boated more than a hundred frogs and had covered but a small portion of the area. When Charlie passed one back, a loud clamoring and commotion started and the boat rocked so violently that it almost threw him from his feet and into the water. Seth shouted, "Charlie, you durn idiot, get that thing out of here! It's a cottonmouth, not a frog!" Seth had already grabbed the deadly snake before he realized what it was.

Charlie jerked the pole upward and flicked the snake high into the air away from the boat. " 'Gator will get him now," he said casually.

"Well, something sides a 'gator's goin' to get you, you do that again," Seth said, breathing heavily. "I durn near loaded my pants. Yore eyes ain't that old you can't tell a snake from a frog!"

"I knew it was a snake," Charlie chuckled. "I just wanted to see if you were awake."

"I'm durn sure awake now, so's you cut that out!" Seth sighed and said, "Gawd, that calls for a beer." He reached into the cooler, opened a can, drained it dry in one gulp, and opened another. "Let's rest a spell afore we go on."

Charlie sat down on the front seat, and they listened for a few moments as two wildcats started a screaming war dance against each other somewhere close by in the darkness. Seth finished the beer and they moved on, working the south side of the pond. Then they recrossed the swamp shallows and searched the banks of the creek on the way back to the chickees. It was after midnight when they reached the landing.

Charlie put the lantern on the bank and they cleaned the frogs, throwing the bodies into the water for the fish and snakes to eat. They had more than four hundred. Seth put the cleaned legs into the cooler to take back to his camp and keep in the refrigerator before taking them with him the next morning.

Seth put the engine back down into the water, started it, and moved off slowly up the creek. Charlie stood on the landing and watched until the lantern

light moved around a bend and disappeared. The fire
in the cooking chickee had burned down to gray em-
bers as he walked stiffly toward his bed.

It was noon when Seth's old truck rambled down
the path and stopped by the cooking chickee. Charlie
was sitting on the ground, starting another little dugout, and Lillie was at the cooking fire. Seth got out
and said, "Did pretty good for you folks." Charlie got
up and came to the truck.

Seth took the money from his pocket and handed it
to Charlie. He grinned and said, "Got fifteen dollars for
the canoe and ten dollars apiece for the two jackets.
We had forty-one pounds of dressed legs, and they
brought 75¢ a pound. That made $30.75 for the lot.
With the other stuff, you got $65.75 total."

"Did you take out your share of the legs?" Charlie
asked.

"Naw, I didn't want nothin' out of it. It was fun to
me, excep'in' when you flung that snake in my lap.
We'll do it again any night you want to."

Charlie gave the money to Lillie, and she put it in a
tin can on the shelf.

"Got something else, too," Seth said, grinning even
more broadly. "Friend of mine who runs a store in Naples gave me this here old refrigerator to get it out of
the way 'cause it looks so bad he couldn't sell it. Shore
don't look like much, but it runs good. Thought you
might like to have it for when your electric line comes
in."

"You mean it did not cost anything?" Charlie asked.

"Naw. Them old things won't bring nothin' any-more. Anybody wants one, they get a new one. But this one will do you fine as new, if you don't mind the paint being gone. Help me get it off the truck."

Seth had bought the refrigerator for twenty-five dollars from an appliance dealer, but he knew Charlie wouldn't accept it if he told him this.

Lillie smiled as they took the old refrigerator from the truck and placed it beside the sewing platform in the chickee. She opened the door, closed it, then opened it again. "It's even cool without the electric line," she said. "I can store things in it until we can make it run."

"We sure thank you, Seth," Charlie said, as proud of the old refrigerator as he would have been with a new one. "Will you eat now?"

Lillie had cut sweet potatoes into thick slices, dipped them in flour and fried them along with a chicken, and there was still a pot of fish stew and a fresh pone of corn bread.

Seth looked at the food on the grill, then he sniffed deeply and sighed, "Don't mind if I do." He sat at the log table as Lillie heaped a plate and handed it to him.

Several days later, on his next visit to Little George, Charlie could hear the dull booms far in the east where the warden was firing a shotgun to frighten the birds away from Muscadine Slough. It reminded him of the days when the white men had come into the Glades to slaughter the snowy egret for its feathers, only this time the gun was firing in an effort to save the birds.

The constant sound disturbed him and sent fear through him, for it brought back memories of a time he hoped would never return. He did not linger after feeding the alligator, and on his return he poled the dugout swiftly so that he could get beyond the range of the sound. When he reached the south end of the creek he again noticed fresh gashes on a line of trees leading eastward into the swamp. He started to investigate this, but decided to push on to the chickees.

Late that afternoon Fred Henderson came by and informed Charlie that the firing would stop. The wardens in this area had been told by the district office in West Palm that they might be frightening infected birds into other parts of the swamp and marsh, thus possibly spreading the deadly bacteria instead of containing it. Their new orders were to continue burning the birds as they died in the Muscadine Slough area and to let what was happening run its course. There was nothing more that could be done, and only rising water could dissipate the bacteria and end this strange carnage.

FIVE

I T WAS THE MIDDLE of the following week when Kenneth Riles left his real estate office and came into the office of the Everglades Gazette. Albert Lykes was sitting at his desk, reading proof for the next issue of the newspaper. He looked up and motioned for Riles to take a seat.

Riles remained silent while Lykes finished reading a column of proof, then Lykes pushed the copy aside. "What can I do for you, Ken?" he asked.

"I've got a story for this week's edition," Riles said, his voice excited.

"What's that?"

"I've received notice that the ten thousand acres of Potter land out in Big Cypress that has changed hands has been purchased by Surf Development Corporation, and they're going to turn it into a new development with houses, condominiums, a recreational complex with a golf course—the whole works! It'll be called Everglades Villas. Al, we're going to have a real boom here in Collier County. With the twenty thousand acres already under development by Trans-Pacific, this will make thirty thousand acres under development at one time. If this keeps up we'll soon be as big as the Fort Lauderdale and Miami area."

Lykes leaned back in his chair. He had suspected this, but its confirmation still came as a shock. He finally said gruffly, "That boom you're talking about is going to be the Everglades exploding. Don't you know what this really means?"

Riles said emphatically, "It means more people and more jobs and more businesses and more tax money for the county and more money in circulation. It means progress."

For a moment Lykes just shook his head, then he said, "It means more drainage canals and more streets and more garbage to dump somewhere and more sewers flowing south and more animals retreating. Is that what you call progress?"

Riles was shocked and annoyed by Lykes' attitude. He said harshly, "Hell, Al, it's only a swamp, and there's plenty more swamp left!"

"Is there really?" Lykes asked. "It was twenty thousand acres yesterday and ten thousand today and maybe another thirty thousand gone tomorrow. When is it going to stop, Ken, when there's nothing left?"

"Well, what about the National Park?" Riles asked, the excitement now gone from his face. "Isn't that enough just for people to look at?"

"What good will there be in a park where nothing grows and no animals can live. Who would want to see that? If Big Cypress dies, the park dies. And that's a fact."

Riles got up from the chair. "I didn't come in here to argue, Al. I just thought you might be interested. But from your attitude I'd say you have a closed mind and that you're against this project regardless, just like you were dead set against the Trans-Pacific project and against the construction of Alligator Alley. You've just got a negative attitude all the way."

Lykes leaned forward and said, "Oh, I'm interested all right, Ken. But let me ask you one question. Are you going to be connected with this Surf project?"

"Yes," Riles said defensively. "I've been given a contract as one of the sales representatives."

"That's what I thought," Lykes said sadly.

"My being connected with the Surf project doesn't have anything to do with it. I'm for anything that brings progress to the county. As I said, though, I didn't come here to argue," Riles went on, his voice calmer. "If you want any more details on this project I'll be in my office."

As Riles started to leave, Lykes said, "Do Billy Joe Jumper and those other people who live out there have any idea of this yet?"

"No. I'll get around to telling them as soon as I can."

"I don't envy you that task," Lykes said, leaning back in the chair.

"Well, I'm sure when they moved onto land they didn't own they knew it wouldn't last forever."

"I guess you're right on that point. Nothing seems to last forever anymore."

For several minutes after Riles was gone, Lykes remained motionless in his chair, thinking back to the time when this development business first started. He was old enough to remember what the country once looked like from Big Cypress to Lake Okeechobee when most of the area was undeveloped and was the natural watershed for Big Cypress and the Everglades. He thought of the lush tropical growths and the clear lakes and springs and the woods teeming with animals and birds. Then came the drainage canals to trap the water and carry it off to the Gulf on the west and the Atlantic on the east, stopping this natural flow that was the lifeblood for hundreds of square miles to the south; and then the dike around Lake Okeechobee so that no more water flowed south; and then more and more drainage canals, more and more dikes, then the thousands and thousands of vegetable fields, each surrounded by a small dike and a drainage ditch; and when the rain came it flowed from the fields and into the drainage ditches, carrying with it the pesticides and the fertilizer, the phosphates and the overflow from thousands and thousands of septic tanks, seeping slowly into the drainage canals and poisioning the land. Great areas of the drained land became bone dry, and the marshland muck dried up layer by layer and blew away, leaving only bare limestone rock; and the muck fires raged over hundreds of thousands of acres, some burning downward for years, ruining the land as a home for the birds and the animals and the reptiles and the men who tried to live there; and then came more land developers with their concrete block houses and St. Augustine lawns, moving northward from Homestead, westward from Miami and Hollywood and Fort Lauderdale and West Palm Beach, draining and building right out into the River of Grass, moving eastward from Fort Myers and Naples, and now it was coming from north of the swamp.

Lykes suddenly leaned forward and reached for a sheaf of clean paper. He knew that the only thing he could do to fight the Surf project was to try to sway public opinion against it through the editorial voice of his small newspaper. This effort might be useless, but at least he would try. He put a sheet of paper into his battered old typewriter.

SIX

MAY PASSED INTO JUNE and still there was no rain. A fire had broken out in the woods adjoining Alligator Alley just sixteen miles north of the east end of Gopher Creek, and it had been brought under control only after Forest Service rangers from over the state had fought it for three days. Smoke from the smoldering trees, stumps, and muck was still drifting through the swamp.

Billy Joe had gotten a job cutting bushes and grass along Highway 29, and this prevented Timmy from coming to the chickees as much as he had previously. He now had the task of feeding the chickens and hogs and watering the few vegetable plants that were being nurtured for home consumption. The other plants in the field had wilted to the ground and were dead.

Seth and Charlie had made three more trips into the swamp at night gigging frogs, and the proceeds from this, along with the extra jackets Lillie had made and the canoes Charlie had carved, had pushed the secret television fund to a hundred and eighty dollars. Charlie thought if they could get two hundred and fifty dollars it would be a fair share of the cost and not place too much of a burden on Billy Joe, especially since the vegetable crop was now a total loss.

Seth and Charlie had planned another money making venture for that afternoon, a trip into the east swamp to gather cypress knees, but that morning Charlie had to cut more cypress for the little canoes. He had promised Timmy he could go with him, and now he was waiting for Timmy to finish his morning chores before coming to the chickees.

The refrigerator Seth had brought was still standing beside the sewing platform without power. Billy Joe had contacted the power company from the telephone in the Janes Store in Copeland and had been told, since there were no crews working in the Copeland area at the time, it might be two or three weeks before a crew could be sent in to run the line from the road to the chickee. This news did not disturb Charlie or Lillie. They had gotten along fine without the electricity for many decades, and a few weeks more would make no difference.

Timmy finally came trotting down the dirt trail and went to the landing where his grandfather was waiting. Charlie put the axe into the canoe and then pushed them away from the bank.

Charlie had decided to go to a different place this time to gather his logs in order to follow the deepest sloughs, for the water level had dropped even more. When he reached the area where the creek widened out into the swamp he turned left and went far to the south of Muscadine Slough. He had never before taken Timmy into this part of the swamp, and each passing

pond or island of button bush and pickerel weed was a
new adventure for Timmy.

They came to a small glade of higher ground and
Charlie stopped the dugout. The ground was covered
with lush ferns and a carpet of velvety green moss so
thick that their bare feet sank into it as they walked. A
giant live oak was entwined by a strangler fig that had
sent its runners upward through the limbs. The vine
would eventually kill the majestic tree and bring it
crashing to the ground.

Timmy suddenly stopped and said, "Granpappa, I
smell skunk. We better turn and run."

Charlie chuckled and said, "It is not skunk, Timmy.
It is the stopper tree. When the wind blows toward
you the tree gives off the odor of a skunk, but the smell
will not cling like the skunk. Maybe the tree wants us
to go away and not bother it."

They crossed the glade and waded out into a small
shallow pond filled with the dwarf cypress, where
Charlie cut three with the axe and brought them back
to the dugout. Then they headed south again, moving
close to the line where the swamp ends and the great
sawgrass marsh begins.

Charlie stopped again and said to Timmy, "Here I
will show you a thing you have not seen."

They walked into an area dotted with huge royal
palms, their stark trunks soaring above the roof of the
swamp. Charlie led Timmy to one tree so old that its
foilage was gone and its dead trunk riddled with holes
drilled by woodpeckers. The center of the bottom of
the trunk had encased an ancient machete, and al-

though the wooden handle was black with decay, the rust-covered blade was still solid.

Timmy immediately grabbed the handle and tried to pull the blade free, but it had long before become a part of the trunk.

"Where did it come from?" he asked excitedly.

"I do not know," Charlie said. "I found it here many years ago when I was a boy, and it had grown into the tree even then. Perhaps it has been here since the days of the first Seminole war. Someone, maybe a white soldier or an explorer, tried to chop down the tree and could not pull the blade out again."

"Can I have it, Granpappa?" Timmy asked. "We can chop the trunk away from it with the axe and I will carry it home with me."

"Let the tree that took it from the man keep it. It belongs to the tree."

"But the tree is dead, Granpappa."

"And so is the man. Let it stay here, Timmy. It is part of a time that will be no more."

Timmy agreed reluctantly and they walked to the dugout and headed back toward Gopher Creek.

Early that afternoon Charlie poled the dugout up the creek to meet Seth for the trip to gather cypress knees. Seth had said he knew a part of the swamp where there was a small stand of bald cypress remaining, and the knees there were plentiful. There were many knees on his land but he did not want them cut.

When Charlie landed, Seth greeted him with "How about a beer?" Charlie declined; then they climbed onto the swamp buggy. Seth cranked the engine, put it in gear, pushed the accelerator to the floor, and released the clutch. At first the odd vehicle remained motionless, its huge rear tires spinning wildly in the soft earth, and then it leaped three feet off the ground and crashed through a clump of bushes.

Charlie grabbed an overhead guard rail and hung on as Seth drove them southeast into the swamp, the accelerator still halfway to the floorboard. Mud was flying everywhere, and Seth crashed the vehicle into bushes and head on into the smaller pond cypress, sending up thick sprays of bark and bits of boughs.

Ponds were not skirted but simply crossed as they came, the wheels creating two streaks of bubbling muddy water right through the lily pads. Once Charlie looked back and shouted, "I think you hit the alligator!"

"Don't worry 'bout it," Seth shot back. "He can't hurt this contraption."

They slammed, bucked, and skidded for five miles, then Seth suddenly pushed in the clutch and jammed on the brakes. The buggy spun around and around and then came to a stop when its rear end rammed into a tree. Charlie left his seat abruptly and landed ten feet away, flat on his back.

For a moment Charlie was afraid to move. The wind was knocked from him, and he was sure that something must be broken. He could hear Seth say loudly, "Haw, haw, I gotcha that time, didn't I!"

Getting slowly to his feet, Charlie discovered that he was intact although his rear was caked with mud.

He looked at Seth and said, "I think my butt is broke. Do you always drive the buggy that way?"

"Naw," Seth chuckled, "I usually try to make some time, but I didn't want to go too fast with you along."

"You travel like the alligator," Charlie said, trying to brush the mud from himself but only smearing it. "What you could go around you just smash over. I think it is best that I walk back."

"Ain't no need to do that. I'll let you drive if you want to."

"You know I cannot drive that thing."

"Well, then, 'pears that you ain't got no choice except to ride or to walk." He laughed again, then he said, "I'll take it easy going back. I were just foolin' around, payin' you back for dropping that snake in my lap."

They took saws from the buggy and went about the task of cutting the knees, which were clustered around a small stand of not more than a half dozen bald cypress. They found knees of all sizes and shapes, some shaped like human heads, some in the form of animals, one resembling a troupe of ballet dancers, and many that had grown into twisted, grotesque patterns. A total of about twenty-five were collected.

Seth drove back much slower and by a different route. He stopped the buggy when he noticed a fresh gash cut into the side of a tree. South from this there were more such cuts, and to the west, across a treeless area of marsh, there was a line of stakes with red cloth streamers nailed to their tops.

Charlie said, "Those cuts are the same as I have seen twice on the south end of Gopher Creek."

"Them's survey lines," Seth said. "Somebody has been running section lines out here. What the thunder fer, you reckon?"

"I do not know," Charlie said, "but I have found them twice. I have seen no men in the swamp doing this."

"Ain't no sense in it," Seth said, getting down from the buggy. "Suppose you and me just mess them things up a mite. I'll take an axe and cut another line on the trees off to the east, and you pull up them stakes and move them a couple of hundred yards to the north of where they are."

"Will this not bring trouble?" Charlie asked.

"Shoot, no. Ain't nobody going to see us. And besides, we'll just be having a little fun. Ain't no harm in it."

"I will move the stakes, then," Charlie said, "while you mark the trees."

A half hour later they returned to the buggy, their tasks completed. Before he cranked the engine Seth said, "Ever time you see them marks down in the south swamp, cut a new line like I done there. And I'll be on the lookout for new ones, too. Ain't nobody ought to be running them lines out here, but we can shore have some fun out of them.

As soon as they reached the camp, Seth went to the store and brought out two beers. This time Charlie accepted gratefully. He was much relieved when he

jumped safely from the buggy, and had already decided against making any further trips into the swamp
on this vehicle.

Seth took one of the knees from the buggy, turned
it over in his hands and said, "Best way to get the bark
off is to steam 'um first. I've got a big pot out back so
I'll do it here. After we get the bark off we'll polish 'um
down real good. Them things is getting scarce and
ought to bring a couple of bucks apiece. The tourist
folks sure like to buy them. You'd think they ain't
never seen a cypress tree, the way they carry on so
over a hunk of wood."

"I'll come back in the morning and help peel the
bark," Charlie said. "I'm going home now and wash in
the creek. My britches are filled with mud."

Charlie could hear a rumble of thunder far in the
south as he poled the dugout away from Seth's camp.
Dark thunderheads had also formed, and the moss
hanging from the oak limbs was blowing northward.
Birds along the creekbank scurried along faster than
usual, and the wind felt damp and cool.

Just after dark the rain came. It was only a gentle
shower and not the downpour they so badly needed,
but it cooled the swamp and washed the limestone
dust from the roofs of the chickees.

~~~~~~

SEVEN

IT WAS TEN DAYS after Kenneth Riles talked to
Albert Lykes about the Surf Development
Corporation project before he drove south
to tell Billy Joe Jumper that he would have to move
from the land. He turned east at Copeland and then
took the narrow winding road that ran from the Turner River Grade into the swamp. This was his first time
in this area, and he was apprehensive about finding his
way. He was also worried about how Billy Joe would
react when told that he would have to abandon his
home. Facing an angry Seminole was not within his
realm of experience. At first he thought of asking
someone from Surf to perform this task but decided it
should not be done by a total stranger. That could
well make matters worse.

When he arrived at the wooden frame house he
found, almost to his relief, that Billy Joe was not at
home. His unpleasant task had been put off for a while
longer. He drove on to Seth Thompson's fishing camp.

A few days earlier Riles had looked up land deeds
for this area and had discovered the ten acres owned
by Seth Thompson. The little plot was an island right
in the center of the Surf property, and Riles knew that
its value would skyrocket when the new development

got underway. He had decided it would be well worth his time to try to purchase the property and later sell it to Surf. In time it would bring thousands of dollars per acre.

Soon after he had moved to the swamp, Seth's father had thought of buying more land and putting in an orange grove. As a windbreak he had planted a mile-long line of Australian pines on each side of the path leading to the house. The orange grove idea had been abandoned, but the pines thrived, their trunks shooting upward and their limbs growing into each other to form a thick canopy over the road. An eighty-year accumulation of fallen needles lay three inches deep on the ground.

Riles entered this tree tunnel and felt as if he had driven his car onto a deep pile carpet. He also felt as if he had moved back several decades in time. The sun was completely blocked out and the only sound was a soft moaning as the wind swept through the trees.

He drove very slowly as he neared the end of the road; then he parked the car in front of the little store and got out. For a moment he studied the house and the surrounding area; then he noticed the old fat man coming toward him from down at the creek.

Seth said, "Howdy, mister. Something I can do for you?"

"Are you Mr. Thompson?" Riles asked, thinking that from Seth's appearance, this old man would be an easy person to deal with, especially if he offered a fair price.

"That's right. I'm Seth Thompson. What can I do for you?"

"Well, Mr. Thompson, I'm Kenneth Riles, owner of Riles Real Estate Agency. Have you thought of selling this land?"

"Nope. I ain't never thought nothin' about it."

"I'm kinda interested in picking up some property in this area. Would you be interested in an offer?"

"As I said, I ain't never thought nothin' about it."

"What would you say to an offer of two hundred dollars per acre cash?"

"I'd say I ain't interested."

"Mr. Thompson, this is nothing but swampland. What do you think is a fair price?"

"To be honest, fellow, I just ain't interested at all. Now is there something I can do for you? I got some boats to work on."

Riles shuffled his feet and clasped his hands behind his back. "Mr. Thompson, I'll make one more offer. I'll give you a thousand dollars per acre cash. That's ten thousand for this piece of swamp. That's a real fine price, isn't it?"

"I done told you I ain't interested at all," Seth said finally. "Me and my pappy before me has been on this land since 1890. That's eighty-two years. And I intend to stay here a few more and be buried right over yonder under that big oak tree. Now excuse me. I got work to do."

Riles became angry. He had not intended to say anything about the Surf project, but emotion overruled this intent. "Mr. Thompson, you're soon going to have to sell this property or live right in the middle of a housing project! Maybe smack in the center of a golf course!"

It took several moments for what Riles had said to even vaguely register, then Seth asked, "What are you talkin' about?"

"Surf Development Corporation has purchased ten thousand acres of this swamp and is turning it into a housing development. You've got one little speck right in the middle of it."

"That's not true," Seth said, his fat jaw sagging.

"Yes, it is true. Some of the work will begin within a week."

"Well, it don't matter none," Seth said in a guarded tone. "As long as the creek is here I can make a living. It don't matter none about them houses."

"Mr. Thompson, don't you understand?" Riles asked, his tone now condescending. "There's not going to be any more creek. Drainage canals will be put in, and this entire area of the swamp will be drained and cleared of everything. There won't be any more creek and there won't be any more swamp."

"Does this include where Charlie Jumper and Billy Joe lives too?" Seth asked.

"Yes. They will have to move. I came out here now to tell Billy Joe." Riles assumed a look of deep sympathy and said, "Mr. Thompson, I understand how you must feel. You've lived here a long time, and you're fond of this place. But ten thousand dollars is a lot of

money. You could move into town and get a job somewhere."

"Fellow," Seth said slowly, his age now showing in
his eyes and face, "I ain't had on a pair of shoes in
more than twenty years. What kind of a job you think
anybody would give me?"

"Well, I don't know, Mr. Thompson, but that much
money ought to do you for quite some time. You want
to sell now?"

"No. No, I don't. I'd have to study on it some."

Riles took a card from his wallet and handed it to
Seth. "When you decide, here's where you can reach
me in Immokalee. And Mr. Thompson, I've offered you
a real good price. Remember now, you should give me
first chance when you make up your mind."

Seth watched as the car turned and entered the
stand of Australian pines and disappeared. For several moments he remained immobile, wondering if
what he had just heard was real or some sort of wild
dream. He went into the store and opened a beer.
When he came out, blinking in the sunlight, he looked
toward the weathered old house and noticed, as if for
the first time, that the front porch was sagging badly.

Billy Joe was swinging a machete, cutting bushes
along the canal that paralleled the highway, when the
car pulled onto the shoulder and stopped. He had removed his shirt, and his brown chest and forearms
were glistening with sweat. Several other men were
working in a line on down the canal.

He immediately recognized Kenneth Riles and wondered why he had stopped. Riles got out of the car and came down to him. He said, "Hello, Billy Joe. I went out to your house to see you and your wife said you were working down here."

"Yessir, Mr. Riles," Billy Joe nodded.

Riles felt uneasy. He didn't want to let his emotions run away with him like he had with Seth Thompson. But this was different. This was only a matter of passing on information. The other was an attempted business deal.

"Billy Joe," he said slowly, "you remember me telling you that the land you've been renting has been sold?"

"Yes, Mr. Riles, I remember. I've thought about it a lot. Has the rent gone up?"

"No, it's not that." Riles paused for a moment; then he said, "The company that bought the land is going to develop the whole area into a housing complex. You can't stay there. You'll have to move."

"When is this going to happen?"

Riles was surprised by Billy Joe's calm reaction. He now spoke with more confidence, "Right away. Preliminary work will begin next week, and the land clearing part will be in full swing within a month."

"How much time do I have?"

"They're going to work around your place and give you as much time as possible. You'll have at least three or four weeks."

Billy Joe wiped sweat from his forehead. "Mr. Riles, what about my house?"

"Well, the company has authorized me to pay five hundred dollars to each person who is a renter and has improved the land."

"You mean five hundred dollars for my house, my sheds, my fences and everything? Mr. Riles, that place is all I've got for twenty-two years of work."

"I'm sorry, Billy Joe," Riles said, his eyes cast downward. "I'm just telling you what the company has authorized me to do. Maybe you could take the money and have the house moved to another location."

It was the inherited nature of Billy Joe's generation of Seminoles to take things stoically, but anger was beginning to germinate deep within him. He said harshly, "Where would I move the house to, Mr. Riles? Is somebody going to give me free land? And even if I could find some place, it would cost five times more than you have offered just to move the house and put in a new well. There's nowhere I could get that kind of money."

This change of mood startled Riles, and he suddenly felt extremely uncomfortable. Sweat stains were showing on his pale blue shirt. He said defensively, "Billy Joe, I sympathize with your situation, but as I said, I'm only following instructions. You know I would do better for you if I could, but I can't. All you have to do to receive the five hundred dollars is come by my office and sign a paper. I hope things work out well for you, and if I can be of assistance, just let me know." With that he walked quickly to his car.

As soon as the car pulled away, Billy Joe went to the foreman and asked permission to quit early. His sudden flash of anger had now turned to deep fear, and he was dumbfounded as to what he could do.

When he reached the Turner River Grade he stopped and got out of the truck. He sat on the bank and threw rocks into the river, thinking and wondering. His first inclination was to retreat further into the swamp, but he knew instantly that he must not do this for Timmy's sake. If he ran, like many of his people had run in the past, there would be no future life for Timmy. And he knew that he could not live along the Tamiami Trail. He had driven that highway many times, and he had seen many of his people reduced to the status of freaks in a circus, not by choice but by necessity to live. He closed his eyes and he could see the signs, Visit Joe Osceola's Indian Village, stop five miles ahead and See John Tiger Tail's Indian Village, the group of chickees behind the board fence, the souvenir shop in front, pay fifty cents and go through this door into the village, watch the Seminole wash his clothes, watch the Seminole cook, watch the Seminole eat, pay an extra quarter and watch the Seminole brave wrestle the alligator.

He knew also that he could not live in the labor camps to the north. He had once been to Pahokee, and he had seen the shacks one on top of another, stacked together like cordwood, the cheap whitewash gone and the roofs sagging, the bare dirt yards, the shacks so close together that they seemed to touch, crushing the life out of a man; and coming back, between Pahokee and Clewiston, he had seen the sugar cane fields stretch away to the horizon, mile after mile of muck so black that it looked like soot, and the land without trees or any place where a man could be alone; then the orange groves and the vegetable fields and more labor camps with their shacks jammed together row upon row.

There would also be no place for him on the reservation, where most of the land was either under water or so poor that it would grow only wiregrass and scrub cattle, and would not sustain even those who lived there now in scattered clusters of chickees and block houses.

The more he thought the more confused he became. This plot of land was all he had ever known. It did not produce much, but it was enough, and it was all that he needed or had ever wanted. It was here that his children had been born, and it was here that he had broken away from the old life of his father. Now his whole world must end and start anew in some strange and as yet undecided place.

He got back into the truck and drove along the narrow road leading into the swamp and to what had been his home, driving slowly, wondering what to say to Watsie and Lucy and Timmy, perplexed even more by what he could say to his father and mother.

When he came into the house Watsie was at the sewing machine, making the wedding shirt for Frank Willie. Lucy was in the kitchen, and Timmy was down at the pen, feeding the hogs. He took a can of Coca-Cola from the refrigerator and sat at the table. For a moment he sipped the cool drink in silence, and then he said to Lucy, "Have you and Frank decided on the date yet?"

Lucy turned from the stove. "No, Pappa, not yet." She noticed the grave expression on her father's face. "Is there something wrong?"

"Could you set the wedding for early next month?"

"Yes, Pappa. We are only waiting until the cattle branding is finished on the ranch where Frank works. He can speak to the preacher any time."

Billy Joe then turned to Watsie. "I have a thing to tell all of you, and I want no one to mention it to my father or mother. I will speak to them myself tomorrow."

Watsie stopped the sewing machine and came over to the table.

EIGHT

HE NEXT DAY Billy Joe drove alone to his father's chickees. He found Lillie at the sewing machine and Charlie down by the creek cleaning a turtle he had brought in from the swamp.

Charlie brought the meat to the chickee and put it into a pan. Then he sat at the table across from Billy Joe.

"I have something I must tell you, Pappa," Billy Joe said.

"We have something for you," Charlie said, his wrinkled face beaming. He reached to the shelf and took down a tin can, then he dumped the bills and coins onto the table. "We have sold many things, and we have over two hundred and sixty dollars to help pay for the television for Lucy and Frank Willie."

Billy Joe looked at the money, and then he looked up at his father. "Ah, Pappa, you and Mamma didn't have to do that. I could have managed it somehow."

"It is what we wanted to do," Charlie said, still grinning.

"Why don't you and Mamma keep this money. There are things you could do with it."

"It is our part of the gift," Charlie said, his voice firm. "It is what we want to do."

"All right, Pappa. It is appreciated. Thank you very much. Lucy will be proud that you and Mamma helped." Billy Joe was surprised by the money, but he wanted to shift the conversation back to his purpose in being there. He said, "Do you have coffee, Pappa?"

"Yes." Charlie poured two cups and came back to the table.

"I have something I must tell you now," Billy Joe said, sipping the steaming liquid. "You've always known that we don't own this land, haven't you, Pappa?"

"Yes, I have known."

"And you know that the land belongs to someone else?"

"The land belongs to those who love it."

"That is not exactly true, Pappa. The land belongs to those who have a legal paper in the courthouse. Pappa, this land we live on has been sold, and the new owners are going to clear the swamp and build houses here. We must leave this land no later than three or four weeks from now."

Charlie sat still for a moment, trying to digest what had been said. Lillie stopped the sewing machine and just stared at Billy Joe. Charlie finally said, "That is not true."

"It is true, Pappa. We must leave this land. Mr. Riles, the land man in Immokalee where I pay rent, has told me this."

"But we have been here all our lives. We know no other place."

"I know, Pappa," Billy Joe said, shaking his head. "But it is ended. I will get work somewhere, and you and Mamma will come and live with us."

Lillie was listening carefully to each word, but she remained silent.

"I will not leave the swamp!" Charlie said, defiance now coming into his voice.

"Pappa, there is no choice. The bulldozers will come soon and there will be nothing left here. You cannot stay, and you must accept that."

"I will speak of this no more."

"Pappa, don't make it any harder than it is," Billy Joe pleaded. "We'll discuss it some more later. There is time yet to decide what to do." He picked up the money and put it into his pocket. "This was a real fine thing for you to do. Now we can buy a television with the wooden cabinet. Lucy will be so proud of you. I will see you again tomorrow."

As soon as the truck was out of sight, Charlie went down to the creek and poled away in the dugout. He pushed the thin cypress pole in and out of the muck, moving swiftly. He still could not believe what Billy Joe had said, and his wrinkled face suddenly looked so old as to be beyond time itself, as ageless as the swamp.

Billy Joe had come to grips with reality and accepted what must be, and he had done this without bitterness; but he was of a different generation and a

different time than Charlie. The older Seminoles har-
bored a deep distrust for the white man, and even a
hatred. Charlie had heard his father and his grandfather speak of the time when the Seminole lived on
the land far to the north, the rich rolling hills with fer-
tile soil that grew corn and squash and pumpkin in
abundance, and the game was plentiful and the
streams as clear as an open sky, and then the white
man came and took the land, and there was fighting
and blood and death and hunger; then the Seminole
moved south, giving way to the white man, settling on
the land north of the big lake, but the white man came
again and wanted the land, more fighting and more running and more hunger, and they moved south again.
Then the white man said they could have this land and
be bothered no more; but he came again and the blood
ran red, and the white man brought in dogs to track
the Seminole like an animal. Then they placed a
bounty on the Seminole, fifty dollars for a man, twenty-five dollars for a woman, fifteen dollars for a child,
bands of white hunters surrounding the chickees at
night, capturing the men and women and children,
binding their hands and feet with rope, throwing them
into wagons like sacks of feed and hauling them to the
fort in the north where they collected the bounty and
returned to the swamp for another hunt; then the fighting and the running until the Seminole disappeared
into the heart of the swamp and into the Sea of Grass
and did not come out again until it was safe to do so,
and some had not come out yet.

Charlie himself had seen the white man come into

this land and slaughter the egret for its feathers, shooting them only when nesting on the rookery, killing
them by the hundreds of thousands and leaving the
young either to die in the nest and be eaten by vultures or fall out of the nest and drown, and the water
around the mangroves turning red with blood; and he
had seen the white man come into this land and
slaughter the alligator, shipping out their hides fifty
thousand at a time to be made into wallets and shoes,
and he had once seen a thousand alligators killed in
one pond in one day, but this time not for the hides,
for the white men pulled out the alligator's teeth to be
sold as watch fobs and left the bodies with their hides
to rot in the blistering sun; and he had seen the white
man come with his mules and his curses and his saws
and his puffing trains and strip the land of the giant
bald cypress, cutting them down like fields of sugar
cane; and he had seen the white man wipe out the tree
snails so that their shells could be sold as trinkets; and
he had seen the white man dig the canals and drain
the land and come closer and closer until he was now
here again, once more telling the Seminole that he
could not live on this land because the white man
wanted it.

Before he realized it he had moved all the way
through the swamp and come to the edge of the great
marsh. He gazed for a long time across the swaying
River of Grass, looking far to the south and even past
where his eyes could see. The sun was beginning to
set, and brilliant hues of red and orange and yellow
were streaking through the clouds and downward into

the hammocks, making the tops of the palms sparkle and glisten like tiny bits of rainbow. Even the somber sawgrass was changing color as the sun dropped lower into the west. There was a quietness about the marsh that made it seem not a part of this world, a land and a time completely unto itself. Darkness had almost descended when the old man turned and left, moving back into the swamp.

When he reached the chickees, Charlie ignored the turtle stew he always relished and sat by the fire. Lillie watched him but said nothing. It was late into the night when he finally lay down on the blanket and stared upward into the thatched roof. When Gumbo jumped up beside him, he put his arms around the furry little animal and held him tightly.

The next morning Charlie poled the dugout up Gopher Creek to Seth's camp. He found Seth out by the swamp buggy and walked up to him.

Seth said, "Howdy, Charlie. You O.K. this morning?" The usual smile was gone from his face.

"I am fine," Charlie said.

Both men squatted down and faced each other. Seth poked at the ground with a stick. "You heard about the land?" he asked solemnly.

"Yes, I have heard. Billy Joe told me."

"What you goin' to do?"

"I do not know, but I will not leave the swamp."

Seth suddenly jabbed the stick into the soft earth. He muttered, "Hell of a note, that's what it is. That's

how come them survey lines has been run everwhere.
They ain't got no right."

Charlie asked, "When are you going to Immokalee
again?"

"I was planning on going this morning. You need
me to bring you something?"

"No. I wish to go with you. I have a thing to do
there."

"Well, you're plumb welcome," Seth said, struggling to get up. "We might as well go on right now and
get back. I've got stuff to do here this afternoon."

Both men got into the battered pickup and Seth
drove westward over the narrow limestone road. No
further mention was made of the sale of the land, and
the trip to Immokalee was made in silence.

When they reached the outskirts of the town, Charlie said, "Will you let me off at the office of the land
man, Mr. Riles?"

"Shore," Seth grunted. "What you goin' to do there,
buy up the swamp so's they won't run you off?" He
said it without mirth.

"No, I just wish to talk. I will be waiting for you
later in front of the building."

"I won't be long," Seth said. "I just got to pick up a
few things at the hardware."

Charlie got out of the truck in front of the small
concrete block building and went inside. The secretary
glanced at his bare feet with distaste; then she asked,
"Can I help you?"

"I wish to see Mr. Riles," Charlie replied.

"Just a moment and I'll see if he's busy."

The woman went into an adjoining room and returned momentarily. "Would you go in, please," she
said, motioning toward the open door.

Kenneth Riles was sitting at his desk when Charlie
entered. He looked up and said, "What can I do for
you?"

Charlie stood in front of the desk and said, "I am
Charlie Jumper, father of Billy Joe."

"Oh, yes," Riles said. "I'm glad to know you. Billy
Joe is a fine man." He wondered immediately why this
old man was in his office.

"I have come about the land," Charlie said. "Billy
Joe has told me about the land and the houses, and he
says that we can no longer live there. If you will forget
this thing and leave the land alone, I will make it up to
you."

Riles asked cautiously, "Just what do you mean,
Mr. Jumper?"

"I will send fish and the animal hides and the jackets that Lillie makes and snake skins if you wish. Seth
Thompson can bring them to you each week. I will do
this as long as you want me to."

Riles scratched his forehead and said, "Mr. Jumper,
I don't think you understand. I don't really have anything to do with that land except act as an agent. I'm
not the owner and I have no say-so whatsoever in
this."

"Will you speak to the owner?"

Riles was trying to think of a way to calmly end
this ludicrous visit and conversation. He said, "Mr.

Jumper, the new owner of that land is not a man; it's a corporation. I can't speak to a corporation about fish and pelts and snake skins. They'd think I've lost my mind."

"I do not understand," Charlie said, puzzled. "Why would they not consider this offer? The things I speak of are worth money, and I will send more if they say I must. I would also make the little canoes. I will do whatever they say, and I could also send some cash each week."

Riles got up from the desk. He said slowly, "Mr. Jumper, I appreciate your coming by to see me, but there is absolutely nothing I can do. You should go on and make your plans to move."

"Will you not even speak to the owners about this?" Charlie asked, his voice subdued.

"There is absolutely nothing I can do, Mr. Jumper," Riles repeated. He put his hand on Charlie's shoulder and guided him through the door. "Good to have seen you, Mr. Jumper."

For a few minutes Charlie glanced up and down the street, watching the unfamiliar people and the rumbling cars and trucks. He felt uncomfortable, alien, and very foolish, and he wished that Seth would hurry on and take him back to the swamp.

NINE

IT WAS EARLY MORNING at the beginning of the next week when Charlie heard the truck amble along the limestone road, heading east. He listened intensely and knew it was not Seth Thompson, for he could recognize the sound of Seth's pickup. He went to the storage chickee, took out his bow and several arrows, and entered the woods between his camp and the road.

For several minutes he squatted behind a bush and saw nothing; then he heard the rumble of another truck as it approached. It was a pickup loaded with gasoline drums. He fitted an arrow into the bow and waited.

Charlie fired the arrow just as the truck passed. The thin wooden shaft struck the top of the cab, careened forward, and landed in the middle of the road. The truck slowed for a moment, then it picked up speed again and disappeared around a curve.

Another pickup followed fifty yards behind this one. As it passed, Charlie fired an arrow that struck the right door and bounced off. The truck screeched to a halt, and a man jumped from the cab, came around the side of the truck, and picked up the arrow. He ran his hand over the slight dent in the door; then he walked toward the bush where Charlie was hiding.

For a moment Charlie did not know what to do. He had not expected the truck to stop. He was not sure just what he did expect, or what he hoped to accomplish with his attack, but the approaching man loomed suddenly as a menace that addled his mind. He put another arrow into the bow and pulled back on the string.

The man stopped and stared at the bush, then he turned and walked back to the truck, carrying the arrow with him. The bow string was still taut as the man got in the truck and drove away.

For several moments Charlie remained rigid, his eyes glinting with a strange and faraway look. He began to breathe heavily, and his hands trembled. He thought of how close he had come to firing the third arrow, firing at a form he had never before shot at in anger.

Very slowly he released the tension on the bow and dropped the remaining arrows. He turned and crept back through the thick woods toward the chickees, leaving the arrows on the ground where they had fallen from his sweating hands.

The pickup was parked to the side of his house when Billy Joe arrived home that afternoon. As soon as he stopped, a man jumped from the cab of the truck and came over to him. He held an arrow in his hand.

"You Billy Joe Jumper?" the man asked.

"Yes, I am Billy Joe."

"I'm Lawton, the foreman of the land-clearing

crew," the man said brusquely. "I got something to say
to you, and I ain't going to say it but once, so you listen real good."

"What is it?" Billy Joe asked, alarmed by the angry
tone of the man's voice.

"Your old man's been squattin' up there behind a
bush, shooting arrows at my trucks. Here's one of
them. We ain't got time out here to be playing no
damned cowboys and Indians with some loco old man.
You better put a stop to this silly crap right now or
we'll have that old man locked up. You hear?"

The words stunned Billy Joe. He said with diffi-
culty, "How do you know who it was who did this?
What makes you think it was my father?"

"Well, it was an old Indian squattin' behind a bush
right up there where that dirt trail leads down to them
chickees. I seen him myself, and started to go knock his
brains out but decided I'd let it go and speak to you
first. If it ain't your paw, who is it? Don't no other
Indians live up there, do they?"

"I can't believe he did this," Billy Joe said, his voice
subdued.

"Well, that ain't all," the foreman said. "Somebody
has been messing up the section lines we've surveyed,
and it wouldn't be hard to guess who. You better speak
to that old man right away. We don't want no trouble.
We're just doing a job, but if he pesters us anymore
we'll have to do something about it."

"I will speak to him now," Billy Joe said. "It will
not happen again, I promise you. Just leave this to me.
I am sorry."

"Well, ain't no real harm done yet," the man said in

a calmer tone. He turned toward his truck. "But for Christ sake, shooting at trucks with arrows! The old man must be getting daffy."

"I will speak to him now," Billy Joe said again, grateful that the matter would be dropped.

Billy Joe did not go into the house, and as soon as the man was gone he drove quickly up the road toward the chickees. The truck raced down the dirt trail and slammed to a stop, sending a cloud of dust into the cooking chickee where his mother and father sat.

He jumped from the cab, ran over to the table and shouted angrily, "Pappa, what is this thing you have done?"

Both Charlie and Lillie were startled by the loud and unexpected outburst. Charlie put down the bowl and said, "Why is it that you shout, son?"

"Pappa, did you fire arrows at the trucks passing on the road?"

For a moment Charlie didn't answer, surprised that Billy Joe knew of this, and then he said slowly, "Yes, I did this. But what is wrong in shooting the arrow in defense?"

"In defense of what, Pappa?" Billy Joe asked, becoming more exasperated.

"In defense of our land," Charlie answered calmly. "Our people have done this thing many times in the past."

"Oh, Pappa," Billy Joe said, sinking down to one of the stump chairs, "this is not our land, and it never will be. Can't you understand that, Pappa? For what you have done they could lock you in a jail cell or send you away to the crazy house."

"I have done no wrong," Charlie said, looking straight into Billy Joe's eyes.

Billy Joe shook his head. Then he said firmly, "Pappa, promise me you won't do this again. If you won't promise me this I will quit my job and move into the chickees and watch you every minute until we are gone from here. I do not want harm to come to you for such a foolish thing."

"I did not mean to harm those men," Charlie said softly. "I did only what I thought I must do. If I had meant them harm I would have used the rifle. I was only trying to frighten them away. It will not happen again, Billy Joe. I promise you. Do not quit your job because of me. I am sorry if I have disturbed you so."

Billy Joe got up and came around the table. He put his arm around Charlie's shoulder. "Pappa, please let it go," he said, holding the old man tightly. "Things are going to work out for us. You will see. I know how you feel, Pappa, but don't do this again. It can only bring trouble and sorrow."

"I will not shoot at them again, Billy Joe. I have given you my word."

Billy Joe walked to his truck. He turned and said, "I am sorry that I shouted, Pappa. I did not mean to do that."

"It is all right," Charlie said. "Every man has a time when he feels he must shout."

As soon as the pickup disappeared up the trail, Charlie pushed the food away and walked slowly to his dugout. Gumbo jumped into the slim craft, and the two of them moved away into the swamp.

TEN

F OR SEVERAL DAYS Seth had been alternating between surges of anger and periods of deep depression. He spent more and more time sitting on the bank of the creek, staring blankly into the swamp. He fried fish in the deep cast-iron pot over the open grill and ate it automatically, not really knowing or caring if he were eating fish or swamp cabbage or an alligator gar. Slim noticed this change but said nothing.

Many hours were also spent brooding about why this sudden thing must be. To Seth this camp deep in the swamp was a sanctuary, and here and only here could he feel comfortable and safe. He had lived this way of life for so long that change was beyond the realm of possibility. He had been free, totally free to do as he wished and dress as he wished and be alone when he wished. Solitude was no farther away than one of the boats in the creek or the swamp buggy parked by the side of the house. From this camp he could come and go into the outside world as he pleased, and elsewhere he would not have such a freedom of choice.

He was at first startled and then curious when he heard the loud clank of a bulldozer coming down the steel ramp behind a flat-bed truck, and then he heard the high-pitched drone of power saws. He stood motionless for a moment, his head cocked toward the sound, listening. Then he ran into the house and emerged with a shotgun. The pickup truck shot across the clearing and bounded full speed into the tunnel formed by the Australian pines.

When Seth reached the north end of the line of trees, one tree had already been felled, and the bulldozer was starting to push it to one side. He slammed on the brakes and brought the truck to a screeching halt, its tires digging through the deep layers of needles and exposing a streak of bare earth. The shotgun was in his hands when he jumped from the truck.

"What the devil you think you're doin' here?" he shouted. One saw was biting into the base of another tree.

The foreman got out of a pickup parked nearby and came over to Seth. "What's the trouble?" he asked.

Seth waved the shotgun toward the men with the saws. "How come they're cuttin' down my trees?"

"Are you Thompson, the fish camp man?" the foreman asked.

"Yeah, I'm Seth Thompson, and I want to know why you're cuttin' down my trees. You ain't got no right to do this. You're on private property."

"No, we ain't," the man said, eyeing the shotgun. "The survey shows that your property starts a half mile down the road. These trees are not on your property, and we've been told to cut them. We're just doing what we've been told to do, mister, and you better put away that shotgun."

The other workers stopped the saws and listened. Seth said, "I don't give a damn what a survey shows! My pappy planted them trees and you ain't goin' to cut them down. Now you better clear on out of here afore I turn this scatter gun loose on you."

"Old man, you're making a big mistake," the foreman said. "This won't do anything but get you in a heap of trouble."

"You're in a heap of trouble right now," Seth said, cocking the hammer of the shotgun. "You got just one minute to clear on out of here."

"All right," the foreman said, backing off. "We're not going to argue with that shotgun, but we'll be back. This is not your property, and we're just doing what we're paid to do."

The men got into the trucks and drove away, carrying the saws with them. The bulldozer was left to the side of the road. Seth turned the pickup and drove back into the tree tunnel and toward the camp.

It was noon when the green car with the red flasher on top pulled up in front of the little store and stopped. Con Drummond, the deputy sheriff from Immokalee, got out and came inside. Slim was standing behind the counter, swatting flies. "Where's Thompson?" the deputy asked roughly.

"He's up to the house," Slim said, revealing a row of snaggled, rotten front teeth that made him lisp slightly.

"Well, go and fetch him down here."

Slim left and in a few minutes Seth came from the house and down to the store. The deputy was standing outside by the patrol car. He was a man of thirty and wore a pearl-handled .38 Smith & Wesson revolver. He said, "Are you Seth Thompson?" He had never before been to the camp or known Seth.

"Yeah, I'm Thompson. What can I do for you?"

"Sheriff Tate sent me down here," the deputy said. "He couldn't come himself 'cause he's busy in Naples. Says he's a friend of yours."

"That's right," Seth said, pleased by the remark. "Me and Arthur Tate has been fishing together a heap of times."

"Well, what was all the ruckus out here this morning?"

"What ruckus?" Seth asked innocently.

"You know what I mean," the deputy said. "How come you been running around out here waving a shotgun?"

"Ah, that wasn't nothing much," Seth said, shuffling his bare feet. "I just run some men off that was cuttin' down my trees."

"Well, Thompson, those trees aren't on your property, and you've been put under a peace bond."

"What's that?" Seth asked, puzzled.

"It means if you cause any more trouble at all out here we'll have to arrest you and take you to jail."

Seth had a sinking feeling deep inside. "You mean I can't protect my property?" he asked.

"Hell, Thompson, that ain't your property," the deputy said harshly. "Can't you understand that? Those men could have had you arrested for pointing that shotgun, but they didn't. They just made out a peace bond. They really done you a favor, and you ought to be glad of it. Sheriff Tate told me to tell you to stay away from out there where them men are working and keep on your own property. Said he'd really hate to see you locked up, but he wouldn't have no choice."

"Well, I guess if that's what Arthur said, he ought to know," Seth said calmly. His voice then changed back to anger. "But you better tell them men to stay off my land! If they come on my land with them saws and that bulldozer they's going to be a heap of trouble!"

"They know where the line is, and you better be sure you do."

Seth sank down to the bench and said, "You tell Arthur hello for me. And tell him that the next time I come into Naples I'll bring him a mess of fresh catfish."

The deputy got into the patrol car. "Yeah, I'll tell him, Thompson," he replied. "And you stay out of trouble. I'd hate to have to come out here again."

An hour later Seth again heard the high-pitched drone of the saws. He got into one of the boats and disappeared up the creek.

ELEVEN

SINCE THE CONVERSATION with Billy Joe about the shooting of the arrows at the trucks, Charlie had acted on the outside as if any mention of the development of the land had never taken place. Each time Billy Joe came to the chickees to discuss the impending move, Charlie would listen and say nothing, only nodding his head as if to indicate that he understood. He was trying to shut the entire matter out of his mind, hoping if he did not think of it, it would somehow go away. But when he too heard the distant hum of the power saws and the crashing of trees to the ground he knew it was real and that it would not go away.

He did not venture down the road to see what was happening, and he did not want to see. So long as the banana trees and the oaks and the palms and the palmetto shielded his chickees from the sight of anyone traveling the gravel road, and so long as no intruders came down the path from the road, he was safe. He could hear the trucks as they rattled along a mere fifty yards from the chickees, but he would not dare go out again and be seen by anyone. He wanted it to appear that he and his little camp did not exist.

Billy Joe had been spending all of his spare time

away from the road job in building the chickee for the wedding feast for Lucy and Frank Willie, which must take place at the home of the father of the bride. The chickee would be forty feet long and twenty feet wide, and there were many pond cypress poles to be cut for the framing and many palmetto fronds to be gathered for the roof. There were also pits to be dug and spits to be made for the roasting of meats.

Timmy had been the most depressed of all by the news of the land development and the necessity to move. He thought that this would separate him forever from his grandfather, and he feared the unknown that was to come. His father had kept him busy gathering fronds for the chickee they were building, but on this morning he had slipped away and come down to his grandfather's camp.

One log had been left after Charlie had carved the little dugouts which were sold to the souvenir stands, and he was making this last canoe for Timmy. He was driving chips from the center of the log when Timmy trotted down the dirt path and dropped down beside him on the ground.

Charlie looked up from his work and noticed that the constant smile was missing from Timmy's face. He said, "I am making this dugout for you."

"Really, Granpappa?" Timmy said without the expected enthusiasm. "When can I have it?"

"In a day or so. We will see how fast I can finish it." He then put the log aside, looked at Timmy again and said, "I think it is time you climbed the big tree."

When he said this, Timmy became very excited. He asked quickly, "Can we leave now, Granpappa?"

"Yes, we will go now so there will be plenty of time. It is a long climb to the top of the sky."

Any thought Timmy had of ever leaving the swamp vanished completely as they drifted along this stream he loved so much. It was now only he and his grandfather and the trees and the vines and the birds and the turtles, and it would be so forever. No other thing existed as they moved deeper into the swamp, no trucks passing his house and no saws humming and no bulldozers moving about like huge angry tortoises. It seemed all too soon to him before they had crossed the ponds and the sloughs and were at the tree.

He asked his grandfather, "Can I see Forever Island? Which way do I look, Granpappa?"

"It is far away and to the south, but look hard enough and you may find it."

Charlie poled the dugout as far as he could into the thick knees, then Timmy got out and waded through the dark water to the base of the tree. He looked upward and it seemed to him that the tree had no end.

"Climb slowly and with a firm grip," Charlie cautioned. "Do not look down until you reach the top."

Timmy climbed the slanted base and reached the first rung, then one by one he moved upward, gripping one rung and stepping up, gripping another and moving upward again, feeling the wind grow stronger and stronger as he moved steadily upward toward the open sky. He was aware when he passed the roof of the swamp and there were no longer trees to the right and

left of his climb, but he dared not look down. He felt
his arms and legs tremble as he touched the last rung
and knew he had reached the top.

The part of the trunk where the top branches
forked out formed a small flat platform, and Timmy
stepped onto this and steadied himself against a limb.
It was only then that he really opened his eyes, and he
suddenly felt as if he had left the earth and joined a
flight of egrets high above the swamp. He was fifty feet
above the tops of the other trees, and the roof of the
swamp looked like a long flat meadow punctured by
stalks of dandelions which were the royal palms. He
imagined that he could spread his arms and sail outward and upward, swooping and dipping and circling
like a hawk. He looked to the south, and the River of
Grass was a velvety brown mass moving endlessly,
spotted with the green clumps of the hammocks, and
when the wind blew, the strands of sawgrass swayed
and weaved and tumbled. It seemed to Timmy that
this was the world of the Great Spirit or God, and it
would endure. Then he moved his eyes further south
to seek the island, but the horizon was hidden from
view. A solid wall of smoke drifted upward from the
land and into the clouds, forming a link between earth
and sky.

Timmy would have chosen to stay forever on this
platform above the swamp had he not finally heard his
grandfather calling from below. When he reached the
base of the tree and stepped into the cool water he had
to grasp a cypress knee and steady himself from the
dizziness before he could cross to the dugout.

The trip back into the swamp was an anticlimax, and Timmy thought that surely he had just returned from a place where no one else had ever before been, and that he had seen things no one else had ever seen or would ever see. He lay in the bottom of the dugout and closed his eyes, and the things he had witnessed came back just as vividly as he had seen them from the top of the tree. It was a moment before he realized the canoe had stopped.

He sat up and watched as his grandfather chased crawfish up and down a shallow slough. Charlie was putting them into a tin bucket he had brought along. When he had all that he wanted he came back to the dugout and stuffed tree moss into the bucket to cover the flouncing captives. "I have enough this time for us and Gumbo too," he said. "Your grandmother will make us a feast when we return."

As Charlie got back into the dugout, Timmy suddenly reached out and struck at a swarm of dragon flies. His grandfather said, "Do not kill the creatures unless you have need of them. When you kill them without need you destroy a part of yourself."

"They're nothing but pesky old dragon flies," Timmy said.

"They are eating the mosquito," Charlie said to him. "Then the bird will eat the dragon fly, and the bird will help spread the seeds of the plants and trees. The deer will eat the plants, and then we will eat the deer. We all have need of each other, and I have told you this before."

"I didn't know that anything would eat an old mosquito for its meal," Timmy said. "I thought they were only to bite us."

"The minnow will eat the mosquito also," Charlie said. "The bass and the turtle will eat the minnow, and we will eat both of them. The snake will also eat the fish, and the alligator will eat the snake. Many years ago we used the hide of the alligator to make our war shields, and we ate the flesh of its tail. All things in the swamp are important, Timmy, and you should not kill without need."

"Then why are the men with the machines killing the swamp?" Timmy asked.

For a moment Charlie didn't answer; then he said, "Billy Joe says that it is because they will build houses."

"Nothing can eat a house," Timmy said, not satisfied with the answer.

Charlie could not explain to Timmy a thing that he did not understand himself, so he pushed the dugout away from the slough and continued toward the creek.

When they reached the landing Charlie carried the bucket up to Lillie and then took some of the crawfish to Gumbo. He dropped them on the ground and Gumbo grabbed them one at a time, scurrying in and out of the storage chickee to eat them out of sight. He bounded back and forth to the hut until there were no more, then he climbed onto Charlie's shoulder and scratched at his head. "Stop that, Gumbo," Charlie said, putting the 'coon back on the ground. "Go down to the creek and catch a fish if you are still hungry. You have not forgotten how to hunt for yourself." As if he understood, Gumbo rambled off down to the water's edge and paced up and down the bank.

Lillie chopped okra, tomatoes, peppers, and bay leaves into the pot with the crawfish, and put the pot over the fire to simmer. She would also fry halves of bananas over which they would pour wild honey. Charlie and Timmy sat at the table and waited patiently as Lillie whipped the corn meal into a batter to make the hot pone.

Timmy was still reeling from his climb into the tree, but he was disappointed by the smoke wall that blocked his view to the south. He said, "Tell me about Forever Island, Granpappa." He had heard the story once before but he could listen to it again and again.

"Not now, Timmy," Charlie said. "It is a long tale, and we will speak of it some other time."

"Have you seen the island?" Timmy asked.

"I am not sure," Charlie answered. "I could have been born there, but I am not sure of this. I have heard my father tell of the island many times. He knew it well."

"Will you take me there someday, Granpappa?"

"It is possible. Maybe we will go there together someday."

Timmy looked anxious for a moment; then he said, "Will the men take the machines to the island, Granpappa?"

"No, they will not do this," Charlie said. "The island is too far in the marsh for the machines to reach. They will never take the machines to the island."

By then the crawfish bisque was almost done, and

the aroma was drifting over to man and boy. Timmy got up and stuck his head close to the pot, sniffing deeply. "Is it ready now, Granmamma?" he asked.

"It is done enough for you," she said, stopping the sewing machine. "Sit at the table and I will bring it to you."

The distant hum of the power saws went unnoticed as Lillie crossed from the platform to the grill.

TWELVE

BILLY JOE DROVE DOWN the dirt trail and parked the pickup beside the cooking chickee. Lillie was at the sewing machine, and Charlie was sitting at the table sharpening the hunting knife he had used to carve the cypress canoes.

Billy Joe got out and took a seat opposite Charlie. He said, "Frank Willie and Lucy have set their wedding date, Pappa. They will be married a week from this coming Sunday in the Baptist Church on the reservation."

"They should be married at the Green Corn Dance festival," Charlie said, putting the knife aside.

"There won't be a festival this year, Pappa. Times are too hard with the drought, and the people have too much to do. Frank and Lucy want to have their wedding in the church."

"There should always be a Green Corn Dance festival," Charlie said emphatically. "It is a time to be together and sip the Black Drink."

"Pappa, you can get just as much good out of a dose of castor oil. The old customs are fading away. They're just not important anymore, especially to the young people." He got up, poured himself a mug of coffee, and returned to the table. "The wedding feast will be held at my place a week from this Wednesday. We have almost finished the chickee, and we have invited many people from the reservation and a few from the Tamiami Trail and the hammocks."

"I will kill the deer," Charlie said.

"No, Pappa, you don't need to do anything. The men from the reservation are bringing beef and turkeys and I will kill two hogs, and there will be vegetables and fruits enough."

"You cannot have a Seminole feast without venison," Charlie said. "I will kill the deer."

"Pappa, if you think you've got to do something for the feast, gather up a few turtles. Everyone knows that Mamma makes the best turtle stew in the Big Cypress."

"Do you think I am too old to hunt the buck?" Charlie asked, his eyes flashing.

"I didn't mean that, Pappa," Billy Joe said quickly. "Of course I don't think you are too old to hunt."

"I am the grandfather of the bride, and I will kill the deer," Charlie said with finality.

Billy Joe realized he was bucking a stone wall, so he dropped the subject. He turned to Lillie and said, "Mamma, do you need anything from the store?"

"I will need some cloth later this week, but I do not need anything today. Could you bring me a bag of the peppermint sticks? I have the money here."

"Forget the money, Mamma. I will bring them to you late this afternoon."

Charlie got up, went to the storage chickee, and returned with the little canoe. "Give this to Timmy," he said, smiling. "He knows I was making it for him."

"Thanks, Pappa. He'll be real proud. This afternoon he is gathering the last of the fronds for the chickee. I must go now. I will come back late this afternoon."

A few minutes after Billy Joe had left, Seth drove down the path and parked. As Charlie was still at the table, Seth took a seat opposite him.

"Would you like stew and corn bread?" Charlie asked.

"Don't mind if I do," Seth replied, sniffing the aroma coming from the grill.

Charlie dipped a bowl and handed it to Seth along with a huge piece of the hot pone.

Seth handed a brown paper bag to Charlie and said, "I been to Immokalee this morning and I brung you a sack of them sugar buns you like."

Charlie opened the package and took out one of the cinnamon rolls. "It is good," he said, eating half a roll in one bite. "I thank you."

"Well, it ain't near as good as Lillie's cookin'," Seth said. "You got the best dern cook in Collier County. She could stew a wildcat and make it taste good."

Lillie heard the remark and smiled.

Charlie said, "You want to gig frogs tonight? This time we could eat them ourselves."

"I can't make it tonight, Charlie. I got some business to take care of. We'll do it some other time, though."

"We will go whenever you wish," Charlie said. "The moon will be better later this week."

Seth finished the stew and got up. "Well, I got to go now. That was mighty good, Miz Lillie. I sure thank you."

"You are always welcome at our table," Lillie said, still pleased by the compliments.

As Seth walked to the pickup he turned and said, "You want to come with us tonight, Charlie? Me and Slim is goin' after a varmint that has been botherin' us some. We won't be out too late, and you're welcome to come along if you want to. You might enjoy it."

"Yes, I will go," Charlie said. "Will I need to bring my spear or the bow and arrows?"

"Naw, you don't need to bring nothin'. We got plenty to get this critter. I'll pick you up just after dark."

"That will not be necessary," Charlie said. "I will come to your camp in the dugout."

When Seth reached the camp he parked the pickup by the side of the house. Slim came from the store, and Seth handed him a package. He said, "Put this in the store, Slim, and you be real careful. It's dynamite. Them fellows ain't the only ones who knows how to use this stuff."

The moon would not come up until late that night, and it was pitch dark as Seth, Slim, and Charlie climbed onto the swamp buggy. Seth cranked the engine and turned on the lights. Then he headed down the road where the Australian pines had stood a few days before. The buggy stopped when they reached the place where the first tree had been cut.

Seth said, "You sure you brung it all, Slim?"

"I got everything you tole me to," Slim answered, "but I shore don't like ridin' on this buggy with a lap full of dynamite and blastin' caps. You take it easy, now. I know how you like to drive this thing."

Charlie was totally confused. He had surmised they were going after a panther or a bear that had been invading Seth's camp, and he could not understand why they were bringing dynamite and no rifles.

Seth drove for a mile through a section of dwarf cypress, following a set of tracks that looked as if they had been made by a dozen bull alligators. He stopped again when the tracks led off into a marsh area.

"Wouldn't nothin' but a dern fool try to drive a bulldozer through a bog," Seth said. "But they ain't going to have to worry 'bout getting it out." He gunned the engine and the swamp buggy shot out into the marsh, the beams of its headlights bouncing through tall clumps of cattails.

"Take it easy, Seth!" Slim shouted, the box bouncing on his lap.

The bulldozer had traveled a hundred yards into the marsh before its left track slipped into a sink hole, causing it to tilt badly to one side. Seth pulled up to the huge yellow machine and aimed the buggy lights at its gas tank.

"Hand me that stuff, Slim," Seth said, excitement in his voice.

Charlie was by then so mystified as to the purpose

of the trip that he remained silent and watched with increasing perplexity.

Seth took the package from Slim and walked to the bulldozer, his feet sinking out of sight into the muck. He worked for a few minutes in the beam of the lights, and then he hurried back to the buggy. "That fuse is long enough for us to get slam to China," he said, panting.

He gunned the engine and let off on the clutch with the accelerator full down, spinning the buggy around and almost throwing Slim and Charlie out. The little vehicle bounded off into the dwarf cypress as if it had been stung by a drove of hornets.

Seth stopped when they reached the road again. He turned off the lights, and the moment the beams went out they were engulfed in total darkness. It was as if the entire swamp had turned into a sea of ink, and Seth could not see Slim or Charlie sitting beside him on the buggy.

They sat in silence for several minutes. Then Charlie said apprehensively, "What is this thing you are doing, Seth? I thought we were going after the panther or the bear."

"That dern thing out there is a heap worse than either one of them critters," Seth said, "but I guess I ought to have tole you what we was up to. I thought you'd enjoy it."

For several moments they waited in silence, and nothing happened. Slim said, "I knew it wouldn't work, Seth. You don't know how to use that stuff."

"I know how to use it, and it's got to work," Seth

said, his voice agitated. "Maybe it ain't had enough time yet. It was a powerful long fuse."

Several more seconds passed, and then Seth said, "Let's go back and take a look. The wind could have blowed that thing out."

Just as Seth reached for the ignition key a mushroom cloud of fire shot upward above the trees, and was followed by a tremendous boom that rushed out of the swamp. The night faded away, and the entire area was bathed with orange light. The sound seemed to come again and again and shake the buggy.

After the fire cloud had dissipated high in the air it was replaced by a steady glow. They could not see the bulldozer itself from where they were parked, and the orange dome a mile away in the swamp looked like the reflection of a giant campfire.

"That's the first bulldozer I've ever seen blow up 'cause of a faulty gas tank," Seth chuckled.

"It do look kind of purty out there at night, don't it," Slim said.

Charlie was so frightened by the whole thing that he could not speak. He wished that Seth would drive the buggy back to the camp quickly so he could get in the dugout and leave behind the sight of the flames.

The three of them watched for a few minutes more; then Seth cranked the buggy and headed back to the camp.

Charlie wasted no time in leaving when Seth finally parked the swamp buggy beside the house, and the trip down Gopher Creek seemed to take only minutes. Lillie did not move when he lay down beside her in the sleeping chickee, and for a long while he stared upward into the fronds, thinking of what he had seen, wondering if his being present when this thing happened was a violation of his pledge to Billie Joe. This was what worried him the most, the possibility that he had broken his word to Billy Joe. But he did not believe he had dishonored his promise against further violence since he was completely unaware of the purpose of Seth's trip, and he had only watched.

It was late in the night when sleep finally began to come, and Charlie was only partially aware when he heard the flutter of wings coming out of the darkness of the swamp. He bolted upright when the owl lit on the roof of the chickee and hooted.

Lillie also stirred at the sound of it, and Charlie said to her, "Did you hear it? The owl lit on the roof of the chickee and cried out."

"Yes, I heard."

"It is the worst of all bad omens," Charlie said, deep fear in his voice.

"Maybe it is not so," Lillie said, also afraid but attempting to appear unconcerned. "Maybe it is just a tale."

"It is not just a tale," Charlie said emphatically. "The truth is written on the lives of our people. It is the worst of all bad omens."

She knew what he said was truth according to the customs of their people, but she did not want to increase his fear by showing her own. She said, "We must sleep now. Maybe the omen was not meant for us."

"This could be so," he said, "but it is bad for some-one."

It was hours later before either of them went to sleep.

It was mid-afternoon when the green patrol car with the red flasher on top came down the road and parked in front of the fish camp store. Seth was sitting on the bench, and he felt a tingle of fear as the vehicle approached. He was greatly relieved, however, when he saw that it was Arthur Tate. Somehow Tate repre-sented to Seth much less of a threat than the deputy, for he had fished with Tate many times but did not know the younger man.

The sheriff got out and took a seat beside Seth. "Good to see you, Seth," he said cheerfully. "Been a long time since I've been in these woods. Looks like there's a lot of stuff going on out here." Tate was a man in his mid-fifties, of medium height with gray-flecked hair and a yet trim waistline.

"Mighty lot going on," Seth said, his voice appre-hensive.

"Well, it's a shame the way they're chopping up the woods. Pretty soon there won't be any swamp left."

This remark put Seth's mind at ease, for it appeared to him that the sheriff was in agreement with his own feelings. "It shore is a shame, Arthur," Seth said ear-nestly. "Just a dern shame. They ain't got no right to be doing this."

Tate leaned back against the wall of the store. "How's fishing?" he asked.

"It ain't no good right now. Water's too low."

"I've sure made some good catches out here. Haven't had much time for fishing lately, though. Seems that folks just can't stay out of trouble, and they keep me busy all the time. I don't see why some people are so anxious to get inside a jail cell. I know I wouldn't enjoy it."

"I wouldn't enjoy it neither," Seth agreed, "but some folks just ain't got no sense."

"You ever use any dynamite around here, Seth?" the sheriff asked casually.

"I use some, but not a whole lot. Sometimes I blow out deep holes to trap the water when it gets down real low, like an ole 'gator will wallow out a hole to trap hisself some water, and sometimes I get rid of stumps to make trails for my buggy, but I don't use a whole lot of it."

"Looks like somebody planted about a dozen sticks on that bulldozer that blew up out here last night."

Seth said unsteadily, "Is that right, Arthur? That explosion mighty near throwed me out of the bed. I couldn't figure out what in the world done it till I went up there this morning and looked."

Tate looked directly at Seth and said, "Deputy Drummond tells me he checked around and found out that you bought some dynamite yesterday at the hardware store in Immokalee. You used it yet?"

Sweat was beginning to pour off Seth's face. "I shore have, Arthur. I blowed out a hole yesterday afternoon down close to an otter pond south of here."

"Well, I can't understand why anybody would want

to blow up a bulldozer, except maybe for pure mean-ness," Tate said. "It sure wouldn't stop this work out here because those big development companies have got a hundred other machines just like that one, and nobody could blow them all up."

"Don't seem like there's much point to it, does it?"

"Nope. No point at all. But somebody's going to get himself either killed or put in jail if he tries that stunt again. The company is putting guards out here at night, and I'm going to have a patrol in this area for a few days too."

"A man must be mighty crazy to do a thing like that," Seth said, trying hard to sound convincing.

"He sure is, Seth." Tate looked directly into Seth's eyes again. "We know that whoever planted that dy-namite used a swamp buggy to go out there, and we know he wasn't wearing shoes, because he left his prints all over the place, but that's not enough yet to make an arrest and go into court. There's buggy tracks all over the swamp, and half the Indians around here don't wear shoes. But we're still looking, and we'll be waiting for him the next time he tries it."

Seth glanced down at his bare feet, then over to the mud-covered swamp buggy parked by the house. He said slowly, "Man'd be a fool to try something like that again, wouldn't he, Arthur?"

"He sure would, Seth," the sheriff said. "It's just not worth it."

"If I see anything going on I'll let you know. I'll keep on the lookout."

"You do that, Seth. And you take good care of yourself. You've always been my friend, and I want it to stay that way. We've got to go fishing together again one of these days. There's not many good guides like you left."

"Anytime you want to go fishing, Arthur, you just let me know."

As soon as the patrol car was gone, Seth drove the swamp buggy down to the fish-cleaning stand and tried to wash the mud from it.

The pickup stopped at a small shack that had been placed beside the road and served as an office for the crew working this section of the swamp. A man got out of the truck and went inside. Two other men were in the shack, one sitting behind a small desk and the other standing.

The truck driver said, "Mr. Lawton, we're having some trouble around that marsh flat on the north end of the creek where we're trying to get that dragline in."

"How's that?"

"Well, the men have threatened not to go in there again. That whole place is swarming with cotton-mouths and rattlesnakes, and there's 'gators in there and ticks and chiggers and all kinds of varmints."

"You mean they're afraid of a few snakes?"

"They're not exactly afraid, Mr. Lawton, but have you ever seen a man after he's been hit by a cotton-mouth or a rattler? It ain't no pretty sight. And that place is a hotbed of them snakes."

"Well, take the pickup and drive up to Immokalee and hire one of those crop dusters. Tell him to come down here and drop some dieldrin and some DDT and anything else he's got to throw in the pot. We'll mark the right area with red flags. And while you're up there, get some arsenic and some meat and bait that place real good. We'll work around that marsh for a day or so, and by then all the snakes should be cleared out."

"O.K., Mr. Lawton. I'll go on up there right away. The men sure don't want to work in a hotbed of rattlers and cottonmouths. That place must be a regular breeding ground."

As the truck pulled away, the man behind the desk said, "Christ! First it's Indians shooting arrows, then it's a bulldozer blowing up, and now it's snakes. Next thing you know the men will be demanding hot lunches. But for Christ sake, snakes!"

THIRTEEN

CHARLIE HAD NOT HUNTED the deer in more than ten years, and the preparations for once again stalking this cunning prey were occupying all of his time. He had spent hours sharpening and sharpening again the tips of the arrows, and he had tested the strength of the bow at least a dozen times. In his lifetime he had killed hundreds of deer, and it had been a commonplace thing without excitement simply to obtain food, but this hunt would be different. It would provide the venison for the wedding feast of his granddaughter.

In his younger days the preparations for hunting the deer had consisted of simply picking up the bow and arrows and walking into the woods. Now he had spent two days doing the things that would have taken him five minutes in past times. Lillie watched him with amusement, comparing his anticipation with that of Timmy each time he set off into the swamp with his grandfather.

Billy Joe had said no more to him about the hunt, for he thought that Charlie would spend a few hours in the woods, fail, and then be satisfied that he had at least tried. There would be plenty of beef and pork and turkeys without the venison.

Charlie knew of a rye grass meadow on the south edge of Copeland Prairie where the deer grazed during the early summer months, and he would go there that afternoon to see if there were signs. He skirted around the area where the men were working and entered the woods to the north of the burned-out bulldozer.

The ground here was higher than the south swamp, and there were thick growths of buck vines and thorn bushes. As he moved further north the woods thinned out and there were more pines, and he knew he was near the edge of the prairie.

When he found the small clearing, he examined the wild rye grass and saw that the deer had been grazing there. Then he circled the meadow and found the trail the deer were using to go back into the swamp. The bark was skinned from several small trees where the buck antlers had struck them. Further down the trail he found a thick clump of palmetto that would be the best spot to lie in wait and ambush the buck as it came from its night feeding on the meadow.

On the way back to his camp, Charlie planned how he would kill the deer. He knew if he shot one at night while it was feeding and only wounded it, he would not be able to track it in the darkness. He would come before dawn and wait for the sunrise to signal the moving of the deer from the place of feeding to the sanctuary of the swamp.

That night after eating his supper and sitting by the fire, Charlie was too restless to sleep. He strapped on his hunting knife and started a journey that he could have waited hours longer to begin. With him he had the bow and three arrows, although in past days he had needed only one. Now his arms and eyes were not so sure.

The moon was high and full, bathing the swamp with a soft glow and silhouetting the dwarf cypress and the palms one against the other. A slight breeze, blowing from the north, rustled the fronds, creating rattling sounds. He was glad the moon was up and high, for he doubted if his old eyes could carry him safely through the swamp in total darkness.

When he neared the edge of the prairie he did not go to the meadow to see if the deer were there, for he feared he might startle them and run them away into the night. He walked slowly and softly to the palmetto clump and cleared a small circle on the ground; then he sat down and faced the empty trail.

As he waited for the dawn his mind drifted back through the years. There were times when he could hit the squirrel and the duck with the arrow, and he had once killed a black bear with only the knife. For a week before the Green Corn Dance festival the hunters would bring in game to be roasted over open fires, and there would follow five days of feasting and dancing and the purging of body and spirit. He could remember times when the deer were as plentiful as the birds, and he had watched them at play more often than he had hunted them for meat. As he thought of these things and tried to relive in his mind the vanished days of his youth, he gently and imperceptibly fell asleep, the ancient bow and the arrows clutched tightly in his hands.

Charlie awoke with a start and discovered the first red streaks of dawn tinting the eastern sky. The wind was still from the north, and that was good, for the deer would not smell him as they moved to the south. He had thought he heard a soft thumping on the trail, and he listened again and was sure. He inserted an arrow into the bow and waited. The sound moved again and stopped, then it moved forward and a small doe bounded down the trail and passed without seeing the man.

Two more does passed and Charlie waited, the arrow pointed toward the trail. He knew that the bucks always sent the does out ahead of them, and that the bucks would come soon. He waited for several minutes more; then he heard a tinkling sound which he knew to be the antlers of a buck striking vines along the trail. The deer moved forward slowly, its head cocked back as it sniffed the air. For a moment the deer hesitated, sensing danger nearby, and in that split second of caution, the arrow left the bow and struck the buck in its right shoulder.

The buck leaped high into the air and crashed into a clump of vines. Charlie scrambled to his feet and plunged after it, almost landing directly on top of the deer. For a moment the eyes of man and animal met, and before Charlie could plunge the knife in, the buck leaped to its feet and crashed off through the vines toward the swamp.

There was a pool of blood on the ground, and Charlie knew the buck was badly wounded. In other times his arrow would have stopped the deer instantly, but his arms were not now so strong. He would have to track the deer and keep it moving so that it could not stop to rest and gain strength.

The trail was not hard to follow, for there was a steady stream of blood along the ground and smeared on vines and trees. The buck moved south for a short distance. Then it turned east and veered along the edge of the prairie. He could hear the deer ahead of him, and several times he came to a pool of blood where it had stopped to rest, but, moving as fast as he could, he had not seen the buck again since he sent the arrow into it.

He followed the trail eastward for what seemed to be hours, and then the blood trail turned to the south. The line of the swamp between prairie and marsh was narrow here, and Charlie knew that if the buck continued straight south and reached the endless sea of sawgrass he would never find it.

The ground became much softer, and if it had not been for the drought he would not have been able to track through this area at all. The blood trail had almost stopped, but the tracks of the buck in the soft muck were easily visible.

When he finally stopped to rest, Charlie realized it was well past noon. He had no food or water, for he had followed the old custom of not carrying food on the hunt, and he had expected to be back at the chickees by now. He had known deer to run two or three miles after being wounded, but he must have already tracked this buck ten miles. It seemed that the deer

wanted to live as badly as the old man wanted it to die.

A mile from the marsh the trail turned and headed westward, and he moved steadily after the tracks. His throat ached but he dared not drink from the slimy ponds. He found a cocoa plum bush and picked some of the fruit. He did not like its insipid taste, but the kernel was mildly narcotic and would allay the hunger and thirst. After resting for a few minutes and chewing several of the kernels, he continued the pursuit.

Finally the trail came to the northeast end of Gopher Creek, and Charlie fell to his hands and knees, drinking deeply of the cool water. He bathed the cuts that covered his face and arms, cuts that he had not noticed until now. He could see the tracks continue on the opposite side of the creek, and for a moment he was not sure what he should do. The sun was now low in the sky, and if he turned for home, even without the deer, it would be dark before he reached the chickees. Perhaps Lillie would be worried and tell Billy Joe, and Billy Joe would come looking for him. He would not like this. He sat on the ground and cupped his head in his hands, trying to decide. If the deer ran much further it would be impossible to track at night, and he would lose it. But if he could not furnish the venison for the wedding feast of his granddaughter then he should sit on the platform and sew the jackets to be sold to the souvenir stands on the Tamiami Trail. And if he could not finish this hunt then he would not be strong enough to seek the island. He hesitated for a moment more, and then he plunged into the water and came out on the opposite side.

He followed the tracks but a short distance when he came to a spot of warm foam on the ground, and he knew that the buck was dying. Now he was glad he did not turn for home, for the hunt was almost ended. He began to trot instead of walk, and he found the deer lying in a clump of cattails. The buck tried to get to its feet but had no lifeblood left to do so. It struggled briefly and then fell back dead.

Charlie sank the knife into the deer's stomach and cleaned out the insides, then he pulled it by the antlers back to the creek and through the water. Once he could have put the buck on his shoulders and walked with it, but now he could not do so. He tried, but he could not lift it from the ground. He would have to drag it home by the antlers, and he hoped no one would see him doing this. It would not be in keeping with the dignity of a hunter.

It was two hours after dark when he reached the chickees, and he noticed the deep concern in Lillie's eyes. She handed him a steaming bowl of turtle stew, and he went to the table and ate ravenously. His arms and legs ached, but this did not matter. He would furnish the venison for the wedding feast of his granddaughter. After eating, he skinned the hide from the meat. From the hide Lillie would make a rug to go on the floor of the house trailer where Lucy and Frank Willie would live.

Later in the night, as he lay beside Lillie in the

chickee, Charlie's mind was completely divorced from all the things that had troubled him and given him anguish in recent days. As he hovered in that dream world between sleep and reality, he thought again of the old days and how it had been then when he brought the slain deer into his camp, how his children had gathered around him and stared in awe at the bounty that would soon become a family feast. The thought of the children reminded him of the days when he and Lillie had been lovers, of the nights when they had held each other close and listened to the gentle beat of rain on the thatched roof of the chickee, of the times they had wandered off into the swamp to be alone, and how they had once created life on a bed of thick green moss beneath the canopy of a giant oak.

Although his tired body ached for sleep, he thought of these things for a long while, then he took Lillie's hand in his and held it gently.

FOURTEEN

FINAL PREPARATIONS for the wedding feast were begun the day before the event was to be held. Billy Joe had taken leave from his job for two days, and he was up at dawn to finish the digging of the pits where the meats would be cooked. He had been both surprised and pleased when he went to the chickees and found that his father had made good his vow to furnish venison. He had taken the dressed deer back to his house. It would be roasted on a spit over an open fire.

Although Billy Joe and Timmy could have completed the necessary tasks alone, Charlie was present constantly, issuing instruction as each spade of dirt was turned for the pits and each frame erected for the roasting spits. Billy Joe was glad that his father was so totally occupied with the preparations and not thinking of what was to come in the near future. He pretended each task could not have been finished properly without Charlie's advice.

Jimmy Gopher arrived from the reservation at mid-morning with a dressed steer, and the wild turkeys would be cooked at the reservation and brought the next day. A pit three feet deep had been dug for the cooking of the beef, and a hickory fire in the pit was burning down to glowing coals. Billy Joe had cut thin gumbo limbo poles to put over the pit, and the beef sides would be placed on the poles and barbecued slowly for twenty-four hours. Shallow pits would be used for the cooking of the hogs and the deer, but this cooking would not begin until the next morning.

Lillie was making a pot of her turtle stew, for this was a favorite of everyone. There would also be a huge pot of boiled corn on the cob. This wedding feast was to be a substitute for the Green Corn Dance festival that would not be held, and there would be an abundance of all the favorite dishes associated with the festive event.

The traditional wedding shirt for Frank Willie was finished, and Watsie was busy in the kitchen making guava jelly to be served with the roasted meats. She would also make several pans of cornbread dressing laced with wild sage and the inner bark of the gumbo limbo tree. This would be baked and stuffed into the wild turkeys.

The huge chickee was also completed, and its size overshadowed the small wooden frame house. It would be used only once before the arrival of the bulldozers, but Billy Joe and Timmy had given no thought to this as they cut the cypress framing, gathered the fronds, and devoted so much time to its construction. A wedding was an important happening in the culture of the Seminole, and Billy Joe was determined not to let the impending move dampen the festivity of his daughter's marriage. As much as he could within his physical means, he would make this an event Lucy and Frank

Willie would always remember with pleasure and pride.

The activities continued throughout the day, Charlie trotting back and forth from one task to another, even invading Watsie's kitchen to sample the jelly and give it his stamp of approval. He tested the strength of the spits over and over again, and personally selected and cut the hickory limbs to be used in roasting the venison.

The next morning at dawn, Charlie and Billy Joe put the deer and the hogs over glowing fires and started them roasting, and soon the entire clearing became enveloped with blue smoke. The smell of the meats as they slowly browned was almost more than Timmy could bear.

The first to arrive at noon was Frank Willie and his family, then came Jimmy Gopher and Charlie Snow and Sam Huff and Richard Osceola and Josie Billie and Bird Fraser and John Tiger and Keith Whoyah and Billy Bowlegs and Miami Billie and Jimmy Cypress and Billie Tommie and Frank Jim and Jack Tiger Tail and John Poole and Ingraham Billie and Doctor John and Abraham Lincoln Jumper. There would be more than a hundred people present. All of the men were dressed in the traditional Seminole shirts that looked as if they had been cut from a rainbow, and the women wore the equally colorful ankle-length dresses. Even the young girls had abandoned their modern short skirts for this special occasion and were dressed the same as their mothers.

The guests arrived in bright red Mustangs and bat-

tered old Fords and Chevrolets and Dodges and pickups and two-ton cattle trucks with their high board
sides, some clean and shining and others coated a dull
gray with the limestone dust or caked with mud. Construction workers passing on the gravel road wondered
what was happening here in this remote section of the
swamp to bring together such an assemblage.

The older men at first wandered around the clearing, inspecting the fences and the sheds and the cattle
and hogs, staring dejectedly at the blistered vegetable
field, sucking grass stems as they moved from one area
of the property to another. Then they came back to the
house and huddled in a group, talking freely about
hunting and fishing and cattle prices and crops and the
drought. Some of the women busied themselves around
the cooking fires while others ran after the younger
children, scolding them for throwing rocks at the hogs
or chasing the chickens, threatening them with dire
things to come if they went into the swamp and ruined
their freshly starched clothes. The older boys and girls
began a game of stick ball, in spite of the heat. Charlie
partook of it all, leaving the cluster of men where he
enjoyed the esteem of the patriarch, going next to the
cooking fire where he cautioned the women not to
burn the venison, then shouting encouragement to the
stick ball players before returning to the gathering of
men.

Charlie had invited Seth to attend, and he arrived
two hours after noon. In the back of Seth's pickup
there were four washtubs of iced beer. From that point
on the men seemed to move steadily from the shade of

the chickee to the rear of Seth's truck and back into the shade again.

At four in the afternoon the meal began, and the eating continued for more than three hours. Knives were placed by each roast of meat so the guests could carve their own portions, and Charlie urged each person to take a larger cut. The only concession to modern times was the paper plates Billy Joe had purchased at the store in Copeland.

All of the men ate together in one section of the chickee, but the women separated themselves into small groups according to clans. It was against the old customs for women of different clans to eat together, and the little groups off to themselves represented the Panther, Wildcat, Tiger, Bird, Otter, Wolf, Snake, Wind, and Town Clans. This custom was seldom observed anymore, but all of the people were following the old ways as closely as possible for the last gathering here in this part of the swamp.

When the feasting was finally finished, everyone came together and sat on the ground beneath the chickee, the men in the front rows and the women and children behind them. Charlie wanted Billy Joe to present the wedding gift before the telling of the tales, and he and Timmy brought it from the feed shed where it had been hidden for the past several days. Lillie clapped her hands with joy as Billy Joe stripped away the cardboard box, revealing the new television set with the gleaming wooden cabinet. Lucy ran to her father and threw her arms around his neck.

"Don't thank me," Billy Joe said, embarrassed but

pleased by his daughter's open display of emotion. "This is mostly the doings of your grandfather and grandmother. It is their gift also, and you should thank them."

She ran to the old man and the old woman and kissed them on wrinkled cheeks. Charlie grinned broadly, and Lillie clapped her hands again.

The gift presented, it was now time for what they had all looked forward to, the telling of the tales. Everyone suddenly became attentive, and a silence fell over the chickee as they waited for someone to speak. Ingraham Billie then led off, saying, "I will tell of a man named Roosevelt Otter, and of the wildest ride in the Everglades. It was in the days when we caught the alligator alive and sold him to the tourist places in Miami and on the Trail. This Roosevelt Otter would come up to the alligator in his canoe, and he would leap on its back and wear it down until he could close its jaws and tie them. He was far to the south one day when he came to a giant 'gator. When he leaped on its back he found that it was not a 'gator, but a crocodile. He knew right away he had committed a grievous error. The crock's jaws were flailing like the blades of a windmill, and if he jumped off there would soon be no more of him than dinner in the belly of the crock. The only thing to do was ride it out as best he could. The crock was jumping and bucking like a stallion, but Roosevelt Otter hung on, his legs locked around the belly of the crock. They flattened several square miles of sawgrass, and two hammocks were destroyed completely. The ground for miles around looked as if the hurricane had come through."

Ingraham Billie stopped, and John Tiger, expecting more, asked, "Well, what became of Roosevelt Otter?"

"I do not know. The last anyone saw of him he was still on the crock's back, heading across Whitewater Bay and toward the Keys."

Seth spoke up and said, "Shoot, that fellow wasn't so tough. Once they was a catfisher up at Lake Okeechobee who could whup any ten men standing. Nobody never did know his name, but they called him Pogy, and he was something else. Didn't nobody mess with Pogy and come away with less than two broken arms or a busted head. Ole Pogy could pick up a two-hundred pound barrel of fish with his left hand.

"Well sir, back in them days Okeechobee City was about the wildest place this side of hell and back. Things went on there that folks nowdays just wouldn't believe. Ever Saturday all the cowpokes from north of the lake would come in, and all of the catfishers from down south would come in, and they had a standin' agreement to fight ever Saturday night soon as they got likkered up enough.

"Well sir, one Saturday night they'd all got skonked and gone to fist city about ten o'clock, and after they got done fighting, about a dozen of them catfishers decided they was hongry for some sweet stuff, so they goes to Albert's Bakery and bangs on the door till ole Albert comes out of the back of the store, where he lived. When Albert seed what was out there, he knowed he were in a heap of trouble if he didn't let them in and in a heap of trouble if he did, but he didn't want his door smashed, so he lets them in and starts dishin' up them pies and cakes. Soon as they got done eatin' somebody pulls out a pistol and starts shootin' up a shelf of canned peaches, and then the whole crew starts blastin' peach halves and syrup all over the place. I come by the store about then and seed what was goin' on, so I goes inside and takes advantage of the situation. Whilst all the ruckus is goin' on I eats me a half dozen of them blueberry pies. And all the while ole Albert is standin' in a corner, shakin' like a pine tree in a hurricane.

"When everbody leaves I follow them down to Gussy's joint where they all start drinkin' again. Well sir, ole Albert and Pogy is good friends, and when Pogy finds out what them catfishers done, he comes into Gussy's madder'n a bee-stung wildcat. He tells them fellows to dish up twenty dollars apiece to pay for the damages, and if they don't he'll make their heads look like a sack of hickernuts. And he woulda, too. One of them fellows says he ain't goin' to pay no twenty bucks just for some canned peaches, so Pogy picks him up and slams him clear through the wall, right out into a pen full of hogs. Then Pogy says it'll be another ten dollars apiece to pay for Gussy's wall. Them fellows seed right away the longer they waited the more it was goin' to cost them, so they all dished up the cash on a table.

"Pogy picked up that money and started out to give it to ole Albert, and one of them fellows spoke up and said, 'What about Seth? He et six pies and didn't pay nothin'.' With that Pogy looks at me and says, 'That'll be two bucks each for the pies, Seth.' I didn't have a cent on me, so I says, 'I ain't got no money, Pogy. I swear I'll pay Albert next Saturday soon as I get my fish pay.' Ole Pogy looks at me even harder and says, 'Seth, you mean you et six of Albert's pies and ain't got no money to pay?'

"Well sir, when I says 'yes,' ole Pogy moves closer and says, 'Seth, if you done et them pies and you ain't got the money to pay, best I can do is see to it that you don't enjoy them.' With that he hauls off and hits me in the stomach so hard his fist goes plumb through my gut and rattles my backbone. And you know, ole Pogy wasn't tellin' no lie 'bout me not enjoyin' them pies. As soon as that big fist comes out of my belly I double up and start pukin' everwhere. I throwed them pies up all over the floor and all over Pogy's shoes, and that done it. Pogy he makes me take off my shirt and clean that puke off his shoes, then he tells me I got to wear that shirt without washin' it until I pay Albert or he'd knock me slam down to Big Cypress. And I knowed he'd do it, too. So I wears that shirt for a week out in that broilin' sun. You ever smelt week-old blueberry puke? I swear to this day I ain't never et no more blueberry pie, and I ain't likely to, neither. But that Pogy was something else, fellows. Could whup any ten men standing."

Sam Huff then said, "That is a good tale, Seth Thompson, but this sickness you speak of is nothing. I have seen worse. Before we moved to the hammock we lived in chickees along the Tamiami Trail, and the tourist people were always stopping and tromping through our place, just like it was some kind of a public zoo. Early one morning this man stopped his car and came to the chickee and said he was some sort of a writer, and that he wanted to know about the Seminole. We didn't pay him any mind, but he kept following us around, writing in a notebook and playing one of those recording machines. Every time I made a move he was right behind me. I believe if I had pooted he would have run up and smelled it just so he could say that he had smelled Indian poot.

"He kept this up all morning, and at noon he said he would give me five dollars to let him squat down in the chickee and eat Seminole food like we eat. I told him I didn't run a cafe but if he was hungry we would give him food. Sara had a big pot of rabbit stew going, so she dished him up a bowl and he squatted down and started eating. He really made a big show of it, too. It wasn't anything but plain rabbit stew, but he kept groaning and grunting about how good it was and what a surprise it was to know that Seminoles ate such good food. Then he asked me what was in the stew so he could make it himself sometime.

"I looked real solemn and said, 'This is a favorite old Seminole dish. It is part skunk, part cottonmouth, part dog, and part buzzard. If you like it so much we will give you a jar to take with you.'

"That tourist man dropped the bowl, and for a few seconds I thought he was going to faint. He just swayed back and forth, his face as white as the egret's feather. Then he started to vomit. Seth Thompson, you think you did something with those pies; you did nothing. That fellow beat all I have ever seen. He finally ran down to the canal and stuck his whole head beneath the water, plumb down to his shoulders, and he just squatted there for five minutes with his head under the water. I thought he had drowned himself. Then he jumped up and ran for his car, and didn't say another word to anyone. He even left his notebook and the recording machine and didn't come back for them, either. We never saw him again, and I gave the recording machine to my cousin Tommie Toby. His wife uses it to store her needles and thread."

Josie Billie, the Baptist preacher on the reservation, spoke up and said, "I will tell a tale of religion."

Charlie interrupted, "I would rather hear a hunting tale instead."

The preacher looked at Charlie. "Are you not a religious man, Mr. Charlie?" he asked.

"I was once a Baptist, like you," Charlie answered. "It was long ago, and the white missionary came to me and told me that the Indian way was all wrong, that if I ever wanted to see the Great Spirit I would have to become the Baptist and do it the white man's way. So I became the Baptist. And then another white missionary came, and he was the Methodist. He told me that the Baptist way was not the right way, and if I wanted to see the Great Spirit I would have to become the Methodist. So I became the Methodist. And then yet another white missionary came, and he was the Presbyterian, and he told me that the Methodist way was not the right way, and if I wanted to see the Great

Spirit I would have to become the Presbyterian. I said
to him that if the white men cannot decide among
themselves which is the right way I will become the
Indian again and seek the Great Spirit in my own way.
And that is what I have done, Josie Billie, and I will
see the Great Spirit when the time comes."

The preacher laughed, then he said, "Well, Mr.
Charlie, if you ever decide you want to start all over
again and be a Baptist, you will be welcome at our
church on the reservation. I am no missionary, only a
simple preacher, and I will not tell you that only one
way is right."

Timmy jumped up and said, "Let Granpappa tell of
Forever Island."

"I have heard of it," John Hicks said. "It is in the
Ten Thousand Islands."

"No, it is not," Charlie said quickly. "It is in Pa-
Hay-Okee. My father once lived there, and I have
heard him speak of it many times."

"There is no such place," Billy Joe interrupted.
"When our people had to hide from the white soldiers,
all of the swamp and all of the Glades was Forever Island. It is everywhere, and there is no such one place.
Forever Island is only a tale that has grown with time."

"You are wrong, Billy Joe," Keith Whoyah said. "I
have also heard my father speak of it."

"Let Charlie tell it," Bird Fraser said. "I want to
hear it from him."

"It was many years ago, in the days of my father
and before," Charlie began, his eyes taking on a faraway look as if he were now in the top of the giant tree

himself, seeing over and beyond the roof of the world and through the borders of time, seeking something far in the past. "The third war with the white soldiers had ended, and our people were living here in the edges of the great cypress swamp. But the white men passed a law that none of our people could remain, and an offer of money was made for the capture of the Seminole man, woman, and child. Our people were to be sent to the lands in the west where others of our nation had already been sent by the white soldiers.

"Our people would not leave, and they fled deeper into the swamp. They had to eat snakes and roots and whatever they could find, and they ate the fish raw for fear that smoke from the cooking fire would give them away to the white hunters. Then the white soldiers came again, and the people moved south once more. Some fled to the Ten Thousand Islands and hid there, and some went many days travel into Pa-Hay-Okee, and it was there in the River of Grass that they found Forever Island. It was the largest of all hammocks, and it had never been seen by the white man.

"The island was surrounded by a reef of limestone rock, and a shallow moat ran from the rock to the shore. The game was plentiful, and the fish as thick as the blades of sawgrass. There were deer and rabbit and squirrels and the turkey flew among the trees. In the center of the island a deep spring brought forth great quantities of cool water. From the rich soil they grew corn and beans and pumpkin, and there was a large grove of banana trees and also guava, mango, and pa-paya.

"The trees were of many kinds, the oak and the strong mahogany and the gumbo limbo and the palm and the lancewood from which the fish spears were made. The muscadine was plentiful, and there were wild oranges on a hammock nearby. It was an island unlike all others.

"Our people lived there for many years. Then a great fire in the sawgrass came out of the south, near where the white man had built the village called Miami. It came toward the island with a great roar, and the people fled to the north, leaving behind all but their spears and their tools. From a distance they watched the flames leap into the trees and through the village, and then they could see no more. They went to other hammocks out of reach of the fire, and many came back to the swamp. That was many years ago, and now the island would show no scars from the great fire. It should be now as it was then."

"But how would you ever know this island today?" John Tiger asked. "Would it not look the same as many other hammocks?"

Charlie responded, "It is said that the people built a stone pyramid ten feet high in the middle of the island as the center of the Green Corn Dance. The fire would not have harmed the stone, and you would know the island by the pyramid."

"That is a good tale, Pappa," Billy Joe said, "but it is nothing more than a tale. You are right now in the center of Forever Island."

Two more tales were told, one of hunting and one of the great war. Then Charlie suddenly jumped to his feet and said, "Let us do the Green Corn Dance! It is not a proper wedding feast without the dance."

"Yes, let us do it!" Miami Billie echoed.

"But we will need the beat, and we have no drums," Sam Huff said.

"We can use tubs," Jimmy Cypress said, the enthusiasm spreading quickly.

"I will bring two tubs from the feed shed," Billy Joe said.

Several of the men gathered limbs and small logs and threw them onto the coals in the pit where the beef had been cooked, causing a stream of sparks to shoot upward into the darkness.

Billy Joe returned with the tin tubs and handed one to John Tiger and one to Josie Billie. The women and children moved from the chickee and sat on the ground, forming a huge circle around the growing fire.

As an irregular, staccato beat came from the tubs and echoed around the clearing, Charlie stepped inside the circle, standing rigidly erect for a moment, his arms reaching upward into the night sky as if trying to grasp the darkness. Then his feet began to move, slowly at first, like a child playing hopscotch, then faster and faster, his feet barely touching the ground.

One by one the men joined the dance, all of them now chanting as their arms flailed the air. The tempo of the dance increased as the flames shot higher, bathing the clearing with an orange glow and sending shadows through the trees and into the swamp. Faster and faster they danced until they were mesmerized, performing a ritual that had been repeated a hundred times before in other glades across this swamp but would not be repeated again. The dancers sensed that this night was the beginning and the end and they wanted to make the most of it.

Charlie danced wildly, as if testing his old body to the limits of its endurance. Then he fell exhausted to the outside of the circle. His eyes gleamed as he watched the other men continue until they too, one by one, dropped out and fell to the ground, panting and sweating. Just as suddenly as it had begun, the Green Corn Dance was then ended.

It was after midnight when the procession of bright red Mustangs and battered old Fords and Chevrolets and Dodges and pickups and limestone-coated cattle trucks left this remote spot in the swamp and started back toward the Turner River Grade and another world.

FIFTEEN

THE MORNING AFTER the wedding feast Seth walked down to the creek to take one of the boats and check a fish trap north of the camp. He suddenly started shouting, "Goddammit! Slim! You come down here, Slim!"

The lanky man scrambled from the store and ran down to the water, wondering what had brought on this unexpected outburst.

"Look at that, Slim!" Seth bellowed. "Look at that! They're ruining the creek!"

A gray streak of mud silt had come down the center of the creek and was widening out toward the banks.

"It's that damned dragline they got workin' up north of here," Seth said. "They'll run ever fish out of here for ten miles around."

Seth paced back and forth for a few minutes, then he said to Slim, "I'll go take up them lines and traps afore they get covered by the mud. You take the truck and go down to Copeland and get me two five-gallon cans of gas. We'll do it this time with something everybody uses; then they won't be able to trace nothin' to me. Goddammit!"

It was just after dark when Seth and Slim put the gasoline cans into the boat and started up the creek. Seth said, "A boat sure don't leave no tracks, do it, Slim?"

"It sure don't," Slim answered, as unconcerned as if they were starting out to set fish traps.

"And I'll fool 'um this time with these shoes."

Seth had put on a pair of brogans so old that the leather had decayed in several places. He had slipped them on without laces so they wouldn't hurt his feet. As soon as the job was finished and he was back in the boat, he would take them off and sink them in the creek.

They used a boat without an engine so as to make no noise, and Seth sat in the rear and paddled while Slim rode the elevated bow. It was two miles up the creek to where the dragline was stationed.

As they rounded a bend they could see the dragline silhouetted by the moonlight. Seth turned the boat into the bank and they got out, Slim bringing the two cans.

Seth said, "I'll slosh the stuff on this side and you slosh it on the other. Then you get back in the boat and I'll throw the match. That thing ought to go up like a bunch of dried sawgrass. Then we'll hightail it back down the creek and nobody'll know the difference."

Slim went around behind the dragline while Seth poured gasoline on one side. Seth was halfway through the can when a brilliant beam of light came from about fifty yards across the marsh and centered on him. He heard someone shout, "Hey! What you doing out there? Drop that can and come on over this way!"

For a moment Seth froze, thoroughly frightened and addled by the unexpected light and the shouting from the darkness. He turned toward the beam and was blinded, and then he dropped the can and jumped from the dragline.

He heard the shouting again, "Hey, fellow, you! Stop right there!"

Seth's eyes were blinded by the light, but he ran toward where he thought the boat should be. There was a thin flash of fire followed by a loud explosion. He felt something hit him hard in the left chest, and he went down to his knees. For a moment he stayed down. Then he struggled to his feet and stumbled into the creek.

The boat was not there, and he could hear no sound from Slim. Then he waded across the shallow water and disappeared into a thick clump of willows on the opposite side.

Seth's foot had struck the right side of the boat when he entered the water, and now the boat was floating slowly down the creek, empty.

Charlie was sitting at the table the next morning, eating a bowl of corn grits, when the green patrol car came down the lane and stopped. Sheriff Tate got out and came over to him.

"You been out in the swamp yet this morning, Mr. Jumper?" the sheriff asked.

"Yes, I have been there," Charlie answered, pushing the bowl aside. He had been to the pond to feed Little George.

"You see anything of Seth Thompson?"

"No, I have not seen him. Is something wrong?"

"Yes, I'm afraid so," the sheriff said, concern in his voice. "Seth was in a little trouble last night, and I think one of the company guards shot him. He may be needing help very badly."

"Is he in much trouble when you find him?" Charlie asked, dismayed by the news, thinking immediately of the night he had accompanied Seth and Slim when they destroyed the bulldozer.

"Not too much. He hadn't really done anything before this guard popped off his rifle at him. He's in some trouble, but not too much to handle, and he'll be O.K. if I can just talk some sense into him and get him to stop right now. But the important thing is to find him."

"I will help you do this," Charlie said eagerly, getting up from the table.

"We'd sure appreciate it, Mr. Jumper. I've got a swamp buggy up at Seth's camp, and we're going to look in those woods on the north side of the creek. You try anywhere you want, and we'll see you later at the camp."

Charlie got into the dugout and poled swiftly up the creek. The mud had not come down this far yet and the water was clear, but when he approached the camp the creek was a solid gray.

He continued past the camp and moved the dugout even faster. There was a small shack to the south of the creek where Seth sometimes stored fish traps when they were not in use, and Charlie thought that this was where Seth would probably be.

He pushed the dugout onto the bank and walked through an area of dwarf cypress; then he came into a cabbage palm hammock. The little shack was to the left, and he saw Seth sitting on the ground, leaning back against the trunk of a palm.

Charlie ran to him and dropped down to his knees. "Are you bad?" he asked.

"I ain't too good, Charlie," Seth answered, his voice weak, "but it sure is good to see you here." The shoes were gone, sucked off by the muck as Seth fled through the swamp, and his overalls were caked with mud. Blood from a hole in his chest had run down and mixed with the dried mud.

"I will take you back to the camp," Charlie said.

"Ain't no use to try that. I'd just sink that little ole canoe you got. You go to my place and get one of the boats and then come on back. And when you come, Charlie, bring me a can of cold beer. A man can't travel on one leg, you know."

Charlie got up and said, "I will be back quickly, Seth. You will be all right soon."

When Charlie reached the camp the sheriff and three other men were there. "You seen anything of him yet?" Sheriff Tate asked anxiously. "We didn't find a trace of him north of here."

"I have found him," Charlie said. "He is to the south of the creek, and he is hurt badly. We must get him out at once."

The company guard spoke up and said, "There were two of them up there last night, sheriff."

"The other would have been Slim," Sheriff Tate said. "If you missed him with that damned rifle he's probably in Georgia by now."

"I told the fat one to stop," the guard said. "I hollered at him three times."

"You sure did want him to stop, didn't you," the sheriff said angrily. He then turned to one of his deputies. "We better take two boats up there. Seth is a big man, and only one person can ride with him coming back."

Charlie ran to the store and got the can of beer, and then he led them up the creek. When they reached the palm hammock Seth was still sitting on the ground, his eyes closed and his hands dropped down by his sides. Sheriff Tate leaned over him and said, "Well, he didn't make it. He's dead."

Sheriff Tate then put his hands over his eyes and said, "Poor old fellow. He did the only thing he knew to do. If I could have talked to him just once more I might have been able to stop this."

Charlie looked at the guard and said angrily, "You did not have to do this! You will be cursed for the rest of your days!"

"Now wait just a minute," the guard shot back, glaring at Charlie. "Don't you go putting no Indian curse on me, you old bastard! I only did what I had to do, and I ain't going to stand here and . . ."

"Now shut up!" Tate snapped at the guard. "I hear

just one more word out of you I'll be tempted to put a curse on your skull with this pistol butt!"

The guard looked sullen and backed away.

Charlie turned to the sheriff and asked, "What will you do with Seth?"

"I guess we'll bury him down at Copeland. I think his pappy is buried there. So far as I know Seth was alone, and there's nobody who should be informed about this."

It took all of them to lift Seth from the ground, and it was a slow journey from the palm hammock back to the muddied water of Gopher Creek.

Seth was buried the next afternoon in the little cemetery at Copeland, close by the grave of his father. Only five people were there, Billy Joe and Watsie, Charlie and Lillie, and Sheriff Tate. A preacher unknown to Seth said the standard funeral words and then the plain casket was lowered into the ground.

When everyone went back to the cars, leaving the small plot again silent, Charlie took a brown paper bag from the pickup and walked back into the cemetery. He kneeled down and placed beside the fresh grave a piece of fried fish and a can of beer. It was the custom of the Seminole to provide a departing friend with that which he had cherished most.

SIXTEEN

CHARLIE WAS SITTING on the bank of the creek, thinking of the simple wedding ceremony he had witnessed that afternoon in the Baptist Church on the reservation, when the first hard rumble of thunder came out of the north. The wind picked up quickly, and lightening flashes streaked from a high bank of black clouds boiling southward. Charlie got to his feet as a few raindrops pelted down, making little puffs in the dry dust.

In a few minutes the rain came in a downpour. Charlie sat in the chickee and listened as the water pounded onto the thatched roof. It was raining so hard he couldn't see the bank of the creek. The ever present cooking fire sputtered vainly and went out, sending up a spiral of hissing steam. Soon the dead coals were riding the crest of a small riverlet, moving steadily from the chickee and in the direction of the creek.

The heavy rain lasted late into the night, starting a flow of water again. On the marsh north of Gopher Creek, the pesticides and the deadly arsenic trickled slowly into the creek, mixed with the now muddied water, and flowed to the west and the south.

When Charlie went down to the dugout the next morning he noticed dead fish floating on top of the water. He also saw a dead turtle and a small alligator dying on the bank. He poled quickly up the creek and found more dead fish and turtles and alligators. This puzzled him greatly, and he knew that something must be terribly wrong with the water.

When he returned to his landing Billy Joe was there to see if they needed anything from the store in Copeland. He had already been down to the creek and had seen the dead fish. He said to Charlie, "Don't drink any of that water, Pappa. And don't use it for cooking. We'll bring water to you from the well."

"I do not understand this strange thing," Charlie said, looking again at the creek. "I have never seen such as this before."

"When I get to Copeland I'll call Fred Henderson and tell him about this," Billy Joe said. "Maybe he will know what it is and what we must do." His face was also deeply puzzled as he got into the truck and drove away.

Charlie stayed around the chickees all that morning, and just after noon Fred Henderson arrived in a van truck with another man. The van was a portable laboratory operated by the game and fish commission. The men took a sample of the water and several dead fish into the van. After an hour they came outside again.

Henderson said to Charlie, "You haven't got a couple of cups of coffee, have you, Mr. Charlie?"

"We have plenty." He poured three mugs and they took seats at the table.

Henderson took a deep drink, then he said suddenly, "This isn't creek water we're drinking, is it Mr. Charlie?"

"No, it is rain water."

Henderson look relieved.

Charlie then asked anxiously, "Do you know yet what is wrong?"

"We've got a good idea," the biologist said. "I'll have to run a few more tests before we know everything, but we know now there's poison in the water."

"It is not a natural thing, then?" Charlie asked.

"No, it's definitely not natural. There are traces of arsenic in it."

Charlie turned to Henderson. "Could someone have poisioned the creek purposely?" he asked.

"I don't know," Henderson said, deeply concerned, "but we're sure going to try and find out. I've got an idea this is coming from something those land developers are doing. There's just no way arsenic could get into the creek without someone putting it there."

"Don't eat anything from the creek for several days," the biologist said. "The poison may contain itself in the creek proper, but it could spread further into the swamp. You'll have to be very cautious until we complete more tests and tell you it's safe again."

"But we take most of our food from the water," Charlie said.

"You'll have to make do on canned goods," Henderson said. "Maybe it will clear up in a few days."

As soon as the men were gone Charlie poled the dugout down the creek toward the swamp. For several hundred yards below his camp there were more dead fish. When he returned to the landing Lillie was waiting there for him.

"Gumbo is sick," she said with anxiety. "He was eating one of the dead fish from the creek, and something is wrong with him."

"Where is he now?" Charlie asked quickly.

"He is lying beside the storage hut."

Charlie found the 'coon and knelt beside it. He knew immediately that the little animal was dying. Foam was coming from its mouth, and its body was jerking violently. Its feet were pawing the dirt frantically, as it had often done to Charlie's head when it wanted food or attention. He cupped the animal's head in one of his hands and stroked its body. For a moment Gumbo seemed to relax, and then he went into a deep convulsion and died. For several minutes Charlie sat on the ground, holding the animal on his lap. Then he got up and placed the body on the floor of the storage chickee.

Later that afternoon Billy Joe came to the chickees with a barrel of well water. "Did Fred Henderson come?" he asked Charlie.

"Yes, he came with another man. They tested the water and the dead fish."

"Did he say what is wrong?"

"Someone has poisoned the water."

"Poisoned it?" Billy Joe said in disbelief. "Who could do that?"

"They do not know, but will try to find this out. There will be more tests also, but we cannot eat anything from the creek."

"Don't worry about that, Pappa," Billy Joe said. "I'll bring meat. It's too bad we never did get a line run to that refrigerator. You could sure use it now." The refrigerator still sat unused by the sewing platform. Billy Joe had canceled the order for the electric line when he learned they would have to move.

Charlie said, "This is a bad thing, Billy Joe."

"Yes, it is bad, Pappa, but we won't have to put up with this kind of thing much longer. I have been offered a job on the Brown Brothers Ranch and have rented a small house in Immokalee. We will be moving from here in about ten days."

"It is a bad thing," Charlie said absently, as if speaking to no one in particular.

He did not tell Billy Joe about Gumbo, and when he was alone again he sat on the ground and stared at the waters of the creek. Lillie had cooked a vegetable stew and a fresh corn pone, but he ate only a bite. Grief was coming to him too swiftly to bear or understand, and he wanted only to be alone.

That night he took several boards from the storage chickee and sat by the fire, building a small coffin. When he finished he put Gumbo inside, then he took the gourd rattle, broke it in half, and dropped it into the coffin beside the animal. After sealing the coffin he put it into the storage chickee.

Charlie did not eat his bowl of corn grits the next morning or drink a mug of the steaming coffee. He put the little coffin, an axe, and some rope into the dugout and moved away down the creek. There were more dead fish and turtles and alligators; death seemed to have advanced further into the swamp.

He moved steadily, not noticing the birds as they flapped away or the otter catching a water snake for its breakfast. He was now past the range of the poison, but he did not notice this either. The dugout moved quickly through the swamp and into the great marsh.

When he entered the River of Grass he turned east and then south until he came to a large hammock surrounded by a thick growth of mangrove trees, their grotesque roots spreading out and running down into the water like the legs of spiders. Hurricanes of past years had smashed many of the limbs down into the brackish water, and now the rotten-egg smell of decay was overwhelming. He rammed the dugout into the mass of splintered limbs and stepped into the water, carrying with him the coffin, the axe, and the rope. When he had picked his way through the mangroves and stepped onto solid ground, he was no longer Charlie Jumper the old Seminole living beyond his time but was Charlie Jumper the Seminole in the days when there were no modern times.

The hammock was covered with live oaks and cabbage palms, and placed about on the ground at random there were many caskets with cypress frames above them, some still upright and some sagging and some fallen. This was the ancient burial ground of his tribe.

After placing the coffin on the ground he cut a small cypress and built two X-frames, binding them with pieces of rope. Then he put one pole on top to hold them upright. He placed the frame over the coffin and left a brown paper bag of crawfish beside it.

The journey back through the sawgrass was as automatic as it had been to the hammock, and when he reached the line of trees that marked the beginning of the swamp he turned to the right and went to the place where he had taken Timmy to see the royal palm grove and the ancient machete encased in the dead trunk.

He walked to the somber tree and struck it with the axe. Then he struck it again and again, smashing into the dead wood until the trunk toppled backward and crashed to the ground. The machete was now free, and he grasped it in his hand and walked back to the dugout. Suddenly he spun around and around, faster and faster, and when he let the machete go it sailed high into the air, tumbling over and over like a flipped coin. When it reached its peak it hung for a moment, and then it came straight down and splashed into the dark water.

For a few moments he watched silently as the ripples spread outward from the spot where the machete had disappeared; then he suddenly screamed, a wild shrill scream that shattered the quietness of the glade and ricocheted into the swamp. He got into the dugout and moved away quickly.

When he reached the chickees Lillie had cooked a beef roast Billy Joe had brought. Although this was one of his favorites, he ate little. For several hours he sat by the fire, staring into the darkness of the swamp.

SEVENTEEN

DAWN CREPT into the swamp as usual, quietly and without fanfare, at first a steel-gray and then a mixture of orange-red. The birds flew from their night roosts in search of food as the alligators returned to the mudbanks to rest after a night of hunting. The fish moved now, striking at bugs on top of the calm water and chasing minnows into the clumps of pickerel weeds with their blue flags glistening with dew. The squirrels barked as the 'coons and 'possums clambered down from the trees, and high above it all, the crows screamed loudly as if trying to awaken the swamp itself.

Charlie sat on the bank of the creek and watched this awakening, but his eyes did not reflect anticipation as they always had at this time of day. His face was solemn, and he moved as if very tired.

When it became light in the clearing he went to the storage chickee and took out a rifle wrapped in a tight covering of deer hide. It was a model 1870 Winchester that had been given to him by a friend when he was very young. He had never known if the rifle had been found in the swamp or stolen from some white hunter's camp, and he had used it little except for a few times hunting bear.

After examining a box of shells he loaded the chamber and put the rifle in the dugout. Lillie watched in puzzlement. It had been many years since he last touched the gun, and she knew he would not this day hunt the bear.

He moved through the floating bodies of the fish and past the turtles and small alligators that had crawled onto the bank to die. The herons and the water turkeys flapped out of his path, squawking loudly to protest this intrusion. He crossed the dwarf cypress swamp quickly, moving directly towards the pond where Little George lived. He did not stop along the way to spear any garfish.

When he reached the pond he stopped the dugout just off the mudbank. Then he stood ramrod straight and looked into the one eye of the giant alligator. Neither man nor alligator moved for several minutes; then he picked up the rifle and aimed.

When the bullet struck, the alligator remained motionless for a split second. Then his body shot straight upward, twisting over and over frantically. He slammed back onto the mudbank on his back, then righted himself quickly. Blood spurted from a gaping hole in his head and ran down the bank, spreading out into a crimson pool in the black water. His body twitched violently. Then he bellowed loudly and lay still.

Charlie dropped to his knees in the dugout and started swaying back and forth, chanting a sound that

had no meaning save to himself. His motion increased its tempo as the blood continued to spread and came nearer the canoe.

He was not aware that the airboat had come into the pond and was now just behind him. Fred Henderson had been passing in the creek when he heard the shot, and had cut the engine and poled the boat toward the sound of the rifle. Amazed and perplexed, he watched as the old man continued to sway back and forth in the bottom of the dugout, the huge alligator still pumping blood down the mudbank.

Henderson pushed the airboat against the dugout and Charlie looked up, his eyes blank. Henderson said, "What in the world have you done, Mr. Charlie?"

"I have killed him, I have killed him," was all that Charlie answered.

"Why, Mr. Charlie? Why?"

"I have killed him. I have killed my friend."

Henderson knew he would not get a coherent response to any question. For a moment he said nothing more. The color had drained from his face, and his hands were trembling. He finally said, "Mr. Charlie, if that was a deer I would just turn my back and go away, but I can't do it with an alligator. I just can't, Mr. Charlie. Do you understand what I am saying?"

"Do what you must," Charlie said without any trace of emotion. "I have killed my friend."

"God knows I hate this, Mr. Charlie, but there's nothing else I can do. I'll have to place you under arrest."

"What will you do with the alligator?" Charlie asked, this seeming to be his only concern.

"One that big—they'll probably give the hide to the museum in Naples. I've never seen one like him before. I didn't know there was a 'gator that big still left in the swamp."

"He has lived long, and his body was his life. You will not leave him here then?"

"No, Mr. Charlie. I'll use ropes and pull him out with the airboat. You go on back home and I'll see you there later."

Charlie seemed greatly relieved that Little George would not be left in the swamp to rot and be eaten by vultures. He did not look again at the mudbank. As he pushed the dugout out of the pond, Henderson shook his head in bewilderment.

Three hours later the warden arrived at the chickees to take Charlie to the branch courthouse and jail in Immokalee. Lillie said nothing. She could only watch silently as they left.

Henderson stopped and told Watsie what had happened and where Charlie would be. He asked that Billy Joe come to Immokalee as soon as he returned home from his job.

Night was just beginning to fall when Billy Joe arrived at the one-story building that served as a branch courthouse and jail for the eastern section of the county. The parking area was deserted, and the outside lights had come on around the building. Two green patrol cars were parked near the rear entrance.

Billy Joe had never before been involved with a law enforcement officer or a jail or a courtroom, and

his fear now was overwhelming. He did not understand what his father had done, yet he knew that Charlie would never commit such an act without reason.

He walked to a desk in the lobby and asked the officer on duty, "Do you have Charlie Jumper here?"

The man looked up from a magazine he was
reading. "Is that the one Henderson brought in for
shooting an alligator?" he asked.

"Yes. He is my father. Can I see him?"

"Yeah. He's the first one we've had in here for
poaching since the new law was passed. Just come on
back with me."

Billy Joe followed the man through a double door
and to a cell along a white corridor. Charlie was sitting
on a wall bunk. He looked very small and very old,
and there was now fear in his eyes. When he saw Billy
Joe he got up and came to the cell door.

"Pappa, what is this thing you have done?" Billy
Joe asked.

"I killed the alligator," Charlie said simply.

"But why, Pappa? Why did you do this? Did he attack you and force you to shoot him?"

"I was in no danger."

Billy Joe stood silent for a moment, and then he
said, "I'll go see Mr. Lykes. He'll help us. I'll be back as
soon as I can."

He followed the officer back to the front desk and
asked, "What will happen now?"

"Well, if he pleads guilty he can be tried here in
the justice of the peace court. He can put up bond now
and come back for the trial in the morning."

"What would happen after he pleads guilty?"

"The law's been changed, you know. Killing a 'gator is a felony now, and he could get up to five years in prison plus a stiff fine. He's in some pretty bad trouble."

A lump formed in Billy Joe's throat when he heard this, and for a moment he thought he would gag. "I'll be back as soon as I can," he finally managed to say.

Albert Lykes was just leaving his office when Billy Joe parked in front of the building. He said, "Hello, Billy Joe. What brings you up here this late in the day?"

"Pappa is in jail, Mr. Lykes."

"What's he charged with?" Lykes asked, startled by the stark fear in Billy Joe's eyes.

"Killing an alligator."

"Killing an alligator?" Lykes repeated, puzzled. "Have you talked to your father yet?"

"Just briefly in the jail."

"Did he say why he did this?"

"No, he didn't. He would only say that he killed the alligator." Billy Joe paused for a moment, then he said emphatically, "But Pappa would never do a thing like this without reason, Mr. Lykes. You've got to believe that."

"What reason could there be, Billy Joe?" Lykes asked, becoming even more perplexed by the whole situation.

"I don't know, but something must have made him do it. We'll just have to find out why."

"Who made the arrest?"

"Fred Henderson, the game warden."

"The only thing your father can do here is plead guilty and go before the justice of the peace. That way he's almost certain to get a stiff sentence. I'll post his bond and ask for a jury trial in Naples, then I'll talk to Henderson and find out what this is all about. I believe the court meets next Monday in Naples."

Billy Joe walked to the pickup as Lykes got into his car. He turned the truck and followed Lykes back along the now deserted streets toward the jail.

EIGHTEEN

IT WAS TWO DAYS before Albert Lykes could get away from his office and drive to the swamp to talk to Charlie Jumper. Fred Henderson had told him about the poisoned creek and how they had traced it to the actions of the land clearers. He surmised that in some way the two incidents were connected; but if this one possibility proved to be negative, then he had no idea what he would do.

It seemed to Lykes that with all the punishment the white man had already inflicted on the Seminole they should not bring Charlie Jumper into court even if he had killed a boxcar full of alligators. But Lykes was lawyer enough to realize that he would have to base his defense on something more concrete and more positive than what had happened in the past to the Seminole.

Lykes' spirits were a degree higher that morning than they had been during the past few weeks. He had received a letter from the governor concerning his Big Cypress editorial campaign, and he knew now that his articles and editorials had generated letters that had at least been noticed and read outside the city limits of Immokalee. The governor wrote that he had been concerned for some time about the plight of Big Cypress and the Everglades, but there was not much the state could do about how private property was developed. He would, however, study and pursue the possibility of the federal government and the state jointly purchasing as much as possible of the swamp and either creating a wildlife refuge or making it a part of the National Park. Lykes thought that this was at least a faint glimmer of hope, that finally someone was now looking and listening, but he also knew it might already be too late.

He had taken one action that, if successful, would preserve at least ten acres of swamp so that in future years people could come and look and marvel at what this entire land had once been. Seth had died with no will and no heirs; thus his property would go to the state. Lykes had petitioned the state to make the property into a park after the land development around it was completed. He remembered once when he had been fishing at Seth's camp he had suggested to Seth that he could make money by charging people a dollar each to walk through the stand of virgin bald cypress, just as they pay to see other such spots around the state. Seth had said to him, "A man ought not have to pay to walk in the woods, Mistuh Lykes. God put it there free." He believed that the creation of a nature park from Seth's woods would have pleased Seth, and that the park would be of much more value to everyone than the money the state could get from the sale of the property.

When he reached the chickees Lykes found that although the poison had been stopped the mud-silt had not, and now the once clear little stream was a solid gray, resembling dirty dishwater. He could also see the lifeless bodies of turtles and small alligators rotting on the banks.

Charlie was sitting at the table beneath the cooking chickee, and Lykes walked over to him. He said pleasantly, "Hello, Mr. Jumper. May I join you?"

"You are welcome in my camp," Charlie said, his voice listless. "Would you have coffee?"

Lykes sat down and said, "Yes, thank you."

Charlie poured two mugs and came back to the table. He was not enthusiastic about this visitor, for he knew why he had come and he didn't want to talk about it.

Lykes said, "Looks as if the creek is about shot."

"Yes, the mud has moved another half mile since yesterday. It will soon be in the swamp."

Lykes sensed that he would have a difficult time drawing from Charlie the clue he was seeking. He said, "It's a shame what is happening here, Mr. Jumper. I have fished many times from Seth Thompson's camp, and this was always my favorite place."

"Seth was my friend," Charlie said sadly. "They did not have to kill him."

Lykes felt he was getting further and further away from the old man and that he must change his tack. He said, "Would you show me the place where the alligator lived?"

"If you wish."

Lykes sat in the front of the dugout as Charlie poled them down the creek and finally out of range of the mud. There was no conversation between the two of them as the dugout crossed the dwarf cypress swamp and entered the pond where Little George had lived and died.

They remained silent for a moment more, then Charlie pointed toward the mudbank and said, "It was there."

Lykes could see the impression in the soft mud where the alligator had been. He looked around at the other edges of the pond and the woods surrounding them. The soft filtered light and the stillness of the place reminded him of the interior of a cathedral.

When he looked up again and noticed the pain and the anguish in the old man's eyes, Lykes suddenly realized just what this crime and this trial was all about. He said softly, "If I had been you, Mr. Jumper, I would have done the same thing."

Charlie looked down at him and smiled, the tension and fear and distrust draining from his face.

The trip back to the chickees was then one long and intimate conversation.

NINETEEN

CHARLIE ARRIVED at the courthouse in Naples an hour before the appointed 9 A.M. time to meet Lykes. With him were Billy Joe, Watsie, and Timmy. Lillie had refused to come. Her fear of what might happen was too great for her to leave the sanctuary of the sewing platform. She would spend these anxious hours alone.

The small group stood on the sidewalk in front of the courthouse, waiting in silence. They were soon joined by Frank Willie and Lucy, who had come to be with Charlie during the trial and give what moral support they could.

When Lykes arrived he led them into the building and into the fluorescent-flooded courtroom with its padded seats and polished wood. To all but the small flock brought in by Lykes, this trial was of no importance. The prosecutor had spent only five minutes studying the file, and the judge had merely glanced at the trial on the docket. It would be a routine matter of no significance.

Also in the courtroom were Kenneth Riles, Ron Simmons of Surf Development, and Will Lawton, foreman of the land-clearing crews. Lykes had issued subpoenas to Simmons and Lawton to appear, and both were puzzled since there was no apparent connection between them and a trial for alligator poaching. Riles had accompanied them out of curiosity.

Promptly at ten the judge occupied the bench and Lykes took Charlie to the defense table past a bannister that separated this area from the rows of spectator seats.

To Charlie the preliminaries of beginning the trial were only more things he did not understand, and soon the prosecutor was calling his first and only witness, Fred Henderson, to the stand.

The prosecutor began, "Mr. Henderson, what is your occupation?"

"I am a game warden."

"Did you arrest the defendant, Charlie Jumper, for killing an alligator?"

"Yes, I did."

"Did you actually see him kill the alligator?"

"No, but I arrived moments after the alligator had been shot."

"Could anyone else have committed this act beside the defendant?"

Lykes rose to his feet and said, "Your honor, this line of questioning is unnecessary. We admit that the defendant, Charlie Jumper, did actually kill the alligator."

The judge said, "Well, counselor, if you admit the guilt of your client, what is the purpose of this trial? Why was this case not handled by the justice of the peace in Immokalee?"

"We intend to prove mitigating circumstances, your honor."

The judge asked, "Was your client's life endangered by this alligator?"

"No, sir, it was not," Lykes answered.

"Then I don't understand how there could be mitigating circumstances in a case such as this. I hope you are not wasting this court's time by bringing this case to trial. We have a very busy docket, Mr. Lykes."

"I am aware of that, your honor, and if you will allow this trial to proceed we will establish the defense."

"Very well," the judge said reluctantly. "We will proceed with the trial."

The prosecutor said, "Your honor, if the defense admits the guilt of the defendant, there is nothing more we can ask the witness. We have no more questions."

Lykes got to his feet and said, "As our first witness we call Will Lawton."

Lawton came forward to the stand and was sworn in, then Lykes said to him, "Is your name Will Lawton?"

"That's right, and you know that already," Lawton said belligerently.

"Just answer the questions, Mr. Lawton," the judge cautioned.

Lykes continued, "What is your present occupation?"

"I'm the foreman of several land-clearing crews working for Surf Development Corporation."

"And where are you presently working?"

"At a new project in Big Cypress."

Lykes paused for a moment, then he said, "Mr. Lawton, do you consider yourself to be a responsible man?"

"I don't know what you mean," the foreman responded.

"I mean, do you think things out and take full responsibility for your acts?"

"I always have. I don't depend on nobody else to do my thinking, if that's what you mean."

The prosecutor rose and said, "Your honor, I don't see how the appearance of this witness or this line of questioning has anything to do with the case."

The judge turned to Lykes. "Counselor, what is the purpose of your questions?"

"This witness is pertinent to the case," Lykes said. "If your honor will allow me to proceed I will make the connection."

"Very well," the judge said, "but at this point your questions seem to be completely irrelevant."

Lykes turned back to Lawton and said, "Did you or did you not order your men to place poison in the form of arsenic, as well as heavy pesticides, in a marsh adjoining Gopher Creek?"

"Yeah, I did," Lawton said cautiously, now wondering what Lykes was leading to.

"Why did you do this?"

"My men had complained about snakes in that area."

"Were there also alligators in that area?"

"Yeah, they was some 'gators there too, but the men was mostly concerned with the snakes."

"Do you advocate putting out deadly poison everywhere there is a possibility of snakes?"

"If it takes that to get a job done, yes."

Lykes looked directly at Lawton and said, "Were you not aware that this poison would eventually find its way into the creek and poison the water?"

"What difference does it make if it did poison the creek?" Lawton shot back. "The creek ain't going to be there much longer anyway."

Lykes looked toward the jury box, then he turned to the judge and said, "Your honor, I submit that this man's actions are the direct cause of this trial being held, and that he should be on trial and not the defendant. I also submit that he is guilty of the premeditated murder of not one but more than fifty alligators and countless other species of wildlife. I further submit that he should be charged with criminal negligence and prosecuted with vigor!"

Lawton jumped to his feet and shouted, "I ain't going to sit here and . . ."

"That's enough, Mr. Lawton!" the judge interrupted quickly.

The prosecutor had also jumped to his feet and come to the front of the courtroom. The judge looked at both him and Lykes and said, "This trial is recessed for fifteen minutes while I consult with the prosecutor and the defense counsel in my chambers. You are dismissed, Mr. Lawton."

The prosecutor and Lykes followed the judge to an

office in the rear of the building. As soon as they entered the room the prosecutor said, "What the hell you trying to do, Lykes? You know damned well that Lawton or his actions have nothing to do with this case. Maybe he should be charged and brought into court, but he's not on trial here this morning."

"I think he's got everything to do with the case," Lykes said, "but you won't let me . . ."

"Just a minute, both of you," the judge said. He took a seat in a black leather chair behind his desk. He turned to Lykes and said, "Albert, I read the *Everglades Gazette* every week, and I'm well aware of your personal opinion of the development of Big Cypress. Are you trying to use my court as a soapbox for expressing those opinions?"

Lykes answered, "No, I'm not. There are things that must be brought out if my client is to receive a fair hearing, and that man's testimony was a part of it."

"I still say you are wasting the court's time," the prosecutor said.

"I can assure you I am not," Lykes said firmly. "This man Lawton is vital to the circumstances of my client's actions, but I certainly am not going to reveal to you at this point the whole basis of my defense. If I did that, what's the use of proceeding with the trial? If you will give me time I will bring my case into focus."

"How many witnesses do you intend to call?" the judge asked.

"Only two more. Ron Simmons of Surf Development and the defendant."

The prosecutor said, "I still say that all of this malarkey is a waste of time."

"What the hell is your hurry?" Lykes snapped. "How come you want this trial over so quickly? You want that old man out there sent to jail just so it won't take too much time?"

The judge said, "Let's not get emotional. I've never seen such a ruckus over a simple poaching case."

"This is not a simple poaching case!" Lykes said emphatically. He was surprised himself by the tone he had directed toward the judge.

The judge said, "I'm going to let you proceed, Albert, but you had better bring some relevancy into your case, and do it soon. If you don't, I'm going to overrule you at every turn and put a swift end to this trial. I don't see your point yet, and as I said before, I'm not going to allow you to use my courtroom as a platform to get something personal off your chest. Do you understand that?"

"Yes, I understand," Lykes said.

"Very well. Let's proceed with the trial."

After they returned to the courtroom and the judge was seated, Lykes called Ron Simmons to the stand. Simmons appeared apprehensive and ill at ease. Lykes said to him, "Your name, please?"

"Ron Simmons."

"And your present occupation?"

"I am vice-president of Surf Development Corporation."

"And just what is your responsibility with this company, Mr. Simmons?"

"Public relations and sales promotion."

"Just exactly what do you mean by public relations?"

"Well, you know. Good will. Making the public like us and support our projects."

"Does it make the public like you when you slaughter wildlife?" Lykes asked.

The prosecutor said quickly, "I object to such a question, your honor. It has no point in this trial."

"Objection sustained," the judge said. "You will ask no more questions such as that, counselor."

"Very well, your honor," Lykes said. He turned back to Simmons. "At the present time, Mr. Simmons, do your responsibilities go beyond these public relations duties?"

"Yes. I have been given the responsibility of overseeing the initial land development of Everglades Villas."

"In that case, the men working out there now are your direct responsibility. Is that correct?"

"At this point, yes. But it is only temporary."

"Have you been out to the project to see firsthand what is being done?"

"No."

"Why not?"

"I don't have the time. And besides that, the foreman has that responsibility."

"But isn't the foreman responsible to you?"

"In a way, yes."

"Yet you really don't know what he is doing out there?"

"I know that he is clearing the land, like he is being paid to do. And he is an expert in his job."

Lykes paused a moment, then he said, "Mr. Simmons, did you have any feelings of guilt when the foreman poisoned the creek and all those alligators and other creatures died? Were you concerned about this?"

"I see no point in answering such a question."

"Would you see a point if it had been human beings who died instead of creatures?"

"That would have been an entirely different matter. Of course I would have been concerned."

"Did not one of your guards needlessly shoot to death a human being out there?"

"That's enough!" the judge said harshly. "The witness is excused. This line of questioning cannot proceed." He turned to Lykes. "It is already near noon, and the defense has not yet called a valid witness or established a line of defense. Court is recessed until 2 P.M., and I would like a word with the defense counselor."

Lykes walked slowly toward the bench. He knew he had been legally and ethically wrong on what he had done thus far in the trial, but he also knew he must get certain things into the jurors' minds before he put Charlie Jumper on the stand. And to do this he was willing to risk a lecture from the judge.

When he approached the bench the judge said to him, "Albert, dammit, I gave you leeway and you tricked me! I am not going to stand for any more of these circus antics, and you are not going to use me!

Now you either get on with the direct defense of your client or remove yourself from the case!"

"So help me, John," Lykes said earnestly, "all of this is a valid part of the trial. I have not tricked anyone. You will see the point when I call the defendant to the stand."

"You had better be right!" the judge said sternly.

Lykes left the courtroom with Charlie, Billy Joe, Watsie, Timmy, Frank Willie, and Lucy, and they walked to a small cafe two blocks from the courthouse. They took seats at a table and Lykes said, "Well, what'll it be, everyone? Lunch is on me."

"Could I have the meat that is between the bread and the fried potatoes?" Charlie asked. "I had this once in Immokalee, and it was good."

"That will be fine," Lykes said. He turned to the waitress. "Make it two hamburgers and fries for everyone."

After the order was taken, Billy Joe said, "Mr. Lykes, I don't understand what all that meant this morning. How come the judge and the other man got so angry at you?"

"It was nothing but the way lawyers sometimes play games," Lykes said.

Charlie looked at Lykes and said, "Do not bring trouble to yourself because of me, Mr. Lykes. I have committed the act which they say, and I have told this to Fred Henderson and to others."

"Don't worry about me," Lykes said to Charlie. "I think I can take care of myself in a courtroom. Our concern is with you, not me."

"Are they going to send Granpappa away, Mr. Lykes?" Timmy asked apprehensively.

"I don't know, Timmy," Lykes said slowly. "But don't you worry about your grandfather yet. This trial is not finished by a long way."

When the court was reconvened, Lawton was no longer in the audience, but Riles and Simmons had returned to watch the conclusion of the trial. A group of Billy Joe's and Charlie's friends from the reservation had come late to Naples to witness the proceedings and were now seated in a group in the rear of the room. Fred Henderson had also returned, although his part in the trial was ended.

Lykes rose to his feet and said, "Your honor, we would like to bring a piece of evidence into the court."

"Very well, counselor," the judge said warily, still unhappy with the morning's proceedings.

Two bailiffs brought in the huge alligator hide and placed it on the floor in front of the jury box. The jurors and the judge stared at the enormous size of the hide.

Lykes then placed Charlie on the stand and asked his first question, "Mr. Jumper, how old are you?"

Charlie answered slowly, the fear of being on the stand causing his hands to tremble. "I am not sure, but I know of eighty-six years."

"How long have you lived in Big Cypress Swamp or the Everglades?"

"All of my years."

Lykes pointed to the hide. "Is this the alligator you killed?" he asked.

"Yes, that is the one."

"How can you be sure? There are many alligators and many alligator hides."

"Because of the scar on his head. That is Little George."

"Who is Little George?" Lykes asked.

"The alligator," Charlie said, pointing to the hide. "That is the name of the alligator."

The prosecutor arose and said, "Your honor, this line of questioning is irrelevant to the case and serves no purpose. The name of the alligator is of no concern to the court."

The judge had become mildly interested in this unique presentation tied to the alligator hide, and he wanted to hear more. He said, "You may proceed, counselor."

Lykes then said, "Mr. Jumper, how long have you known of this alligator?"

"Sixty years or more. Little George was very old."

"Would you please tell the court how that scar came to be on the alligator's head."

Charlie spoke slowly, forming his words carefully as if in deep remembrance, "I took the alligator from the swamp when he was but a foot long and kept him in the village. One day a white boy came to the chickees and saw the alligator on the ground. I had never seen this boy before. He took a burning stick from the fire and put it to the back of the alligator's head. The little 'gator screamed like a child, but the boy kept pushing the stick in until he had burned out one eye and set the back of his head on fire. I knocked the stick away, and Little George was almost dead. I made medicine from herbs and roots and mud and kept it on the burned place for many weeks, and the alligator lived. When he became larger I took him to the pond in the swamp and set him free."

Lykes asked, "Did you see the alligator between the time you put him in the pond and the day you shot him?"

"Yes. I would feed him each week. Mostly I would take him the garfish, and sometimes a rabbit. When we had one to spare, I would give him a chicken."

"You mean you have been feeding this alligator each week for sixty years?"

"He was my friend, and he could not see to hunt as well as the others."

Lykes then asked, "Mr. Jumper, what first made you think of killing the alligator?"

"It was because of Gumbo."

"And who is Gumbo?"

"The little 'coon that lived in my chickee."

The prosecutor arose and said, "Your honor, I object again. These questions are irrelevant and a waste of the court's time."

By now the judge was thoroughly absorbed in the proceedings. He said briskly, "Objection overruled. You may proceed with the questioning, counselor."

Lykes focused his attention again on Charlie. He asked, "What did the 'coon called Gumbo have to do with the alligator?"

"When the men who are clearing the swamp poisoned the creek, they killed the fish and the turtles and the alligators. Gumbo ate one of the fish from the creek, and he died. Before he died he was in great pain and suffered much, and I did not want Little George to suffer as Gumbo had suffered."

Lykes then said, "No more questions."

The prosecutor had not intended to cross-examine the defendant, but now decided to do so in order to focus the jury's attention back to the fact that there had been a violation of the law. He crossed to the witness stand and said, "Mr. Jumper, do you believe that this alligator you call your friend would have preferred to live rather than have you put a bullet into its head?"

"He would have liked to live the rest of his life in the swamp, but this was not to be."

"Did you know that the poison would penetrate further into the swamp and kill the alligator?"

"No, I did not know this."

"Then you might have killed him for no purpose. Isn't this right, Mr. Jumper?"

"If he had not been killed by the poison, then he would have been killed by the machines."

"Not all alligators are killed when land is cleared, are they, Mr. Jumper. Many must survive."

"Some would get away, but Little George was very old and could not see as well as the others. He did not know any other place but the pond where he lived, and he would not have left when the machines came. He would have been crushed by the bulldozer, and I did not want him to die in this way or by the poison. He was my friend."

The prosecutor sensed that Charlie's simple, direct answers were having an effect on the jury even beyond his previous testimony. He looked toward the jury box and thought he detected a hostility against his line of questioning. He said quickly, "No more questions."

Lykes arose and said, "We have no more witnesses, your honor. The defense rests."

Charlie came from the witness stand in great relief that his part in this strange drama was ended. He sipped from a glass of water as the courtroom fell silent, waiting for the summations.

The prosecutor knew that he had been put into an almost impossible position, but the fact remained that the law had been violated and he must try to impress this fact into the minds of the jurors. He got up hesitantly, faced the jury box, and spoke without fervor, "Ladies and gentlemen of the jury, the one important fact in this case is that the law has been violated. If we allow a law to be broken and then not convict the guilty party, then we may as well not have the law. A law is either a law or it is not, and that is the only thing for you to decide in this case. There is no possible way for you to rule but guilty." With this brief statement he returned to his table.

Lykes had been trying to plan his summation while the prosecutor was speaking. He concluded that anything he could say would merely detract from the honesty of Charlie's testimony and could actually do harm. He was willing to take his chances with the jury without speaking at all, but he rose and said, "We have admitted that the defendant, Charlie Jumper, did actually kill the alligator in violation of a law. But this violation of the law is not the important thing in this case. The only thing you must consider is whether Charlie Jumper was right or wrong in doing what he did. There are times in life when all of us must act according to what we know is right. I ask only that you consider what he did, and consider what you would have done."

Both the prosecutor and Lykes declined a rebuttal on the summations, and, following the judge's instructions, the jurors filed out to begin their deliberation of the case.

A hushed atmosphere prevailed in the courtroom as one minute passed into five, five into thirty, and a half hour into an hour. To Lykes this was good. He knew that if the jurors were concerning themselves with only the one point of law violation, they would not have been out of the room for more than ten minutes.

Another hour passed, and still the jury box was empty. Long shadows were beginning to form outside the building, and the western sky was streaked with red. Lykes left the table and purchased two sodas from a machine in the hall. Charlie drank the cold liquid gratefully, his face reflecting both apprehension and fatigue. No one left the courtroom. Everyone, even those spectators who were spending the day listening to trials simply out of curiosity and had no personal interest in this case, wanted to remain and hear the verdict.

Lykes was concerned now that the trial might end with a hung jury. If this happened, and a second trial became necessary, he knew he would not have the leeway in a second trial that he had enjoyed in this first. A second trial would be confined strictly to the one point of law violation, and chances for an acquittal would be greatly reduced.

Another fifteen minutes passed; then the jurors filed back into the room. The judge asked for the verdict, and the foreman said, "Your honor, we find the defendant not guilty." Lykes slumped forward against the table, and Charlie looked down at his bare feet.

No one in the courtroom seemed to move or breathe for a moment. Then a sudden outburst of applause came from the spectators and the jury. The judge rapped hard with his gavel. When the noise subsided, he said, "Will the defendant please rise and face the court." Charlie pushed himself to a standing position, and the judge continued, "Mr. Jumper, in a verdict such as this it is not customary for the judge to make further comment. I do, however, wish to issue a word of caution. I would not like to see you back in this courtroom again. You might not be so fortunate the next time. You are now free to go."

For a moment more the courtroom remained motionless, then there was a sudden rush of movement. Billy Joe ran to Lykes and grabbed his hand, and the group on the back row moved in mass to the front.

Charlie was still confused by it all, but he did hear the words "free to go." He moved away from the table as Timmy threw his arms around him. The second to reach him was Lucy, and then Fred Henderson.

Lykes looked around and noticed Kenneth Riles and Ron Simmons standing in the rear of the room. Both looked as if they wanted to come forward and say something to him or to Charlie. They hesitated for a moment more; then they left the building.

Night had fallen when the courtroom was finally cleared. Charlie's entourage of followers went outside to the parking area. They all stood around the dusty pickup, at first discussing the trial with Lykes, then talking about hunting and fishing and the price of cattle and crops and the weather. The bright street lights and flashing neons fascinated Charlie. For several minutes he watched them with interest; then he was swept with an overwhelming desire to leave this place quickly and return to the darkness and the quiet of the swamp.

TWENTY

OR TWO DAYS AFTER the trial Charlie seemed to be his old self again. He ate his food with relish, and each day he took Timmy into the swamp, exploring the same ponds and sloughs they each had always loved.

On the third morning he came from the chickee wearing the knee-length dress instead of the dungarees. When Lillie looked up from the grill and saw this, she knew. He ate his corn grits and fried beef strips and drank the steaming coffee, then he put his spear and the bow and arrows into the dugout.

He came back to the chickee and said, "It is time to go. Will you come?"

"I am too old," she said, her eyes misty. "I will go and live in the house of Billy Joe."

"You will give the rifle to Timmy."

"I will do this if you wish." She went to the grill and said, "You will need food for the journey."

She wrapped corn bread and beef strips in a piece of brown paper and handed it to him. He took her hands in his and gripped them tightly; then he turned and walked to the dugout.

For several minutes after he was gone she continued to look after him, watching the flow of muddy water and knowing he would not come this way again.

She turned when the pickup came down the dirt path and stopped. Billy Joe came to her and said, "We will be ready soon. Where is Pappa?"

"He is gone."

"Gone where?"

"To seek the island."

After a moment's silence Billy Joe said, "Oh, Mamma, why did you let him go? There is no Forever Island. It is just an old man's memory playing tricks on him. It is only a dream, Mamma."

"You are wrong, son," she said. "It is not a dream. It is pride."

Billy Joe shook his head. "We will go after him. I will get Fred Henderson to help. He cannot survive out there, Mamma."

"He would not survive in the house in Immokalee."

He said again, "We will go after him."

"Let him go, Billy Joe!" she said firmly. "He will return if he wishes."

"But there will be nothing left here for him to return to, and he will not know where we are. Don't you understand that, Mamma?"

"He will find the way."

Billy Joe walked back to the pickup. He turned and said, "Timmy and I will be back for you in about two hours. We will load the things then, and we will talk more about Pappa."

For several moments after he was gone she stood still, listening to the roar of the bulldozer as it came closer. Soon now it would crash over the chickees and smash them into the ground. For a moment more she listened, then she went back to the ancient sewing machine and started making the jacket that would be sold to the souvenir stand on the Tamiami Trail.

ALLAPATTAH

ONE

A glowing orange dawn was invading the swamp when Toby Tiger walked across the small clearing and approached the chickee hut. Thin wisps of fog were clinging to tree limbs like blobs of cotton candy, and a light dew created puffy little beads in the limestone dust. Birds were moving now, and several chickens ventured into the edge of the woods in search of food. When one grabbed a small green snake and ran, others followed, cackling loudly.

Toby's wife, Lucy, was at an iron grill beneath the chickee, finishing a breakfast of grits, salt bacon and corn dodgers. She handed Toby a plate and then took one for herself.

They sat at a table beside the chickee and ate in silence, and then Lucy said, "Will you be gone all day?"

"I'll go by Allapattah Flats first and then to Grandfather's hammock. I should be back shortly after noon."

Lucy said, "I wish you wouldn't go to Allapattah Flats just to stare at those crocodiles. They're dangerous, and could do you great harm. You're the only Seminole man I've ever known who would go so far just to visit crocodiles."

"That's because before you married me you knew

only reservation Indians," Toby said, "and I'm one of the wild ones from the swamp. There's a great difference. And besides that, the crocodiles will leave me alone if I leave them alone. I don't bother them when I go there. I only look."

"I still wish you wouldn't go, but I know you will," Lucy said, resigned. "I don't understand what pleasure anyone gets from looking at such ugly creatures." She then changed the subject. "Please give my love to your grandfather. I wish he would come and live with us. He's too old to be out there in the Everglades alone, and I worry about his safety."

"I'll speak to him about this again, but I don't think he will listen. He's a stubborn old man and will do only as he wishes."

As soon as he finished eating, Toby took a bag from the table and entered a narrow trail leading into the swamp. Darkness almost came again as he walked beneath thick growths of pond cypress and cabbage palms and palmetto interlaced with vines. Bordering the trail there were lush beds of ferns, and in places the ground was covered solidly with green moss. Squirrels barked at him as Toby walked slowly and carefully to avoid snakes.

After a mile the woods became thinner, and here the path led across an open area of meadow dotted with cypress. In normal times this ground would have been soggy with a thin covering of water, but now the earth cracked beneath Toby's footsteps.

Soon he came to the bank of Lost Creek, a narrow black stream bordered thickly with willow and button brush. An airboat was partially hidden in a clump of pickerel weeds. Toby put the bag into the boat, shoved it away from the bank, and inserted the key. When he hit the starter, the airplane engine mounted on the rear of the boat thundered to life.

Toby had purchased the boat three years ago for the low price of $300 because the engine pistons were cracked. He had rebuilt the engine himself, and now the old boat would make a top speed of forty miles per hour. It was his most valued possession and his only means of getting around the Glades quickly. Before he had purchased the boat he made his weekly trip to his grandfather's hammock in an ancient cypress dugout canoe which still rested on the creek bank.

He guided the boat slowly along the winding stream, watching for signs of bass and turtles. Huge herons and snowy egrets, frightened by the roar, flapped away as he moved past them. Soon the stream blended into endless sawgrass, forming the vast Pa-Hay-Okee, the River of Grass flowing southward through the Florida Everglades to a point where marsh meets sea at Florida Bay.

For a few hundred yards Toby continued to drive the boat slowly, and then he rammed the throttle full forward. Staccato bursts of thunder roared from the engine, and the boat sprang forward like a horse stung by a hornet. Toby's eyes widened as he sat on the elevated driver's seat and skimmed along the top of the water, crashing through the solid wall of sawgrass as if it were not there at all. This was what he loved most, running wild with the wind, racing forward across the marsh as if nothing could block his way.

He turned westward, continuing to run the airboat at top speed. The open marsh was dotted with hammocks, which were islands covered with cabbage palms and lancewood and clumps of palmetto. Some were very small and some large, and occasionally he circled one, causing waves to rush into the bushes lining the shore.

Gradually he came into an area of mangrove islands, the inner reaches of the Ten Thousand Islands. Here the water was brackish. Soon he slowed the boat as he approached an elevated island known as Allapattah Flats.

Toby moved slowly until he came to a cove leading inward, then he rammed the bow of the boat onto the shore and stepped out. He made his way carefully along a narrow path until he reached a point where the cove ended. On a bank on the opposite side of the cove, two huge crocodiles lay motionless, their jaws open wide and their eyes closed.

Toby looked across the cove, and then he squatted on his haunches and said, "Allapattah. Old long snouts. You may be called allapattah by some, but your real meaning is death. You would like to eat me, heh? You would kill all you touch, like instant death. But in the end you'll die too. You'll see. Only four of you are left, and someday soon there will be none. They will kill you, just as they are killing me, and there's nothing for both of us but death."

For several minutes more Toby watched the crocodiles, then he picked up a stick and threw it into the water. When the crocodiles hissed menacingly, he said, "That's not me in the water, only a stick. If I jump into a pond with the alligator, he'll leave and go into another pond, but if I jump in there with you, you'll cut me in half. But that's not to be today, so you can stop your silly hissing. I am not afraid, for now is not the time. Someday I'll test you, and you will win, but you will go also. You kill all you touch, but someday the white men will get you. They also kill all that they touch."

Toby stared at the crocodiles as if mesmerized, and it was a half hour before he finally got up and went back to the airboat. As he walked away he said, "I'll see you again soon, long snouts. When they return, tell your two friends that Toby Tiger was here."

Toby Tiger was a twenty-five-year-old Seminole Indian, five feet ten inches tall, with deeply browned skin, high cheekbones and the almost oriental look of pure Seminoles. His body was hard and muscular, his legs slightly bowed, and his eyes as black as his raven hair.

Toby had been born on a Florida Everglades hammock southwest of the Tamiami Trail, the highway running through the Everglades from Naples to Miami. He had always loved all things about this land, and his boyhood days were filled with hunting and fishing and running free with the wind and sleeping beneath the open-sided chickee huts and exploring the vast River of Grass and the hammocks. By the time he was ten, he knew almost every hammock and mangrove swamp from the Ten Thousand Islands to Whitewater Bay.

Toby's mother and father had insisted that he get as much schooling as possible, and when he reached school age, they forced him to go out to the Tamiami Trail each

morning and catch the yellow bus that transported
Indian children to the white school in Everglades City.
Each day as he rode the bus his mind was filled only
with anticipation of returning that afternoon to the
Glades. He studied the books and the figures by the light
of an open fire each night, but he did so only to please
his mother and father.

In 1965, when Toby was fifteen and in the ninth
grade, a flash fire swept over the hammock, killing his
parents and reducing the chickees to ashes. It was said
that the fire was set by white hunters trying to flush deer
from the sawgrass. Toby escaped death by being in
school that day, and when he returned to the hammock
and found what had happened, his schooling was ended
forever. He buried his mother and father on a remote
hammock in the old Seminole way, in crude cypress
coffins placed on top of the ground and then covered by
a small frame of pond cypress poles.

Toby went to live in the camp of his grandfather and
grandmother north of the Tamiami Trail, and his days
were spent in exploring this new land; but the grief of his
mother and father's deaths always lingered. Although the
bitterness and sadness never really left, he spent many
happy days with his grandparents and came to love them
as he did his parents.

Several years later his grandfather's camp was selected as the site of the new Miami International Airport, and they were told they must move because the
land was to be drained and cleared and filled. The giant
concrete runways were eventually built, but the international airport was never to be. Protests by conservation

groups halted the project but not before a large section of the swamp's heart had been destroyed. The runways were now used as training facilities by several airlines.

Toby's grandfather decided to build his new camp on a hammock southwest of the Trail where destruction would be slower in coming. At the time of the move, the grandmother became ill, and less than a month after the new chickees were completed and the ground cleared, she died. Toby's grandfather lived by the old Seminole ways, and he would not remain in the camp after a death. They buried the grandmother on the hammock with Toby's mother and father, then they burned the chickees and moved once again to a hammock several miles west of the deserted camp.

Toby remained on the hammock with his grandfather for two years, but it became increasingly difficult for them to live off the land. The drainage canals and dikes built by white men turned the water away from the marsh. During periods of draught, which came more and more often, the land dried up, killing the deer and other animals and the fish. Then when great rains did come, and water could not escape the diked areas quickly enough, the flooding drowned the deer and small animals. But Toby's grandfather refused to even discuss going elsewhere, insisting that he had moved enough and would spend his remaining days here regardless.

Toby then left the hammock and took odd jobs wherever he could find them, returning to the camp each weekend with what supplies he could buy. He worked on road repair crews and in service stations and on cattle ranches, living temporarily in the chickees of any Seminole family who would accept him. Most often he would sleep on the ground alone beneath cabbage palms. For a time he wrestled alligators for tourists along the Tamiami Trail and in the Seminole Indian Village on the small reservation at Dania, but none of the jobs he would hold for long. As soon as he had money, he would return to his grandfather's hammock with supplies and remain there until he was forced to seek work again.

While helping with a cattle roundup on the Big Cypress Reservation, he met Lucy Cypress, daughter of Reverend Charlie Cypress, the reservation's Seminole Baptist preacher. He went back as often as possible to visit her, sometimes even missing the weekend with his grandfather, and two years ago they were married by her father in the concrete-block church on the reservation.

Toby then rented for fifty dollars a month an abandoned hunting camp belonging to a man in Miami, and he took Lucy there to make their home. The camp was located on the Loop Road, which was a twenty-four mile stretch of limestone dirt that left the Tamiami Trail at Monroe Station, looped out through the swamp and came back to the Trail at Forty Mile Bend. Most of the Loop Road was uninhabited except for a few hunting cabins and the small village of Pinecrest, which contained only a cafe catering to hunters, a small general store, and the Gator Hook Lodge. But more and more lots along the road were being sold for weekend cabins.

Lucy did not want to live in this remote place so far from her mother and father and the type of reservation life she knew, but she loved Toby deeply and would follow him wherever he chose to go and live however he wished to live.

For the past year Toby had worked with a state highway department crew, chopping bushes, cutting grass and cleaning drainage canals alongside the highway. And each Saturday morning he took supplies to his grandfather's hammock.

When Toby left Allapattah Flats he headed eastward, again driving the airboat at full speed. He slowed only once when he came to a small pond partially covered with water lilies.

Toby cut the engine and picked up a cypress pole in the bottom of the boat, then he pushed the boat slowly into the center of the pond. Suddenly he dove from the boat and disappeared beneath the surface. A startled black bass bolted from a clump of pickerel weeds, sending a turbulent wave rushing across the top of the water.

In a moment Toby came up clutching a large snapping turtle. He threw the turtle into the boat on its back, then he climbed in and said, "You'll make a good stew for Grandfather. I almost missed sight of you, but you didn't hide quick enough."

He did not stop again until he reached a large hammock several miles to the east. From a distance he could see the smoke of a fire drifting above the cabbage palms, and then he made the engine backfire several times. When he reached the shore, the old man was waiting for him.

Toby rammed the boat ashore, jumped out and hugged his grandfather. The old man said, "I am glad to see you, Toby. I always hear you coming. No one but Toby Tiger drives the airboat with such thunder." He spoke in the old Seminole way, pronouncing each word slowly and distinctly, as if reading from an unseen book.

Toby climbed back into the boat, picked up the package and said, "I've brought many things this time, Grandfather. I have corn meal and flour, sugar and salt, rice, a package of sliced ham, two boxes of shotgun shells, bread and coffee."

The old man smiled at the sight of the sack. He said, "Did you bring tobacco?"

"Yes. I have a large tin. And before you ask, I also brought sugar buns."

"That is good. You are a fine grandson, Toby. I have thanked my son many times for bringing you to life."

They walked along a path to the center of the hammock where there were two chickees, one for cooking and one for sleeping. Toby put the package on a plank shelf in the cooking chickee, then they sat on benches at a cypress table beneath a cabbage palm. Each time Toby returned to the hammock it brought floods of memories of the days he lived here. He said, "How've you been this week, Grandfather?"

"For one who has lived seventy-eight or more summers, I seem to manage well enough. But it is getting harder each day to find food, and I have a great fear now of fire." The old man was about the same height as Toby, but his body was as frail as bamboo. His skin was baked black and deeply wrinkled, and his hair a solid white. His misty eyes were squinting and tired.

"It is very dry and dangerous everywhere," Toby said.

"I cannot count the days it has been since we had rain, and the water in places is down three feet and more. We need much rain."

"It is not just the rain," the grandfather said. "The white men's canals and dikes have turned the water away from the marsh. Someday all this will be no more. There were times when food out here was plentiful, fish so thick I caught them with my hands, and deer so many that I killed them easily with the bow and arrow anytime I needed meat. Now I cannot find even one deer to kill with the shotgun."

For a moment Toby hesitated to say what he promised Lucy he would ask once again, then he spoke cautiously, "What you say is true, Grandfather. The land out here is dying. This is no longer a fit place for you. Will you not come now and live in my camp, or move to the reservation if you would rather do that? There are many people on the reservation you know from the old days."

Just as Toby expected, the old man's eyes flashed. He said, "I will never do this thing, Toby! I have lived all my years as I live now, and what time I have left will be spent here. I will die here, and then I will lie with your grandmother and your mother and father on the hammock in the marsh."

Toby felt no surprise from the words. He said, "As you wish, Grandfather. But if you ever decide to leave, you must tell me this. I only wish I could live here with you, but this is not to be."

"No, it is not to be. You have a child in your woman now. This would be no place for you or for them. Those days are gone forever, Toby. Soon now it will be no more."

"Are you hungry?" Toby asked, wanting to change the subject and cause no further disturbance to the old man. "I'll fix a nice dinner of ham and rice."

"I already have a stew of rabbit. We will eat together, but I wish that the stew was turtle."

Toby jumped up and said, "I forgot that I brought you a turtle, a large one about thirty pounds. It's in the boat. I'll get it while you dish up the stew."

When Toby returned with the turtle, two steaming bowls were on the table. The old man said, "Just leave him on his back and I will clean him later." When Toby put him down, the turtle's legs kicked frantically, trying to right itself.

After they finished eating, the old man went to the chickee and returned with a wooden box resembling an old army trunk. He placed it on the table, opened it and removed a bundle wrapped tightly in deer hide. He said, "I am old, Toby, and I am becoming very tired. The days are not many. There are things here I want you to have. They have always been for you, but I have waited for the time, and the time is now."

Toby watched curiously as his grandfather untied the package. He placed on the table a multi-colored knee-length dress, a pair of knee-length buckskin moccasins, a buckskin belt with a sheathed knife, a ceremonial sash, and a turban with three egret plumes. Toby stared at the items with wonder.

"These were the warrior clothes of my grandfather," the old man said. "He wore them beside Osceola, and then in battles at the side of Wild Cat and Billy Bowlegs.

He was an honorable warrior, and he was never defeated until the time came when he had to flee with others and hide in the swamps to escape the white soldiers, and he was not defeated then. It was a long war, and it also touched my father. But in the end it was all for nothing. The white soldiers were too many and too strong, and there was no way to stop them. But if my grandfather and father and others had not refused defeat and hidden in the swamps, there would be none of us here now. They did an honorable thing. The warrior clothes were passed down from my grandfather to my father and to me. They are for you now, Toby, and your son after you. Keep them with honor."

Toby did not know what to say. He ran his hands across the cloth which was still firm after so many decades. "Are you sure you want to do this, Grandfather?" he asked.

"They are yours now," the old man repeated. "And there is one thing more." From the bundle he took a small buckskin pouch attached to a thin strap and put it gently onto the table. "This is the sacred medicine bag," he said. "There have never been more than three true ones among our people. When I was but a young man, and we lived on a hammock many days' journey from here, the wind for several days was filled with the pollen of the sawgrass, so thick it was hard to see. We knew this to be a bad omen, a sign of great wind. Many left the hammock and went deep into the swamp, but others did not leave. A great hurricane came out of the south, bringing both wind and water, and much death. All the people who remained on the hammock were killed, and among them was the medicine man. When I went back after the storm, I found this hanging on the limb of a gumbo limbo tree. I have kept it all these years, and now it is yours. It is very sacred, and it has great power. Use it only for good, and never for evil. It will show you the way to the Great Spirit in the sky."

Toby picked up the pouch and turned it over and over in his hands. He said, "If it will do what you say, Grandfather, you need it more than I."

"I need it no more. I have seen the way and I know the way. When you live my years, and you live alone on the marsh as I have lived, you see many things others cannot see. Since the death of your father and mother, your heart has been troubled, my grandson. I know this. I have seen anguish and hatred in your eyes many times. You have not accepted things as they must be. What you wish most is gone forever. The peace you seek must be found only within yourself. Know this, Toby. Use the medicine bag wisely, and it will help you find the way."

Toby wrapped all of the things in the deer hide and tied them tightly, then he rose and said, "I'll keep all these things as you have kept them, Grandfather. They'll be passed to my son with honor. And I thank you more than you can know. But I must go now."

The old man said, "The next time you come, Toby, can you bring pork chops? I have wanted this very much lately."

"I'll bring a whole hog," Toby said, watching his grandfather carefully. "We'll cook it and eat it together."

"We could not eat a whole hog," the old man chuckled. "Pork chops would do fine."

They walked back to the boat together. Toby once again hugged the old man, then he got into the airboat and shot away quickly across the marsh.

TWO

Toby's camp was located on a half acre of cleared ground, and the main facility was an old City of Miami bus with the seats removed and the tireless wheels resting four feet off the ground on cypress blocks. Inside the bus there was a small refrigerator, several shelves for canned goods and other staples, a counter with an electric hotplate, a small wall cabinet, a table with four chairs, another small table holding a portable Singer sewing machine, and a sagging double bed. Blue cotton curtains covered the windows facing the road.

Behind the bus Toby had built a chickee from thin cypress poles with a roof of thatched palmetto fronds. An iron gate propped up on concrete blocks was beneath the chickee, and here Lucy did most of the cooking over an open fire because it was usually too hot to cook inside the bus. Also, Toby preferred his food cooked this way. There was a cypress table with two benches beside the chickee.

Water came from a faucet above a well just to the east of the bus, and here Toby had built a small enclosed shower stall which operated from the same faucet. This was done at the insistence of Lucy. At the back of the clearing there was an outdoor privy with a tin roof.

A small section of the clearing was used as a garden where Lucy grew tomatoes, corn, squash, okra, and peppers. Chickens roamed freely, pecking at anything that moved.

It was just past noon when Toby returned from his grandfather's hammock. When he came into the clearing, Lucy was sitting beside the grate, stirring stew in a blackened iron pot. He went into the bus and put the buckskin bundle into a cabinet, then he took a can of beer from the refrigerator and came back to the table.

Lucy looked up and said, "How was your grandfather?"

"I'm not sure if he is well or not. But he wouldn't even talk about coming here to live."

"I wish he'd change his mind," she said.

Lucy, six years younger than Toby, was five feet tall with black hair flowing halfway down her back. Her slim body was beginning to show the child she had carried within her for five months. Her skin was pale and not deeply burned by wind and sun as was Toby's. Her wide black eyes and high cheekbones accentuated a face of unusual beauty. Instead of the traditional long Seminole skirt, she wore a pair of black slacks, an orange blouse and leather sandals.

Toby took a deep drink of beer and said, "Are you feeling well?" He was pleased about the baby and overly concerned for her condition.

"Yes. I'm fine." She put the wooden spoon into the pot and came over to the table. "Are you still going to take me to see my mother and father tomorrow?" she asked.

"Yes. We'll leave as early as you wish."

"Josie Billie came by here this morning," Lucy said. "He wanted to see you, and said he would come again later. Do you wish to eat now?"

"I'm not hungry. I ate with Grandfather before I left the hammock."

"I'm not hungry either," Lucy said. "And I have sewing to do." She got up and went into the bus.

Toby had just started carving an alligator from a block of cypress wood when the 1970 Ford Mustang pulled into the camp and stopped. Josie Billie got out of the car and came over to the table. He was a Seminole the same age and build as Toby, but he wore a thin beard along his lower jaws. He lived in a village along the Trail that was open to tourists. One of the attractions inside the village was alligator wrestling, and Josie was in charge of this part of the tourist trade.

Toby motioned for his visitor to sit down. He said, "Hello, Josie. How are you and the 'gators?"

"Not too good right now," Josie said. "That's why I came to see you."

"You want a beer?" Toby asked.

"Yes. And I've got a fifth of Old Crow in the car. I'll get it too."

Toby went into the bus to get the beer while Josie brought the bottle from the car. They took seats at the table, passed the bottle and then opened the beers.

Josie said, "We've got an old bull 'gator in one of the pits who thinks he wants to mate. It's making him so ornery he's snapping at anything that moves. He almost bit the tail off another bull. We've got to get him out of the pit with the other bulls and into the big pen, but nobody can handle him. Can you come to the village and help?"

"Yes, I can do this," Toby replied. "I have nothing to do this afternoon. But if he does make love when we get him into the pen, don't watch it. My grandfather once told me that if you watch someone make love, either a man or an animal, you'll go blind."

"That doesn't bother me," Josie said. "The only thing I want to see of that old bull is his tail going over the side of the pit. You want to come down and wrestle for the tourists tomorrow? Sunday is usually a good day. You can make yourself a few bucks."

"No," Toby replied. "I'm taking Lucy to the reservation to see her mother and father."

Josie took another drink from the bottle and pushed it toward Toby. He said, "You ought to come to the village and wrestle every day. You could make as much doing that as you make working on the road. You're the best 'gator man in the Glades, and you know it."

"I couldn't stand having those white tourists stare at me that much," Toby said. "I'll do it for you sometimes, but not all of the time."

"You'd get used to the tourists. Most of the time I don't even know they're there. We take their money and that's the end of it."

Toby drank again from the bottle, then he said, "I would never get used to it. Whites are the lowest of all things. They're chicken snakes."

Josie looked at Toby curiously and said, "They're not

so bad as that, Toby. I thought you liked Big Jim Bentley and several other whites living on the Loop."

"They're different," Toby said. "Sometimes I think they're part Indian. But I couldn't stand those white tourists. I'll wrestle for you sometimes, but not all of the time."

"Anytime you want to make a few extra bucks it's up to you. Money is money no matter whose pocket it comes from. And I'll sure appreciate it if you'll help get that loco 'gator out of the pit."

Toby got up and said, "I'll leave in a few minutes. I can't go as fast as that Mustang, but I'll be there shortly after you."

As soon as Josie pulled out of the clearing, Toby went into the bus and said to Lucy, "I'm going to the Osceola Village to help Josie with a bad 'gator. I'll be back as soon as I can."

Lucy stopped the sewing machine. "Are you coming back by Monroe Station?" she asked.

"Yes. I haven't cashed my check and paid the rent."

"There are things we need," she said. "I've made a list. Will you get them?"

"I'll stop at Monroe Station on the way back."

Toby went outside and walked to his old 1960 Ford pickup. The truck had originally been red, but now it was covered solidly with white limestone dust. He got into the cab and cranked the engine, sending a huge puff of smoke out of the exhaust pipe and across the clearing.

THREE

Toby turned south on the Tamiami Trail and stopped several miles later when he reached a paved road leading off the left side of the highway. A tall cyclone fence guarded the property, but the gate was open. This was the entrance to the airport that had taken the land of his grandfather. A sign beside the gate read: "No trespassing except for official airport business. Gates closed from 7 p.m. to 7 a.m. For information call Miami International Airport Administrative Office in Miami." For a moment Toby stared at the strip of black asphalt leading into the swamp, then he cursed to himself and drove away quickly.

When he reached Forty Mile Bend, the highway turned directly east and ran arrow-straight across the Everglades toward Miami. It was along this section that many Indians lived, and their chickees could be seen in clumps of banana trees along the highway. Several Indians were fishing in the drainage canal paralleling the highway, and others walked aimlessly along the borders of the road. Brightly colored signs offered airboat rides, alligator wrestling, village tours, souvenirs and cold beer.

Toby pulled in when he reached the John Osceola

Indian Village. Facing the highway there was a souvenir store, and a tall board fence surrounded the rest of the village. Inside the store there were racks of handmade Seminole skirts, blouses and jackets. Counters were piled high with Indian dolls and a variety of items carved from cypress. A sign over a rear door inside the shop read: "$1.25 each to enter village. Alligator wrestling 50¢ extra."

It was here that Josie Billie and six other Seminole families lived. Toby greeted John Osceola and his wife as he went through the souvenir store and into the village. Several groups of tourists were walking about, looking into the chickees and snapping pictures. Indian children chased each other around the compound, throwing rocks and ignoring the tourists until offered twenty-five cents to stand before a camera; then they stopped and smiled into the lens, palms outstretched.

The wrestling pits were located behind another fence on the west side of the village. Behind the pits there was a three-acre pen containing more than two hundred alligators.

Toby found Josie Billie standing beside the second of three wrestling pits. Several other Seminole men were also there, but no tourists. They were all looking into the pit. When he saw Toby approaching, Josie turned and said, "He's even worse than before, Toby. We're glad you're here. We can't do a thing with this old fool."

Toby walked to the low concrete wall surrounding the pit. Inside, there were five bull alligators, one with a nasty red gash across its tail. The largest was about sixteen feet long, and he looked to be very old.

Josie said, "There's nothing worse than a bull 'gator in heat, and this idiot is too old to even have it on his mind. I don't know what's the matter with him. He acts plumb loco, and he's been this way for several days."

"Maybe he just wants out of that pit for a while," Toby said, studying the alligator carefully. "If he does, I would sure know how he feels."

"Maybe so, but he won't let anybody give him any help in getting out."

Toby took off his shirt, kicked off his old brogan shoes, and removed a leather thong holding a large crocodile tooth that he always wore around his neck. Then he picked up a stick and jumped into the pit, approaching the old bull from the rear. When he touched him on the back with the stick, the 'gator wheeled around quickly and snapped the stick in half, then he opened his jaws and hissed menacingly, snapping again at Toby. Toby stepped back and said, "He may be old, but he's still filled with fire. Do you have rope ready?"

"We have rope," Josie replied. "We're ready when you are."

Toby walked slowly around the alligator several times, and each time the 'gator turned to face him. The other alligators in the pit paid no heed to what was happening. Toby finally turned to Josie and said, "He's following me, and I have to get behind him. Come in here and get his attention."

Josie climbed into the pit and waved a stick at the alligator, and Toby eased away slowly. The 'gator sprang at Josie, snapping at the stick and hissing. The moment the 'gator's attention was turned away from him, Toby sprang catlike onto its back, locking his arms and legs around the bull's huge body.

For a split second the alligator lay still, then the pit exploded in violence. The 'gator twisted over and over, jumping and bucking and then tumbling again and again. Toby felt his body being rammed into the ground. The 'gator's hide cut into his flesh, sending sharp pains through his chest, but he locked his arms and legs around the body tighter and tighter and held on desperately. The other alligators scrambled out of the way as Toby and the old bull thrashed around and around the pit. Several times the breath was knocked from Toby, and his mouth was clogged with dirt.

Finally the violence slowed. Toby pulled himself forward and snapped the 'gator's jaws shut, then he flipped him on his back. Josie and four other men pounced on the 'gator immediately, tying his jaws with rope. Toby was still holding on as Josie shouted, "Let go, Toby! It's done!"

Toby pushed himself to his feet. He stared at the old bull, now lying motionless, then he walked over to the wall. Blood was oozing from several cuts on his chest, and he was covered with dirt. He spat dirt from his mouth and said, "Damn! That was a rough ride. The old devil was almost more than I could handle."

The other men picked up the bull and dragged him over the wall and into the large pen. Josie looked after them and said, "I hope the old fool soon works off his mad. I could never have stayed on him like that. We should have let the tourists in here and charged five bucks a head to watch. You can clean up at my chickee, and you probably need a drink after that ride."

Toby picked up the leather thong with the crocodile tooth and put it back around his neck. He gathered up his shirt and shoes, and then he followed Josie back into the village where he bathed himself at a hydrant, letting the cool water gush over his head. Josie took a carton of beer from an ice box, then they went outside the rear of the village fence and sat on the bank of the drainage canal.

For several minutes they drank in silence, and then Toby said, "Someday I'll try that with a crocodile."

Josie said, "You do, and that will be the end of you. There would be nothing left but cracked bones and your flesh in the croc's belly. You wouldn't stand a chance."

"You're probably right," Toby said, "but I'd try. And I'd rather end my days in the belly of a croc than be dead on the ground and eaten by vultures."

Josie looked at Toby curiously and said, "Toby, sometimes you're as strange as the old 'gator we took out of the pit." He finished his beer and opened another. "But you ought to come here and wrestle all the time. You could make good money. Nobody can handle a 'gator like you can."

Toby spoke absently, the words directed not to Josie or to anyone, "I'll wrestle for you some of the time, but not all of the time. I couldn't stand the white tourists."

Toby stopped the truck when he reached the store at Monroe Station. The two-story wooden structure, housing a combination grocery and cafe, was plastered with dozens of garish signs designed to attract the attention of tourists. One large sign in front offered wild hog ham and eggs for breakfast, and a wild hog bar-b-que dinner. The second story served as living quarters for the owners, Big Jim and Suzie Bentley. There were also gas pumps and a small garage adjoining the main building, and this was the only facility for ten miles in either direction. Across the highway there was a grouping of ten chickees where several Seminole families lived.

Toby parked beside the building and went inside. Several people were sitting at tables eating, and two men were at the cafe counter drinking beer. The inside of the building was just as cluttered as the outside. Deer antlers and photos of hunting kills and fish strings covered the walls. When he went into the grocery section, Toby found Big Jim Bentley sitting on the counter, munching a piece of cheese and drinking beer from a paper milkshake cup. Bentley was a tall man with a tough, muscular body and penetrating brown eyes. He was in his middle forties, but a short-cropped brown beard made it difficult to judge his true age.

Bentley flicked his hand in greeting and said, "Hi, Toby. What can I do for you?"

"I need to cash my check and get supplies. I have a list that Lucy sent. And I also want two cartons of beer."

Bentley took the slip of paper and studied the list of supplies. He said, "You know you're behind with the rent, don't you? You want me to take it out of the check first?" He acted as a broker and collected rent from several people along the Loop Road, sending the money on to the owners after deducting a small fee. He also collected electric bills for the power company serving the Loop.

After deductions, Toby's weekly check from the road department was just under sixty dollars, and from this he also had to supply his grandfather. He said, "There won't be enough, Mr. Bentley. Besides the supplies, I need gas for the truck and the airboat. Take out half the rent, and I'll pay the rest Monday afternoon. I gigged frogs last night, and I'll gig again tonight and tomorrow night. Then I'll sell the legs to the restaurant in Ochopee on my way to work Monday and give you the money that afternoon."

Bentley seemed unconcerned. Toby was often late with the rent but he always paid. "That suits me, Toby. While I'm filling the list, go in there and tell Suzie to give you a cold beer on the house."

"That would be good," Toby smiled. "It's been a long hot day, and I wrestled a real bad alligator this afternoon."

"Don't see how you can do anything like that in this heat. I don't think I've ever seen it so hot for June. I could fry eggs on the highway. This morning I was out in the swamp and saw smoke coming off a wild hog's back. If we don't get rain soon, this whole damned place is going to explode. I'd rather stay under the air conditioner and drink beer."

Toby sat at the counter while Bentley gathered the supplies. Those in the cafe who were tourists watched Toby with interest. This was the closest they had come to a Seminole, and they relished the opportunity to stare.

Bentley helped Toby take the bags outside and load them into the truck. Before he left, Toby filled the truck and two ten-gallon cans with gasoline, then he turned to Bentley and said, "Thanks, Mr. Bentley. I'll bring the rest of the rent Monday afternoon."

"Don't worry about it," Bentley replied. "And you might save a couple of frog legs for me."

"I'll bring a dozen for your dinner," Toby said, "and there'll be no charge."

As soon as Toby turned down the Loop Road, the truck churned up a billowing cloud of white limestone dust. Trees and bushes beside the road were solid white with dust and looked as if they were covered with snow. The constant holes in the road caused the old pickup to bang, rattle and buck as if it would fall apart at any moment.

Both sides of the road led into an almost impenetrable swamp of pond cypress and wax-myrtle and palmetto. There had been no rain for more than four months, and the entire area was a tinderbox. Several small bridges that once carried traffic over flowing streams now led over powder-dry, cracked earth.

Toby's place was about halfway along the Loop Road, and the stretch of road just to the north of his camp narrowed to little more than one lane. Limbs of trees formed a solid canopy over the road, creating a dimly lit tunnel. Dust drifting from the limbs made it look as if ice were dripping from the trees.

When Toby pulled from the road, the boiling dust cloud followed him, bathing everything in his camp with an additional layer of white. He parked the truck behind the bus and took the packages inside, then he opened a beer and came out to the table beside the chickee.

Lucy was sitting on the ground beneath the chickee. She said to him, "Did you get all of the things?"

"Yes. But I didn't have enough left to pay all the rent. I'll gig frogs again tonight and tomorrow night and sell the legs on my way to work Monday, then I'll pay the rest of the rent."

"I wish you wouldn't go into the swamp so much at night. It's dangerous, and one of these nights a bugger will get you."

"I'm not afraid of buggers," Toby said. "I'm a bugger myself. And we need the extra money. Everything costs so much now, and I never seem to have enough."

Lucy got up and came over to the table. "You're drinking too much, Toby," she said without emotion or threat.

For a moment Toby made no response. He looked across the darkening clearing and into the woods, as if something had suddenly caught his attention. Then he said, "Yes, I know." For the past year his drinking had become steady but had caused no harm to himself or others. The only time he didn't drink or wish to drink was when he was alone in the swamp or in the Glades with his grandfather.

Lucy said nothing more of this. "Do you wish to eat now?" she asked.

"I'm very hungry. It was a bad afternoon with Josie."

She went to the grill and dished up two plates of chicken stew, then she brought over a Dutch oven of hot biscuits. Toby took the plate and ate eagerly.

As soon as the meal was done and the dishes cleaned, Lucy went into the bus and started running the sewing machine. Toby walked to the back of the chickee and returned with a gig mounted on a long cane pole. He called to the bus, "I'm going now. I'll return soon."

Lucy looked out the door and said, "Be careful, Toby."

Toby picked up one of the gasoline cans and walked across the clearing and into the darkness of the swamp. Far in the distance, somewhere close by the bank of Lost Creek, the shrill cry of a panther broke the stillness of the night.

FOUR

D awn had not come the next morning when Toby and Lucy climbed into the pickup truck for the trip to the Big Cypress Reservation. Lucy wanted to start early so she could spend as much time as possible with her parents. They did not go to the reservation often, and she had been homesick lately, although she would never mention this to Toby.

Toby did not share Lucy's enthusiasm for the trips to the reservation. He liked and respected her parents, but he had never accepted the Christian faith, looking upon it as the white man's religion. His parents and grandparents had lived by the old Seminole traditions, believing in a supreme being but not accepting the Christian preachings as the only true faith. Lucy's father knew of Toby's reluctance to accept Christian faith, and he wished to convert him if possible. But Toby resisted his efforts.

Toby followed the Trail until it met Highway 29, then he turned north toward Immokalee. The sky was streaked with red as he passed Copeland, and soon they reached the junction of Alligator Alley, the toll road running from Naples to Fort Lauderdale, cutting a wide swath through the heart of the Big Cypress Swamp. At this hour on a Sunday morning the highway was empty, and Toby pulled through the usually dangerous but now deserted intersection and continued north.

From Immokalee he headed east on a narrow paved road running through vast areas of cattle country. The open prairie was broken occasionally by clumps of cabbage palms and pines, and cow egrets swarmed after herds of grazing cattle, eating whatever insects the cattle exposed.

The entrance to the reservation was marked by a sign warning visitors against hunting or fishing on reservation land. Soon they came to the residential section where some of the Indian families had built concrete-block houses, some lived in house trailers, and others still lived in the open-sided chickees. There were also two small trading posts and the Baptist Church.

Lucy's parents lived in a concrete-block house beside the small church. In another section of the churchyard there was a large chickee where families gathered to spread dinner after services, and for other social occasions. Most of the Seminoles who had built concrete houses had also built a chickee in the yard.

When Toby arrived at the house, he remained in the truck and said to Lucy, "I'm going to visit some friends for a while. I'll be back later."

Lucy said, "The services begin at ten. Pappa will be disappointed if you're not there."

"I know," Toby said. "I'll be back in time for the services."

As he watched Lucy go into the house, Toby regretted his decision not to go in with her. He hesitated for a moment, thinking of getting out and following her, then he pulled from the yard and moved along the paved road.

Toby drove slowly, looking at the block houses and the clusters of chickees. He turned when he came to a road leading to the maintenance barn for the cattle trucks and farm equipment. The place was deserted, so he drove back to one of the stores, and it was also closed. Then he drove a half-mile east and parked beside a narrow dirt trail leading through a thick grove of oaks.

The ground beneath the trees was thickly covered with leaves, and he made no sound as he approached the cluster of chickees. A dog suddenly ran into the path and snarled. A voice called from the camp, and the dog retreated.

This was the camp of Miami Billie, the tribal medicine man. Toby had met him once during a cattle roundup but did not really know him. When he entered the camp, Miami Billie was sitting at a table beneath one of the chickees. Nearby, an old woman, dressed in an ankle length dress with pounds of glass beads around her neck, was cooking on an open grill.

Toby sat across from the man and said, "I'm Toby Tiger, grandson of Keith Tiger who lives in the marsh west of the Trail. I'm married to Lucy Cypress, daughter of Charlie Cypress, the Baptist preacher."

Miami Billie was in his late sixties but looked much older. His hair was white, and his face deeply lined. He looked across at Toby and said, "How is your grandfather?"

"He seems to be fine. I've heard him speak of you."
Toby thought for a moment of telling Miami Billie about
the ancient medicine bag his grandfather had given him,
but he decided against this for fear that the old man
might want it.

For a moment there was no further conversation, and
then the medicine man said, "Do you want a love potion?
I can make you one for two dollars."

Toby laughed. "No. I have no need of that. My wife
is five months with child."

Miami Billie's stern expression did not change. He
said, "Have you had dreams lately?"

"No. I have had no dreams."

"Then what is your problem?"

"I have no problem," Toby said, beginning to feel
uneasy. "This is just a visit."

"Oh," the medicine man said, immediately losing
interest in his visitor.

Toby got up and said, "It's been good to see you,
Miami Billie. I'll tell grandfather when I see him again."

"Come back if you have dreams. If you have dreams,
I can make a cure for you."

Toby walked back through the grove and then drove
east again. When he came to a large drainage canal he
parked, sat on the bank and threw rocks into the water.
He knew that the services would begin soon and that he
should return to the church, but he continued to sit on
the bank for another hour.

People were beneath the giant chickee, spreading
food on long tables, when Toby returned to the house.
He joined Lucy and her parents at one of the tables.

After eating, they all went to the house and sat in cane rockers on the front porch.

Lucy's father was a tall man with a lean, wiry body. During the week he helped with the cattle operation, and his face was burned deep brown by sun and wind.

For several minutes they all rocked in silence, and then Lucy's father said, "We missed you at the services, Toby."

This was the conversation Toby had tried to avoid. He said, "I was visiting friends and lost track of the time. I'm sorry."

Lucy's father continued to rock. He said, "Lucy tells me you're still working on the road, and also that it's very dry now on the Loop. If you want to come and live on the reservation for a while, you're always welcome. There's less danger here of fire."

Toby wanted to get up and walk away but knew that he must not do this. He feared the effect of his words as he said, "What would I do if I came here, become a white man? Take up the white ways and live in a concrete house? They're making white men out of all of you who live on the reservation. I'll never do this so long as the marsh is still there."

Lucy glanced at Toby nervously but remained silent. Her father said, "You have much bitterness in your heart, Toby. Do you still blame the white people for the death of your parents? That was a bad thing, but it was many years ago and is best forgotten now."

"I'll never forget. They were the cause of it, and they're not friends of the Indian."

"That's not true," the reverend said, his voice still

calm. "The white man has done many good things for our people. They're now building schools and medical clinics and other things. And did they not give us this land?"

"They gave us this land?" Toby questioned. "They gave us nothing! Once we owned all the land, and they took it from us. Then they gave us back this small part, and now they're taking this back too, bit by bit. First it was canals and dikes, and then a highway, and then another highway, and then power lines. Soon there will be nothing left but what is useless to them. They destroy all that they touch."

Lucy's father was becoming as uncomfortable as Toby, but he knew he must pursue the conversation as best he could and try to change Toby's attitude. He said, "Toby, the Christian way is to forgive. That is what most of our people have done. If you do not have it in your heart to do this, then you don't understand the ways of God."

Toby calmed his voice and said, "I know that God is everything. God is the land and the water and the trees and the animals, and they are destroying Him. God will soon be dead."

"Do not believe such a thing, Toby!" the reverend admonished. "That's not true. God will never be dead, and if you believe what you say, then you've never seen the true face of God as I have."

Toby stopped rocking. Sweat formed on his forehead, and he wished the conversation had never started. He said slowly, "I've seen the face of God, the true face. It was in the swamp during a dry spell. I came to a pond with no water. Fish were flouncing about in the mud, dying. A huge cotton-mouth came over the bank and into the pond. His body was as big as my leg. I said to myself, 'Now the snake will feast on the fish.' He took a fish in his mouth, but he did not eat it. Instead, he carried it over the bank and to a nearby pond with water, and then he turned it loose. He came back and did this again and again. I had never seen such a thing before, and I knew this must be the face of God. While I watched, a white man came up behind me. He too watched the snake take the fish to the other pond and set them free. Then he aimed his rifle and shot the snake through the head. He went into the pond, picked up the remaining fish, put them into a sack and walked away. I couldn't believe what I'd seen. He killed God for a few fish."

Lucy's father didn't make an immediate response. He rubbed the side of his head and looked deeply worried. He finally said, "Toby, you're the husband of my daughter, and you'll soon be the father of my grandchild. We all love you. We're concerned for your life and the life that comes after. If you ever have need of me, I am here."

Toby felt relief that the conversation was ended. He said, "I thank you for your concern, and I haven't meant to offend you. I've only spoken what I feel." Then he got up and said to Lucy, "It is time for us to go now."

Lucy kissed her mother and father and then followed Toby to the truck. They both remained silent during the drive back to Immokalee. Toby was anguished, wishing that he had attended the services whether he wanted to or not, and then enjoyed a pleasant visit with Lucy's parents. He could find no excuse for his behavior regardless of how he felt inside, and worst of all, he also knew that Lucy had been shamed in front of her parents.

Finally he reached over and touched her hand. "I'm sorry, Lucy," he said. "I didn't mean to ruin your visit. I don't know what's wrong with me. I mean only love for your parents."

Tears welled in her eyes as she said, "Pappa was only trying to help. He's a good man, and he meant you no harm."

"I know. And I'm sorry. I'll tell him this the next time we visit, and I'll also listen to him and not argue."

No further words were spoken during the remainder of the trip. When they reached the camp, Lucy prepared a supper of fried chicken and boiled corn she brought back from the reservation, but Toby only picked at the food. For a while he sat at the table beside the chickee and carved on a block of cypress, then he took the gig from the chickee and vanished into the swamp.

FIVE

I t was the middle of the next week before Lucy's coolness toward Toby subsided. Toby worked those few days with no thought of what he was doing. His mind was dominated by the way he acted at the reservation, and several times the road foreman admonished him for careless work. He knew that what he had done was useless and foolish, and he was determined to never again become argumentative with Lucy's father about religion. He would simply listen and let that be the end of it. Although he regretted what he had done, he still believed there was only truth in what he said.

Toby had not yet shown Lucy the things his grandfather had given him. He had placed the buckskin bundle in the cabinet and covered it with a blanket. It was now late in the afternoon after supper, and Lucy was at the outdoor faucet, washing dishes in a tin tub.

Toby went inside and took the bundle from the cabinet. He untied it carefully and placed each item on the bed, then he slipped off his faded jeans and put on the knee-length dress. It fit perfectly. The knee-length moccasins were also a perfect fit. He strapped on the belt with the knife, put the ceremonial sash over his shoulder, and put on the turban with the plumes. All of it seemed as if it had been made for him. Then he put the medicine bag strap around his neck and looked at himself in a mirror on one wall of the bus.

Just then Lucy came inside. She was startled by his appearance, and she said quizzically, "What is that you've got on, Toby? Where did you get such things?"

"Grandfather gave them to me," he said, puffing out his chest. "This is the warrior dress of Grandfather's grandfather. He wore these things when he fought with Osceola and Wild Cat and Billy Bowlegs. They were passed down to his son and then to Grandfather, and now he has given them to me."

"I haven't seen such things before except in picture books," Lucy said. "They're very old and must have great value. It's a wonder they didn't rot."

"They were wrapped tightly in buckskin," Toby said, strutting around the bus, "and they seem to be as good as new. Do you know what this is around my neck?"

Lucy looked at the pouch. "No. I've seen nothing like it before."

"It's the ancient medicine bag," Toby said, fingering the pouch. "Grandfather said there have been only three true ones among our people. He also said it will show the way to the Great Spirit in the sky."

"I don't believe that," Lucy said tartly. "The Christian church is the way. But your grandfather was no medicine man. How did he come to have this thing?"

"When he was very young, he found it in a hammock after all the people had been killed by a hurricane, and he has kept it ever since. He says it is a sacred thing, and

I have always heard that the true medicine bag has great power. Grandfather cautioned me to never use it for evil."

"I don't know how you could use it for anything," Lucy said. "There's no telling what's inside that thing. It's probably filled with crushed bones and frog's tongues and feathers and eyeballs and alligator teeth and no telling what else."

"I'll treat it as a sacred thing," Toby said, disregarding her comment. "Grandfather has lived many years, and he knows the power of the old ways. There are few left so wise as he."

Lucy sat at the sewing machine and inserted a spool of red thread. "Leave the dress out and I'll wash it for you," she said. "It smells musty. I'll be very careful with it."

"I must show these things to Josie Billie," Toby said, again looking into the mirror. "I know he would like to see them."

"If you ever wear them away from the camp, someone will throw a net over you."

"Why?" Toby asked, turning to Lucy. "They're fine things, and they were worn by an honorable man. I'm not ashamed of them."

"It's not a matter of shame. Those things are from the past, and the past is gone forever. They aren't worn anymore. But they are very old and valuable, and I'll be careful when I wash the dress."

Toby took off the things and rewrapped all but the dress, then he put on his jeans.

Lucy said, "Do you plan to gig frogs tonight?"

"Yes. We need the extra money, and the gigging

hasn't been good lately. Most of the ponds are almost dry, and I have seen more snakes than frogs."

Lucy stopped the machine. "I forgot to tell you this morning, but we're out of milk. I should drink milk every day now for the baby. And I also need a spool of blue thread. Can you get these things before you go?"

"Yes. There's plenty of time before the frogs come out. I'll get them at the Hughes Store."

The small store in Pinecrest was closer to Toby's camp than the one on the highway at Monroe Station. He usually traded with Bentley because he could stop there on the way home from work, but he often picked up needed items at Hughes.

The sun dropped from sight into the cypress trees as Toby drove slowly along the pocked road. The lights of the pickup bounced from dust into overhanging limbs and back into dust each time the truck banged loudly into a hole or crossed sections of rutted rock. A family of raccoons ambled slowly across the road and then disappeared quickly in order to escape the choking cloud of white dust following the truck.

After he reached the store and purchased the things for Lucy, he stopped at Don's Bar-B-Que, a rustic wooden building located on a stretch of road halfway between Pinecrest and Toby's camp. It was owned by a man in his early forties, Don Lowry. His cabin was directly across the road from the bar-b-que place, and he also operated a small sawmill where he cut cypress planks and poles which he sold in Naples.

Most of the cafe business was on weekends when the swamp was invaded by hunters and campers from

Miami and Fort Lauderdale and Naples. Now there was a lone station wagon parked in front of the building.

The inside of the cafe contained a long, narrow room with exposed cypress rafters. There were two rows of plank tables and benches, and in one end there was a pool table. The other end was crossed with a cypress counter for serving food and beer. The walls were covered with deer antlers and the stuffed heads of bear and wild hogs.

Don Lowry was behind the counter when Toby entered, and three men were sitting at one of the tables, drinking beer. Toby walked to the counter and said, "Hello, Mr. Lowry. How've you been lately?"

"Dry," Lowry answered. "Don't see you down this way much at night, Toby. You still working on the road?"

"Yes. I had to get some things for Lucy at Hughes."

"Doing any gigging?" Lowry asked.

"Almost every night, but it hasn't been good lately."

"Jim Steelman told me today he isn't having much luck either. He goes every night too. Fact is, that's all he does anymore, sell frogs. We need some real rain to bring the water back up. Ain't no way frogs can live on dry land. You want something, Toby?"

"A six-pack of Bud."

Lowry took a carton of beer from the cooler and handed it to Toby. Toby opened one and put the others in a paper sack, then he paid Lowry and took a seat at one of the tables.

The three men had been watching Toby. They were all dressed in gray khaki pants and shirts, high-topped leather boots, and each wore a long hunting knife at his side.

Toby glanced at the men as he drank the beer. He had never seen any of them before, but this was not unusual. There had been an increasing flow of strangers along the Loop during the past few years.

The men continued to watch Toby closely, then one of them said loudly, "Seems like a stink's come up in here, don't it?"

"Yeah," another replied. "Smells downright bad. Got to where you can't go nowhere anymore and drink a beer without running into a nigger or an Indian. But Indians is the worst of all. You take a Indian, put him in a nice house with a nice yard, and first thing you know the whole place is covered with chicken shit, including his feet. I've seen it happen in Fort Lauderdale. They pure stink, and that's the truth of it."

Toby felt his grip tightening on the beer can, and Lowry got up from a chair and came around the counter.

One of the men said, "I hear tell you try to make one of them Indian broads, she'll fill herself with dirt to keep you from it. Don't know who'd want one of them noway, the way they stink. I couldn't get that close."

Toby suddenly slammed his fist onto the table and said, "Go to hell, you chicken snakes!"

One of the men said, "Well, looka here, fellows. We got us a real live Injun. You going to scalp us, chief? You got a tommy hawk hid in your britches?"

Lowry came over to the table and said, "That's enough, dammit! He hasn't bothered you. You think you can come in here and shoot that kind of crap for the price of a beer? Now get the hell out! And I don't want to see you back again! You understand me?"

The three men got up. One said, "Don't see why you're so worked up, fellow. We didn't do nothing but carry on a private conversation. But we'll tell all our friends who come out here to stay away from your joint. It pure stinks."

"You do that!" Lowry snapped, his face flushed with anger.

Toby was still clutching the beer can with trembling hands as he watched the men go out the door, then he listened as they started the station wagon and drove off toward Monroe Station.

Lowry went back behind the counter and opened a beer for himself, then he came over and sat at the table with Toby. He said, "I'm sorry about that, Toby. Every once in a while I get bastards like that in here. Most folks mind their own business, but there's some who just look for trouble."

"It doesn't matter," Toby said. "There's no harm done. I thought it would end worse than it did." He finished the beer and got up. "I have to go now. Lucy needs the thread."

There was a fraternalistic bond between the few people who lived permanently along the Loop. As Toby went outside, Lowry said with concern, "You take care, Toby."

The anger had finally drained away when Toby rounded a curve and his headlights revealed the station wagon parked along the edge of the road. He approached slowly, and just before he was to pass, the vehicle pulled sideways, blocking his way. The three men got out and walked into the dim glare of the headlights. One turned a flashlight into the pickup cab. "It's him," he said.

The other two men came to the side of the pickup, and one said, "We was hopin' you'd come this way."

"What is it you want?" Toby asked. "I've done nothing to you."

"We don't want anything to cause you to fret. All we want is just to visit a spell. Now why don't you come on out of there and let's talk things over peaceful like?"

"I don't wish trouble with you," Toby said. "Please move your car and let me pass."

"Are you comin' out, or are we comin' in — chicken snake?"

Toby said, "If that's the only way, I'll come out." He stepped out of the truck. "Now what is it you want of me?"

One of the men moved closer and said, "I can handle this by myself, fellows. You just watch and enjoy it." He moved quickly and struck Toby in the face.

The blow caused Toby's ears to ring. He shook his head for a moment, then he pounced on the man as he would an alligator, locking his arms and legs around the man's body. Both of them fell hard into the dust.

As Toby tightened his grip, the man screamed frantically. "Get him off of me! Get him off of me! He's breaking my ribs! Get him off!"

Toby felt the boot smash into his face, then a rain of blows poured onto his head, back and sides. He exerted all of his strength in one final crushing grip, and he could feel bones crack. He heard the man scream once more in agony, and then he heard no more.

When Toby finally became conscious, he pushed himself to a sitting position. Warm blood trickled from the side of his mouth. He sat still for several minutes, wondering how long he had been on the ground.

He got up slowly, walked to the truck and found that the headlights were still on and the motor running. Then he eased himself behind the steering wheel and felt the crunch of broken glass. The windshield was smashed. He swept glass from the seat with his hand, and then he moved the truck forward.

When he came into the bus, Lucy jumped to her feet and gasped, "What has happened to you, Toby?" His body was white with dust, and streaks of red blood creased his face.

He put the package on the table. "Here's the things you wanted," he said. "I'm sorry it took so long."

"For God's sake, Toby, tell me what has happened!"

He leaned against the counter. "I met some white Christian brothers," he said bitterly, "and they didn't like the way I smell."

She could tell he was in pain. She asked anxiously, "Are you hurt badly?"

"No. It is nothing. I'll be fine."

"Do you know who did this to you?"

"I'd never seen any of them before."

Lucy took a cloth and dabbed at his face. She said, "Go and wash yourself, and then I'll treat the cuts."

He pushed her hand away. "I'll do this later, after I have gigged frogs. We need even more extra money now. They smashed my windshield, and I will have to replace it."

She put her hands on his shoulders. "Toby, please don't go off like this," she pleaded. "Go and wash yourself and let me treat the cuts. The frogs don't matter."

"Maybe my smell will drive away the snakes," he said. "The white men said that I stink. I have the smell of chicken shit."

"Toby, please . . ."

Before she could finish, he turned and went outside, then he took the gig from the chickee and disappeared across the clearing and into the swamp.

Lucy put the milk in the refrigerator and returned to the sewing machine. For several minutes she stared at the spool of blue thread, then she dropped her head into her hands and cried softly.

SIX

Toby stopped by Monroe Station the next afternoon after work. Big Jim Bentley was outside in the garage shed, working on a swamp buggy engine. For a moment he didn't notice Toby standing there, and then he looked up and said, "What happened to you, Toby? You look like a bulldozer ran over you."

Both Toby's eyes were blackened and his nose and lips badly swollen. "It's nothing. Just an accident at my camp last night. I tripped and fell into a bench."

Bentley put down the tools and looked at Toby quizzically. "Lots of accidents down your way last night. 'Bout nine o'clock three men from Fort Lauderdale came in here asking about the nearest doctor. One of 'em was in bad shape. Ribs was busted. He was carrying on something awful, muttering something about 'stinkin' Injuns.' They said he tripped and fell across a stump. Must of been a bad night on the Loop with all them accidents. You need something?"

"I need a windshield for my truck."

Bentley looked over at the pickup. "How'd you do that?" he asked. "You trip and fall through it?"

"It was a loose rock on the road."

"Must of been some rock to wipe out a whole wind-shield. You want a new one or a used?"

"I don't know. How much would each cost?"

Bentley scratched his head. "Well, I'd say about forty or fifty bucks used, if I can find one. That truck's a pretty old model, and it might be hard to find. A new one would cost somewhere around a hundred and fifty."

"A used one," Toby said quickly. "The truck wouldn't bring a hundred fifty. When would you know if you can find one?"

"I'm going to Naples and to Fort Myers Saturday morning. I'll check all the places there. If I don't find one, I'll try the next time I'm in Miami. If I find one, you want me to put it in?"

"No. I could do this myself."

"In that case, it would cost you only what I have to pay for it. Those things can be a pain to install. I'll get the cheapest one I can find, and I sure better get it pretty quick if I can. You get behind a car on the Loop with this dust the way it is, it'll run you right out of the cab without a windshield."

"It already has," Toby said. "I got behind a car this morning and had to park for more than fifteen minutes to let the dust settle. It almost made me late for work." He stopped and hesitated for a moment, and then he said, "Do you have red paint and a brush in the store?"

"Sure. We stock paint. Won't do you much good to paint anything, though, with the dust so bad."

"I need to paint some things for Lucy inside the bus."

"Just go in the store and tell Suzie what you want."

As Toby started off, Bentley called after him, "Toby!

If you have any more trouble with accidents down your way, you let me know. I've got a whole box full of crowbars and tire tools, and I know how to use them. You hear?"

Toby wished that Bentley didn't suspect the truth. He frowned. "Yes, Mr. Bentley. I'll let you know. But it was only an accident."

After supper that afternoon, Toby took the buckskin bundle from the cabinet. He said to Lucy, "I'm going to the Osceola Village and show these things to Josie. I'll be back in time to gig frogs. Do you need anything from the store?"

"No, I need nothing. But I think you should stay here and rest. You shouldn't have even gone to work today with your face so bad."

"I'm fine, and it doesn't bother me. I'll not be gone long."

On the way to the village, Toby made a mental note of signs along the highway. Although he had traveled the Trail hundreds of times, he had never paid much attention to road signs.

When he reached the village he went through the souvenir store and to the chickee, where he found Josie sitting at a table, finishing a plate of fried fish and corn pone. Josie motioned to Toby to sit down.

"You hungry?" Josie asked. "If you want some fish, we have plenty."

Toby sat on the bench and said, "No thanks. I've already eaten."

Josie plopped a piece of pone into his mouth. "What

happened to you?" he asked curiously, staring at Toby's battered face. "You look like somebody really put one on you."

"It is nothing," Toby replied. "It was only an accident at the camp."

"Last time I saw somebody looking like you, it was after an accident in the Big Coon Bar in Everglades City. It took six deputy sheriffs to break up the accident. I've never seen a 'gator do you up like that. Must of been some accident."

"It is nothing," Toby repeated, not wishing to discuss it further. "I brought something to show you." He opened the bundle and laid the things out on the table.

"What's all this?" Josie exclaimed, running his hand across the dress.

Toby was pleased by Josie's reaction. He said, "These are the warrior clothes of my grandfather's grandfather. He wore them with Osceola and Wild Cat and Billy Bowlegs. Grandfather has given them to me."

"Have you tried them on?" Josie asked, examining the turban.

"Yes. And they fit perfect. It's as if they were made for me. And the cloth is still as good as new."

"There's probably no other like this. You could get a big price for these things in the souvenir store."

"They'll never be for sale," Toby said quickly. "They've been passed down to me, and I'll pass them on to my son."

Josie picked up the pouch. "What's this thing?" he asked.

"It is the ancient medicine bag," Toby replied, "and

it's sacred. Grandfather found it many decades ago when the medicine man was killed by a hurricane. There's no way of knowing how old it is. The bags were passed down from medicine man to medicine man in the old days, and Grandfather says there were never more than three true ones among our people. It's supposed to have great power, and it will show the way to the Great Spirit in the sky."

"Well, you can keep this thing," Josie said, putting the pouch back on the table. "I would probably say the wrong words, or do the wrong dance, and it would explode in my face — or send me down below instead of into the sky. But I have heard from the old people that these things do have magic."

"I will treat it as Grandfather says, as a sacred thing, then maybe I'll find its power."

Josie got up, went to a shelf in the chickee and returned with a bottle of Old Crow. He said, "Let's go sit by the canal and have a drink. I'm dog tired after being in the pits all day. Some days I wish the alligators would win."

Toby followed Josie across the village and out the back gate. Josie took a drink, handed the bottle to Toby and said, "What brings you down here at night? Did you come just to show me the warrior clothes?"

"No, not just that," Toby replied. "There's a thing I'm going to do tonight, and I thought you might want to come along with me."

"Gig frogs?"

"No."

"Then what is it you plan to do?"

"I'm going to paint something on the road signs."

"What?" Josie asked, wondering why Toby was hesitating to say what he meant. "I don't understand what you're trying to say."

Toby said casually, "I am going to paint 'allapattah' on all the signs."

"You've got to be kidding," Josie said, giving Toby a penetrating look. "Have you had too much to drink already? That's just an old word for the long snout crocodile, or maybe even the 'gator. I'm not sure, for I haven't kept up with the old language. But why would you paint this word on a sign? It makes no sense to me."

"The word doesn't really mean crocodile," Toby said. "What it really means is death. The end of all things."

Josie shook his head, disbelieving the whole conversation. Then he realized Toby was serious. He said, "Even if what you say is true, what would be the point? No one but another Seminole would recognize the word as anything. You had as soon write 'yeehaw' as 'allapattah,' for no one would know the difference between 'wolf' and 'crocodile.' The whole thing is silly."

"They will know the difference someday," Toby insisted. "Do you want to come with me or not?"

Josie took another drink from the bottle. After a moment's silence he said, "Toby, I've had accidents too. When I was young, and my mother and father made me go to the white school in Miami, there was a white boy who stopped me outside the building every morning. He would throw up his hand and say, 'How', and then he'd do a war whoop and dance around me in a circle. He did this to me every day, and all the other white boys and girls would watch and laugh. Finally I had enough. When he stopped me one morning and said, 'How,' I said, 'Up your ass, white trash.' For a moment he looked surprised, and then he spit right in my face. It made me so mad I pulled out my pecker and pissed all over his britches. When that white boy looked down and saw that he had Indian piss all over him, he went plumb crazy, then he hit me in the face so hard I thought he'd knocked my head off. But I flew into him like I'd never flown into anyone before. I was getting the best of it, too, until ten of his friends pulled me off and stomped me into the ground like I was a snake. The teacher took me into a room, beat me with a paddle and then kicked me out of school for the rest of the year. When I got home I went out in the marsh alone. I sat on the ground and cried. The more I cried, the madder I got, and I wanted to take a knife and stick a hole in every white skin I could find. But I didn't. If I had, I wouldn't be here now. I would have been blamed again for starting the fight."

Toby had only half listened. He said, "What has all this to do with painting signs?"

Josie reached over, touched Toby's shoulder and said, "Toby, what I mean is that I sometimes feel as you do. I understand. But you're fighting the wind, and no one can fight the wind. You have to bend with it. Even the trees know this."

Toby became pensive, staring across the canal into the darkness of the marsh. "If you do nothing, the wind will blow you away. And already the sawgrass is sending up great clouds of pollen. Are you coming with me or not?"

Josie put the cap back on the bottle and said, "I'll go with you because I don't have anything else to do. But let this be the end of it. I'd rather sit here and drink."

They walked back to the table beside the chickee, and Toby repacked all of the things except the medicine bag. He put the strap over his neck, and the pouch hung just below the giant crocodile tooth he already wore.

When they reached the pickup, Toby drove east toward the Highway 27 junction leading to Miami. Wind gushed through the open space of the missing windshield. Josie opened the bottle, took a drink and said, "Toby, are you sure you want to waste our time on something as useless and foolish as this? There are other things we could do. We could gig frogs or catch fish. Or we could sit by the canal and drink."

Toby replied, "They will know the meaning of the word someday."

It was long after midnight when Toby returned to his camp. Lucy aroused herself and said sleepily, "Have you already gigged the frogs?"

"No," he answered softly. "I helped Josie with some things at the village, and it took longer than I expected. I'll go now."

"But it's so late. You should stay here and rest."

Toby put the buckskin bundle back into the cabinet and said, "It's not so late as you think. You've been asleep. I will go now and be back to you soon. We need the extra money."

He was far into the swamp before he realized that he still had the medicine bag around his neck.

SEVEN

June passed into July and still there was no rain except for one late-afternoon sprinkle that succeeded only in making the dust on Toby's bus run in thin streaks like mascara.

Two days after the sign painting episode, the road foreman said that some high school students had pulled a foolish prank and painted an odd word on highway markers all the way from the Highway 27 junction to Monroe Station. It angered Toby to know that what he had done was passed off merely as a prank, and even worse, he had been made part of a special crew assigned to take paint remover and clean all of the signs.

Bentley found a windshield for Toby in Naples, and Toby spent an entire Sunday trying to fit the old, brittle glass into the frame without breaking it. The windshield cost fifty dollars, and Bentley accepted ten dollars down with ten dollars due each Saturday.

Lucy noticed that Toby was spending more and more time in brooding moods. He would eat his food silently and then sit alone by the side of the chickee, staring at something in the distance she could not see. Always before, they enjoyed long conversations about things that happened during the day, but now he talked little. She sensed he did not want to discuss whatever it was that bothered him. She thought she knew, but all she could do was talk whenever he wished to talk and hope that his depressed mood would soon pass.

Each night now he would put on the warrior clothes, sometimes wearing them as he watched the night creep through the cypress trees and invade the clearing. One night he wore the clothes into the swamp. He also spent much time turning the medicine bag over and over in his hands, pressing it gently as if to find its secret power and make it come alive. Lucy watched silently, wishing that his grandfather had never given it to him.

Toby still gigged frogs each night, but the catch was poor and not worth the effort. As the drought continued and the water level dropped, the frogs retreated into the dense sawgrass where they were impossible to find.

In order to make extra money, Toby promised Josie Billie he would wrestle alligators for the tourists a half-day each Saturday. He arose early and arrived at the village while Josie was eating breakfast. With him he had a box containing figures of alligators, herons and deer he had carved from cypress.

Toby sat at the table and drank coffee while Josie finished eating. He took several of the figures from the box and asked, "Are these worth anything, Josie?"

Josie examined one carefully. "These are the best I have seen. Did you carve them?"

"Yes. I sometimes make them at night. Can you sell them?"

"I'm sure we can sell them. The tourists don't spend

their money as quickly now as they used to, but we'll get all we can for them. Maybe fifteen or twenty dollars each. Whatever we get, you'll keep half. How many do you have?"

Toby was pleased by the response. He said, "More than a dozen."

"Leave them in the store. You should do more of this."

"Maybe I will if these sell."

"They will sell. It may take a little time, but we can sell all you make. These are the best I have seen."

Toby asked, "How much are the jackets in the store? I may buy one for Lucy. I haven't been good to her lately."

"From the tourists we get fifty dollars and up. You can have any one on the rack for twenty-five."

"Could you take this out of the carvings when they're sold?"

"Sure. And you'll have extra money coming too. Before you leave, pick out any one you want. This will make a nice gift for Lucy. Have you been mean to her?"

"No, it's not that. I can't really explain it. More and more lately I've been thinking of things in the past. I try not to, but I do. I know it's lonely for Lucy being at the camp alone so much, and she would like to talk at night and see more of me. But I must have the extra money gigging frogs, and when I am at the camp, my mind wanders. I thought maybe the jacket would make her happy."

"They're very nice," Josie said. "They're hand-made by Tanya Gopher and Lillie Jumper, and no one is better than them when it comes to cloth."

"I'll select one before I leave." He then asked, "Who

will wrestle this morning?"

"You and me and Frank Willie. It should be a good day. The tourist traffic has picked up lately."

"I hope we make some money. The truck windshield cost fifty dollars, and I've paid only ten. And soon the rent will be due again."

Josie pushed the plate aside, got up and said, "Well, we better go on down to the pits and warm up the 'gators. The tourists expect a good show for their fifty cents."

At noon they came back to the chickee, and Josie heaped two tin plates with fried chicken. He said, "If I stay in the pit all afternoon, I need a stiff drink. You want one?"

"Yes," Toby replied.

Josie took a bottle from the shelf, poured two tin coffee mugs full, and handed one to Toby. Then they sat at the table. Josie stripped a chicken leg in one bite, threw the bone to a dog and said, "The 'gators seemed to be frisky this morning."

"I noticed that," Toby said. "I'm a little sore. You should have seen the look on a woman's face when I threw a 'gator on his back, rubbed his stomach and made him go limp. I believe she thought I had broken his neck. She shouted for me not to hurt him, and the 'gator was only sleeping."

Josie chuckled. "I have seen women scream and faint while watching. Once when a 'gator grabbed me by the leg, an old man filled his pants. The smell was awful. We had to take him to the chickee and clean him up before he could leave the village. Sometimes the tourists put on a better show than the 'gators."

Toby asked, "Do you know yet how much we made this morning?"

"It wasn't too bad. Your part is seven dollars. Stay this afternoon and you'll make more. The traffic is better in the afternoon."

Toby took a drink of the whiskey. "I am going into the Glades for a few days next week, and I've got a lot of things to do this afternoon."

"Where are you going?"

"First I'll visit Grandfather, and then I don't know where I'll go. Just into the Glades. I'm tired of my job on the road, and I just want to go away for a few days."

"I can't see why you don't quit that kind of work. You could wrestle and carve figures and gig frogs and make enough money to get by."

"Maybe I could quit if the rains come. The gigging isn't good now, and the frogs I get won't even pay for the gasoline I use going and coming from my road job. But with the baby coming, I need a steady job. I have to save money for the baby."

"You could make enough," Josie insisted.

"Maybe," Toby replied. "Someday I may try this. I'll go now and pick out the jacket for Lucy, then I have to get back to the camp."

"You want another drink first?" Josie said.

"One. And then I must go."

Josie refilled the mugs. He said, "I wouldn't work on the roads cutting bushes for anyone. I would rather skin snakes for a living."

When Toby left the village, he stopped a mile up the road at a small chickee on the bank of the drainage canal. Beside the chickee there was a sign, "Willie Tigertail's Airboat Rides — See The Everglades — $2.50 Each."

Willie Tigertail was sitting on a bench beneath the chickee. Toby got out of the pickup, walked over to him and said, "Hello, Willie. How's business?"

"Not too bad, Toby. But if we don't get rain soon, I'll need a jeep or a swamp buggy instead of the airboat. What brings you down this way?"

"I've been wrestling at the Osceola Village this morning. I saw you sitting here and just thought I'd stop for a minute."

Willie frowned. "Well, you can have all that wrestling. I'd rather run an airboat for a living than get in a pit and flop around with a 'gator. You in a hurry?"

"Not too much," Toby said.

"I forgot to bring my lunch, and I need to go get it. Can you watch the airboat? I won't be gone long."

"Yes, I have time to do this."

Willie got up and said, "If anyone comes along before I get back, don't make a trip unless you have at least four. The gasoline's so high now I can't make money with less than that." He walked to his car and drove off.

Toby sat on the bench and shuffled his feet in the dust. The two mugs of whiskey, combined with the heat, were making his head swim. He watched idly as cars raced along the highway in both directions.

One car coming from the east slowed and pulled off the highway, making a crunching sound as the tires bounced over the bed of limestone gravel lining the edge of the road. The car bore an Ohio license plate, and there were two couples inside, both in their fifties.

The driver got out and walked to the chickee. He was dressed in a white knit shirt, blue walking shorts and white canvas shoes, and his arms and face were badly sunburned. He said to Toby, "How much does a ride cost?"

"There on the sign," Toby replied, pointing to the large sign the man had obviously seen. "Two-fifty each."

The man looked briefly at the airboat and then back to Toby. "That's a bit steep just for a ride, isn't it? But I'll tell you what I'll do. How about six dollars for the four of us?"

The question irritated Toby. He said flatly, "It's two-fifty each!"

"Well, I guess we could pay that price. How long does a trip take?"

"About fifteen minutes."

"Could we go now, or do we have to wait for others to fill the boat?"

"You can go now. For the four of you it's ten dollars, and you pay in advance."

The man handed Toby a ten-dollar bill and then motioned for the others to get out of the car. Toby went down to the canal and cranked the airboat engine.

Willie Tigertail's boat was much larger than Toby's. It had five rows of wooden seats and was designed to carry up to fifteen passengers, and it also had a larger and more powerful engine.

Directly across from the landing, a water path

opened into the sawgrass and moved to the north. It made a winding circle two miles into the marsh and came back to the canal a hundred yards south of the landing. The path was eight feet wide and had been used so much that it was totally free of sawgrass. The usual ride was to move along the path dead slow so the tourists could watch the water birds and the small alligators as they poked their snouts out of the sawgrass or from lily ponds along the way.

Toby guided the boat into the path's entrance and moved forward slowly. He had driven the path many times before for Willie Tigertail and knew it well. He shouted over the roar of the engine, "Look close and you will see the alligator!" One of the women shielded her ears from the booming noise of the engine.

When he reached the point where the water path turned south back toward the highway, Toby did not turn with the path. Instead, he shoved the throttle full forward and bounded off over the solid sawgrass with a roar. All of the passengers looked startled, and one woman's straw hat blew off and sailed over the grass.

Toby continued north for two miles with the boat crashing forward at better than fifty miles an hour. Sawgrass smashing into the boat's bow sounded like the sharp pop of firecrackers. Then he turned east toward a mud island. When he reached the island he hit the inclined bank at full speed, causing the boat to shoot upward and become airborne. It sailed for forty feet over the small island and came down with a loud thud in a thick growth of water lilies. The passengers left their seats and tumbled into the bottom of the boat.

One of the men jumped up and shouted, "God-dammit, fellow! What the hell are you trying to do, kill us all?"

Toby tried to suppress a grin that was breaking across his face. He shouted back over the roar of the engine, "It's part of the ride! It's called jumping the 'gator hump!"

"Take this damned thing back where we came from!" the man said angrily, helping his wife back onto the seat. "Now!"

Toby retraced his way back to the water path at no more than five miles an hour, then he finished the ride at dead slow. As soon as the bow of the boat touched the landing, both couples jumped out simultaneously and headed for the car. One man muttered, "Crazy Indian!"

Toby had not finished securing the boat when the car's rear tires screeched wildly, sending a shower of rocks into the canal. He smiled as the car reached the highway and sped swiftly away over the hot asphalt.

Willie Tigertail had driven up just as the car roared away from the landing. He walked to the bench beneath the chickee and said, "What was that all about?"

"They were four tourists I took for a ride. One man said they were in a hurry to get to Naples."

"They must of been," Willie said, scratching his head. "Looks like they dug two ruts right through the rock. Crazy tourists. Always in a hurry."

Toby handed Willie the money. "Well, see you later. I hope business is good this afternoon."

Willie reached into a brown paper bag. "You want a fish sandwich and a beer before you go?"

"No thanks. I ate at the village."

"Well, I sure appreciate this, Toby. Stop by next time you're down this way."

"I will," Toby said, "and I enjoyed the ride. You have a fine boat, Willie. It runs real good."

Toby turned onto the Loop Road at Forty Mile Bend, and when he reached Pinecrest he stopped at the Hughes Store and purchased five pounds of pork chops and two cartons of eggs. Further down the road, as he passed Don Lowry's place, he thought of the night when the strange men had pounded him into the dust.

But even this recollection couldn't dim his high spirits. He was exhilarated with the anticipation of the coming trip into the Glades and of not reporting to work Monday morning.

Toby had not yet told Lucy what he planned to do, but he stopped Friday afternoon on his way home from work and spent half his paycheck at Big Jim Bentley's for twice the amount of supplies he usually brought home. The refrigerator and the shelf were well stocked, and Lucy wondered about his sudden change of appetite.

When he reached the camp Lucy was in the garden, watering a row of tomato plants. He went inside the bus and put the pork chops and eggs into the refrigerator, then he hid the jacket beneath Lucy's pillow on the bed.

Toby then went outside to the grill and poured himself a cup of coffee. Lucy came over to him, immediately aware of his change of mood. She said, "You must have had a good morning at the village. Your eyes are sparkling."

"It wasn't bad. Six women tourists fainted, and two

men went crazy and ran off into the sawgrass behind the pits." He thought of the airboat ride and chuckled. "And I took four tourists on the boat of Willie Tigertail and showed them how to do the 'gator hump jump."

Lucy sat down beside him and said, "You're being silly, Toby. You act like a little boy who has seen his first deer in the woods."

"I've seen many deer." He put his arm around her, pulled her close and said, "There's something for you hidden in the bus."

"Stop teasing me, Toby," she said. "What is it?"

"First, there's something else you must know. I'm not going to work Monday. I'll spend that day and the night with Grandfather, and then I'll stay in the Glades for a few days."

She was not surprised by Toby's words, but now she knew why his mood had changed. Several times in the past he had gone off alone for a few days, and she did not mind. To her this was the natural way of Seminole men. She said, "Have you told this to the road foreman?"

"Yes. I told him yesterday morning. Mr. Simpson said it would be all right. He said he would keep my job open for me if I didn't miss but a few days."

"It was good of him to do that. Steady jobs are hard to find, and there are many others who would like to take your place." She took his hand and said, childlike, "But tell me now, Toby. What is it you've hidden in the bus?"

He enjoyed her eagerness. He said, "Let's go and see."

They walked together to the bus and went inside. Toby said, "I'll give you a clue. It's not in the refrigerator, and it's not something you can eat."

Lucy opened the cabinets and searched them, then she looked along the shelves. She even looked beneath the bed. Finally she said, "Toby, is there really something here?"

He said, "Search the top of the bed."

She immediately grabbed the pillow and found a rainbow of color beneath it. The jacket was patterned after the colors of a tree snail. She picked it up and ran her fingers across the cloth. "It's beautiful," she said, her voice excited. "But I've seen these in the store on the reservation, and I know what they cost. Pappa could never afford to buy one for me, and you shouldn't have spent so much money just to bring me a gift."

"It cost nothing," Toby said, pleased that she liked the jacket. "I left a box of my wood carvings with Josie. He says they are the best he has seen, and he can get fifteen or twenty dollars each from the tourists. I'll get half. When the carvings are sold, Josie will take out the cost of the jacket and I'll still have money coming." He put his hands on her shoulders and said enthusiastically, "Lucy, I could carve at least a dozen of these each week if I did nothing else. That would be as much or maybe more than I make on the road."

She smiled, and then she slipped on the jacket. It was a perfect fit. She said, "Toby . . . I'll love it always. It's the nicest present I've ever known. And I'm happy about the carvings. I always knew they were good. But you've never done this for money. It would mean sitting at the table all day every day. Are you sure this is what you wish to do?"

He knew she was right. He had carved the figures only for pleasure, and maybe he couldn't do so well under the pressure of money. He would continue to carve them only at his own pace. He said, "We'll see. Maybe they wouldn't be so good if I hurry. But I'll carve as many as I can, and they will bring extra money for the baby."

Toby's jubilant mood infected Lucy. She said, "I have fresh okra in the garden, and also peppers and tomato. And there's still turtle meat in the refrigerator. If you will get crawfish I'll make your favorite gumbo. Do you think you can do this?"

His face brightened at the mention of turtle and crawfish gumbo. He said eagerly, "I will get you a bushel. I know where they are plentiful if I can run the 'coons away from them."

She smiled again as she watched him take a bucket from the chickee and trot across the clearing toward the swamp.

After supper Toby drove to Monroe Station and filled the gas cans for the airboat. When he returned, Lucy had finished cleaning the dishes and was sitting at the table beside the chickee. He put the cans down, sat beside her and said, "I must take the gasoline to the airboat. Come and go with me. There is a thing I want you to see."

The sun had sunk below the horizon but was sending fingers of red into the clouds where they were filtered downward, bathing the cypress with a mystic orange glow. A flight of white egrets winging westward looked pink against the darkening sky. Trees and vines changed color constantly as the swamp absorbed the last of the day and prepared for night. Lucy followed Toby along the narrow path as this daily phenomenon created a twilight fairyland. Then they entered the open area leading to Lost Creek.

When they reached the airboat landing, all light was gone, and they were in total darkness. Lucy felt a pang of fear as Toby left her and went down the bank to put the cans in the airboat. She could see nothing, and she was afraid Toby would not be able to find her when he came back up the bank. But he had eyes that could see as well as the panther or the nighthawk, and she was relieved when she felt his hand grasp hers.

Toby led her along a trail that bordered the creek. Frogs were beginning to bellow, and from somewhere in the distance there came the sound of an alligator grunting. Then they turned from the path and walked through a thick forest of cabbage palms, feeling their feet sink into a solid matting of fallen fronds. Soon they came to a small knoll of high land just at the point where swamp merged into the great open marsh.

"We'll sit here," Toby said softly.

Lucy dropped down to the ground and moved close to Toby. She leaned against his shoulder and said, "I can see nothing. Why have we come to this place?"

"It will be only a few minutes, and then you will see."

From far across the black distance there suddenly appeared a small tip of silver. The dim glow moved upward and became larger, and soon a ghostly scene of vast sawgrass flats dotted with palm hammocks emerged from the darkness. There was a slight breeze blowing, causing the sawgrass to sway gently. Drops of moonlight seemed to be catching in the tops of the grass like luminous beads lacing the heads of dancers.

Lucy was spellbound. "It's beautiful," she whispered, as if the sound of her voice might shatter the scene and cause it to vanish.

"When I was a boy this was my favorite time of night," Toby said. "I would slip from the chickee and watch as the moon came up through the palms. I come to this place often when I'm gigging frogs."

Lucy put her hand on his and said, "Toby, we'll go and live on a hammock if that is what you wish. I'll do whatever you want to do."

He pushed her backward to the ground gently and moved close beside her, then he cupped her face in his hands. He said, "No, Lucy. That will never be. I only dream. Out there would be no place for you or the baby. It's a hard life now on a hammock, not like the old days. And soon it will be no more. I'm even afraid for Grandfather."

"If you would be happy, I would go."

She felt his arms move around her, and her eyes closed as his face touched hers. They paid no notice as the full moon gathered strength and invaded the knoll of high ground, and it was past midnight when they returned to the camp.

EIGHT

⌇⌇⌇⌇⌇⌇⌇⌇⌇⌇⌇⌇⌇⌇

When the airboat reached Allapattah Flats at mid-morning, Toby pulled the boat onto the shore and walked quietly along the path leading to the back of the cove.

None of the crocodiles were on the opposite bank, but he could see the eyes of one protruding from the water. He squatted behind a cocoplum bush and watched.

"Where are your friends, old one?" he said. "Are they in the bushes, waiting for me? Or somewhere down there with you? Would you like my arm, or a leg, or all of me? But you will have to catch me first. I'm not so dumb as you think."

Toby continued to squat, staring at the two eyes just above the surface of the still water. The crocodile wasn't creating even a ripple, and it remained motionless as a coot flew into the cove.

Toby watched with interest as the small black bird paddled around in circles, dipping its head beneath the surface in search of food. He said, "You best be careful, little one. You're getting too close. There's instant death awaiting you."

The coot popped beneath the surface and came up

three feet in front of the eyes. An explosion suddenly ripped the water as two giant jaws shot upward and clamped over the bird. The coot screamed briefly, then it disappeared downward.

"I told you so, little one," Toby said, watching waves spread across the surface. "I warned you, but you wouldn't listen. And there was nothing I could do for you. Now you're only food in the belly of allapattah."

He watched for a few minutes more, then he got up and went back to the airboat.

From the flats he headed straight toward the hammock of his grandfather. As he approached the island he pushed the throttle back and forth, causing the engine to pop like the sound of cannons. The old man was waiting when he rammed the bow of the boat onto the landing.

Toby hugged his grandfather in greeting, and then his grandfather said, "Many airboats pass this way, but I always know when it is you. No one else rides on such a wave of thunder. It is as if the gods are coming out of the sky."

"I am no god, Grandfather," Toby said. "I only know how to make the engine backfire."

Toby took two packages from the boat and followed his grandfather along the path leading to the camp. When they reached the cooking chickee, Toby put the packages on the table and sat on the bench.

"Would you like coffee?" the old man asked.

"Yes. That would be fine."

They sat at the table and sipped from the steaming mugs. Toby said, "I will stay here with you tonight,

Grandfather, and then I will spend a few days in the Glades before returning home."

"That is good. I will enjoy your company, and we will talk of many things."

"Do you know what I've brought?" Toby asked. "I will tell you. I have five pounds of pork chops and two dozen eggs. We'll have pork chops tonight and eggs in the morning. How does that sound to you?"

The old man smiled. "I have not eaten eggs in more than a year. Do we have to wait until morning? Could we not have some of them tonight?"

"Yes. We'll have eggs tonight with the pork chops. How many can you eat?"

"I will eat six tonight and six in the morning."

Toby laughed. "You have a big stomach for such a slender man, Grandfather. It will be pork chops and eggs tonight, and then I will gig frogs. In the morning we'll have fried legs with our eggs. And I will also make a pot of corn grits. What else would you have?"

"That would be enough," the old man said, still smiling. "Unless you brought some of the cake buns with sugar on top."

"There are two packages of them in the bag. I thought you'd want them. I will get them now."

Toby brought a package of sweet buns back to the table and handed them to his grandfather, then he watched as the old man opened them and ate eagerly. He said, "Would you like to go for a ride in the airboat this afternoon? I have enough gasoline to go from here to Cape Sable if you'd like." He knew his grandfather loved to ride in an airboat.

"That would be fine," the old man replied, smiling again. "But I would not wish to go so far."

"We will go wherever you like, and I will take you on a wave of thunder such as you've never seen or heard."

"Do not make it too loud, Toby. You would frighten away all the rabbits and fish, and then I would have nothing to eat." He suddenly became serious. "Could we go to the hammock of your mother and father and your grandmother? I have wished to visit them lately, but it is too far for the dugout canoe. I am too old now to travel so far with a pole."

"Yes, we will go there," Toby answered. "I haven't seen this ground myself for a long time. We will go as soon as you finish eating."

The fire had burned down to a bed of glowing coals when Toby placed the frying pan on the grill. His grandfather was in the chickee resting from the afternoon's trip. The pork chops sizzled and popped as the pan became hotter. When he finished cooking them he placed the chops on a cypress platter and dropped in the eggs. Biscuits were baking in a Dutch oven on the edge of the grill.

The meal was on the table when Toby beckoned his grandfather. The old man just sat and looked for a moment, and then he ate with relish. Pork chop after pork chop hit his plate until soon there was nothing left but a pile of bones. Then he dipped up the egg yolk with hot biscuits. Toby received more pleasure from watching his grandfather than he did from the meal itself.

When they finished eating they sat on the ground

and leaned back against the trunks of cabbage palms.
Night had come completely, and the fire sent flickering
shadows around the camp. The old man said, "You are a
good cook, Toby. Almost as good as your grandmother.
But not quite so good. Do you remember the stews that
she made?"

"Yes, I remember," Toby replied. "I could never
forget. And I am nothing like her. Anyone can cook pork
chops and fry eggs, but I'm glad you enjoyed it. I wish
you could eat a meal prepared by Lucy. She is as good
as mother or grandmother."

The old man lit his pipe and said, "I am glad you are
here, Toby. Many nights now I get lonely."

For a moment Toby thought of again asking his
grandfather to come and live in his camp, but he knew
this would be useless. He said instead, "Would you like
to go with me for a day or so? I would bring you back
here on the way home. We will go many places and see
many things you haven't seen now for a long time but
remember from the old days."

"No, I would not do this," he replied, his voice tired.
"I do not go far from the hammock anymore, except to
a nearby island to hunt rabbit or spear a fish. I would
only be in your way. But when I was as young as you I
made many trips. Sometimes we went south to the place
where the marsh meets the sea, and it was many days'
journey in the dugout canoes. We would come back by
the west to the place of many islands, and there we
would have great feasts of oysters and clams. And each
year we would go to the ocean in the east when the giant
turtles crawled onto the sand to lay eggs. One turtle was

enough to feed all of the people for many days. And some years we held the Green Corn Dance on the south shore of the great Okeechobee. There were many things there of wonder. The moon vines were so thick they covered the tops of trees, and I often walked on them over the roof of the forest. Keith Huff told me many years ago that it is all gone now. He said the white men have built a giant dike around the lake, and there is nothing left there now but houses and farms. I would not like to see it again. I will stay here on the hammock and remember things as they once were."

Toby got up and said, "I'm going to the airboat and get my gig and lantern, then I will gig frogs for our breakfast."

"There should be many around the shore. I would help you, but I cannot see now in the darkness."

When Toby returned, the old man was still sitting against the tree, but he had slumped forward, sound asleep. The pipe lay at his feet. He did not awaken as Toby picked him up gently and placed him on the palmetto bed beneath the chickee. Toby looked at him for a long time, realizing just how frail he had become. Then he lit the lantern and moved off toward the sound of the croaking frogs.

Toby did not leave his grandfather's hammock until early the next afternoon. They spent part of the morning spearing fish together from the old cypress canoe. Toby still marveled at his grandfather's ability with a lancewood spear. He saw fish Toby could not see, and sometimes he rammed the long shaft downward into seemingly empty water. But he always brought it back into the canoe with a flouncing bass attached to the tip.

In late morning they sat at the table drinking coffee and talking of things in the past, then at noon Toby's grandfather fried the fish and made a pone of cornbread. Soon afterward, he was asleep when Toby left. Toby did not start the airboat engine until he had poled the boat two miles from the hammock, and then he ran it dead slow for another mile to lessen the noise.

Toby had no particular destination as he pointed the boat west and gave it full throttle. His long hair straightened out as the airboat skimmed through the sawgrass, stirring up flights of ducks and rails and cormorants that hid along his path. When he passed two miles off the shore of Allapattah Flats, he muttered, "I'll not stop with you this day, long snouts. I wish no sight of you today."

He did not slow the airboat until he was well into the area of the Ten Thousand Islands. Finally he cut the engine and let the boat drift. Trees on some of the mangrove islands were white with ibis and snowy egrets, and the shallows were filled with herons and roseate spoonbills searching for food. He laughed when two anhingas engaged in a noisy squabble over a fish one of them had caught.

He poled the boat into a clump of mangrove trees and picked oysters from the roots until the bottom of the boat was covered with shells, then he moved into the shallows, looking for fish. He finally found an unaware snook and slammed the gig into its back. When he cleaned the fish and threw its insides into the water, it caused a swarm of pelicans to surround the boat, clacking their bills loudly for a handout.

When he left this area he turned south, moving aimlessly again, then he began searching for a place to spend the night. Many of the mangrove islands were inaccessible because of dense barriers of rotted limbs smashed into the water by hurricanes. Once he saw a houseboat anchored in the distance, and he turned away from it.

He finally came to an island with a clear cove. After securing the boat, he gathered wood for a fire. The sun had now dropped low in the sky, and all of the islands were alive with birds seeking a roost for the night. A family of raccoons watched with interest as he brought his supplies ashore, waiting patiently for an opportunity to steal whatever food they could find.

After he built a fire, Toby went back to the shore, stripped naked and waded into the black water. At first it was warm to his body, but as he waded deeper, it became cool. He turned on his back and drifted, looking upward as the sky changed from red to orange. Then he swam back to the shore and put on the faded cut-off jeans.

He threw heaps of oysters into the fire, and when the shells cracked open, he removed them from the fire and scraped off the meat with a knife. It tasted good, and he remembered the times his mother had used oysters in a pot of stew. He then cut the fish into chunks, speared the flesh with a stick and roasted it over the coals. At this moment it seemed to him that all a man ever needed, all there really was to life, was here free for the taking.

The approach of night created a flurry of activity. Flights of birds hurried by over the island, and fish snapped at minnows and bugs on top of the water. For a while Toby sat on the shore by the airboat and watched all of this. Then when the last trace of light was dying, all motion stopped. No living thing moved, and the great marsh became soundless. Even the sawgrass seemed somber, and the palm islands in the distance looked not real but like objects painted onto a giant canvas. Stars and the moon gradually coming into the sky caught his interest momentarily. But suddenly he felt alone.

He thought of the time only two nights ago when he held Lucy in his arms as this same moon drove the darkness from the marsh. He could still smell her and feel her swollen body pressed tightly against him. And then he thought of his grandfather, an old man excited because of a supper of pork chops and chicken eggs, then asleep alone against the trunk of a cabbage palm. There were no longer any children to brighten his camp-fire, no longer a woman to share life, no companions to exchange tales. And there never would be.

A realization came to Toby that being here on this remote mangrove island was a selfish thing. He could not run forever. He knew that the past was dead, and he would not find it out here or elsewhere. It lay on the hammock with his mother and his father and his grand-mother, and soon now his grandfather. He wished he had not left the old man alone. It also bothered him that he was thinking of these things. Always before when he went away alone for a few days, it gave him a feeling of freedom; but now something was different, and he could not understand.

He got up and threw more sticks onto the fire, causing sparks to dance over the dying coals. Then he lay back on the blanket and watched as a jetliner roared through the night, making its way swiftly across the silent marsh toward Miami. The airplane's lights blinked and sparkled like fast moving stars, and soon it dropped below the horizon and was no more.

Toby was not aware when sleep finally came, but it was closer to dawn than to midnight.

The next morning, Toby pointed the airboat eastward. He had intended to make his way south to Whitewater Bay and cut back north from there, but now he headed straight for the hammock of his grandfather.

He did not slow the boat as he passed Allapattah Flats, and the speeding craft bounded across the marsh like a frightened deer. When he approached the hammock, he pushed the throttle back and forth, causing booming backfires to shoot from the engine's exhaust. In the distance, Toby could see his grandfather standing by the landing, waiting.

NINE

Toby stayed with his grandfather for two days and nights, and returned home Thursday afternoon. Lucy was fine, and she was happy to see that Toby seemed relaxed. That night they sat by the chickee, talking about the trip. He carved on a block of cypress as he told her how his grandfather had eaten a dozen eggs in two meals, remarking that perhaps he should take chickens to the hammock.

At dawn the next morning Toby left for his job, but he returned to the camp before noon. He walked from the pickup and sat on the bench beside the chickee.

Lucy came outside, and when she looked at Toby she was alarmed by the dejected expression on his face. She said, "Why are you back so soon? What has happened?"

He spoke angrily, "He gave my job away! Someone else has my job! Mr. Simpson lied to me!"

Lucy sat beside him. "Did he tell you why he did this?"

"He said they had an emergency job to do on a bridge, and he had to have a full crew. He told me to come back in about a month and maybe there would be something open then. But he lied to me! If I had known this would happen, I wouldn't have gone on the trip."

"Maybe it is as he says," Lucy said, trying to calm him. "Maybe he couldn't help what he did."

"He lied to me!" Toby repeated. "The rent's due again, and I still owe Mr. Bentley on the windshield. How much money do we have?"

"I'm not sure." She went into the bus and returned with a coffee can. "We have twenty dollars and some change."

"Then I'll take what we have to Mr. Bentley and ask him to wait for the rest. He has always done this before."

Toby got up, put the money into his pocket and started for the truck. Lucy said, "There are other things you can do, Toby. The job on the road was not all there is."

He replied, "I know. But Mr. Simpson lied to me! He didn't have to do that."

Big Jim Bentley was in the garage shed when Toby arrived at Monroe Station. Toby walked over to him and said immediately, "Mr. Bentley, I don't have all that I owe you this week, and I've lost my job on the road. I can give you ten dollars now and the rest soon. I'll wrestle alligators for the tourists at the Osceola Village."

Bentley leaned against a car fender. "How come you lost your job?" he asked. "Are they cutting back on the crew?"

"No, it's not that. When I went into the Glades for a few days, Mr. Simpson said he would hold my job for me, but he gave it to someone else."

"That's too bad," Bentley said. "But it's O.K. about the money. You know I won't press you. And I'll have some work you can do in about a week. I've got a contract to check over all the swamp buggies at the Everglades Hunting Club. That's about three dozen buggies, and some of them will probably need engine overhauls. I know you can do this kind of work, Toby. You did as good an overhaul on that airboat engine as anyone could do. If you work hard at this job, you can make fifty or sixty dollars a week, and the job will last at least a couple of months. That should pull you out of the hole with a little to spare. I've got to hire someone, and the job is yours if you want it."

"That would be fine," Toby said, greatly relieved. "I will do this, and I thank you. I will work hard as you say. When do I start?"

"Probably a week from next Monday. I'll start getting parts next week. And there's something else you might want to do, too. A couple of men came in here this morning asking about a guide with an airboat. Said they wanted to tour the Glades for a few days. They offered twenty dollars a day for a guide and a boat, and I told them I'd try to find someone. I was going to ask Sam Gopher, but you can have it if you want it. They'll be back here early tomorrow morning."

"What is it they want to do?" Toby asked, interested but having doubts.

"I don't know. I didn't question them. They were in a camper van with a Texas tag, so I guess they're just a couple of tourists wanting to see some of the Glades. But twenty bucks a day isn't bad money for running an airboat, and that tourist money spends just like all the rest."

Ordinarily Toby would not have hired himself to

tourists, but now he needed the money. He said without enthusiasm, "I guess I'll do it. Maybe they'll not wish to stay long. I've already been away from my camp for five days."

Bentley asked, "Where do you keep the airboat now?"

"On Lost Creek, close to the edge of the swamp."

"I'll tell you what, then," Bentley said. "Why don't you just meet them in the morning and leave your pickup here while you're gone? I'm not going to be using my buggy for a few days, so you can take them to the airboat in it from here. Shouldn't take you more than an hour to get to Lost Creek. The men can leave their camper here too, and you can get your truck when you bring the buggy back."

"I will be here in the morning," Toby said as he handed Bentley a ten-dollar bill. "I'll try to have all of the money I owe sometime next week. And I thank you for waiting."

"That's O.K.," Bentley said. "There's plenty of ways to make money if you try."

Toby then went into the store, and with the other money he purchased a bucket of red paint and two cartons of beer. When he returned to the camp he put the beer in the refrigerator, opened one and went out to the chickee. Lucy looked up from the grill and said, "Are you hungry now?"

"No, I'm not hungry. I will eat later."

"What did Mr. Bentley say about the money?"

Toby sipped the beer. "He will wait. And he offered me a job in a week working on swamp buggies. He says

I can make fifty or sixty dollars a week, and the job will last two months or more."

Lucy smiled. She didn't think he would find something so soon, and she was pleased. "That is good, Toby. That's about the same as you made on the road. I knew there would be other things for you to do."

"That is not all," Toby said. "I'm to meet two men at Monroe Station in the morning and be their guide for a few days. It pays twenty dollars a day, and maybe with this we can pay some of the rent."

"How did you come to get this?" she asked curiously.

"Mr. Bentley arranged it." Toby got up, went into the bus and returned with his hunting knife and a block of cypress. "I am going to carve a crocodile," he said, "but this one I will make for the baby."

Lucy sat beside him and said, "I knew things would work out, Toby."

"We'll be fine," he replied. "But Mr. Simpson didn't have to lie to me."

TEN

The brown camper van was parked beside the building when Toby arrived at the store the next morning. When he went inside, there were two men seated at a table, eating ham and eggs and drinking beer. Toby said to them, "Are you the ones who need a guide?"

The two men studied Toby carefully. One said, "Yeah, that's us. I'm Jesse Thornton and this is Carl Avery. We're from Texas. What's your name?"

"Toby. Toby Tiger."

"Tiger?" The man chuckled. "Now that's a good old Irish name. You know these swamps well?"

"I've known them all my life. I was born in the marsh."

"That's good," Thornton said. "We just want to poke around a bit out there and see if you've got anything here we don't have back in Texas. We've heard this place is kind of weird, and we want to see."

"I can take you wherever you wish," Toby said.

"Fifteen a day O.K. with you?" Thornton asked, assuming the role of spokesman for the two.

For a moment Toby was perplexed, then he said, "Mr. Bentley said it would be twenty dollars a day including my airboat."

"Well, if that's what he told you, O.K. It's a deal. We don't want to cheat anyone. And maybe we'll give you a little something extra if you show us a good time."

The two men got up. Both were in their middle forties, and both were more than six feet tall and heavy built. They wore gray hunting clothes and high-topped leather boots.

As they followed Toby outside, Toby said, "We'll go from here to Lost Creek in the swamp buggy, then we will go into the Glades in my airboat."

"Good," Avery said. "We didn't come down here to go hikin'. We could of done that in Texas. We'll get our things from the camper."

Toby went behind the building and put two cans of gasoline into the buggy. When the two men came around the side of the garage, they both carried large canvas packs and .270 rifles. Toby took the packs and put them into the back of the buggy.

Thornton looked curiously at the huge airplane tires on the small vehicle. He said, "Will this thing go through water? It ought to float with them tires."

"It will go anywhere in the swamp," Toby said, "but we won't run through much water. The swamp is very dry now."

Toby got behind the wheel and cranked the engine, then the two men climbed in beside him and they headed south.

For several miles Toby ran parallel to the Loop Road. The land here was mostly open and dotted with dwarf cypress. In normal times the ground would have been mushy with a thin covering of water, but now the buggy was leaving a dust trail.

For a while the two men studied the landscape with interest, and then they became bored. Avery said to Toby, "Is this all there is out here? I thought this was supposed to be a swamp."

"We're not really in the swamp yet," Toby replied. "It won't be long now."

Thornton looked over at Toby and asked casually, "You a full-blooded Seminole?"

"Yes. My parents and my grandparents and those before them have lived on this land." He thought of telling them of the warrior clothes that had been passed down to him but decided against it.

Thornton then said, "Well, we don't have Seminoles in my part of Texas so far as I know, but we've had about every other kind of Indian at one time or another. Most of the Indians left in Texas are good Indians. They're planted six feet under the ground." Thornton and Avery both laughed, and then Thornton said, "No offense, fellow. Just an old Texas joke, that's all."

Toby said nothing.

When they crossed the Loop Road, the swamp became thicker, and several times they ran through stretches of shallow water. Toby could no longer drive in a fairly straight line. He had to weave the buggy around thick growths of trees and vines, and twice he had to backtrack and find another way.

Avery suddenly said, "Jesus, fellow, stop this thing a minute!" He was slapping at his arms and neck. "How the hell can you stand skeeters like this? I got to put something on before they suck the blood out of me."

Toby stopped the buggy beneath a thick clump of pond cypress. He had paid no heed to the mosquitoes. "They will not be so bad when we reach the open Glades," he said.

Avery opened one of the packs, took out a can of repellent and sprayed himself, then he handed it to Thornton. "You want a drink?" he asked.

"Yeah, I could use one," Thornton replied.

While Avery was taking a bottle of whiskey from the pack, Thornton suddenly threw up his rifle and fired. The unexpected explosion startled Toby. He looked up quickly and saw a large raccoon fall from a limb and hit the ground with a thud.

"Got him!" Thornton exclaimed excitedly.

The high-caliber rifle had knocked half the raccoon's head off. Toby watched as blood gushed from the small animal and stained the ground. He said, "Do you want the 'coon for your supper? If you do, I will clean it."

"Are you kiddin'?" Thornton said, staring at Toby. "Me eat a 'coon? Back where we come from, that's nigger food. I was just testin' my sight."

Both men took deep drinks from the bottle, then Toby cranked the engine and moved forward again. He soon reached Lost Creek and parked the buggy on the bank beside the airboat.

Toby loaded the gas cans and packs into the boat, and then the two men climbed in. He said, "Where is it you wish to go?"

"Anywhere you want to take us," Thornton replied. "You're the guide. We're just along for the ride."

When he reached the marsh, Toby gunned the engine and headed south. The boat was overloaded and couldn't reach top speed, so he cruised steadily at about twenty-five miles an hour, circling several hammocks before he turned west. Thornton then motioned for him to stop, and he pulled back on the throttle.

Thornton said, "What's on them little islands?"

Toby replied, "Some have nothing, and some have deer and rabbit."

"Let's go in and have a closer look," Thornton said.

Toby guided the boat to a small hammock and circled at dead slow. Several coots popped in and out of clumps of pickerel weed, and a few egrets rested in trees. A great blue heron walked slowly along the shore, pecking at the bottom with its long beak. Avery threw up his rifle and fired, then the giant bird toppled forward into the shallow water and lay still.

Toby shook his head. He said, "The heron is no good to eat. If you want bird, we'll have to find ducks. But it's out of season now for all game."

"We got food in the packs," Avery said. "If we want to shoot ducks, we can do that in Texas. I never got a crack at one of them big birds before."

Thornton said, "Is this whole place nothin' but grass and islands? I've had about enough of this already. We want to see somethin' different."

Toby thought for a moment, and then he said, "Would you like to see crocodiles?"

"Are you kiddin'?" Thornton exclaimed. "You'd have to take us to Africa for that."

"There are a few left here," Toby said.

"Crocodiles?" Thornton questioned again.

"Yes. There are but a few left. Would you like to see them?"

"Sure," Thornton replied. "How far is it?"

Toby said, "They live on Allapattah Flats, only a short distance from here."

"Well, then, let's have a look," Thornton said, still doubtful.

Toby gave the engine full throttle, and he soon guided the boat ashore at the island. When the two men got out he said to them, "You must be very quiet and very careful. Crocodiles are dangerous. They are not like alligators."

Toby guided them along the narrow path to the back of the cove. Only one crocodile was on the opposite bank. He said quietly, "This is their den, and no one but me knows they are here. There are also three others."

Both men stared across the water. Thornton exclaimed, "Well I'm damned! It is a croc. I've seen pictures of them with that pointed snout."

Before Toby realized what was happening, Thornton put three bullets into the crocodile's head. The croc jumped backward as the first bullet shattered its brain, and then it lay still.

For a moment Toby just stared, not believing what he had seen. Then the sight of the lifeless body pumping blood down the bank brought reality to what he witnessed. Anger boiled within him, and he shouted, "You've killed him! You've killed him for nothing! There were only four, and now you've killed one for no reason!"

Thornton and Avery were startled by Toby's unexpected outburst. Thornton stepped back and said, "Now just cool down a bit, fellow. Don't blow your cork. You think I could pass up a chance like this? Something like this is what we came here for."

Toby repeated, "You've killed him for nothing! There were only four! I shouldn't have brought you here!"

Thornton then disregarded Toby and turned to Avery. He said, "We'll skin him out and slip the hide back to the camper. Can you imagine what they'll say back home when they see this souvenir?"

Toby wanted to grab the rifle and smash the butt into Thornton's face, but he knew instantly that that would be a foolish act. He steadied his trembling hands and said as calmly as possible, "That wouldn't be a wise thing to do. To kill a crocodile or an alligator is a felony. If you're caught with the hide you will be in deep trouble, and you could spend much time in jail for this. It would be best to leave him here now, wait on a nearby hammock, and come back tonight. Then we can skin the crocodile and take the hide out in the darkness."

"That makes sense," Thornton said, impressed by Toby's warning of a prison sentence for what he had done, and also glad that Toby had calmed himself. "When we get that croc hide back to the camper, it'll mean an extra hundred dollars for you." He felt sure that money would close Toby's mouth and gain his cooperation in getting the hide back to Monroe Station.

They followed Toby back to the airboat, then he cranked the engine and headed south. For two miles he ran the boat as fast as it would go, and then he pulled into a large hammock.

Toby picked up the two packs and carried them to a small clearing beneath cabbage palms. He put them down and said, "We will stay here until dark. I must go now and secure the boat."

The two men sat on the ground beside the packs. Thornton opened one, took out a bottle and said, "Man, I could sure use a drink after that. This trip was worth it after all." He turned up the bottle and drank deeply.

Toby walked back to the airboat, shoved it out as far as it would go and cranked the engine. He rammed the throttle forward and gained full speed instantly. When he was a half mile out, he looked back and could see the two men on the shore, waving their arms wildly.

It was mid-afternoon when Toby reached Monroe Station. He parked the swamp buggy and started toward his truck. Bentley came from the garage and said, "How come you're back so soon, Toby? And where are the two men?"

"They decided to camp for a few days on a hammock," Toby answered. "I'll go back for them Tuesday."

Bentley said, "They must be some kind of nuts, wanting to spend that much time on a hammock. Well, it takes all kinds, and they all show up out here sooner or later. You can use the buggy when you need it to go after them."

Toby said nothing more as he got into the pickup and drove off. When he reached his camp he told Lucy the same thing he had told Bentley, that the men wanted to camp for several days on a hammock.

For several minutes after the airboat disappeared from sight, Thornton and Avery stared across the silent sawgrass in disbelief. Finally Thornton bellowed, "Dammit to hell! That fool Indian must be loco!"

His booming voice caused a swarm of egrets to flap out of a dwarf cypress and rush away from the hammock.

Avery said, "He was really pissed off about you shootin' the crocodile, but I thought the offer of extra money would buy him. I didn't think he would pull something like this on us. What do we do now?"

"What the hell you think we'll do," Thornton shot back irritably. "We'll walk, that's what! All the way back to the camper. There ain't no bus line runnin' out here, stupid!"

Avery resented the outburst Thornton directed to him, and he said coolly, "What about the equipment?"

"We'll leave it. We can't carry it across the marsh. Could be we might even have to swim some. When we get back to the camper we'll hire someone else to bring us back out here and pick it up."

The two men placed the packs and rifles against the base of a palm. Thornton said, "Strap your knife to your belt. We'll go back to that place and skin out the croc. If we can't drag the hide out with us, we'll pick it up when we come after the packs."

As they left the hammock and waded into the sawgrass, both were surprised by the shallow depth of the water. It came only to their knees. But the sharp blades of sawgrass cut through their clothes and made thin slashes in their flesh, and it seemed to them to be an almost impenetrable barrier. Both men cursed constantly as they made their way foot by foot to the north.

It was late afternoon when they finally reached Allapattah Flats and climbed up the bank to the cove. Only the one dead crocodile was in sight. The two men rolled it onto its back and rammed their knives into the tough hide.

Thornton said, "I've never tried to skin out anything like this. He's sure a tough cuss, ain't he?"

Avery struggled with his knife. "I'll say. What we need is a hatchet or an axe, or maybe even a chain saw."

When finally they succeeded in slicing open the stomach, sweat was pouring from both of them. Avery wiped his brow, smearing blood over his face. He said, "Man, I quit! At this rate it'll take us a week to skin this thing. We better get on out of here and bring something back with us besides these knives."

"I guess you're right," Thornton agreed. "This is a bigger job than I thought it would be."

Avery went down to the cove to wash his hands and face. As he splashed the water he did not notice the two eyes just off the bank. Horror twisted his face as the giant jaws burst suddenly from the still water, grabbed his arm and jerked him headlong into the cove. He screamed once before his body was pulled beneath the surface.

Thornton wheeled around quickly. At first he didn't realize what was happening. Then as he stared into the cove in puzzlement, Avery's thrashing body broke the surface. The crocodile shook him violently and pulled him under again. Thornton's flesh turned white, and his hands trembled. He felt hot vomit rush through his throat and pour out. He tried to scream but could make no sound. Finally he grabbed a stick and started beating the ground hysterically.

ELEVEN

The next morning Toby drove to the Osceola Village to tell Josie he would wrestle alligators for the next week. Josie was in the large pen behind the pits, feeding garfish to the alligators. He came outside when he saw Toby.

As they walked to the wall surrounding one of the pits, Toby said, "I'll wrestle for the next week if you need me."

"We always need you," Josie said, pleased with the news. "But what of your job on the road?"

"When I went into the Glades for a few days, the foreman gave it to someone else."

"That's the best thing that could happen," Josie said. "You don't need to work on the road. Now you can come here all of the time."

"I'm going to start working for Mr. Bentley at Monroe Station a week from Monday. I will fix swamp buggies, and he says I can make fifty or sixty dollars each week."

"That's not bad money," Josie said, "but you can come here any time you wish. The trade has slowed lately, though. Maybe the tourists don't want to stop in this heat."

"Have you sold any of the carvings yet?" Toby asked.

"We sold all of them. One woman even bought four. But we could only get ten dollars each. There were thirteen, so taking out for the jacket, you still have forty dollars coming. Maybe next time we can get more."

"That's good enough," Toby said, disappointed at the price but glad they had been sold. "Now I can pay the rest of the money for the windshield, but I'm still short for the rent."

Josie said, "If you would move here and live in the village, there would be no rent."

Toby thought of what happened with the two men and the crocodile. He said, "I couldn't stand the white tourists that much. I'd rather live on the Loop and pay rent."

Josie asked, "Are you going to stay today and wrestle?"

"Yes."

"Then you can have first turn. The 'gators are always mean during the first show, and you can handle them better than anyone else."

It was late afternoon when the last group of tourists left the village and the wrestling was ended for the day. Toby and Josie were both tired as they walked to the chickee. Josie took a bottle from the shelf inside the chickee, and then they sat at the table. Josie said, "Do you want food? There's a big pot of spare ribs on the grill."

"I'm not hungry now," Toby replied wearily. He poured a mug full of whiskey and downed it in one gulp. He had not eaten at noon either, and he immediately felt the bite of the whiskey in his empty stomach.

Josie said, "Well, I'm hungry, and I'm not so tired I can't eat." He got himself a heaping plate of ribs and then came back to the table.

Toby poured another mug of whiskey, and as he sipped it he became thoughtful. He said, "I saw a bad thing yesterday."

"What was that?"

"Two men hired me as a guide. They were tourists from Texas. I took them to Allapattah Flats, and one of them killed a crocodile."

Josie stopped eating. "Killed a croc?" he questioned. "Why would he do that? You can't sell a hide anymore without going to jail."

"He did it for no reason — just to kill it. And they also shot a raccoon and a heron. After the crocodile was killed, I took them to a hammock south of the flats and left them there."

"You left them on a hammock?"

"Yes."

Josie shook his head. "Well, you'd best not be around when they return. That's a long trek through the sawgrass and the swamp." He dismissed this news from his mind and started eating again. "How was your trip into the Glades?" he asked.

"I didn't go far like I planned. Instead of going south, I spent most of the time with Grandfather." Toby finished the drink and poured another. He continued, "I'm worried for him, Josie. He has become very frail. I think he eats nothing anymore but a fish now and then, and he won't go more than a mile from the hammock. There is no game left out there for him to hunt. I try to take him all the food I can afford, but I am still worried. He shouldn't be out there alone."

"Could he not live at your camp?" Josie asked.

"I have asked this of him many times and he won't even speak of it. You would have to tie him with ropes to get him off that hammock."

Josie threw several bones on the ground and watched as two dogs fought over them. He said, "Well, you can't tell an old man what to do. It's his life. But it is a bad thing to be out there alone in the marsh at his age."

Toby drank again from the mug, and then he said, "He wouldn't be alone out there if they hadn't built the airport in the swamp. When they told us we must leave, my grandmother didn't eat or sleep for many days. She would only sit around the chickee, grieving and saying nothing to anyone. Then she became ill. It was a long trip to the new hammock, and we hadn't been there a month before she died. They killed her for the airport, and the airport ended up as nothing."

"You can't be sure of this, Toby," Josie said. It worried him that Toby even had such thoughts. "Was she not old when you left the land?"

Toby replied, "You can't be sure of anything anymore. But she was not ill before they built the airport and ran us away from the land. They killed her for no more reason than the men killed the crocodile. It was for nothing."

Toby was feeling the whiskey. He started to ask Josie for food but changed his mind and said, "I am going to do another thing tonight. I have thought of it much lately, and I will need your help."

"What is it this time?" Josie asked curiously, noticing also that Toby was drinking more than usual without eating.

"I am going to paint 'allapattah' on the airport runway."

Josie sighed with exasperation. "Toby, you have to be kidding me. Why would you do this? We did it once before with the highway signs, and it meant nothing."

"It will mean something someday."

"Even if you're foolish enough to do this, you can't get into the airport at night with the gate locked."

"I have a hacksaw in the truck. Also the paint."

Josie poured himself a cup of whiskey and downed it quickly, then he went to the grill and came back with a plate of ribs. "Eat this, Toby," he insisted. "And then if you still want to do this foolish thing, I will go with you — but only to keep you out of trouble. I can see no sense in this. Maybe it is only the whiskey."

"It is not the whiskey!" Toby said harshly, pushing the plate back across the table. "This is a thing I must do, a warning to them, and they will know the meaning some-day. If you don't come with me I will go alone."

Josie realized he couldn't convince Toby otherwise, and he knew from Toby's voice that he would do this thing alone. He said, "I will go with you. I don't wish to, but I will. I will go only to keep you out of trouble if I can. Sometimes I think you are crazy to even have such things in your mind."

Toby made no response. Then they walked to the front of the souvenir store. At night there was little traffic on the Trail. Josie looked at the empty highway and said,

"I will drive the truck, but I'll do none of the painting. If you wish to paint a silly word on a strip of concrete, that is your affair."

"I will do the painting alone," Toby said. He took the medicine bag from a paper sack inside the truck and put it around his neck.

They drove west for several miles, and just before they reached the airport gate, Josie pulled to the side of the highway and stopped. He turned off the headlights and said, "I'll wait here. If someone passes and sees you cutting the lock, run back to the truck. I'll keep the motor going."

Toby got out and walked along the edge of the highway. The moon had not yet come up, and he had to feel his way slowly to the gate. No cars passed as he sawed off the lock and swung the gate open. Then he walked back to the truck.

Josie drove the pickup through the gate and along the road leading to the airstrip. The road had been built wide enough to accommodate heavy passenger traffic to and from an international facility which never came into being. It was flanked by a row of tall lamp posts without bulbs. Josie kept the headlights off and drove in darkness. He said to Toby, "If we're seen by a guard, I am going to come out of here so fast it will sling the pistons out of this old truck."

Toby said, "No one will see us if we're careful, and there may not even be guards in here at night. I don't know. But the medicine bag will protect us."

"I'd rather depend on the truck engine than that bag of junk," Josie retorted.

It was an eerie feeling to Josie driving along a super road leading to nowhere in the heart of a black swamp. He had a strong impulse to turn back, but he knew Toby wouldn't allow this. He moved the truck forward slowly, straining his eyes to see through the darkness.

The road cut to the east before it reached the open area of the runways. Toby said, "I have seen this place in the daytime. There is a meadow to the north. Go that way and we'll enter a runway.

Josie left the asphalt road and cut across open ground. It seemed to him that he was driving through a pond of ink, and he expected at any moment to crash into a tree. He said, "I can't see anything, Toby, and I don't know where we are. How can you paint a sign in such darkness?"

"The moon is coming up now. I will be able to see well enough."

Josie finally felt the wheels of the pickup touch concrete. He stopped and said, "Is this far enough?"

"This will do fine. We're near the end of the runway."

Josie cut the engine as Toby took the bucket of paint and a brush from the truck. Josie said, "Hurry with this foolishness, Toby. I want to leave this place."

The moon came up just enough to cut the darkness, but Josie still couldn't understand how Toby could see well enough to paint. He remained in the truck and could distinguish only a dim shadow as Toby smeared red paint across the concrete strip.

Toby was half finished when a row of blue lights flanking both sides of the runway suddenly came on. Josie jumped from the truck and shouted, "What is this thing, Toby? Why have they turned on the lights?"

Toby stopped the brush and listened to the roar of a jet approaching from the north. He turned to Josie and said, "I'm not finished. It will only take a minute or so more."

Josie said urgently, "Let's get out of here, Toby! Let's get out of here now!"

Toby continued to paint as the roar became louder, not looking up until the airplane's landing lights flooded the edge of the swamp. The jet came in fifty feet over the top of the truck and then suddenly pulled up. The sound of the straining engines was deafening as the huge airplane stopped its downward glide and slowly moved upward again.

Josie fell to the ground and watched as the landing lights bathed the runway to the south. As Toby jumped up and ran for the truck, his foot struck the bucket of red paint, sending it tumbling across the runway. Paint sloshed across his shoe.

Josie had already started the truck forward when Toby jumped onto the running board and climbed inside. They both remained silent as the old pickup shot through the darkness of the meadow and finally reached the asphalt road leading back to the highway. Josie looked back and could see a red flashing light far behind him. He pushed the accelerator to the floor and it sounded as if the engine would come out of the truck. When he reached the gate he slammed on the brakes, sending the pickup screaming sideways onto the Trail. He was three miles down the highway before he finally turned on the headlights.

When they reached the village, Josie stopped in front of the souvenir store. He cut off the engine and the lights, then he slumped forward against the steering wheel and said, "Toby, we are both as crazy as that old bull 'gator in heat! I will never do this thing again! Don't even ask me! Do you understand?"

"It was close," Toby said calmly. "For a minute I thought the airplane would land in the back of the truck. But the medicine bag kept us safe."

"Medicine bag, hell! Did you see the flashing red light coming after us? If they had caught us in there, I don't know what they would have done to us. But it would have been something bad, you can count on that. I will not do this again! Never! They are not going to put me in a cage because of a silly sign."

"I won't go there again myself," Toby said.

Josie became calmer. "Do you want a drink before you go?" he asked.

"No. I have had enough, and I should have eaten. I will get food as soon as I reach the camp."

Josie opened the door and got out. He said shakily, "Well, I am going to the chickee and get myself as drunk as a squirrel eating cocoplum nuts. I will see you in the morning."

Toby cranked the engine and turned on the headlights. He waited until Josie disappeared into the village before driving onto the highway.

TWELVE

I t was early Monday afternoon when Thornton limped across the meadow behind the store at Monroe Station. Big Jim Bentley was inside, eating a plate of bar-b-que and drinking a beer.

When Thornton entered the cafe, Bentley was startled by his appearance. His pants were in shreds, and his legs covered with cuts made by sawgrass. Arms, neck and face were solid mosquito welts.

Thornton slammed his fist onto a table and bellowed wildly, "Where is he?"

Bentley stopped eating. "Where is who?" he asked, puzzled as to why Thornton was even there.

"You know damned well who! That goddam Indian!"

Bentley still didn't understand. He said, "You mean Toby Tiger?"

"Yes, dammit! Where is the bastard?"

Bentley shoved the plate away and stood up. He said, "Now just calm down a bit, fellow. What's this all about? Toby came back here Saturday afternoon and said you wanted to camp on a hammock for a few days and that he'd pick you up Tuesday. I haven't seen him since then."

"He ran off and left us out there!" Thornton ex-

ploded. "He left us on a hammock, and I've been walkin'
for two days tryin' to find my way out of that goddam
swamp! I'm goin' to put the law on him! And if I find him
first, I'm goin' to put some fist in his teeth!"

Bentley became even more perplexed. He knew Toby
Tiger would never abandon anyone in the marsh without
reason. He said, "Did he steal something from you?"

"No," Thornton answered. "He didn't steal anything;
but our equipment is lost."

Bentley then said, "Did he take your money as a
guide and then run off and leave you?"

"No. We were goin' to pay him when we got back."

Bentley picked up the can, took a drink of beer and
said, "Well, if he didn't steal anything, and if you didn't
pay him, what's he done to break the law?"

Thornton became even angrier. He said, "He's a
murderer, that's what! He left us on an island full of
crocodiles, and two of them attacked us! I shot one, but
the other one killed Carl! That Indian is a goddam
murderer!"

"What?" Bentley exclaimed, wondering if he had actually heard the accusation. "You mean to tell me your
friend's been killed by a crocodile?"

"That's right!" Thornton snapped. "I saw it with my
own eyes. The crocodile killed him and ate him."

To Bentley the whole scene was becoming ridicu-
lous. He said, "I don't believe that for a second! There's
no way that two grown men armed with high-powered
rifles can stand on a piece of open ground and let one
man be killed and eaten by a croc. No way! You tell that
tale to someone around here and they'll laugh you right

out of the county."

Thornton bristled. "Are you callin' me a liar?"

"Yes, I'm calling you a liar! When they attacked you — if they attacked you — why didn't you just shoot them?"

For a moment Thornton didn't answer, and then he said, "They came out of the bushes like lightnin'. Carl didn't have time to shoot, and after I killed the first one, my gun jammed. I couldn't do nothin' but stand there and watch."

"You sure they didn't jump down on top of you from out of a tree?" Bentley asked. "If the gun jammed, let's have a look at it and see what's wrong."

"I lost it comin' out of the swamp." Thornton's face again flushed with anger, and he said, "What the hell you mean questionin' me anyway? You're just takin' up for that goddam Indian. Now tell me where he lives!"

"His camp is about ten miles down the Loop Road, but he won't be there now. He's working this week at the Osceola Village on the Trail."

Thornton said, "Well, I'm goin' to put the law on him, and if the law won't do nothin', I will! Back where I come from we know how to handle something like this. I got a forty-four pistol out there in the camper. I'll put some hot lead in his guts, and that's a fact! I'm goin' to leave now, but I'll be back!"

The words angered Bentley, and he said harshly, "You sure are going to leave! We know how to handle things out here too. It's a swamp game we play called 'gator stomp, and I've been champion for the past five years. And that's a fact! Now you get the hell out of here before

I stomp a mudhole in you and then bounce you around
the walls like a hickernut!"

Thornton stormed out. Bentley went to the door and
watched as he got into the camper and drove off hurriedly toward Naples, then he went back to the table. He
scratched his head absently, trying to make some sense
from all of this.

Just before dark, Toby stopped at Monroe Station on
his way home from the Osceola Village. When he
entered the store, Bentley was sitting on a counter in the
grocery section. Toby walked up to him and said, "Mr.
Bentley, I have the rest of the money for the windshield,
but I can pay only ten dollars on the rent. Here's fifty
dollars, and I will pay more by this weekend."

Bentley took the bills, put them into his pocket and
said, "You make all this wrestling 'gators?"

"No. Most of it came from wood carvings I sold, but
I also made some wrestling. I would have come by and
paid you last night but I was late getting back from the
village."

"That's good, Toby," Bentley said. "I know you'll clear
this up before long. You'll make good money fixing the
buggies, and things'll work out O.K. for you."

Toby took a five-dollar bill from his pocket, handed
it to Bentley and said, "I need a gallon of milk, two
loaves of bread and a pound of bacon."

Bentley put the things into a paper bag and then
handed Toby his change. He said, "By the way, Toby, a
man was in here this afternoon looking for you."

"Who was that?"

"One of those fellows you took out in the Glades. Thornton. Seems they didn't really want to camp on a hammock. When Thornton came in here he looked like he'd been in a pit full of wildcats."

Toby had started to pick up the package but stopped. "He was here?" he asked.

"Yeah, he was here. And I ain't never seen a man madder than him. He claimed you just dumped them on a hammock and took off. He also told me a wild tale about you leaving them on an island full of crocodiles. Said his partner, Avery, was killed and eaten by a croc."

Toby was shocked by the words. He said, "That's not true, Mr. Bentley. I left them two miles from Allapattah Flats. What he says isn't possible. There are no crocodiles anywhere now but at Allapattah Flats, and I didn't leave them there."

Bentley looked straight into Toby's eyes and said, "What happened out there, Toby? I know Thornton didn't tell me the truth, and I don't think you've told me everything either."

"They were bad men," Toby said, knowing that he must tell Bentley exactly what happened. "In the swamp they killed a raccoon for no reason, and later they shot a heron. I took them to Allapattah Flats, and there Thornton killed a crocodile. There were only four left, and he killed one for no reason but just to kill. It was after this that I left them on a hammock two miles from the flats."

"He killed a croc?" Bentley questioned.

"Yes. They were going to bring the hide back here after dark and put it in the camper. They offered me a hundred dollars to help. I took them to the hammock to wait until night before skinning the crocodile, then I left them there."

"Well I'm damned!" Bentley exclaimed. "No wonder he made up such a lie. He probably knows he's committed a felony. They must have gone back to the flats to skin the croc, and whatever happened, it happened there. But why didn't you just come on back here and report them to the law?"

"I thought what I did was best."

Bentley said, "He said he was going to put the law on you for this, and I'm sure he will. You'll hear more from this before it's over, but I don't think you're in any trouble because of it. If the truth is found out, then Thornton will be the one in hot water. But he also threatened to kill you, so when you're around him again, Toby, be careful."

"I didn't mean them harm," Toby said. "But they did bad things. They killed without reason."

As Toby started to pick up the package, Bentley said, "Something else I wanted to mention, Toby. One of the guards who works a night shift down at the airport stopped in here early this morning for breakfast on his way to Ochopee. He said somebody busted in down there last night and dumped a bucket of red paint on a runway. That's all they did, just dump paint and make a few letters. This guy said nobody down there could figure out why the hell anybody would do that, unless it was some high school kids pulling a prank. But they almost got hit by a jet making a practice landing."

Toby gripped the sack, suddenly wanting to get out

of the store quickly. Bentley then said, "That paint sounded like the same kind somebody used to paint an Indian word all over the highway signs not long ago. I know you've been painting some cabinets or something for Lucy inside the bus, but you better clean that red paint off your shoe. Somebody might get the wrong idea."

Toby looked down at his shoe. He stammered, "Mr. Bentley . . . I don't know how that paint got there . . . I must have . . ."

Bentley interrupted, "Toby, if you ever want to talk about anything that's bothering you, I'm a good listener. We all have to look out for each other here in the swamp. If we don't, nobody will. I'm just a dumb old coot and I know it, but sometimes I can help. You hear?"

Toby said, "Yes, Mr. Bentley, I hear. And I will clean the shoe as soon as I get to the camp." Then he turned and walked quickly from the store.

THIRTEEN

Toby was standing by one of the wrestling pits the next morning when the deputy sheriff and Thornton entered the village. As soon as Thornton recognized Toby, he exclaimed loudly, "That's him! He's the one!"

Josie walked over and stood by Toby as the two men approached. The deputy said, "Are you Toby Tiger?"

"Yes," Toby answered, expecting this would happen.

"Have you seen this man before?"

"Yes. He hired me last week as a guide."

"How many men were there?"

"There were two. This one and another."

The deputy then said, "Thornton here has a pretty wild tale about you leaving them someplace where there were crocodiles, and about his friend being killed by a croc."

"Yes, I know," Toby said. "Mr. Bentley at Monroe Station told me last night. But what this man says is not true. I didn't leave them where there were crocodiles."

"I told you he'd lie about it!" Thornton snapped, stepping toward Toby. "I told you, didn't I?"

"Now just a minute, Thornton," the deputy said, stepping between Thornton and Toby. "Simmer down and let me handle this." He turned back to Toby. "Let's hear your side of what happened."

Toby said, "I took them to Allapattah Flats to see the crocodiles. This man killed one of them. They were going to skin out the hide and take it back to their camper, and they offered me a hundred dollars to help. I told them they would be in deep trouble if caught with the hide, that it would be better to wait until after dark. Then I took them to a hammock two miles away. After I had taken their gear into a clearing I went back to the airboat and left them. I did this because I wanted no part of what they had done. But there has never been a crocodile at the place where I left them."

"That's a damned lie!" Thornton exploded. "I ought to knock the livin'. . ."

"That's enough!" the deputy said, grabbing Thornton's arm. Several Indians in the village came forward to watch the commotion. The deputy then said to Thornton, "How the hell do you think I'm going to find out what happened if I don't ask questions? Now you calm yourself down and keep it that way!"

"He's lyin'!" Thornton repeated.

"We'll see about that," the deputy said. "We'll go out there where this happened and see what we can find." He turned to Toby. "You got a place here where I can launch my airboat?"

"There's a landing just behind the village," Toby replied.

"I'll bring the car and trailer around there," the deputy said. "You two wait at the landing."

Toby said to Josie, "I'll see you later."

"Is there anything I can do?" Josie asked, concerned for Toby.

"No. There is nothing."

Toby helped the deputy slide the airboat off the trailer and into the canal. The deputy took a .44 magnum rifle from the patrol car, and then they all got into the boat. The engine thundered to life, and the deputy guided the boat along a narrow creek. When they reached the sawgrass he shoved the throttle forward, and the airboat dashed away quickly.

It took them an hour to cross the marsh, and when they approached the area of Lost Creek, Toby pointed the way to Allapattah Flats. Soon the deputy guided the boat ashore at the island, and they all got out.

Toby led them along the path to the cove. The dead crocodile was on the opposite bank, lying on its back, and another crocodile was asleep just to the left of the carcass.

The deputy said to Thornton, "Well, at least part of what you say is true. Somebody sure as hell did kill a croc, and there's another one still here."

"This is the place he left us," Thornton said. "Carl was killed right there on the bank and dragged into the water by that other crocodile."

"That's not true!" Toby said. "This is where he killed the crocodile, but this is not where I left them."

The deputy said, "There's just one way to find out for sure about your friend." He raised the rifle and aimed it across the cove.

Toby sprang forward and grabbed the deputy's arm. He shouted, "No! Don't kill him! You cannot do this!

There will soon be none left!"

The deputy shoved Toby away. "Dammit, Tiger, stay out of this! I don't want to kill him, but there's no other way."

"Please don't do this," Toby pleaded. "This is not the place I left them. I swear it! Please don't kill him."

The deputy paid no heed to Toby's words as he aimed the rifle and fired. The magnum bullet knocked a hole as big as a grapefruit in the crocodile's head. It jumped forward and struggled for a moment, and then gushes of blood pumped from its head.

Toby's brown skin paled. He sank to his knees as the deputy went back to the airboat and returned with an axe and a large knife. Toby couldn't watch as the axe blade smashed downward again and again. He heard the thump of steel meeting flesh, but he kept his eyes cast downward.

Finally the deputy came back around the cove and said, "Wasn't nothing in there but gar fish, two coots and a possum." He turned to Thornton. "If that croc is supposed to have eaten your friend, where is he?"

"I don't know," Thornton said. "Maybe he's already digested him."

"Nope. I would have found bones and other evidence."

"Maybe that was the wrong croc."

"I don' see any others," the deputy said, putting down the axe. "Are you real sure your friend was killed?" he asked.

"I stood right over yonder and watched it."

"I mean did you actually see the crocodile eat him?"

"What do you want me to say?" Thornton said, becoming irritated. "I saw the crocodile jerk him into the water, and I saw him go under. If you mean did I run down there, stick my head under the water and watch it, the answer is hell no!"

"What did you do after your friend was jerked into the water?" the deputy asked.

"I tried to shoot, but my gun jammed. Then I guess I sort of blacked out for a while. I don't remember."

"For all you know, then, your friend could have got out of there and run off into the sawgrass, scared out of his wits."

"What the hell's this?" Thornton said angrily. "You tryin' to make me out a liar? I told you I stood right over yonder and watched him jerked into the water."

The deputy said nothing more. He walked around the cove and looked carefully, then he went into the brush and searched for a hundred yards around the island. When he returned, he said, "If this is the place Tiger left you, where is your gear and rifles?"

For a moment Thornton looked unsure of himself, and then he said cautiously, "I lost my rifle on the way out of the swamp. The gear was right over yonder. I guess somebody must have come along after I left here and stole it."

"Something else puzzles me," the deputy said. "How come that dead croc's stomach is cut open? Somebody started to skin out the hide but quit. Now who do you think could have done that?"

Thornton again spoke cautiously, "I don't know. Somebody must have come along after I left."

Toby was still squatting on the ground, listening. He

looked up and said, "This isn't the place I left them. The gear is not here. They must have come back here and tried to skin the crocodile after I left them on the other hammock."

Thornton glared at Toby and said, "Damn you, you stinkin' liar, I'm goin' to . . ."

"You're not going to do anything!" the deputy snapped. He turned to Toby. "Show me where it is you say you left them."

"You goin' to let that crazy Indian lead us on a wild goose chase all over this marsh?" Thornton asked. "I ain't got time to go on a sight-seein' tour."

The deputy ignored Thornton's remark and said to Toby, "You point the way, Tiger."

It took the fast airboat only a few minutes to reach the hammock. Toby walked straight from the shore to the small clearing and pointed to the two packs and rifles on the ground beside a palm trunk.

The deputy looked at the equipment and said to Thornton, "Is this your stuff?"

"I never saw it before."

After examining the packs, the deputy said, "If this isn't your stuff, why the hell is your name tag sewed onto this pack?"

Thornton stepped forward and looked at the pack. "Well, I guess it's mine. I just didn't recognize it at first. But I don't know how it got here. That Indian must have come back after I left that other place, stole the stuff and brought it here."

"If he stole it, why would he lead me straight to it now?" the deputy asked.

Thornton moved closer to the palm. He said, "Seems to me you're doin' nothin' but takin' up for that lyin' Indian. If you won't do nothin' about this, I will." He suddenly grabbed his rifle.

Before Thornton could throw the bolt, the deputy had a .44 pistol pointed directly into his face. The deputy said harshly, "Now you just put that rifle down, fellow! You try something like that again, I'll put cuffs on you!" Thornton leaned the rifle against the palm.

"I'm going to give you some good advice," the deputy said to Thornton. "Killing a crocodile or an alligator is a felony. For what you did you could spend a long time in jail plus pay a stiff fine. I could go over there and get the bullet from that croc's head, send it to the lab and match it to your rifle, and then you'd be in hot water up to your neck. Now as far as your friend is concerned, I'll get two more patrol boats out here this afternoon, and we'll search every foot of marsh for several miles around that island. If we find him, we'll bring him in. If we don't, he'll just have to be reported as a missing person. Either way, we'll send you a final report. As soon as we get back to Naples, I'd advise you to get into that camper and get the hell away from here as fast as you can, else I might change my mind and file charges against you. Do you understand what I'm saying?"

"I understand," Thornton said sullenly.

The deputy then turned to Toby and said, "As for you, I'm going to warn you to never again leave anyone out here alone no matter what the reason! Do you understand? After they killed the crocodile, you should have come straight back and reported them to the law."

Toby said, "I meant them no harm, but they did bad things. They killed without reason. And I was afraid that if I stayed with them, and they were caught with the hide, they would blame it on me."

"Well, you two get that stuff loaded into the boat," the deputy said, shaking his head. "This is the damnedest thing I've ever had to investigate. Let's get on out of here before I change my mind and arrest both of you."

As soon as they reached the village, Thornton and the deputy left in the patrol car. No further words were spoken among the three of them. Toby walked to Josie's chickee and sat on the bench.

Josie came from the pit, sat beside Toby and said, "Well, what happened out there?"

"The deputy found that what I said was truth. It is ended now."

"I'll bet you're glad of that."

"I am glad of nothing. The deputy killed another of the crocodiles and cut him open, and now only two are left. And he killed this one for nothing — the missing man was not there."

"You sure do take on about those crocodiles," Josie said. "You would think they are your kin."

"They are as all things I know and have known, even of the marsh itself," Toby said. "Soon it will all be ended, and there will be no more. The white men destroy all that they touch."

Josie got up and said, "Toby, why don't you go back to your camp and not wrestle today. Just spend the day taking it easy."

"No. I will stay here and wrestle. I need the money."

The two of them then walked through the village and to the pits.

FOURTEEN

Toby told Bentley the conclusion of the investigation by the deputy, but he didn't mention the affair to Lucy, not wanting her to even know that he had been taken into the marsh with Thornton and the deputy.

The next Monday morning he started his new job with anticipation. He had always liked to work with engines and anything mechanical, and he proved to be so good that Bentley let him do all of the buggy repairs in order to keep himself free to service regular garage and gasoline customers and help in the store.

The Everglades Hunting Club compound was located a mile down the Loop Road from Monroe Station, and Toby brought the swamp buggies to the garage one at a time. As soon as one was repaired, he returned it to the club storage shed and drove back with another. Bentley helped tow in the ones that wouldn't crank.

For the first week Toby worked from dawn to sunset each day, and he also worked Saturday and Sunday. His pay for the period came to eighty-five dollars. He didn't like to miss the weekend trip to his grandfather's hammock, and he determined that he wouldn't work again on weekend days; but it pleased him to know he would be able to pay the next rent on time and the bills and maybe save a little for the birth of the baby. When the time came, he would take Lucy to the medical clinic in Everglades City.

Toby stopped gigging frogs because of the continued drought, but he spent some time each night carving the wooden figures. He finished the crocodile he was making for the baby, and when he showed it to Lucy, she thought it to be the most perfect thing he had done. It was two feet long, and each minute detail of a crocodile's hide and body was as distinct as the real thing.

It was in the middle of his second week at Bentley's when Big Jim came into the garage one morning extremely worried. He said to Toby, "I just got back from the south swamp, and some damned fools have fired the woods. I was about a half-mile away when they saw me. They dropped their torches and high-tailed it out on a buggy. They were probably going to shoot wild hogs in front of the fire, but if we don't get it stopped before it spreads, that south wind will bring it right on up here. I've called the rangers and they should be out here soon."

Toby put down his tools and said, "What do you want me to do, Mr. Bentley? You want me to help with the fire or keep working on the buggies? I will do whatever you say."

Bentley thought for a moment, and then he said, "The woods are so dry that fire could move like it's running over spilled gasoline. I'll take the tractor and a disc and cut a fire lane around the meadow. You better get down to your camp and see about things there. If the fire comes that way, get out of there as quick as you can and bring Lucy back up here."

As Toby started for his truck, Bentley said, "Take one of those long lengths of hose from the shed and wet down your camp as best you can."

Toby got the hose and drove down the Loop Road. He could smell smoke although he couldn't see a smoke cloud or signs of fire. He churned up white dust as he pushed the pickup hurriedly along the rutted road.

When he reached the camp, Lucy was outside by the chickee. She ran to him immediately and said, "Toby, I have smelled smoke. Where is it coming from?"

"Someone has fired the woods south of Monroe Station, and I don't know if it will come this way or not."

Toby went to the faucet and hooked on the hose. When he turned the handle, a thin stream of water shot across the dry ground. He handed the hose to Lucy and said, "Keep the water running and wet everything in the camp. I'll go into the swamp and see what is happening."

Lucy was frightened just by the thought of fire. She said with concern, "Be careful, Toby. The woods are so dry you could be trapped out there."

"I'll be careful, and I will return soon. Keep the water running and wet everything."

Toby crossed the road in front of his camp and walked north. He did not come into this section of the swamp often, and he didn't know this land as well as the area to the south. The ground here was drier and more open than the dense swamp leading south to his airboat landing on Lost Creek.

He began to trot rapidly, and as he moved further

north, the smell of smoke became stronger. He had covered almost four miles before he saw the first sign of fire.

Even at the distance of a half-mile, Toby could feel the heat. Beads of sweat rolled down his chest, and his long hair was clinging to his neck. He watched as the top of a cabbage palm exploded like dynamite, sending a shower of sparks high into the air. The fire roared like the sound of the jet that night on the airport runway.

The wind was from the south, pushing the fire northward. Toby knew this presented no danger to his camp, but if the wind didn't change, Monroe Station would be in serious trouble. He watched for several minutes more as exploding trees made deep booming sounds, then he turned and ran back toward his camp.

Toby had a constant fear of such a fire breaking out in the Glades, rushing over the sawgrass and consuming the hammock of his grandfather. He knew that if this ever happened, the old man would be helpless to save himself. The sight of the hammock and the charred bodies of his mother and father came back into his mind vividly.

When he reached the camp, Lucy was spraying water onto the top of the chickee. He said to her, "The fire is moving northward. There is no danger here except for sparks drifting from the sky, but we must keep everything wet."

Toby got into the pickup and drove back toward Monroe Station to see if he could help Bentley. As he moved north the smoke became thicker until finally he couldn't see the road, then he turned the truck and went back to his camp.

Just at dusk the wind changed to the south, bringing with it clouds of choking smoke. Smoke poured into Toby's camp so thickly that Lucy went into the steaming bus and closed all of the windows. A dull glow lighted the sky to the north. As sparks drifted down into the camp, Toby put them out with the hose. His sweating body was black with soot as he moved about the clearing constantly, and it was long past midnight when he finally washed himself with the hose and went into the bus.

At daylight he was on his way to Bentley's place. The land just south of Monroe Station was charred black, and still smoldering. Smoke drifted on the air like fog, and soot covered the whiteness of the limestone road. As he drove nearer he dreaded what he might find, wondering if the building would be still standing or in ashes. He was greatly relieved when he came to the highway and found the old two-story structure still there.

Bentley was standing by the garage, gazing at the blackened pasture where the fire had finally stopped. He looked exhausted. When Toby came to him, Bentley said, "I guess we lucked out on this one. If the wind hadn't changed and backfired the fire, it would have jumped right over this place no matter what we did."

Toby followed Bentley into the store. Bentley went behind the counter and opened two beers, then they sat at a table as Bentley handed a beer to Toby and said, "You look like you could use one too. After last night, I need something cold instead of hot."

Bentley became silent for a moment, and then he said thoughtfully, "You know, Toby, sometimes I think it's just not worth it even trying to stay out here. You work your butt off to make a go of it, and then some damned fool comes along and fires the woods just for a few scrawny wild hogs that ain't worth a tinker's damn to nobody. Sometimes I feel like taking a torch, burning this place to the ground, saying to hell with it and moving on. It just ain't worth it."

Toby had never seen Bentley like this. He suddenly felt a closeness to him that he had never before felt toward any white man. He wanted to reach out and touch him, to establish a bond of understanding between the two of them. He also wanted to say something that would ease Bentley's depression, but he couldn't express himself as he wished. He only said, "I know, Mr. Bentley. Sometimes I have such thoughts myself."

Bentley took a deep drink of beer and said, "Your job went up in smoke too. Before we could stop it, the fire got into the hunting club grounds and burned the buggy storage sheds. Burned them right down to the ground, and there was nothing we could do. Now all of the buggies are gone. Seems like you've had nothing but hard knocks lately, and now this happens just so some bastard can take a shot at a pig running for its life."

The news shocked Toby, but he didn't want it to show. He said, "That's too bad, Mr. Bentley. I don't mind not having the work, but I'm sorry the fire did such a bad thing."

Bentley noticed the fear in Toby's eyes despite his attempt to hide it. He said, "I've been needing some help around the gas pumps and the garage. Suzie has a hard time when she has to handle the cafe and the grocery by herself. I couldn't pay much, maybe twenty bucks a week, but this would at least keep you in groceries till you find work. Could be your road job will be open again soon. You think about it, Toby, and let me know. You could start the first of next week."

Toby was already thinking before Bentley finished. He said, "I could also do carvings at night, and wrestle in the village on Sunday. And there are rabbits and turtles in the swamp, and we still have chickens. Maybe we can get by until something comes along. I will do this, Mr. Bentley. I will start the first of next week."

Bentley got up and said, "Let's go take a closer look at the damage."

Toby followed him outside, then they climbed onto the swamp buggy and headed south. Bentley drove rapidly over the smouldering ground, the buggy tires creating little black clouds of soot. They could see the charred bodies of rabbits, raccoons, armadillos, opossums, snakes and turtles. The deer, bear and wild hogs seemed to have outrun the fire to safety.

Bentley made a wide circle through the blackened swamp and then returned to the garage. He climbed off the buggy and said, "Well, I better find something to do and get with it before I change my mind and put a match to this place. It gets harder all the time just to survive, and sometimes it seems it just ain't worth the effort."

Toby went into the garage and put away his tools.

FIFTEEN

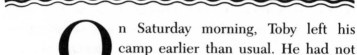

On Saturday morning, Toby left his camp earlier than usual. He had not visited his grandfather in more than two weeks and wanted to spend as much time with him this day as possible. He carried two bags of supplies he had purchased the night before.

He first turned the airboat west toward Allapattah Flats. When he reached the cove he took the cypress pole from the boat and made his way along the path.

Neither of the two remaining crocodiles were on the mud bank, but the dead ones were still there. Their flesh was rotted and torn into strips by vultures, and where the eyes had been there were now hollow sockets. Flies swarmed around the carcasses.

Toby knelt on the bank and searched the water for some sign of the others, then he looked at the carcasses and said, "I am sorry, old ones. I didn't want it to end this way for you. What happened to you is my fault. It was wrong for me to bring the white men here, and I will never do this again. I am sorry. But you shouldn't be there now where the others must lie."

He made his way around the end of the cove and approached the carcasses carefully. When he reached them he said, "I do not wish to come suddenly on your brothers in the bushes. Now is not the day for that."

The stink was overwhelming. Toby held his breath as he put the pole beneath one body and turned the crocodile over and over until he pushed it down a slight incline and into the water of the open bay. Then he rolled the other one in. "You will rest better in the water," he said. "It is not right for you to lie in the sun and be food for buzzards."

He then left the flats immediately and moved eastward. As he approached his grandfather's hammock he created his usual engine backfire and could see the old man come out of the palms and stand by the landing.

Toby embraced his grandfather and then took the packages from the boat. He said, "I am sorry to have been gone so long, Grandfather, but I worked on the weekend." The old man looked even more frail than during the last visit.

They walked up the path to the chickee and sat at the table. The old man said, "I saw great smoke in the north, and at night the sky was as red as the sunset. I was afraid you had been done harm."

"The fire didn't reach my camp," Toby said. "The south wind blew it north, and it did much damage around Monroe Station. All of the swamp buggies were burned at the hunting club, and many animals died in the woods."

"Fire is a bad thing," his grandfather said. "I have seen it leap over hammocks and race across the marsh like the wind, killing all in its way. I am glad it did you no harm."

Toby said, "I have brought many supplies, Grand-father. What would you like for your dinner?"

"You do not have it, but I would like deer. Many times lately I have hungered for the meat of the deer. That is what I liked most in my younger days. But I can hunt them no longer. I cannot go so far from the hammock."

Toby thought for a moment, and then he said, "If you want deer, you will have deer. I know a hammock where I've seen them lately. I will go kill one and then roast it over a fire. Is your shotgun in the chickee?"

"I did not mean for you to do that," the old man said quickly. "It was only foolish talk. I do not want you to go to such trouble for me."

"It will be no trouble at all. I will kill a buck and be back soon, and tonight you will have your fill of deer and eat until your stomach swells."

Toby went to the chickee and returned with an old double-barreled 12-gauge shotgun. He put a shell into each barrel, snapped the breech shut and said, "Gather some firewood while I'm gone, Grandfather. It will take a big fire to cook a whole deer."

The old man smiled. "I will have wood, and I will also make a spit for the roasting."

Toby pointed the airboat north toward a hammock a mile from the mouth of Lost Creek where he had seen deer the last time he passed that way. When he ap-proached the area he stopped the engine and poled the airboat through the sawgrass, not wanting the noise of the engine to frighten away the deer if they were still there.

He moved to the shore slowly, and then he crept into a thick clump of palmetto. At this time of morning the deer would be lying on the ground, resting after a night of feeding, and they wouldn't be as alert as they were at first dawn.

Toby moved catlike from bush to bush, making his way toward the center of the hammock; then he moved to one side of a muscadine vine and stopped. Fifty feet to his left, a spike buck and two does were lying on a bed of bear grass. The buck's ears were turned back, and his head was tilted upward in an alert position.

When Toby cocked the hammers, the buck jumped to its feet. Both barrels fired at once. The two does bounded off into a thicket as the buck fell to the ground and kicked violently. Toby dropped the shotgun and ran forward, then he grabbed the buck's antlers and slit its throat with his hunting knife.

As soon as the kicking stopped, Toby cut open the buck's stomach and cleaned out the insides. He would wait until he reached the hammock before skinning out the meat. It was a small deer, weighing no more than sixty pounds on the hoof, but it would do. He retrieved the shotgun and carried the carcass back to the boat.

He gave the airboat full throttle, wanting to reach the hammock as quickly as possible. It would take several hours for the deer to cook, and he hoped his grandfather had already started the fire.

Toby was not aware of the airboat coming up swiftly behind him. It was a sleek craft much faster than his, and he was surprised when it shot in front of him and the driver signalled for him to stop. Painted across the side were the words, "Game and Fish Commission."

Toby eased back on the throttle and cut the engine, gliding his boat to a stop. The other boat turned and came along side of him. The driver wore a green uniform and had a .38 pistol strapped to his belt.

The game warden looked into Toby's boat and said, "I heard your shots back there. Got a deer, huh?"

"Yes," Toby said, looking down at the buck. "I killed it for my grandfather. He is very old, and he lives on a hammock alone. He has wanted deer meat badly and can no longer hunt for himself."

The warden said, "Well, I guess you know deer's out of season now. That's an illegal kill."

Toby felt a pang of fear. He had not even thought of the season. He said, "I know it's not the season, but I killed only for food. It is for my grandfather, and it is only a very small deer."

"Size doesn't matter. A deer's a deer. I'll have to place you under arrest."

Toby was startled. He studied the man for a moment, noticing that the warden was the same age as himself. He said, "In the past I killed one out of season for Grandfather and was stopped by a warden. When I told him why I shot the deer, he only warned me not to do this again and let me go. I haven't killed one out of season since then, but now Grandfather has hungered for deer."

The warden said, "If someone else turned his back on something like this, he shouldn't have. He could have gotten himself in trouble. We're out here to enforce the law. What's your name?"

"Toby Tiger. I live on the Loop Road, and I come out

here each week to bring supplies to Grandfather."

"Well, I'm afraid you're in for a bit of trouble. Indians have to obey the game laws just like everyone else, and if you wanted to kill a deer for your grandfather this time of year, you should have driven up to the reservation where the game laws don't apply. I'm sorry, but you're in possession of an illegal kill."

"What does this mean you will do?" Toby asked, now thoroughly frightened.

"You'll have to go to court. You could get a fine or a sentence or both, or the whole thing could be dropped. It depends on the judge. But we'll also have to take the shotgun and your airboat. That's the law."

It took a moment for Toby to digest the meaning of what the warden said. "You cannot do this!" he finally exclaimed. "It's my grandfather's gun, and I only borrowed it. Without the gun he cannot shoot the rabbit. He kills only for food. And without the airboat I cannot bring supplies each week."

"You should have thought about all that before you killed the deer," the warden replied. He noticed Toby's deep anguish and said, "Tell you what I'll do, though. I'll give you a break. I'm supposed to take you in right now and let you post bond until the hearing. I'll write you up and let you report on your own Monday morning in Everglades City."

"You cannot do this!" Toby repeated angrily. "It is only one small deer! It's for my grandfather, and he is very old! He doesn't have many days left!"

The warden eyed the shotgun lying in Toby's boat, and then his hand moved to the pistol. He had been a game warden for only six months and had just been transferred into the Everglades from Ocala. This was his first encounter with a Seminole. For a moment he wished he hadn't stopped the airboat, or that he had let Toby go when he explained about his grandfather; but he surmised that if he let him go now, it would appear that he had backed away from a problem. He said, "Listen, fellow, I'm just doing my job, and I'm also trying to do you a favor. I've given you a choice. I can take you in right now, or I can let you come in on your own. Which will it be?"

Toby realized there was no way out except to do as the warden instructed, that to resist would only make things worse. He said, "I will come next Monday to Everglades City. Can I go now and take the deer to my grandfather?"

"I'll have to keep the deer in case it's needed as evidence." The warden reached across and pulled the small buck into his boat. "Where do you dock this airboat?"

"On Lost Creek, near the entrance to the marsh."

"Well, just leave it there and we'll pick it up later today. I need the shotgun now."

Toby handed him the gun.

The warden seemed relieved that the shotgun was now in his boat. He wrote on a pad and handed a copy to Toby, then he said, "Report to the justice of the peace court in Everglades City at eight Monday morning, and I want to tell you something for your own good. If you're not there, you'll be in deep trouble. This could be a very simple thing, and for your sake I hope it is. But you must be in the court Monday morning. Do you understand?"

"Yes, I understand," Toby replied. "I will be there."

The warden cranked his engine, and as he moved away he shouted over the roar, "Be sure you leave the key in the airboat!"

As Toby watched the boat speed away to the east, he had a deep sickening feeling. It would have hurt less if the warden had only let him keep the deer. The warden was of his own generation, not of the time of the ruthless destroyers his grandfather spoke of, yet the warden didn't understand. It seemed to Toby that the warden had no sympathy for his grandfather and those before him who had lived on this land for centuries before the game laws were passed, laws created and designed only to keep other white men from destroying all that lived in nature. He knew it was not his people who raped the land, and the Seminoles had lived always by their own law of killing only for need. Over the years Toby had seen hundreds of deer die from the drought or drown in floods caused by the white men and their dikes and canals, but now only one deer killed for food presented him such trouble. He was angry at himself for being caught, and he also felt deep hatred for the warden and all others who enforced the white man's law. He couldn't believe the small buck to be worth the shotgun and his airboat, plus a fine and whatever else lay before him in Everglades City.

He finally started his boat and went back to the hammock, this time keeping the engine as quiet as possible when he approached. He found his grandfather still sitting at the table, sipping a cup of freshly brewed coffee.

To one side of the chickee there was a pile of wood with a spit of lancewood constructed over it.

Toby took a seat opposite his grandfather and said, "I have done a bad thing, Grandfather. I let the gun fall out of the boat, and I couldn't hunt the deer. I have lost your shotgun."

The old man showed no surprise or anger. He said, "It does not matter about the gun, Toby. I have not needed it lately. The gun was old and had no value."

Toby said, "In the packages I have corned beef and potatoes. Would you like for me to make a pot of stew?"

"If you wish," he replied. "I have not felt well lately, and I am not hungry. If you make the stew, I will try some later."

"You'll be hungry as soon as the heat of the day passes. It is only the heat. I will make the stew and leave it for you. And I am sorry about the deer and the shotgun."

When he finished cooking, Toby came back to the table. The old man was slumped forward, asleep. Toby touched his shoulder and said, "I must go now, Grandfather. There are things I must do."

He snapped awake. "I am glad you came, Toby. It is always good when you are here."

Toby walked back to the airboat with his arm around the old man's shoulder. Before he got into the boat he said, "Grandfather, I'll be back next Saturday and bring you a rifle from my camp. On the way I will kill a deer, then I'll spend the night and we will have a feast together."

"That would be good," his grandfather said, smiling.

"The wood will be waiting, and I have already made a spit for the roasting."

When he reached the camp, Toby went into the bus, opened a beer and came back out to the chickee. Lucy was sitting by the grill. She said, "I didn't expect you back so soon. How is your grandfather?"

"I don't think he is well. He fell asleep at the table while I was cooking his stew, and he wouldn't eat. I have never seen him do this. Always before he has had an appetite. I have heard that when old Seminole men know they are dying, they wander off into the swamp alone, searching for the place of their birth. It wouldn't surprise me to go out there soon and find him gone."

"I wish he would come and live here," Lucy said. "He would be good company for me, and I would see that he gets proper food."

Toby took another drink of beer, not wanting to speak of what happened but knowing he must. He said, "Lucy, I'm in some trouble and you will have to know of it."

She looked up quickly, and then she came over and sat at the table. "What is it?"

He spoke hesitantly, "Grandfather said that he has hungered lately for venison. I took his shotgun, went to a hammock and killed a small deer. On the way back I was stopped by a warden, and he placed me under arrest. He also took grandfather's gun and will take my airboat later today. I have to be in court next Monday morning in Everglades City."

Lucy's face flushed with fear. She said, "What does

this mean? What will they do to you?"

"I do not know. The warden said I could get a fine or a jail sentence or both, or even nothing. It is up to the judge. But I'm sure they won't put me in jail for killing one deer. I will tell the judge why I did it and he will probably let me go with a warning."

"Why don't you see Mr. Bentley about this? He would go with you and help."

Toby shook his head in disapproval and said, "No, I'll not do that. Mr. Bentley has done enough for me already. I'll not bother him with this."

"He will help if you ask," Lucy insisted.

Toby wanted to minimize his trouble to Lucy and ease her concern. He said, "I am not worried about what will happen in the court Monday. We have more than enough money in the coffee can to pay the fine if that is what they do to me. What bothers me most is the airboat. I need it as much as the pickup. Maybe I can find another airboat with a bad engine and rebuild it myself as I did before. When I get back Monday I'll go down to the airboat place on the Trail and see what they have."

"Will you at least tell Mr. Bentley about this?" Lucy asked.

"Yes. I'll stop by there Monday morning and tell him, but there's no need for you to worry. The fine will not be so much for one deer, and I can soon save money again for the baby."

SIXTEEN

Dawn was breaking as Toby arrived at Monroe Station Monday morning. The garage was locked, so he went into the store. Several men were seated at tables, eating breakfast. Suzie Bentley was behind the cafe counter, but Big Jim wasn't there.

Toby sat on a stool and said, "Where can I find Mr. Bentley?"

Suzie turned away from a skillet of eggs and said, "He's not here right now, Toby. He went down to the south swamp just a few minutes ago, but he should be back in an hour. You need the garage key?"

"No, I don't need the key. When he gets back, please tell Mr. Bentley I can't work this morning. I have a trip to make and I'll be back as soon as I can."

"Yeah, I'll tell him, Toby. You want something to eat or some coffee?"

"Thanks, but I've already eaten," Toby replied. "I have to go now. Just tell Mr. Bentley I'll be back as soon as I can."

As Toby drove west he thought of the many times he had traveled this section of highway at dawn on his way to the road maintenance headquarters north of Cope-

land. For a long time he had been angry about the loss
of his job, but now he was glad he no longer had to drive
so far each day to and from work. And he enjoyed working at Bentley's much more than chopping bushes, cutting grass and replacing drainage culverts.

He also tried to convince himself that what he soon
faced in Everglades City would be minor and of no real
consequence. Even if the fine took all of his savings for
the rent and for the baby, he could replace some of it
with his work at Bentley's and by carving cypress figures
at night. Somehow, too, he would replace the airboat. Yet
all of his self-assurances couldn't erase a deep under-
current of fear.

When he reached the Highway 29 junction he
turned south to drive the final three miles into Everglades City. Once before he had been to this same courtroom with Josie Billie when Josie had to appear before
the judge and was fined thirty-five dollars for driving the
Mustang too fast along the Trail.

The streets of the town were deserted as the dust-
covered pickup ambled around a corner and parked in
front of a two-story stucco building that served as
town hall and courthouse. Paint on the windows and
doors was flaked in strips, and the old building seemed
to have settled into the muck earth and tilted to the left.

Toby was thirty minutes early, so he sat in the pickup
and watched as an occasional car rattled along the
street. In the distance he could hear the shrill cry of
sea gulls as they swarmed over the waterfront, searching
for food. When finally several people entered the building, he got out of the truck.

There was no one in the entrance foyer, but an arrow pointed upward to the Justice of the Peace Court. Toby climbed the wooden stairs to the second floor and entered a small room lined with benches. A deputy in uniform sat in a chair beside a closed door leading into an adjoining room. Toby sat on one of the benches and waited.

The deputy leafed through a file of papers, and shortly after eight o'clock he stood up and said, "Toby Tiger."

Toby was startled by the sound of his name coming from the stranger. He said apprehensively, "I am Toby Tiger."

The deputy opened the inner door and said, "In here."

The small room contained a large desk with several wooden chairs in front. On the right corner of the desk there was a small American flag, and on the left a state flag. Behind the desk, the wall was decorated with a framed copy of the Bill of Rights, a membership certificate in the Chamber of Commerce, a Kiwanis plaque, and a calendar from a sporting goods store in Naples. Pictured on the calendar was a scene of a man pointing a shotgun at a flight of ducks.

Toby sat in the room alone for several minutes, and then the judge entered from another door on the left. He was a man in his middle forties with thick hair bleached sun-yellow. His face looked as if he spent much time each day outdoors, and his walk was brisk as he came to the chair behind the desk and sat down.

The judge paid no heed to Toby as he examined papers on the desk, then finally he looked up and said,

"Your name, please."

"Toby Tiger."

The judge then said, "Do you know the nature of this court?"

"I am not sure," Toby replied.

"This is a justice court. We don't have trials by jury here. If you plead guilty, I will hear your case now and decide on the outcome. If you wish, you can request a jury trial in circuit court. In this event, you would then hire an attorney and your case would be heard in Naples. Do you understand?"

"Yes, I understand," Toby replied.

The judge asked, "What is your wish in this matter?"

Toby had not known he would have a choice, and he was not prepared for such a decision. He said, "I have done nothing wrong. What would be the cost of the attorney?"

The judge looked at Toby quizzically. "I can't tell you that. It depends on who you hire. There's no set fee but I'm sure it would run at least a thousand dollars to go into circuit."

"I cannot pay so much," Toby said, surprised by the figure.

The judge remained silent for a moment as he studied a piece of paper, then he looked again at Toby and said, "You are charged with deer poaching. It says here that Warden Simms apprehended you with an illegal deer in your airboat. Is this true?"

"Yes, this is true. He stopped me in the Glades as I was on my way to my grandfather's hammock with the deer."

"If this is true, and you say it is true, you would surely be found guilty in a circuit court. You would fare better here. Do you want me to hear the case or not?"

Toby was confused. He wished now he had done as Lucy insisted and brought Bentley with him. He responded, "If I would be found guilty in the court in Naples, there is no need to go there. And I don't have money for an attorney."

The judge looked annoyed as he said impatiently, "We have a full docket this morning and I can't spend all day on one case. You will have to give me a definite answer."

"We will finish it here," Toby said.

"Good. Now tell me what you have to say about this case."

"I have done nothing wrong."

For a moment the judge looked as Toby remembered the white teacher looking at him each day in the school classroom. He said, "Just tell me what happened. Can you do something as simple as that?"

"Yes." Toby turned his eyes directly to the judge as he spoke. "My grandfather is very old, and he lives on a hammock alone. He is not well, and he can no longer hunt for himself. Each week I carry supplies to him, as much as I can afford. When I went to the hammock that morning, Grandfather said he had hungered lately for deer. I took his shotgun and went to another hammock where I killed a small buck. I was on my way back to Grandfather's hammock to cook the deer when the warden stopped me."

"I understand your concern for your grandfather," the

judge said, "but didn't you know you were killing the
deer out of season?"

"I knew it was not the season, but I didn't think of it
at the time. I killed the deer only for food for my grandfather, and it was a very small deer."

"What you intended to do with the buck is not at
issue," the judge said. "When you killed the deer out of
season you knowingly broke the law. That is the only
thing at issue."

"But it was only for food," Toby stressed. "I didn't kill
without reason."

"There is no 'reason' when it comes to rules of law,"
the judge said. "You have either broken the law or you
haven't, and in this case, you have clearly broken the law.
When a case comes before this court I must act according to law, and the law applies to all people the
same. This is what we call equal justice before the law.
When a person breaks the law for any reason, he must
be prepared to pay the penalty. And we must protect our
wildlife or there will soon be no more. There is little
enough left now for everyone to hunt without someone
killing out of season. It is such acts as you committed
that will soon make our wildlife vanish. Do you understand what I am saying?"

Toby did not understand. He repeated, "I have done
nothing wrong. I killed only for food for my grandfather.
He is very old, and he has but a few days left. He has
lived all of his days in the marsh, but now he is too old
to hunt for himself."

The judge leaned back in the chair and looked
toward the entrance door. He said, "In this case I can do

nothing but find you guilty as charged. You have admitted this yourself. Your sentence will be a five-hundred-dollar fine and thirty days in jail. Because of the circumstances behind your breaking the law, I will suspend the thirty days and place you on one year's probation. You also owe twenty dollars for cost of court, and you can pay the fine and the court cost to the clerk downstairs."

Toby didn't move. For the first time that morning, he felt deep fear. He said, "I don't have five hundred dollars."

"Is there someone who can pay it for you?"

"I know no one who can pay so much."

"If you cannot pay the fine, you will have to serve the time in jail. A deputy will transport you to the jail in Immokalee."

Toby stood up, took a roll of bills from his pocket and said, "I have seventy-five dollars. I can pay this now and some each Saturday." He put the bills on the desk.

The judge picked up the money and handed it back to Toby. "All fines have to be paid in full. If you don't have all of the money, and you can't get someone to put up the rest, then you must serve the time. The deputy will escort you to Immokalee."

Anger suddenly flushed through Toby. He shouted, "No! I will not do this! I must take supplies to my grandfather each week, and my wife is with child!"

"One more outburst like that and you'll get an extra thirty days for contempt of court!" the judge said sternly. "This case is ended! Do you understand that?"

"And what of my wife, Lucy?" Toby asked, his voice now reflecting both defeat and concern. "Will someone tell her that I will be gone for awhile?"

"Where do you live?" the judge asked.

"On the Loop Road, about ten miles from Monroe Station."

"Do you live in chickees?"

"We live in a bus, but there is a chickee behind it. I rent the camp from a man in Miami. It will be easy to find."

The judge said, "I will have a deputy go by there and tell her that I will be gone for a while?"

"Where do you live?" the judge asked.
deputy stepped inside, and the judge said to him, "The prisoner is to be escorted to the jail in Immokalee in his own vehicle."

"Yes, sir, judge," the deputy said. "I'll get someone here right away."

Toby was not aware of the road or the traffic or the scenery or the deputy sitting beside him as he drove north to Immokalee. Even the details of the brief trial were but an incomprehensible blur in his mind. He was remembering the days when he was young and his father came into the camp with a deer he had killed for food for the family, and he was remembering tales told by his grandfather of white men coming into the marsh to slaughter the alligator for its hide and the egret for its plumes, white men killing deer and bear by the hundreds and selling the meat for two cents a pound, sometimes leaving the bodies on the ground to rot when there were too many to carry; but now he must leave Lucy and his grandfather for killing one deer for food.

He also thought of the many skeletons he had found in the marsh because the white men drained the land with canals, diked it and turned the water away, destroying food for the deer and other animals; and then his mind drifted to that morning when he watched helplessly as the white man pumped bullets into the crocodile's brain, shattering the life from it for no reason, and they didn't even take the man's rifle from him. It was impossible for him to put all of the pieces together and make sense or reason or justice from what the judge had done to him. He felt only deep bitterness.

He drove by instinct into the city limits and to the bright modern building housing the county's branch courthouse and jail. The deputy escorted him inside to a room where he was photographed and fingerprinted. His personal belongings were put into a brown envelope, and then he was led down a white corridor lined on both sides with cells.

SEVENTEEN

~~~~~~

Lucy moved the wooden spoon absently, unaware that she had stirred the pot continuously for more than an hour. It contained a small portion of chicken stew, but it was enough for one person. For most meals she ate only a piece of cold chicken or a tomato. In the intense heat it seemed pointless to her to sit by the grill and cook hot meals only for herself.

During the day she watered the garden and cleaned the bus and spent long hours at the sewing machine, mending and then re-mending Toby's clothes, or making something for the baby. Until the time she ran out of thread and cloth, she had made enough things for the birth of twins. She managed to keep busy during the days, but the nights were long and lonely and filled with sleepless hours.

A deputy sheriff did not come by and tell her the results of the trial until three days after Toby was jailed, and she was frantic with fear and anxiety when the green patrol car finally turned into the camp. Afterwards, she sat at the table beside the chickee, crying constantly for the better part of an afternoon. She gradually accepted the fact that Toby wouldn't be with her for a month.

She then went into the bus and examined the shelves and cabinets. There was a fair supply of staples such as flour, cornmeal and salt, and also a few cans of beans. She would have to do without milk, but there were chickens in the clearing, and she could shoot the rifle well enough to kill rabbits in the swamp. And there were vegetables in the garden. There would be enough to survive on for a month until he returned.

Many times during the coming days she thought of asking Bentley to take her to the home of her parents on the reservation so she could pass the time there. But each time she started to stand by the road and catch a ride to Monroe Station, she realized it was a long way to the reservation, and as Toby had said, this was not Bentley's problem. She didn't want to cause him bother.

Toby had been away for two weeks on the morning Lucy got out of bed feeling ill. Her head spun, and she steadied herself against a shelf. She thought immediately of morning sickness and thought it would soon pass.

When the dizziness did not stop, Lucy went to the refrigerator and poured herself a glass of cold water. Even early in the morning, the inside of the bus was like a furnace. Sweat poured from her forehead as she sat at the table and sipped the water.

She finally got up to go outside for fresh air, but when she approached the door, she again had to steady herself against a cabinet.

For several minutes she stood still, thinking perhaps it would be better to go back and lie on the bed. Sweat dripped into her eyes, hazing her sight, then she moved

instinctively toward the outside. Her foot caught on a
thin ledge beneath the door, causing her to pitch forward
and fall headlong to the ground.

She immediately tried to push herself up. Her arms
strained, but her swollen body would not move. Then
the dizziness became worse. When she looked upward,
the tops of cypress trees resembled vague, ghostly flights
of egrets. She then looked across the clearing, her eyes
searching for some sight of Toby coming along the path
from the swamp.

When she realized Toby would not come, she pictured him leaving the clearing at night with his gig,
dressed in the cut-off jeans she had patched so often, his
brown body glistening with shadows from the fire; and
she could see him running with the wind in the airboat,
moving with reckless abandon across vast stretches of
marsh, visiting the crocodiles he spoke of so often, carrying food to his grandfather, sitting by the fire at night
carving blocks of cypress into living things; remembering his defiance of her father . . . *God is everything . . .*
the water the trees the animals the land . . . they are kill-
ing God . . . His face in the swamp . . . shot God through
the head for a few fish . . .; thinking of his love of the old
ways, insisting she wear the traditional ankle-length
dress for their wedding in her father's church on the
reservation, coming to Toby's camp, hesitant, walking
hand in hand past lush beds of thick ferns in the swamp,
then beneath a cypress tree, and again by Lost Creek
with the moon playing its special magic, wondering
about him now, seeing him in all ways except in the jail
cell in Immokalee.

All of these thoughts suddenly merged into a mass of darkness. Her arms jerked as a sharp pain raced through her stomach. She tried once again to push herself up, but it was impossible. She whispered feebly, "Toby . . ." And then she lay still.

EIGHTEEN

~~~~~~

Toby's first few days in the cell were almost unbearable. He paced back and forth constantly, walking from wall to bars and back again, trying desperately to think of some way to get himself out of this impossible situation. The stale air choked his lungs, and he ached to be outside when the sun first reddened the sky and when the magical twilight hour came. He thought much of Lucy, wondering if she had enough to eat, hoping that Bentley or someone would visit her and see to her needs. He also worried about his grandfather and hoped that his supplies would last until he could get out of the cell and visit the hammock once again. Each day passed slowly and miserably as one week merged into another.

Toby was sitting on the bunk, looking without interest through a magazine, when he heard the key click in the cell lock. At first he thought it was his breakfast being served, but the man carried no tray. He motioned for Toby to come outside.

Toby hesitated, and then the guard said, "You can get your things in the office, Tiger. Your fine's been paid."

Realization came slow. "Who has done this?" Toby

asked.

"I don't know," the guard replied. "I was just told to let you out."

Toby followed the guard down the corridor and into a small office. Another man handed him the brown envelope containing his money and personal things. He pointed toward another door and said, "That way."

As soon as he entered the lobby he heard the word spoken loudly, "Toby!" It was Lucy's father. He came to Toby quickly and said, "We didn't know of this, Toby. If we had, you wouldn't be here. You should have sent word somehow."

"I didn't know of a way to do this," Toby said. "But who paid the fine? It was so much money."

"I paid half, and Mr. Bentley half. I wanted to pay it all myself, and he also wanted to send all of it. Then he insisted he at least pay half. Mr. Bentley didn't know of this until two days ago. When you didn't show up for work, he thought you had gone off to stay with your grandfather. He said had he known in the beginning, you would never have come to this jail."

"I will repay both of you," Toby said. "It was so much money."

"There is time later to think of that, and there's no hurry." Lucy's father then touched Toby's shoulder and said, "Let's sit over here for a moment, Toby."

They walked to a line of chairs against the lobby wall. Toby was anxious to get out of the building and return to his camp, but he knew that Lucy's father had something he wished to say, and Toby appreciated what he had done. He would listen patiently.

The reverend seemed hesitant, not wanting to speak further, and for a moment he just looked at Toby. Then he put his hand on Toby's arm and said, "It is about Lucy."

Toby said immediately, "Has something happened to her?"

"She will be fine," the reverend said quickly. "She is at our house on the reservation."

"Tell me what has happened!" Toby urged.

Lucy's father spoke slowly. "She got up one morning feeling sick, and then she fell from the bus. It was Mr. Bentley who found her. He had gone to the camp to inquire of you. Lucy had dragged herself to the chickee, and that is where the baby came."

"The baby came?" Toby questioned, his voice trembling with fear of what he would hear next.

"Yes, beneath the chickee. It was a boy. But he died, Toby. It was not his time, and he died before anything could be done for him. I am sorry. I hated to tell you of this."

Toby was silent with shock, feeling as if lead had been poured into his veins. "When did this happen?" he finally asked.

"Two days ago. I would have come here yesterday, but I broke the axle on my truck just as I left the reservation and had to fix it."

"And what of the baby?" Toby asked. "What was done with my son?"

"Mr. Bentley brought Lucy and the baby to the reservation. I buried him there in the cemetery beside the church."

Toby jumped up and said, "I will go there now!"

"Leave the truck and ride with me," Lucy's father said. "You shouldn't be driving now. We can return for your truck at another time."

Toby said nothing more as he rushed from the building and to his pickup. When he turned onto the road leading to the reservation, he pushed the old truck's accelerator to the floor, not caring if he broke the speed limit or if he smashed into a stray cow that wandered into his way. The hot asphalt zipped by in a blur, and soon he raced past the reservation entrance and skidded the truck to a stop in the clearing beside the church.

Dust drifted onto the porch as he ran up the steps and into the house. Lucy was in the parlor with her mother. She came to him quickly and cried, "Toby . . . Toby . . ."

As he held her in his arms he could feel fear draining from her as her frail body trembled against him. He said to her, "I'm sorry, Lucy. This would not have happened if I had been at the camp, and there is no reason for this."

Lucy looked at the anger and the hostility in his eyes, and then she said, "It was an accident, Toby. Don't blame yourself or anyone. It was only an accident. And I am so sorry about the baby."

"Where is the grave?" Toby asked.

"Beside the church, just inside the front gate. Pappa gave him a Christian burial."

"I will dig him up, and then he will lie on the hammock with my mother and my father and my grand-mother!"

Lucy stepped back, shocked and horrified by what

he said. She said, "Do not do this thing, Toby! Wait until Pappa gets here and speak with him first."

"I will dig him up!" Toby repeated. "He is my son and the grandson of my father, and he will lie with the others!"

Lucy's face whitened. She said, "Toby, please listen to me! Do not do this."

Before she could finish he raced from the room and to a shed behind the house. He grasped the shovel firmly as he ran to the side of the church and into the small cemetery. After removing a vase of flowers from the fresh grave, he struck the ground savagely. Dirt flew aside wildly as he started unearthing the coffin.

Just then Lucy's father ran into the cemetery. He pleaded, "Do not do this, Toby! You're on sacred ground! It is God's will the baby is dead, and now he is with the Lord!"

Toby stopped for a moment and said angrily, "It is not God's will! It is the will of the devil! It is the will of the white men who took me from Lucy!"

Lucy's father shook his head in anguish as Toby struck the ground again and again. Then Toby threw the shovel aside and snatched the small coffin from the grave. He took it in his arms, rushed back to the house and placed it in the back of the truck.

Lucy came outside. Toby turned to her and said, "We will go now."

Her eyes were moist as she said, "I cannot come with you, Toby. I am not well enough for the trip. I must stay here for a few days, and then Pappa will bring me home."

As Toby climbed into the cab, Lucy started to run

to him and try to reason with him again. Her father grabbed her arm and said, "No, Lucy! Now is not the time to interfere. He would not hear you. Let him go."

She watched as the pickup sped away from the house and disappeared down the road, then her father steadied her as she almost toppled forward into the dust.

NINETEEN

I t was noon when Toby reached the camp. He went into the bus and put on the warrior clothes and the medicine bag, then he opened a cabinet and took out the carved crocodile he had made for the baby. He put the wood against his knee and snapped it in half, carrying it with him out to the coffin.

He walked swiftly through the swamp, not seeing the birds or the barking squirrels or the rabbits that scurried out of his way. When he reached Lost Creek he went automatically to the airboat landing, but the boat was not there. Then he pushed the cypress dugout canoe into the water and placed the small coffin and the broken carving in the bow. He picked up the slender cypress pole and moved away silently down the creek.

When he reached the beginning of the marsh he paused for a moment, looking down at the coffin and the broken crocodile. He breathed deeply, as if trying to draw the marsh itself into his body, and then he moved the canoe swiftly into the sawgrass.

Night had come when Toby returned to the deserted camp. He went into the bus and flicked on the light switch. When nothing happened and the bus remained in darkness, he realized he had not paid the electric bill and the power had been cut off. This also meant that the well pump wouldn't work, and there would be no water in the camp. He lit a kerosene lamp and placed it on the table, then he opened the refrigerator for a beer, but there was none. He then went outside to the truck and drove away toward Monroe Station.

Several tables in the cafe were filled with people when Toby entered. He walked through the room and into the grocery section, finding Bentley behind the counter. Bentley noticed Toby's strange clothes and the turban but made no comment. He waited, and finally Toby said, "I thank you for what you have done, Mr. Bentley."

Bentley said, "It's O.K., Toby. But why didn't you let me know about this when it happened? If I'd known, you would never have gone to Immokalee."

"I didn't want to bother you with it," Toby said. He handed Bentley a roll of bills. "I have seventy-five dollars here, and I'll work out the rest as soon as I can."

Bentley refused the money. He handed it back and said, "Keep it, Toby. You might need it now for something else. We'll square up later."

"It is yours if you wish," Toby said.

"No," Bentley said again. "We'll square up later."

"The electricity has been cut off at my camp," Toby said. "Do you know how much it is that I owe?"

Bentley looked in a card file on a shelf, then he said, "It's twenty-five dollars. I didn't realize it was past due."

Toby counted out the money and handed it to

Bentley, and then Bentley said, "I'll see to it that the power is turned on again first thing in the morning."

Toby handed another bill to Bentley and said, "I would like two cartons of beer."

Bentley took the beer from a cooler, put it into a paper bag and handed it and the change to Toby. He said, "I'm sorry about Lucy and the baby. Real sorry. That was a bad thing to happen."

"He is fine now. I took him this afternoon to the hammock of my mother and my father and my grandmother. He is with the others now, and he is at peace."

Bentley said, "Toby, take a few days to yourself before you come back to work."

Toby picked up the package. "I may do this. And I thank you again for what you have done for me and for Lucy."

All of the people in the cafe had noticed Toby when he had entered and had watched him curiously. As he passed back through the room, one man sitting alone laughed and said loudly, "What kind of an outfit is that you got on, chief? I didn't know they had a cowboy and Indian circus going on out here in the swamp."

Toby turned to the man. He whipped the knife from its sheath and slammed it into the top of the table, and then he said bitterly, "Shut your mouth, you goddam chicken snake! Or I will slit you open like a fish!"

The man looked at the intense anger in Toby's face and at the long knife imbedded in the wood. He moved his chair backwards as he said, "I'm sorry, fellow. I didn't mean anything. I was just trying to be funny."

Toby jerked out the knife and tightened his grip on

the handle as he moved the blade towards the man's throat. Steel touched flesh before he hesitated and said, "What is it that's so funny, chicken snake?" Then he rammed the knife back into the sheath and left hurriedly.

For a moment no one in the cafe seemed to breathe, and even the noisy air conditioner lost its sound. The man finally turned to Bentley and said, "What's the matter with that fool Indian? Is he crazy?"

Bentley looked toward the door and then back to the table. He said, "No, he's not crazy. I guess he's just had about all he can cut. You're lucky he didn't slice you up like a watermelon. You better learn when to keep your mouth shut."

The man took a deep drink of beer, wiped his mouth and said again, "I was just trying to be funny, that's all. I didn't mean anything by it."

TWENTY

For two days Toby stayed in the camp alone. He would sit at the table for a time and carve cypress blocks, then he would get up and pace back and forth across the clearing. Several times he walked through the swamp to the empty airboat landing on Lost Creek, poled the old dugout canoe to the edge of the marsh and stared intensely toward a distant hammock. He also wore the medicine bag constantly, sometimes talking to it as if speaking to Lucy or his grandfather.

On the third morning he left the camp early and drove past the Osceola Village to the Gator Airboat Sales. When he reached the place he parked in front of a small office and walked through the sales lot. Several airboats were on trailers, and others rested on the bank of a creek leading into the marsh.

As Toby looked carefully at the boats, a man came from the office and joined him. Toby said, "Hello, Mr. Thompson."

"Hi, Toby," the man replied. "What can I do for you?"

"I need a boat."

Thompson said, "A warden told me what happened with the deer. I didn't know it was you, though, until they brought your boat in here for storage. What'd they do to you?"

Toby was surprised that Thompson knew, and also surprised that his boat was here. He said, "I went to court in Everglades City. The fine was five hundred dollars or thirty days in jail, and I didn't have the money."

Thompson whistled. "Five hundred bucks or thirty days for one deer! You must have caught Judge Lambert. He's a real bastard. Last year him and three other guys got caught shooting doves on a baited field out from Clewiston. Got off scot-free. He fined a friend of mine a hundred bucks for having one bass over the limit. Too bad you didn't have a faster boat, Toby. You could have outrun the warden."

Toby said, "Do you have another boat with a bad engine like I bought before?"

"Sure don't. I only have a few used boats in stock. You want to see what I have?"

"Yes. I must have a boat."

Toby followed Thompson to the bank of the creek, then Thompson pointed and said, "These three."

Toby glanced briefly at the boats and said, "Which is the cheapest?"

"Well, they're all in top shape. The one on the end I could let go for twelve hundred."

The figure was impossible to Toby, but he knew he must have a boat even if it took him the rest of his life to pay for it. He said, "I have forty dollars to pay down, and the rest I'll pay each Saturday."

The man shook his head. "Can't do that, Toby. We have to have a third down on used boats. That would run you four hundred."

"I could pay more each Saturday."

"Just no way. But why don't you buy your old boat back? They'll sell it at auction, and boats don't bring much of nothing that way."

Toby had not thought of this. He asked anxiously, "When will they sell it?"

"Probably three or four weeks. Whenever they get around to it."

"I can't wait that long," Toby said, disappointed. He looked down the bank at his boat. "I will have to do something sooner."

As Toby walked back to his truck, Thompson called after him, "You get some more money, Toby, come back and see me. That boat's in top shape. It can outrun any of those patrol boats."

Toby drove back west and stopped when he reached Osceola Village. As he walked through the souvenir store, he wished he had brought the few finished carvings with him. He met Josie coming from the pits, and they went to the chickee together.

Josie poured two mugs of coffee and said, "I heard what happened. I was up by your camp one day and Lucy told me. That's a hell of a note, so much trouble over one deer. Lucy was very worried. How is she?"

"She's at the reservation."

"Why is she there?" Josie asked.

"You don't know?"

"I know nothing more than I've said. She seemed fine except that she was concerned for you. Why did she go to the reservation?"

Toby said, "She fell from the bus one morning while I was gone. The baby came, and it died. She is spending a few days with her mother and father before she returns to the camp."

Josie was surprised. Sympathy crossed his face as he said, "I didn't know, Toby. I'm sorry. You seem to have much bad luck lately."

Toby didn't want to discuss it further. He said, "I tried to buy a used airboat, but the cheapest was twelve hundred. I couldn't make the down payment and they wouldn't take less. I haven't taken supplies to Grandfather since they let me out of jail, and I must have a boat."

"I can let you have fifty dollars," Josie said.

Toby said, "I appreciate the offer, but that wouldn't be near enough. They want four hundred down and I have only forty. But there is a way. My boat is stored at Gator Sales. Mr. Thompson says it will be sold at auction in a few weeks, and that it will bring little. I might have enough money by then to buy it back, but I can't wait that long. I will take it back."

"You mean steal it?" Josie asked.

"How can I steal what is mine? They shouldn't have taken it from me in the first place. I did nothing wrong. I will take only what is mine."

"Well, if you get caught, you know what will happen," Josie cautioned. "That is as bad as stealing a car."

"I don't give a damn about that!" Toby said harshly. "If someone comes on me, I will stick a knife in them."

Josie eyed Toby curiously, and then he said, "In that case, I hope you're not caught. Then you would be in more trouble than you've ever known."

Toby said, "If you'll drive me down there tonight, I will wire the ignition and go across the marsh in the darkness. I can hide the boat on Lost Creek."

"Is that all you want me to do, take you down there?"

"Yes."

Josie sighed. "I will do that, Toby, but nothing more. You've almost gotten me into jail before. It would seem that you like it in Immokalee."

"No one will see," Toby insisted. "And I must have a boat now."

"I will pick you up at your camp late this afternoon. But if you'll not do this thing, I will pass the hat around the village and try to raise the down payment."

Toby said again, "I will only take what is mine."

It was an hour after dark when Josie let Toby out of the Mustang just west of Gator Sales. Josie said, "Be careful, Toby. Don't let anyone see you or you'll be in great trouble, much more than the deer. And if you do get caught, don't do something foolish. The airboat is not worth it."

Toby made no response. He put on the medicine bag and strapped the long warrior knife to his side, then he took a pair of wire cutters from the car and walked slowly along the edge of the highway. When he reached the creek he went down the bank and directly to his boat. The sales office was bathed with light from several floodlights, but the place was deserted.

Toby's boat was chained and locked to a post. He cut the chain with the wire cutters and pushed the boat backward into the water, then he got in and poled it down the creek.

Two miles out into the marsh he stopped and looked back at the glow of the floodlights. Ahead of him lay vast stretches of darkness. He then wired the ignition, started the engine and moved away slowly.

From this point to Lost Creek was more than twenty-five miles, and he would have to run at less than half speed and be very careful. Once when running the boat on the marsh at night he had hit a stump, thrown himself out and damaged the boat. This night he wanted no injury to himself or to the boat.

There was no moon, and the hammocks were ghostly forms drifting on a sea of darkness. Several times he heard loud thumps beneath the airboat as he ran over either logs or alligators. He drove the boat by instinct, searching constantly for sights of things familiar. When finally he came to a solid line of pond cypress, he knew he had reached the edge of the swamp. From here he veered west, and soon afterwards he found the mouth of Lost Creek.

When he reached his landing he took the airboat farther up the creek than usual, then he pulled it onto the bank and covered it with bushes and palmetto fronds.

He had to feel his way slowly through the black swamp, and when he approached the camp, the clearing was bathed with flickering light from a fire beneath the chickee. This startled him, and he moved forward cautiously. Then he saw that Lucy was there. She was sitting by the grill, cooking something in the pot.

She jumped up when he came from the shadows. "I have wondered where you were," she said, coming to him. "Since your truck is here I thought you would be in the swamp. Pappa brought me late this afternoon."

He took her in his arms and said, "I am glad you are here. I have been lonely without you."

She was pleased that he missed her. "Have you eaten yet?" she asked. "I've been keeping a supper hot for you."

"No, I have not eaten, and I'm starved."

Toby ate ravenously, and then they talked. He said, "I have the airboat back. I will go tomorrow and take supplies to Grandfather."

"How did this happen?" she asked.

"It was stored at the airboat sales place on the Trail. I took it from there."

"You took it?" Lucy questioned. "They didn't give it back to you when the fine was paid?"

"No, I took it. I've just brought it across the marsh to Lost Creek."

Worry crossed Lucy's face. She said, "Toby, do you mean you have stolen the boat?"

"How can I steal what is mine? I took back only what belongs to me. They have no right to my boat."

"Will this not mean great trouble?"

"No. The boat is well hidden. They will not find it if they look. And I must take supplies tomorrow to Grandfather. It would take too long in the canoe and it wouldn't hold as much."

"I'm afraid, Toby," she said, her face creased with concern. "I don't want anything more to happen to us. I wish you would take the boat back right now."

"No, Lucy!" he said. "It is mine, and I must have it to visit Grandfather."

TWENTY-ONE

Toby was at Monroe Station shortly after dawn. He planned to speak to Bentley about his delay in taking the job, but Big Jim was not there; so he purchased two bags of supplies from Suzie Bentley and then drove back to the camp hurriedly.

He left the camp immediately and made his way to the place on Lost Creek where he had hidden the airboat. After uncovering and loading the boat, he moved cautiously to the edge of the marsh. For several minutes he searched the horizon, making sure that no other airboat was nearby, then he gunned the engine and glided swiftly across the sawgrass, watching constantly for the sight of any moving thing.

The marsh remained as deserted as usual, and Toby ran the airboat at top speed. Soon he approached his grandfather's hammock, but when he made the engine backfire in salute, the old man did not appear on the shore.

Toby left the packages in the boat and walked swiftly along the path. He first sighted the cooking chickee, and there was no fire. This filled him with apprehension, for the fire was never allowed to go out. Then he walked directly to the sleeping chickee.

The old man was lying on the palmetto bed, his eyes closed and his face pale. Toby moved toward him with dread. He lay very still, and flies swarmed around his face.

Toby knelt slowly and touched his grandfather's shoulder. He stirred feebly, and then he looked up. For a moment he said nothing, as if he didn't know who was there, and then he whispered, "Is it Toby?"

"Yes, Grandfather, it is me. I have brought many things, and I'm sorry to have been gone for so long."

"Were you not here only yesterday?"

"No, Grandfather, I was not here. But I will stay now as long as you wish. I will build a fire and then cook food."

The old man waved his hand. "No, Toby. I am not hungry. But I would have coffee. I have not had coffee for many days."

"You will have both," Toby said. "I'll go to the boat and get the supplies, then I will make coffee and a stew. You will be hungry when you smell the pot."

Toby's face was drawn as he went to the boat and brought back the two packages. He knew his grandfather was dying, and his mind was tormented with guilt for having been away for so long.

He started a fire and filled the coffee pot, and then he put a pot of beef stew on the grill. When he went back to the chickee, the old man pushed himself to a sitting position. He then arose slowly and said, "I will sit with you beside the fire."

Toby helped him walk to a palm tree beside the table.

He eased himself to the ground, leaned back against the trunk and said, "The water will soon be gone, Toby. I have seen no fish around the hammock. But I do not seem to be hungry lately. I have made a few cakes of the cornmeal."

Toby said, "Well, you will eat now. I have brought enough to last many days. But you'll not need supplies. You will go back to my camp with me."

The old man's eyes flashed. He said firmly, "No, Toby! I will not do this! I will not leave the marsh! If you take me from here, I will never know peace."

Toby understood. He knew that he himself would have known no peace if he had not brought his son into the marsh. He said, "I will do as you wish, Grandfather. But now you must drink your coffee."

He took the cup eagerly and sipped the hot liquid, seeming to gain strength from Toby's presence. He said, "Do not ever grow old and unneeded, Toby. It is a bad thing to be old and alone. All I have ever known is now no more. Sometimes at night I listen to the thunder of the airplanes passing by, and I think of the days when only the egret and the heron crossed the sky. I am no more a part of this world. It is good that I go now."

"Don't say such things, Grandfather. You're needed by me. And you're going nowhere except to eat stew."

The old man watched as Toby dished up a bowl of broth. He said, "Is it the meat of the deer?"

Toby had forgotten his promise to kill another buck, and he noticed that the pile of firewood and the spit were still beside the chickee. He said, "Yes, Grandfather. It is a very small deer, and the meat seems to be tender."

He put his arm around his grandfather's back and then put the spoon to his mouth.

The old man swallowed, and then he said, "It is good, Toby, and just what I wanted. I thank you, but that is enough. I am not hungry. Maybe I will eat more later." He leaned back against the palm trunk. "How is Lucy?" he asked. "And what of the baby? Will you bring him here when the time comes?"

"She's fine, and I will bring my son here soon. You will teach him much, and he will learn to spear fish and to know the marsh as you know it."

"That is good." The old man suddenly grasped Toby's hand. He said, "There is one thing you must promise me, Toby!"

Toby felt the grip tighten. "What is it, Grandfather?"

"You will take me to the hammock with the others, and I will be with them. There is no one left but you to do this. And you must not take me away from here first. I do not wish to leave the marsh."

Toby said, "You're talking foolish, Grandfather. I will take you to the hammock when the time comes, and I have already said that you will never leave the marsh."

The grip on Toby's hand weakened. His grandfather said, "Toby, do you yet have the ancient medicine bag?"

"Yes, Grandfather, it's at my camp, and I have worn it many times since you gave it to me."

"Use it wisely, Toby, for it is a sacred thing. It will take you to the Great Spirit in the sky. There is a place we will be together again. It is but a short journey. We will soon . . ."

He suddenly slumped forward and was dead.

Toby dropped to his knees and buried his face in his hands, crying unashamedly for a long time, then he picked up his grandfather gently and carried him to the palmetto bed beneath the chickee. He covered him with a blanket, and then he touched the still form and said, "You will not leave the marsh, Grandfather. I'll be back soon to do as I promised. You will rest now, and you will never again be alone."

~~~~~~~~~~~~~~~~

As soon as Toby came into the camp, Lucy knew. His face was lined with grief. She said, "He's gone, isn't he?"

"Yes," Toby answered. "He died while I was there. I left him on the hammock because that is what he asked in his last words. There was no food in his chickee, and he wouldn't eat what I prepared. If I hadn't gone there today, he would have died alone."

"I'm sorry," Lucy said. "I should have gone with you to see him more often, but I didn't know he was so ill. I only wish he would have come here and spent his last days with us."

Toby sat at the table and said, "That is not what he wished, Lucy. He was very old, and all that he loved is now gone. He knew only the old ways in the marsh, and that is how he wished his life to end. When he left me there beside the chickee, it was more than the death of an old man, it was the end of a time known only by Grandfather and others before him. There will be no more such as he, and it is now all ended. But it would have been a bad thing for him to die alone."

For a moment Toby became silent, looking back toward the swamp, and then he arose and said, "I will go now to Lowry's sawmill and get planks for the coffin, then I'll go to the Hughes Store and call Josie to come and help. I cannot handle everything alone."

Lucy said, "Should you also call Pappa and ask him to come?"

"No," Toby said quickly. "We will take him to the hammock, and it will be in the old way. You will wear the long dress and also the beads. It will be in the Seminole way, the way of my mother and father and my grandmother. I promised this to Grandfather."

When he returned from the sawmill, Toby sat in the clearing and constructed a crude coffin of cypress planks. It was late afternoon when Josie Billie arrived. Toby immediately said to Lucy, "We'll dress now and then leave for the hammock. I don't want Grandfather to be out there alone."

Toby put on the warrior clothes and the medicine bag and came back outside to wait with Josie. Lucy soon came from the bus wearing the multi-colored long dress. Around her neck there were a dozen strands of glass beads, and she had pulled her long hair into a bun held tight with a hairnet. Josie still wore his usual faded dungarees, but he had on one of the traditional Seminole shirts.

Toby and Josie picked up the coffin, and Lucy followed them down the narrow trail leading through the swamp and to Lost Creek. The sawgrass was undergoing its rainbow change of colors and images as the airboat slowly entered the edge of the marsh. Flights of egrets and herons moved westward into the dim red glow of the day's final light. It would soon be that magical moment when all sound and motion ceases, that brief interlude when day creatures become still and night creatures awaken. Toby and Josie searched the marsh for any sign of other airboats, but there were none.

The airboat cut a steady path through the wall of grass, and soon they approached the hammock. Toby made the engine backfire, and for a moment he expected to look up and see his grandfather standing there on the shore; but the reality of the cypress coffin in the boat told him otherwise.

Lucy went ahead of them and built a fire as Toby and Josie carried the coffin to the chickee. Toby lifted his grandfather and placed him inside, but before he nailed down the top, he placed a carved figure of a deer beside the body.

Lucy made a supper from the supplies Toby had brought that morning, but none of them ate much. Several times Toby left the fire and walked along the dark shore, listening to frogs and searching the night for something that was not there. Sleep came to none of them until close to dawn.

As soon as the first shaft of light cut through the thick caggage palms, Toby and Josie loaded the coffin back into the airboat. Toby gathered all of the pots and dishes and put them into a cloth sack, then he tied his grandfather's old dugout canoe behind the airboat and the procession moved again into the sawgrass.

The hammock was small, not as large as the grandfather's hammock, and it was thickly covered with cabbage palms and dwarf cypress. The edge of the water was lined thickly with button brush, making it necessary for Toby to ram the boat through the foliage to reach the shore.

Once again the coffin was lifted from the airboat, Toby and Josie carrying it inland with Lucy following. They stopped when they entered a small clearing. Placed at random on the ground there were four coffins, three large and one small, and all but the small one were deeply weathered. They placed the new one in the center of the others.

Toby went back to the boat and returned with the cloth sack, a length of rope and a hatchet, then he pulled the cypress canoe into the clearing and placed it beside the coffin. He cut thin cypress poles and tied them with rope, making a frame over the coffin. Then he took a rock, dented all of the pots and threw them on the ground. He smashed the dishes against the edge of the coffin.

For several minutes he stood by the crude box in silence, and then he said, "I'm sorry, Grandfather. I left you alone for too long. You were a good and kind man, and I loved you. There are none left such as you. You will be happy now in the sky, for there are many good things there, and the wind is soft. You are with the others now, and you will never again be alone."

He picked up his grandfather's lancewood spear, snapped it in half and put it on top of the coffin, then he turned to Lucy and said, "It is done. He is where he wished to be. We will go now."

As they started out of the clearing, Toby hesitated for a moment. He grasped the medicine bag tightly, then he looked back at the coffin and said, "I will use it wisely, Grandfather."

TWENTY-THREE

The next morning Toby paced back and forth across the clearing. Several times he went alone into the swamp, and when he returned, he sat at the table in silence. Lucy would speak to him and receive no answer. She knew he was grieving, so she did not try to force herself into his silent and private world.

At noon he refused food, then he got into the pickup and drove away, and it was late afternoon when he returned. He had a thick cardboard box in the back of the truck.

For supper he ate only a few bites of food, and then he went into the bus. When he came back outside he was dressed in the warrior clothes, and the medicine bag hung from his neck. Lucy looked at him quizzically and said, "Why are you wearing those things now? Are you going back to the hammock?"

"I am going to the Osceola Village to see Josie," Toby responded, "and I'll not be gone too long."

It was night when he parked in front of the souvenir store. Children were running around the village chasing each other, and several dogs were fighting over a pile of chicken bones.

Josie and Frank Willie were sitting on the ground beside the chickee, a bottle resting between them. Josie looked up and said, "Hello, Toby. You want a drink? Frank and I are trying to get over the day in the pits."

"I suppose so," Toby said absently, his eyes looking as if he already had too much to drink although he had drunk nothing. Josie noticed this.

Frank Willie got up and said, "I've had enough. I'll go and eat now, and maybe I'll see you later."

Toby sat on the ground and sipped the whiskey. Josie said, "Why are you dressed like that tonight?"

Toby didn't answer. He said instead, "My grandfather didn't weigh even a hundred pounds when he died, and he was once a strong man. There was no food in his chickee, and he said he could no longer find fish. It's the water. Everything will die without water."

Josie said, "It is bad, but maybe we'll get rain soon."

"It is not just that. The white men have turned the water away from the land. I will put it back into the marsh before everything dies just like grandfather."

Josie looked closer at Toby. He said curiously, "And how will you do that?"

"I'll blow a hole in the dike. I have dynamite in the truck that I bought today in Everglades City. Then I will turn water back into the marsh."

Josie shook his head in disbelief of what he was hearing. He said, "Toby, you're not serious, are you? If putting water in the marsh is your purpose, you should as soon stand on the dike and pee. It would do as much good. You would have to fill all the drainage canals and then drop a bomb on the dike at Lake Okeechobee. Then you would get water. But what you say would be only a trickle."

"It would help."

Josie feared for Toby. He said, "Don't do this foolish thing, Toby. You are getting in deeper and deeper. It's not worth it, and sooner or later you're going to get caught. I ask you as my friend, please do not do this thing."

Toby ignored Josie's plea. He said, "Without water, everything out there will die. And the medicine bag will protect me from harm." He got up. "I will see you later. Maybe I'll stop by here on my way back."

Josie watched with anguish as Toby walked from the village.

Five miles east of the village Toby parked the pickup beside the highway. The drainage canal ran parallel to the south side of the road with the dike on the opposite bank.

He put the box on his head and waded into the water, finding that it was no more than chest deep. The long dress clung to his body as he came out on the other side. He took his knife and dug a hole into the side of the dike, then he inserted the dynamite. The fuse was extra long to give him time to go back across the canal and get away, and he hoped it would be enough.

When he finished he climbed to the top of the dike and gazed briefly over the silent marsh, then he went back and put a match to the fuse.

He moved across the water as quickly as possible, and then he ran up the bank to the pickup. He had not noticed the two cars approaching in different directions, and just as he reached the truck, the beaming headlights centered on him. He froze. The light caught in the egret plumes on the turban, causing them to sparkle like fireflies.

Toby had not expected this. He either hesitated too long or the fuse was too short, and suddenly a tremendous boom came out of the darkness. Dirt showered across the highway and onto the top of the pickup, and Toby was knocked flat by the concussion.

One of the cars swerved wildly and then righted itself. It slowed but did not stop. The other was pelted by dirt clods as it sped away from the explosion.

Toby jumped up and scrambled into the truck. Tires screamed as he rammed the accelerator to the floor and raced away into the night. He did not slow the old vehicle as he went past the Osceola Village heading north to his camp.

TWENTY-FOUR

Toby spent all of the next day carving cypress figures. When he arrived at the camp the night before, Lucy noticed the wet, dirt splattered clothes. She wondered about this but did not question him, and he made no comments as she washed them and hung them on a line beside the chickee to dry.

It was after noon the next day when he put the carvings aside. He looked at Lucy as if finally making a decision. "We have no money left in the camp," he said. "Not even a dollar. Tomorrow I'll go to work for Mr. Bentley. I'll go now and tell him, and maybe tomorrow night I can take the carvings to Josie."

It worried Lucy that he did nothing but sit around the camp in a depressed mood, and this news made her smile. She said, "That's good, Toby. I'm glad this is what you wish to do."

When Toby reached Monroe Station, Bentley was not there. He told Suzie Bentley what he intended, and then he purchased milk, bread and bacon, promising to pay for the items at the end of the week.

Toby noticed the car just before he turned into the camp entrance. It was a green patrol car with a red flasher on top. Lucy was standing by its side, talking to the driver. Fear raced through him like fire in the swamp. He gave the pickup gas and moved past the camp quickly; then two miles down the road he pulled to the rear of a deserted cabin and stopped. Sweat poured from his face, and his hands trembled. As he thought of those days he spent in the jail in Immokalee, he was flooded with a feeling of near panic. It was an hour before he turned the truck and drove back toward the camp.

The patrol car was gone, so he pulled the pickup to the rear of the bus. Lucy came to him immediately. Her voice trembled as she said, "Two men from the sheriff's department were here looking for you. They said they must ask questions. What is this, Toby?"

He did not mention that he had already seen the patrol car at the camp. He asked, "What did you tell them?"

"I only said you were not here. They said they will come again. Is it about the airboat? Do they know?"

"It is more than the airboat," Toby said, his voice hesitant. "I have blown up a dike and done other things. But I don't understand how they could know. If they come again, tell them I'm not here. I must have time to decide what to do."

Before she could speak further, Toby turned and hurried across the clearing and into the woods.

Late that afternoon Josie Billie drove into the camp. Toby was in the edge of the swamp, watching the clearing, and at the sight of the red Mustang he came back to the chickee.

They sat at the table for several minutes with no word spoken, as if some silent understanding was passing between them. Josie's face reflected worry. He finally said, "Toby, there were deputies at the village today asking questions. From things they said, I think they know."

Toby showed no surprise. He said, "Know what?"

"About the airboat and maybe the dike."

"How could they know?"

"I can't answer this, but I think they suspect it was you. Maybe they figure it would be only you who would go past a line of new airboats and then take an old one such as you did."

Lucy was sitting by the grill, listening. With each word her face grew paler.

Josie then asked, "Did anyone see you when you blew the dike?"

"Two cars approached from different directions as I came back to the truck. The fuse was too short, and it blew just as the cars reached my pickup."

"They were asking about the clothes," Josie said. "Have you ever worn them elsewhere?"

Toby thought back to the night when he rammed the knife into the table at Bentley's. He said, "You know I have worn them to your village, and I also wore them once in the store at Monroe Station."

"Damn!" Josie exclaimed. "Why did you wear them when you blew the dike? No one else but you has things like that. Why didn't you just put a neon sign on your back?"

"I didn't think anyone would see."

Josie thought for a moment, and then he said, "Well, that's really no problem. You can hide the clothes in the swamp and there's no way they can prove it was you. You can lie like a white man. Swear you have never been near that dike. And they can prove nothing about the airboat if no one saw you. We'll take it into the marsh and leave it on a hammock, then you will be rid of it."

Toby said, "There is nothing you can do they will not know. They have eyes that see everything except what they don't wish to see."

What Toby said had no meaning to Josie. He said, "I'll come here at noon tomorrow. I have to be at the village in the morning or I'd come sooner. You can take the airboat into the marsh, and I will follow in the canoe. We'll leave it on a hammock and that will be the end of it. There is no way they can prove anything if you admit nothing."

Toby spoke absently, "They are like the hawk flying over the marsh, seeing everything that moves. Even the smallest creature isn't safe from them."

Josie got up and said, "Toby, you're not making sense. Just keep out of sight, and hide the clothes in the swamp as soon as possible. After tomorrow, there will be no need to worry. I will see you at noon."

Toby did not watch as Josie got into the Mustang and drove off. Lucy came to the table and said, "What will you do, Toby?"

"I don't know."

"If you don't wish to do as Josie says, you could go see the deputy and tell him what you've done. Maybe it's not so bad as you think. Mr. Bentley would do all he can to help. And if you do as Josie says, they may never know."

Toby looked across the clearing toward the darkening swamp. His eyes were in deep thought as he said, "Lucy, I have done these things, but not without reason, and now the sky is falling on me. I am being crushed by the white men, just as our people were crushed by them in the past; but I cannot fight them as our people fought. If I fight back I will lose, and that would bring shame and dishonor to the name of my father and my grandfather and those before them. They never lost, but there is no way I can win. If there was I would try. But they will never put me in a cage again. Never! I was born free in the marsh, and I cannot live in a cage."

His words caused Lucy to become even more alarmed. She said, "But you have done nothing so bad, Toby. It is not as you think."

He got up from the table and said, "I will stay in the swamp tonight. If they come again, say I'm not here."

"But you must eat first," she insisted.

"I am not hungry now. I will eat when I return at dawn."

Toby stopped several times as he walked through the swamp, picking leaves from ferns, crushing them in his hands and smelling the sharp fragrance. He watched with interest as squirrels jumped from limb to limb, making their way to their nests for the night. He paused once and let a mother raccoon with her young pass in front of him.

When he reached Lost Creek the light faded, bringing on the silent time. He paused momentarily by his airboat landing where the grass was bare from the many times he had pulled the boat onto the bank. Then he made his way along the path by the creek.

A south wind rustled the sawgrass as he moved instinctively toward the knoll of high land where he had watched the moonrise with Lucy. He sat on the ground and waited, but there was no moon. Ahead of him lay only darkness. He tried to distinguish hammocks from sawgrass but could not do so.

As he sat alone his thoughts drifted from fragment to fragment, dwelling on no one thing but briefly remembering happenings long forgotten and some still vivid — the day he speared his first fish and killed his first deer, smells of food cooking over open fires, the blood on his arm when bitten by a small alligator because he was careless, stripping naked and running through clear water, his first ride on the yellow bus to Everglades City, taunts by white children as he entered school, his fascination when first discovering the crocodiles at Allapattah Flats, vomiting violently after the fire, moving again and again to new hammocks, his first sight of Lucy, walking together into the night, loving beneath the cypress tree, the death cry of a coot suddenly caught in the jaws of allapattah, frustration and anger at the death of the crocodiles, the warden and the judge in Everglades City, pacing back and forth in the jail cell after the airboat suddenly came in front of him, the small coffin, death without reason, the frailness of his grandfather as he placed the lifeless form on the palmetto bed beneath the chickee. He looked into the darkness and all of these things paraded silently through the night. He clutched the ancient medicine bag hanging from his neck, seeking guidance. And then it came to him from the marsh, whispered softly across the somber stretches of endless sawgrass, the last words of his grandfather, *There is a place we will be together again. It is but a short journey.*

TWENTY-FIVE

W hen Toby walked into the clearing at dawn, Lucy had already kindled a fire beneath the grill. She noticed that his face was calm, as if he had just arisen from a deep sleep. She said, "Your breakfast will be ready soon. I have eggs and bacon and an oven of biscuits."

He walked past her and into the bus, and when he came back to the chickee, he was dressed in the warrior clothes. The medicine bag was still around his neck. He sat at the table as she served the food, and then he ate as if very hungry. When he finished he went to the side of the chickee and picked up the frog gig.

Lucy watched each move he made, and she could not understand the sudden change. He no longer had fear or anger in his eyes.

He came back to the table and stood before her, the turban plumes moving gently with a slight breeze. She said, "Are you gigging frogs at this time of day? Always before you have gone only at night."

He spoke calmly and in the manner of his grandfather, pronouncing each word slowly and distinctly, as if reading from an unseen book, "I must leave you now, Lucy. I am going on a journey, but I will see you again soon. I have loved you as I love the marsh and the wind. Know this. But I must go now. There is a place we will be together again. It is but a short journey."

His words and his speech pattern seemed strange to her, but he had spoken and done strange things often during the past few days. She said, "Will you be back by noon? Josie will be here then to help hide the airboat, and he cannot do this alone."

"Tell Josie I need the airboat no longer."

What he said and the way he was speaking brought a sudden horrifying realization to her. She felt the same weakness that overcame her that day he drove from her father's house with the small coffin in the back of the truck. She pleaded, "Toby, do not leave now! Josie will be here at noon, and everything will be fine!"

He took her in his arms and held her gently. "There is no need for you to worry," he said, speaking again in the manner of his grandfather. "I am only going on a journey into the marsh. I will be with you again soon."

He moved away from her quickly and walked across the clearing, the gig gripped in his hand. For a moment she started to run after him as he disappeared into the swamp; and then she repeated the words, "It is not so bad as you think, Toby. Everything will be fine. You must be back by noon."

When he reached Lost Creek, Toby walked past the airboat and to the dugout canoe. He poled the slim craft slowly across the water, and the egrets and herons paid no heed as he moved past them silently. He thought of the times when the airboat engine caused them panic.

He paused for a moment when he reached the beginning of the marsh, looking out over the River of Grass stretching into the distant horizon. He imagined he could see a line of men dressed the same as he, moving swiftly through the sawgrass in canoes, standing erect, their plumes waving with the wind. They circled a small hammock and then turned southward. He looked closer and realized it was only a flight of egrets.

For several minutes he continued to gaze across the vastness of the marsh, then he looked back briefly at the mouth of the creek and pointed the bow of the canoe westward.

Josie arrived at the camp just before noon. As soon as he was out of the car, Lucy ran to him. He noticed immediately the desperate apprehension in her eyes as she said, "He's gone, Josie!"

"Where?" he asked. "Do you know where?"

"I'm not sure, but I think he has gone to Allapattah Flats."

"Did he take the airboat?"

"No. He said to tell you he no longer has need of it."

Josie said urgently, "We must go after him, Lucy! And we must hurry!"

They both ran through the swamp and across the open area of dwarf cypress. When they reached the creek Josie snatched the limbs from the airboat and wired the ignition quickly, then he thundered the boat down the narrow stream and into the edge of the marsh.

Josie's way was blocked by another airboat entering the mouth of the creek. It was a sheriff's patrol with two uniformed men, and they signalled for him to stop. Josie cut the engine as the boat came alongside of him.

One of the deputies said, "Are you Toby Tiger?"

Josie answered, "No, I am Josie Billie. This is Lucy Tiger, Toby's wife. We're looking for Toby."

"So are we. There are questions we must ask him. Is that the boat that was stolen from Gator Sales?"

Josie answered cautiously, "It's Toby's boat, but I don't know that it was stolen. We're only using it to find Toby."

"Do you know where he is?" the deputy asked.

Josie did not want to lead the deputies to Toby, but he felt a desperate urge to find him. He said, "We're not sure, but we think we know."

"You lead and we'll follow."

The two boats shot away across the marsh, the patrol boat running just behind Josie. When they reached the edge of the island, Josie cut the engine and glided the boat onto the shore. The cypress canoe was pulled onto the bank.

They walked single file along the path leading to the back of the cove, Lucy and Josie both moving in fear of what they would find. When they reached the black pool of water Josie steadied Lucy.

The frog gig was rammed into the ground, with the medicine bag tied to its shaft. At its base, the warrior clothes were neatly arranged on the ground. One crocodile lay motionless on the opposite bank, and one was partially out of the water.

As the deputies stared at the long dress and the turban, one said, "That must be the stuff he wore when he blew the dike. They said he had on a dress and a crazy hat. You two wait there while we search the island."

Lucy and Josie remained by the cove as the two men went into the brush in opposite directions. They soon returned, and one of them said, "He's not here. He must have changed clothes to throw us off and then gone on without the canoe, but he can't get far out there in the sawgrass. We'll find him and bring him back. Just leave the airboat on Lost Creek and we'll pick it up later."

As soon as the deputies were gone, Lucy turned to Josie and said, "They'll not find him out there. He is here."

"I know," Josie said. "But do you want me to kill the crocodiles and be sure?"

"No!" Lucy said quickly. "That is not what Toby would wish."

Josie said, "Toby believed it a bad thing to kill without reason, and that is what they have done to him. Only you and I can understand this. But it didn't have to be this way. I tried many times, but he wouldn't listen. He was my friend, and I couldn't help him when he needed me most."

Lucy touched Josie's arm and said, "There was nothing anyone could do. Toby was not of this time, and it would have been best if he had lived in the past, in the days of his grandfather. But that time is gone now forever, and Toby couldn't accept this. I hope he has found what he was seeking." She untied the medicine bag from the gig shaft. "Will you tie a rock to this?" she asked.

Josie found an oblong rock, wound the buckskin thong around it, tied it and handed it back to Lucy. She

went down the bank to the edge of the water. For a moment she knelt silently, her arms stretched outward as if
reaching for someone not there. Then she threw the rock
into the center of the cove. It sank immediately, and her
eyes filled with tears as she watched ripples spread
across the water.

When she came back to him, Josie said, "What of
these things? Do you want the clothes?"

She picked up the strap with the crocodile tooth. "I
will keep this," she said, "and we will leave the rest. If he
were on the hammock with the others, I would place
them on the ground beside him. He would wish for them
to be with him now."

Josie said, "I will take you to the reservation, to the
house of your mother and father."

"That would be good," Lucy replied. "I cannot stay in
the swamp without Toby."

As they started along the path, Lucy stopped and
looked back. She said, "Toby . . . Toby . . ." And then she
followed Josie to the boat.

Josie pushed the airboat away from the shore. When
he connected the ignition wires, the engine thundered
to life; then he pushed the throttle forward. For a moment the boat hesitated, and then it shot away rapidly
across the endless stretches of somber sawgrass.